To our sweet rambling rose

❧ PROLOGUE

Colorado Territory
April 1866

THE NIGHT WIND WAILED LIKE A LONELY SPECTER AS IT
swept over the moonlit grassland, carrying a chill from
the snowcapped Rocky Mountains to the west. Jamie
Keegan lifted his hot face to the coolness and drew in a
deep breath.

In all his eleven years, he couldn't remember a single
time when he had been so weary. He'd been working
nonstop since sundown, and from the looks of things, it
would be several more hours before he saw a bed.
Needing a rest, he leaned heavily against the horse he'd
just hitched to his stepfather's covered wagon, then
wiped the sweat from his brow with the back of a dusty
sleeve.

"Easy, Patch," he murmured when the exhausted,
dun-colored gelding snorted in protest at being back in
the traces. "Pa knows what he's doing. Come mornin',
we'll find you horses a nice grassy spot near water. You'll
see. While we laze about under the wagon, you four-
legged beasties can graze and rest your bones."

Even as he uttered those words, Jamie was hard-
pressed to believe them. Judging by what he'd seen, the
folks in these parts were about as friendly as the Yankee
tax collector who'd put them out of their home. They
wouldn't cotton to sharing their water—especially not
with strangers from the South. Since it was a good two-
day wagon ride to reach open country, that put him and
his family in one heck of a pickle.

1

Truth to tell, Jamie was just plain scared. What had begun in St. Louis as a dream come true for everyone was rapidly becoming a nightmare. He wasn't sure his fragile mother could survive the hardships of the return journey east, not without some decent food in her belly and a good long rest before they set out.

"Don't see why Pa won't stand and fight those fellers," he muttered to the still unsettled horses. "Not that I think he's yeller, or nothin', cause he ain't," he hastened to add. "That scar he's got on his arm from a Yankee sabre is proof enough of that."

Patch snorted again and rolled his eyes. Back in Virginia, Joseph had owned a dozen draft horses. Thanks to the thieving Yankees, Patch and his brother were the only two left.

The dun craned its neck to nuzzle Jamie's shirt front. Wishing he had some treats hidden in his pockets, Jamie rubbed the gelding's velvety muzzle. Since the war, times had been hard, and the days when his ma could spare lumps of sugar were a distant memory.

Looking out over the grassland, Jamie blinked to dry his eyes. Only babies cried, and he was no crybaby. It was hard, that was all, turning around and leaving after they'd gone through so much to get here. It didn't make sense. No sense at all, the way he saw it.

This was about the prettiest country he'd ever seen. To the west, the Rockies, their peaks limned by moonlight, rose in craggy silhouette against the slate sky, the sheer granite slopes giving way to foothills and then prairie. His pa said the soil on these rolling flats was rich and fertile, perfect for raising crops or running a herd of cattle. If they looked for a hundred years, Jamie doubted they'd find another piece of land to compare.

How could his pa let a few swindling crooks force him to turn tail and run? The land was theirs, bought and paid for with practically every cent Joseph had been able to scrape together. With his own eyes Jamie had seen Joseph's deed to the land, too. Maybe he didn't understand all the fancy language, but his pa's name was spelled out real clear at the top, and there was a genuine, official-looking seal in one corner, all shiny and gold, with a red ribbon to boot.

No, sir, it wasn't right to let those weasels steal their dream. Jamie wished he were bigger. Big enough to teach that loudmouthed Conor O'Shannessy a few lessons in manners.

After giving Patch a reassuring pat, Jamie crossed behind the now fully loaded wagon and headed for the cookfire where Joseph was repacking the chest holding the staples and some of the cooking utensils.

Hearing Jamie's boots crunch on the grass, Joseph glanced up, his thin shoulders snapping taut. Though the War of Secession had been over for better than a year, he still spooked easy. Jamie figured that was because Joseph was different from most folks, a truly gentle soul from the marrow of his bones. The awfulness of battle ate away at him in quiet moments, never giving him peace.

Looking down at his stepfather now, Jamie wished with all his heart that they had been able to keep the plantation in Virginia. If so, Joseph wouldn't be in such an awful spot, homeless and penniless, with a bunch of hungry mouths to feed.

"Pa, can you and me talk private like?" Jamie asked as he stepped into the lantern light.

Joseph flashed him a curious look. "We can, but first hand me that coffeepot yonder, will you, Son?"

Though Joseph spoke with a soft drawl, his manner more humble than authoritative, Jamie obeyed him without hesitation, saying, "Yessir," in the respectful way his ma had taught him.

"Horses all hitched up?" Joseph asked as Jamie handed over the pot.

"Yessir, all hitched to the wagon, just like you said."

"As soon as your mother and the boys return from the creek, we'll be heading out. I reckon we can make it to No Name in a couple of hours, or near to. I'm thinking we can probably spend the night behind the livery. Who knows? Maybe we can even muck stalls for the owner and make a little money for supplies."

Jamie glanced toward the gully where a pretty little

creek bubbled over rocks the color of rust. As was her custom, his ma had insisted on bathing his little brothers before bedding them down in the back of the wagon. Cocking an ear, Jamie could hear eight-year-old Joseph chortling and the younger boys squalling. Sometimes, though not often, Jamie was glad to be the oldest. At least his ma didn't feel it was necessary to help him wash anymore.

Joseph wiped out the coffeepot with a cloth before placing it in the proper compartment of the custom-made chest. Then, as though privy to Jamie's thoughts, he said, "I know you don't agree with my thinking on this land business, son, but once you're responsible for a family of your own, you'll find yourself looking at things a bit differently."

Jamie dug at the grass with the scuffed toe of his boot. "Yessir."

The weary lines of his face etched in shadow by the bright moonlight, Joseph sighed and sat back on his haunches. "Try to understand, Jamie. I'm one man against five."

"You've got me to stand beside you."

"And I'm lucky to have you. But you're still only a boy, with a boy's strength. Those are grown men, and mean fellows at that." Joseph shook his head. "I have to think of your ma and little brothers. If there were trouble, they could get caught in the crossfire. I'd never forgive myself."

"But, Pa, we can't just walk away! We have to stand and fight. It's our land, bought and paid for in good faith. Without it, what'll we do? We only got a little money. Our food is pert near gone. You keep talkin' about headin' back east, but what'll we eat? If just one of our horses goes lame, we'll be stranded."

"The good Lord will provide, just as he always has." Joseph closed the lid of the wooden cabinet, then pushed to his feet and reached over to rumple Jamie's dark hair. "As for standing and fighting? You take after your real father, sure as rain is wet, boy. From what your ma says, he was a fighter, too. There's not a thing wrong with that, mind you, so don't think I'm saying that there is. According to Scripture, Saint Peter himself lived by the sword."

Jamie shook with an inexpressible frustration. "Sometimes, Pa, you got no choice. It's that or die."

Joseph wagged a finger. "For the godless, perhaps, but the Good Book speaks of a better way, warning that violence begets violence." He held up a hand to keep Jamie from interrupting him. "Come morning, we'll pay a visit to the marshal in No Name. I'll report what those men have done, show him the deed to this land that I paid good money for. If he's a decent, God-fearing man, he'll take them to task, and we'll get to stay here, after all."

"But what if he ain't decent and God-fearin'?" Jamie knotted his hands into fists. "What if he don't help us none?"

"Then we'll have to leave. I can't put your ma and the smaller children at risk. There's not a piece of land on earth worth a single hair on any of their heads. Nor yours, either."

Joseph bent to lift the chest onto his shoulder. Jamie followed him over to the wagon, then helped as best he could to lift the chest over the tailgate and settle it amongst their possessions. Joseph began checking the canvas on one side of the wagon to be certain the tie-downs were secure.

Schooled to assist his parents in whatever way he could, Jamie ran around to the other side of the wagon. As he jerked to tighten the last rope, an odd sound drifted to him. Glancing over his shoulder, he saw four brilliant flares of light bobbing toward their camp.

"How's it looking on that side?" Joseph called.

Jamie swallowed to get the quivery sensation out of his throat. "Pa, riders are coming this way. Fast! Four of 'em, carrying torches."

Joseph stepped around the wagon to investigate. The white of his shirt looked almost blue in the moonlight. Jamie ran to him and grabbed his arm. "Should I get the rifle out of the wagon?"

Joseph patted his hand. "Don't be silly, son. The coffeepot, maybe. That's a bad habit you're developing, thinking the worst of every stranger who comes along."

Jamie looked out into the darkness. The riders were drawing closer by the moment, and all his instincts told him that he and his stepfather should make ready to defend themselves. Instead, as his convictions dictated, Joseph walked out to meet the riders.

At that moment Jamie's mother Dory emerged from the darkness to call anxiously, "Who is it, Joseph?"

"That's what I'm fixin' to find out," Joseph drawled as he turned to offer her a reassuring smile.

"It's rather late for folks to be out and about. Don't you think?"

In the moonlight, Dory's large blue eyes looked like black splashes in her pale face. When she drew up beside Joseph, he curled an arm over her frail shoulders. "A little late, yes." He glanced around. "Where are the boys?"

"Little Joe is helping them dress. The water isn't that deep. When I heard someone coming, I thought I'd best get up here, just in case you needed me."

Joseph chuckled. "It seems everyone is a bit on edge tonight."

Dory glanced back at Jamie, then anxiously at the swiftly advancing torches. "You have to admit, Joseph, that the welcome we received today was less than neighborly."

"True, but I agreed to leave. O'Shannessy left here satisfied that I would do so before morning. We shouldn't have any more trouble from him or any of his—"

"Paxton!" an angry male voice boomed. "You miserable back-shootin' coward!"

So thick it was suffocating, dust billowed up from around the skidding horses' hooves as the riders brought their mounts to a stop. Eyes stinging from the grit, Jamie stared at the four men. The big, broad-shouldered fellow in the lead was Conor O'Shannessy, the man who had warned them off the land earlier that day. Behind him rode Estyn Beiler, one of the two scoundrels who had honey-fuggled Joseph in Saint Louis. His sidekick, a short, rotund man named Camlin Beckett, wasn't present tonight.

Even in the dim light, Jamie could see the taut lines of the men's faces. Their eyes burned with hatred, a mindless hatred that made his heart thud against his ribs. Every instinct urged him to run for the rifle. Joseph was wrong. The good Lord didn't always provide. Sometimes people had to save their own hides.

Spinning on his heel, he raced for the wagon, the wild pounding of his pulse resounding against his eardrums. His breath whistled in his throat by the time he reached the wagon's tailgate. Grasping the wood, he hauled himself upward, barking a shin and elbow as he scrambled for purchase. The rifle. He had to get the rifle.

When Joseph wasn't carrying the Spencer in his saddle boot, he kept the weapon safely wrapped in one of Ma's quilts and stowed under the wagon cot. He maintained that keeping a loaded gun within easy reach wasn't a safe practice when small children were underfoot.

Dimly aware of the angry voices outside, Jamie dropped to his belly and reached under the bed. The wagon jerked, pitching him backward. He realized someone was up front, messing with the horses. He heard Patch whinny as he shoved his arm back under the bed. Fishing frantically through the layers of quilt, he thought for a moment that the rifle wasn't there. Then, finally, he curled his hand over the Spencer carbine's barrel. Scrambling to his knees, he paused to listen. As near as he could make out, O'Shannessy and the others were accusing Joseph of murder.

It was the craziest thing Jamie had ever heard.

Jamie's thoughts were cut short by his mother's scream, which was followed by "Oh, my God, no! Are you mad? Turn loose of my husband. Please! He hasn't murdered anyone! He's never hurt anyone in his entire life. Oh, my God! Stop this. Stop it this instant!"

Spurred into motion by the fear in his mother's voice, Jamie tumbled from the wagon. The instant his feet touched the ground, he froze to get his bearings.

The four men had gotten off their horses and thrust

the ends of their torches into the ground. Patch, Joseph's dun gelding, had been unhitched from his traces and stood at the center of the men, one of whom held fast to the cheek strap of the animal's harness while two others tossed a struggling Joseph, hands tied behind his back, onto the gelding's back.

Fear slammed into Jamie. Like the lawless outlaws in a dime novel his ma had once read to him, these men meant to lynch his pa.

Dory threw herself forward and clung to Joseph's leg, pleading for his life between ragged sobs. One of the men flung her to the side, and she landed hard.

Jamie felt his knees give, but somehow he remained standing, dumb with terror. And then he remembered the rifle. It was his pa's only chance.

"You let my pa go!" he cried as he swung the rifle butt to his shoulder. "Let him go, I said, or I'll shoot. I mean it!"

Jamie had no sooner issued the threat than a beefy hand jerked the gun from his grasp. He looked up to see Conor O'Shannessy looming over him. The burly red-head reeked of whiskey and horse sweat. He staggered slightly as he lifted the rifle in his capable hands.

"Git outa here, boy. You can't help your pa. Nobody can."

Dory sobbed piteously. "Joseph! Oh, dear God, Joseph!"

Jamie whirled back around. His heart nearly stopped when he saw that Joseph, still helplessly astride Patch's broad back, was sitting under a nearby oak tree, a noose dangling before his pale face.

"No! You let my pa go! Lynchin' a man is against the law."

"We are the law," Estyn Beiler hollered. "I'm the marshal in No Name, boy!"

The marshal? Jamie started forward, only to be pulled back by Conor O'Shannessy. "You can't hang my pa," Jamie protested. "He ain't done nothin'!"

"Oh, yes, he has, boy. Murdered Camlin Beckett! Shot him in the back."

"You're wrong! It wasn't Pa. It *wasn't*!"

"Who else would've done it? Camlin was a good man. There isn't a soul for a hundred miles who wished him ill. Nobody except your father. I should've known to expect trouble. Goddamn, no good squatters. There ain't a one of you worth the powder it'd take to blow you straight to hell."

Jamie saw that the other men were lowering the noose over Joseph's head. Fists and feet flying, he threw himself at O'Shannessy. "You let him go! You let him go!"

"Why, you miserable little shit!"

The metal plate of the rifle butt glinted in the torchlight as O'Shannessy drew the weapon back. The next instant, Jamie's head seemed to explode. A horrible, bone-shattering pain radiated from his left cheek to fill his vision with flashes of white. With a *whoosh* of expelled breath, he landed in a loose-jointed sprawl, too dazed even to spit the dirt from his mouth. Curiously, he felt little pain when O'Shannessy followed the blow to his face with a kick to his body, the toe of his boot connecting sharply with Jamie's right hip.

"Jamie!"

Feeling as though he were separated from reality by heat shimmers, Jamie heard his mother's scream, then saw her lift her skirts and run toward him. An instant before she reached him, Conor O'Shannessy snaked out a hand and brought her reeling to a stop. Her petticoats flashed beneath her swirling skirts as he jerked her against him and gave a low, evil laugh.

O'Shannessy tossed away the rifle. "Well, now, aren't you a fine little swatch of calico."

Dory struggled to escape his grasp. "Let go of me! My son—"

"Deserved what he got, just like that no good bastard yonder."

Jamie worked his mouth to tell his ma that he was all right, but for the life of him, he couldn't make the words come out. He looked past her at the oak tree. Joseph was jerking frantically from side to side to avoid having the noose lowered over his head.

"Ma, help Pa," he finally managed to gasp out.

Following his gaze, Dory saw what was happening and stopped struggling. What little color remained in her face drained away. "I'm begging you, mister. Don't do this terrible thing. You have to believe me. Joseph would never, *never* shoot anyone. I swear it. Please, at least allow him a trial before a jury!"

O'Shannessy shook his head. "He's had all the trial he's gonna get, and we've found him guilty."

"Please. Don't kill him. I'll give you anything. The wagon, our horses, what little money we have. Anything!"

O'Shannessy snorted. "I don't want your old wagon and broken-down horses, woman."

"Then what? Anything. Just name it, and it's yours. Please, Mr. O'Shannessy, please."

Dory's plea ended with a horrible, tearing sob. O'Shannessy peered down at her for a moment. Then his broad face creased in another drunken grin. After signaling to his friends that he wanted them to hold off on the hanging for a moment, he said, "Well, now, darlin', that's a mighty tempting offer."

"Dory, no!" Joseph cried. "Dear God in heaven, no. I'd rather—"

One of the other men cut Joseph short by shoving a wadded handkerchief into his mouth. Dory laughed, a horrible, wet, shrill little laugh that didn't sound quite sane. Desperate to stand up, Jamie fought with all his will to move, but even as he struggled, O'Shannessy was leading his ma away from the light.

Sensation slowly returned to Jamie's body, first to his fingers, then to his hands. He managed to push onto his knees, but then another wave of dizziness took him down again.

He had no idea how much time passed before O'Shannessy reappeared. Still fastening his trousers, he staggered toward the oak tree.

"Gentlemen," he said with a flourish of one hand, "you may now hasten to make an honorable man of me. As you know, I don't consort with married ladies. Widows, however, are fair game."

"No!" The bodice of her dress agape, Dory came tearing out of the bushes. "You promised! You gave me your word!"

O'Shannessy let loose with a loud, coarse burst of laughter. One of his cohorts slapped Patch on the rump. Startled, the gentle dun gelding surged forward, taking the man astride his back along with him.

When Joseph reached the end of the rope, he was jerked from Patch's back. As the noose cut cruelly into his windpipe, he arched spasmodically. Then, as though in time to his wife's horrible sobbing, he kicked and twitched, the macabre cast of his shadow dancing across the ground. His gasping mouth seemed to grin around the wad of handkerchief between his teeth.

When at last Joseph hung lifeless, O'Shannessy staggered to his horse. Hollering for his friends to do the same, he climbed into the saddle.

"Leave the torches," he yelled, still laughing. "The boy'll be needin' light to bury the bastard by." With that, they rode away into the darkness.

1

STARTLED AWAKE BY A THUNDEROUS NOISE, CAITLIN O'Shannessy sat bolt upright. Disoriented from sleep, her first thought was that her father had come home drunk again and was storming through the house toward her room. She had already leaped from bed and was throwing on her wrapper when it occurred to her that Conor O'Shannessy had been dead for nearly a year.

Heart still pounding, Caitlin went utterly motionless in the inky darkness and cocked her head to listen. The noise, she realized now, was coming from outside. Horses? Judging by the din, there were six or seven, and all of them seemed to be heading toward the barn.

Pushing a shank of long, curly hair back from her eyes and quickly tying the sash of her wrapper, she padded across the bare wood floor to the window where light from a waning moon shone faintly through Irish lace. As she swept aside the curtains to peer out, several months' accumulation of dust stung her nostrils. Disgusted, she waved a hand to clear the air.

The barn, which sat facing the house about a hundred feet away, looked dark and quiet, just as it should. Above its hip roof, the pale half-moon resembled a broken ivory button dangling by an invisible thread from sequined blue velvet. Though she stared until her eyes started to burn, Caitlin could detect no sign of movement in the patches of darkness under the billowy oak trees scattered about the yard.

13

Strange, that. She felt certain she'd heard horses. So where were they?

The question no sooner presented itself than she saw lantern light flicker faintly inside the barn. As the glow gained brightness, elongated shadows leaped to life upon the interior plank walls. Having spent more than one night in the barn tending sick animals by lantern light, she recognized the distorted shadow shapes as those of men and horses. Several of each, judging by the jumble.

Though it was too dark to see the clock beside her bed, she guessed it to be well after midnight, a late hour for company to come calling. But since her brother Patrick had taken up drinking as his favorite pastime three months ago, very little surprised her.

Thoroughly awake now, she sighed and leaned a shoulder against the window frame. Here she was, in the middle of cutting and baling the season's first stand of grass hay, and Patrick had come home with a passel of friends in tow? He was twenty years old, for Pete's sake, only two years younger than she was. When in heaven's name was he going to stop this infernal carousing and get back to the business of running the ranch?

Since he'd started drinking, Patrick rarely spent much time at home anymore, which left her to do all his work as well as her own. With the additional load, she seldom found opportunity to clean the house. And now he'd brought friends home with him? They would undoubtedly make a big mess in the kitchen, and if any of them spent the night, she'd have linen off all the beds to wash next week as well. As if she had time for things like that? While Patrick was trying to drown his demons in a whiskey bottle, someone had to keep food on the table. It seemed little enough to ask that he at least show her some consideration.

Time, Caitlin. He just needs time.

Even as Caitlin thought those words, she realized they were becoming a familiar refrain. And tonight, she was so bone weary, she didn't have the patience to be understanding. True, Patrick had been going through a lot of turmoil lately, but did that excuse his complete irresponsibility? Usually, she assured herself the answer was yes. But with every muscle in her body aching from doing the work of two men, she felt less inclined to be charitable.

It wasn't easy, accepting the truth about their father. Drunk or sober, he'd been a worthless human being, without scruples or redeeming graces. And Conor's blood flowed in her veins. It made her feel tainted. She'd spent most of her life trying to live down the fact that he was her sire. As a result, she was honest to a fault and would do almost anything rather than break a promise.

Being the only son, Patrick seemed to be having even more difficulty accepting the truth about their father. To Caitlin's dismay, instead of trying to live it down, Patrick now seemed bent on proving to himself and everyone else that bad blood always won out in the end. Conor O'Shannessy's son, a chip off the old block, one hand wrapped around the neck of a bottle, his other knotted into a fist.

In Patrick's mind, his masculinity, his sense of identity, even his pride in bearing the family name, had been destroyed over the last three months. He was angry and resentful. In a way, she even understood his behavior of late, that he was striking out, not only at their new neighbor Ace Keegan, whom he considered to be the source of all his woes, but also at the people in town, by living up to what he believed were their expectations of him.

But enough was enough. She was tired of carrying her brother's share of the load. More importantly, she was beginning to feel truly frightened. With each passing week, Patrick's behavior when he drank was becoming more and more crazy. And, lately, even when he was sober, she sensed a distance between them, as if he were slowly and irrevocably withdrawing from her. Not long ago, he'd been her best friend in the whole world. Now she sometimes felt as if a stranger were living with her— an unlikable stranger who was becoming alarmingly like their late father.

Indescribably weary, she closed her eyes for a moment, wondering how long it might be before the legacy

of heartbreak Conor O'Shannessy had left behind would
be eradicated from their lives. One would have thought
that with their father dead, his power would be destroyed. Instead, he seemed to be grabbing hold of them
even from the grave.

Giving the dusty curtains another swat, Caitlin gulped
back a sudden rush of tears. And if tears weren't silly,
she didn't know what was. As if blubbering would cure
her troubles? Instead it would probably give her a
headache, and wouldn't that be a fine kettle of fish? It
wasn't as if she could laze about all day tomorrow with a
cool cloth draped over her eyes.

Well, she had news for her brother. Some people had
to work in the morning and needed their rest. If he
thought he was going to keep her awake until all hours,
he could think again.

Caitlin was about to drop the curtain and return to
bed when she saw three men come running out of the
barn, one slightly in the lead. Assuming that her brother
and two of his comrades comprised the trio, she was
startled when the three went down in a thrashing tangle
of arms, legs, and flying fists. Eerily illuminated by the
backdrop of lantern light, dust billowed around the
combatants in a golden cloud. Her brother Patrick's red
hair shone like a torch where he lay at the bottom of the
pile.

Caitlin whirled from the window. *Keegan!* The name
tore through her mind like a ricochetting bullet. Who
else would Patrick be fighting in the middle of the night?
Since his arrival in No Name three months ago, the man
had become the focus of all Patrick's anger.

She knotted her hands into throbbing fists. That
brother of hers! How many times had she told him to
leave Ace Keegan alone? So far, she'd managed to avoid
making Keegan's acquaintance herself, but she'd heard
plenty of stories about him, all bad. A notorious gunslinger who'd made a fortune at the gaming tables in San
Francisco, he was undeniably dangerous, and ever since
his return to the area, her brother had been doing his
level best to goad him into a fight. Now it looked as if
Keegan had finally decided to give him one.

Never had Caitlin been so furious with her brother. So furious, in fact, she was tempted to let Keegan beat the stuffing out of him. It was certainly no more than Patrick deserved, and it might be just what he needed.

But no. Even as the thought slipped into her mind, she was giving the sash of her wrapper a tug and groping her way across the room to the door. Right or wrong, Patrick was her brother. Despite his outrageous behavior recently, he was basically a good person and had always been loving and supportive. She couldn't just stand here while a bunch of Barbary Coast ruffians ganged up on him.

The windowless hallway outside her bedroom was as black as stove soot. Like a swimmer pulling herself through water, she groped her way along the wall toward her father's study. The rank smell of soured whiskey blasted her in the face as she stepped into the room.

Just like her bad memories, the scent never seemed to fade. Though she knew it was her imagination, the very air in the study seemed several degrees colder than in the rest of the house, making her skin prickle and her palms go icy. Very little light seeped through the damask curtains. Patting the air to avoid tripping over furniture, Caitlin hurried to the gun cabinet. From outside, she heard the faint sound of men's angry voices.

Fingers gone clumsy with urgency, she fumbled for the cabinet door latch, turned the key, and located her '73 Winchester by touch. The instant her hand curled over the gunmetal, she felt better. If Ace Keegan had come looking for trouble, she would give him more than he had bargained for, fifteen .44-caliber lead bullets, each backed by a forty-grain black powder charge.

Rifle in hand, Caitlin rushed through the dark house. At the front door, she hesitated. There were several men out there. No doubt, they were all armed. A lone woman who went up against such odds had to be crazy.

She touched a hand to her stomach and hauled in a bracing breath. Patrick was out there, and he needed help. What kind of sister would she be if she cowered inside the house? In the past, her brother had put his own safety on the line for her more than once. She could do no less for him.

The hinges creaked eerily as she drew open the heavy oak door. At the sound, the crickets outside stopped singing, the cessation so abrupt and complete that even the wind seemed to hold its breath.

Caitlin slipped soundlessly onto the porch. The coolness of the Rocky Mountain air cut through her nightclothes, making her shiver. After easing the door closed, she stood stock still for a second and scanned the yard. Nothing. Even the doorway of the barn stood empty now. Only the lantern light and shifting shadows inside the building indicated that anything out of the ordinary was going on.

The bunkhouse lay some two hundred yards north of the barn. Caitlin allowed herself one brief glance in that direction. She had kept only two men on the payroll after her father's accident, both elderly fellows who'd worked for the family for years and had been willing to stay on for nominal wages. As tempting as it was to wake them, she knew they would probably be more hindrance than help in a fracas. She didn't want either of them to get hurt.

Gathering her courage, she jumped off the porch and raced across the small patch of lawn, never breaking stride. Out the gate. Across the service yard. Thistles jabbed the soles of her bare feet, but she scarcely felt the sting.

At the barn, she whirled and pressed her back against the rough siding. A sudden gust of wind, carrying scents of alfalfa and freshly mowed grass hay, molded the lightweight cotton of her nightclothes to her body. Gulping for breath, her heart pounding, she got a handier grip on the Winchester, depressed the combined lever and trigger guard, and forced the hammer to full cock. The muted click of the well-oiled mechanism made her wince.

Bracing the rifle butt against her hip, she curled a finger over the trigger and leaped through the open doorway. "What's going on in here?"

To her dismay, Hank Simmons, one of their hired hands, stood just inside the door. The barrel of her rifle was aimed smack dab at his spine.

"Hank! Get out of my way!"

Hank didn't so much as twitch. With a sickening lurch of her stomach, Caitlin remembered the wiry old cowpoke was deaf as a post. Why he was just standing there, she couldn't guess. He had his rifle—she could see the butt extending beyond his right hip—but as near as she could tell, he'd made no attempt to use it.

Wielding her Winchester like a canoe paddle, she forced her way past him. Hank gave a startled gasp and fell back against the wall. Not sparing him a glance, Caitlin halted a few feet shy of the light, momentarily blinded by the sudden brightness. Blinking frantically to clear her vision, she repeated her question.

"What's going on in here, I said? Patrick, are you all right?"

Silence. An awful, terrible silence. Not even a horse nickered in response. As her vision sharpened, she understood why. Surrounded by six men and several milling horses, Patrick sat on his pinto at the center of the barn, his hands tied behind his back, his neck encircled by a rope already looped over the massive rafter above him. Only a sharp slap on the gelding's rump stood between him and a broken neck.

Like little boys caught perpetrating mischief, the men around Patrick stood motionless, their expressions shamefaced. Only, of course, they weren't little boys, and they weren't up to harmless mischief.

For a fleeting instant, Caitlin wondered which of them was Keegan. Then the horror of it all began to sink in. A gunshot might spook Patrick's horse, a fact that rendered her trusty Winchester absolutely useless. Little wonder Hank stood frozen in place behind her, doing nothing. One wrong move from either of them, and her brother was a dead man.

"Oh, God," she said faintly.

She jerked her gaze up to her brother's face. Tears streaked his pale cheeks. His deep red hair, the color so like her own, stood out from his head in a wind-tossed tangle, and his frightened blue eyes looked as big as supper plates. The white shirt he wore was ripped at the shoulder—a shirt she had made for him last winter when the snow was deep. Her brother, her baby brother.

"Oh, Patrick, what have you done?" she asked shakily. Then, to the men standing around him, "Why? What on earth did he do? Are you mad?"

Instead of answering her, the men glanced uneasily into the shadows off to her right. It took Caitlin a moment to realize the significance of that. Startled, she swung around and stared into the unlit area under the stairway that led up to the loft. For a moment, she could see nothing. Then she caught a flash of silver. *Keegan.* She'd heard stories about the fancy six-shooter he wore, nickel plated, with a pearl handle. Silver death, one man in town had called it, and given the number of men Keegan was rumored to have killed, she guessed the comparison wasn't far wrong.

Like an image coming to life under the deft strokes of an artist's charcoal, the man standing in the darkness began to take shape. Though he remained indistinct, she could see him well enough to tell he was dressed all in black and had skin bronzed by the sun to a deep umber. Darkness blending with darkness. Except for his eyes. Like the gun on his hip, they reflected the light as he gave her a slow, almost insolent appraisal.

For an awful moment, Caitlin felt exposed. Then she remembered that she, too, stood in the shadows. Only two lanterns illuminated the barn, both suspended from rafter hooks, one on either side of the feed passage. Keegan might be able to see the white of her gown and wrapper, the darkness of her red hair against the cloth, and the oval of her face, but otherwise very little.

As though to rectify that, he came slowly toward her, his gait lazy and loose-jointed, the heel of one boot scuffing ominously over the packed dirt, the creak of holster leather marking his uneven stride. Her every instinct urged her to run. But for Patrick's sake, she stood her ground.

The muscles along her spine ached with the effort to hold the heavy rifle level at her waist. Not that she would dare use it.

Say something! Do something! her brain commanded her. Instead, she just stared at him, helpless and terrified in a way she'd sworn no man would ever make her feel again.

In some distant part of her mind, she heard Patrick sobbing softly. But she couldn't take her gaze off Keegan. He had obviously positioned himself under the stairs so he might observe the hanging and give orders while his men did the dirty work. The miserable coward. His lack of courage was small comfort, though. Cowards were at their most dangerous when they had the upper hand.

Coming to a stop in the flickering play of lantern light, Keegan looked satanic and deadly dressed all in black, the nickel-plated revolver flashing in the low-slung holster at his hip. The impression was undoubtedly intentional, the better to intimidate his opponents when he went up against them in a gunfight. Caitlin wondered how many men he'd actually killed with that fancy gun and prayed gossip had painted him meaner than he actually was.

With the lower portion of his face illuminated by a swath of amber, the upper cast into shadow by the brim of his hat, she could see only the strong line of his square jaw, a jagged scar on one cheekbone, and the bitter twist of his hard mouth. It was his eyes she wanted to see. They were the windows to a man's soul, or so her father had always said, and judging by personal experience, Caitlin believed that was true.

As she ran her gaze over Keegan's frame, the lump of fear that had lodged in her throat expanded to the size of a hen egg, making it difficult to breathe. Lofty and lean were the first two words that popped into her mind, but those adjectives alone didn't do him justice.

Unlike her father, who'd carried a lot of extra weight on his rangy body, Keegan was powerfully muscled, especially across the shoulders and through the arms. The men in town were rumored to step off the boardwalk when they saw him coming. Now she knew why. Even the way he stood, arms loose at his sides, one lean leg slightly bent, exuded power. Add to that his reputation with a gun, and he was one of the most intimidating individuals she'd ever had the misfortune to clap eyes on.

His sharply chiseled features reflected a chilling expression of absolute control. She wanted to look away, needed to so she might gather her composure, but some intangible force emanated from him, holding her helplessly in its grip.

She squared her shoulders. "Mr. Keegan, I take it?"

He touched the brim of his hat. The gesture seemed absurdly polite, considering he was about to lynch her brother.

"Please, Mr. Keegan. I, um . . . I know Patrick has been making a pest of himself since you returned to No Name. But surely you can't, in good conscience, end a young man's life over some harmless prank."

After several seemingly endless seconds, he finally spoke. "Prank? Did you say 'harmless prank?'" His voice, deep and rough-edged, made her think of whiskey and smoke, each lazily drawled word seeming to curl around her. Planting his hands at his hips, he shifted his weight to his other booted foot, a purely masculine stance that made him look relaxed—and about as harmless as a rattlesnake. "You call his gut-shooting my prize bull a harmless prank?"

"Prize bull?" she said weakly. She squeezed her eyes closed for a second, so sick with fear for Patrick she wanted to vomit. Shooting someone's bull was a hanging offense in a community that owed its survival to the successful breeding of beef cattle. "There must be some mistake. Patrick wouldn't do something so stupid."

Behind her, the men who stood around Patrick's horse seemed to exude malevolence. She sensed their readiness—no, their eagerness—to slap the rump of the pinto and watch her brother kick at the end of a rope.

"Stupid," Keegan said. "Now there's a word. Stupid drunk, to be exact."

Caitlin flashed a horrified glance over her shoulder at Patrick. He said nothing, just gazed at her with imploring eyes. His silence attested to his guilt.

"I, um . . ." She turned back to Keegan. "Please, Mr. Keegan." She gestured toward the hanging noose. "This is no way to settle things. Let's go in the house, have a nice cup of tea, calm down. If we put our heads together, I'm sure we can resolve this matter in a way that will be satisfactory to us all."

She thought she glimpsed a humorous twist of his firm lips. "Tea?"

By the way he said "tea," Caitlin guessed he considered the stuff scarcely better than poison. She searched frantically for an alternative. "Coffee, then?"

He made a low huffing sound under his breath that she presumed was meant to be a laugh. "I don't think so, Miss O'Shannessy. Your brother has been a thorn in my side since the day I got here. You know it, I know it, and so does everybody else in town. In short, I've taken all the shit off of him I'm going to."

"I know Patrick has tried your patience, Mr. Keegan. And I can't really say I blame you for wanting to take a strip out of his hide."

"Caitlin!" Patrick interjected in a hushed voice. "What in God's name are you saying?"

Striving to ignore her brother, she went on, "And if he did kill your bull, I'm in absolute agreement that he should be punished. It's just that hanging him seems a little extreme. Don't you agree?"

"If I agreed, I wouldn't be here." Holding up a large hand, Keegan began to take count on his long, blunted fingers. "In the last three months, your brother has insulted me in public and called me a coward for not meeting him in the street with guns blazing. He's poured rock salt in two of my best watering holes and poisoned another, costing me twenty-three head. He's cut my newly strung fences on countless occasions, spooked my cattle, and taken pot shots at my hired hands. Trust me when I say that, at this point, nothing I might choose to do strikes me as being extreme."

With each count Keegan named off against her brother, Caitlin flinched. Stupid, so stupid. When he got drunk, Patrick didn't have the sense to pour water out of a boot. "I know he's been difficult. But has it occurred to you that perhaps you're as responsible for this ongoing battle between the two of you as he is?"

"Me?" Keegan said incredulously. "Me, responsible? I don't think so."

Her voice going squeaky with desperation, Caitlin plunged on. "Maybe, just maybe, if you tried to put yourself in his shoes, the things Patrick has done would be a little easier to understand."

"I'll tell you what, Miss O'Shannessy. *You* understand him. *I'll* get even for the loss of my bull by hanging his ass. Then we'll both be happy."

Tucking her rifle in the crook of her arm, she held up a shaky hand. "Let's not be hasty. You're about to make a mistake you're bound to regret. Just look at it from Patrick's side. In a manner of speaking, you've provoked my brother into doing most of those things."

Caitlin took it as an encouraging sign that Keegan didn't interrupt her. Her voice still tremulous, she said, "The very first thing out of the bag when you came to town, you lured him into a poker game and relieved him of the deed to several thousand acres of prime ranch land. Then, while he was still upset over that, you began making all sorts of allegations against our father and his friends, accusing them of a swindle, not to mention murder. You even had the effrontery to demand that Patrick let you see our father's ledgers and journals so you might prove your stepfather was swindled and was innocent of Camlin Beckett's death. On the heels of that request, you made no secret of your belief that our father or one of his friends would be implicated in the murder instead!"

When Keegan made no move to speak, Caitlin rushed on to add, "You've accused our father of cold-bloodedly killing a man, Mr. Keegan! Just you think about that. True or false, it's a very serious indictment, and no matter what your personal opinion of Conor O'Shannessy may be, even you must admit it's a charge no dutiful son could let stand uncontested. Our father is no longer alive to defend himself. Naturally the boy has demanded a retraction and hates you for refusing to make one!"

In a perfectly level voice, Keegan replied, "Four things, Miss O'Shannessy. Remember them well. The first is that I didn't twist your brother's arm to make him play poker that night. The minute he learned who I was, he started challenging me to play, not the other way around. I can only assume he believed he was lucky enough at cards to fleece me. It was his choice to put the deed to the Circle Star Ranch into the pot as part of his ante. I didn't suggest he do so, or in any way encourage it."

He shifted his weight and resettled his hands at his hips. "Second, the things I've said about your father are the truth, not mere accusations. Third, it was not effrontery on my part to demand to see his ranch records, but an attempt to uncover evidence that would clear my stepfather's name.

"If your father and his friends were innocent of any wrongdoing, as you obviously believe, there would have been nothing in those records to implicate them. So why all the fuss? Were you and your brother afraid to let me see those records for some reason? Possibly because you feared I might actually find proof that my stepfather *was* innocent?"

The question was one Caitlin had already asked herself, and the truth was, she believed Keegan's stepfather probably had been innocent. Whether or not Conor O'Shannessy had been stupid enough or careless enough to make entries in his ledgers and journals attesting to that, however, was another question entirely, and one she preferred not to address, not because she was afraid to learn the truth, but because she feared doing so might destroy her brother.

Why couldn't this man understand that? Everyone had illusions, her brother's being that his father had been a basically good man whose personality was grossly altered by his consumption of whiskey. Sometimes self-deception was all that kept a person sane.

Camlin Beckett's murder had occurred nearly twenty years ago. Joseph Paxton was long since dead, and her brother was still very much alive. As far as she was concerned, the truth, no matter how damning, had been buried with her father, and it should stay buried. What earthly difference did it make now if Paxton had been innocent? The facts wouldn't bring him back, nor would they undo what had happened. Ace Keegan could leave this place any time he chose and get on with his life. Patrick would have to live with the shame of a scandal until the day he died.

As if he sensed she wasn't going to reply to his question, Keegan hauled in a deep breath and released it with a long sigh. "The last point I want to make, Miss O'Shannessy, is that your brother isn't a boy. He's a grown man. It's time he suffered the consequences of his actions. Maybe next time, he'll think twice before he gets trigger happy."

"Next time?" Caitlin felt a hand on her arm. Believing it to be Hank's, she didn't jerk away. "If you hang him, there won't be a next time! Please. There must be another way to settle this. I will happily compensate you for the bull. How much did it cost you?"

Keegan's mouth drew up at one corner in a humorless smile, his flashing teeth a startling white. "Three thousand, plus shipping."

Caitlin's knees nearly buckled. "Three thousand? You can't be serious."

"Dead serious, and since I doubt you have that much money lying loose around the house, there isn't much point in our discussing it further, is there?" Inclining his head in a gesture of dismissal, he added, "Good night, Miss O'Shannessy. It's been a pleasure."

Too late, she realized the man touching her wasn't Hank, but one of Keegan's men. Before she could react, he wrested the rifle from her grasp. She rounded on him. "You give that back this instant!"

From over her shoulder, she heard Keegan say, "Get her out of here, Esa, and see to it she stays out until we've concluded our business with Mr. O'Shannessy."

The sandy-haired cowboy tossed her rifle to another man. Caitlin whirled to evade his grasp, only to find herself trapped in the strong circle of his arms. Panic washed over her in great crashing waves. Struggling to get free, she forgot everything but Patrick and what would happen to him if she didn't convince Keegan to have mercy.

"No, please!" Digging in with her heels, she fought desperately to hold her ground, her gaze fixed on Keegan. "I'll pay any price for the bull you name! I can't"—she twisted and swung sharply at her captor's midriff with an elbow—"immediately lay my hands on the three thousand! You're right about that. But I have plenty of collateral to put up as security—the cattle, the land, even the house. I'll draw up an IOU. Your men can act as witnesses! We'll make payments, if nothing else."

"And meanwhile, I have no prime breeding bull to cover my cows? That equates to no crop of prime calves next spring, Miss O'Shannessy, which means thousands more in losses for me when I take my cattle to market next fall." Keegan gave another humorless huff of laughter. "I don't want your money. Or your IOU. I came here to teach your brother a lesson, and that's exactly what I'm going to do."

"A lesson?" Caitlin's voice went shrill. "Dear God. You call hanging him a lesson? Please, Mr. Keegan. You can't do this. Please."

She gave a violent twist of her body and somehow managed to jerk free of her captor's hold. Dashing across the earthen floor, she threw herself at Keegan's feet and curled her hands around his black boots, determined to hang on no matter what.

"You have to listen to me! Please, don't do this terrible thing."

The thought of trying to strike a bargain with this man with glittering eyes and a devil's sneer had her insides quaking. But if she meant to save Patrick, she couldn't see that she had a choice.

Quivering at the indignity of being on her knees, she forced herself to lift her head. She was glad for the beam of lantern light that fell across her face; the unaccustomed brightness after standing in the shadows made it difficult to see and spared her the indignity of having to immediately meet Keegan's gaze.

"Please," she pleaded. "Don't hurt my brother. Name your price. Anything. Absolutely anything. Just, please, don't hurt my brother."

As her vision cleared, Caitlin noticed two things, the first that she could see the upper half of Keegan's chiseled face more clearly from this angle, the second that he could evidently see hers more clearly as well. Judging by his expression, he didn't like what he saw. No. That was putting it too mildly. Stunned, that was how he looked. Almost as if an invisible fist had just knocked all the wind out of him.

For a second, Caitlin felt certain all the rumors she'd heard about him were false. But even as she gazed up at him in rising hope, the vulnerability she thought she glimpsed in his eyes gave way to frosty indifference. The slack, almost shocked expression on his face went granite hard, and his full, firm lips twisted into another mocking sneer.

"Anything?" he asked softly. "All I have to do is name my price?"

With slowly dawning terror, Caitlin realized what he was hinting at. When she'd made the offer of "anything," she'd been referring to money, that she would happily compensate him, not only for the cost of his bull, but for his projected losses next year. She and Patrick would even sell the ranch, if necessary, to get their hands on the funds. Losing everything they owned was preferable to seeing her brother killed.

Keegan was clearly not thinking along the same lines.

"I asked you a question, Miss O'Shannessy. Anything?" he repeated with a frightening softness.

Caitlin knew exactly what he was suggesting, and everything within her cried out with revulsion. Wanting to scream, she released her grip on his boots, sat back, and curled her hands over her bent knees, digging in hard with her fingernails. The pain provided a tenuous link with reality while her mind was a jumble of horror.

Patrick. She could still hear him sobbing softly. Unless she agreed to do whatever Keegan suggested, he would hang her brother. *Hang him.* Compared to that, nothing that might happen to her seemed important. Nothing.

Catching the inside of her cheek between her teeth, Caitlin forced herself to nod. It was the most difficult thing she'd ever done in her life.

Keegan's eyes, she noticed inanely, were not obsidian black, but the deep, dark brown of chocolate, her favorite sweet. Unfortunately, there was nothing sweet in the look he gave her. His gaze seared hers, then dropped with insolent slowness to take inventory of her body. Caitlin felt shame burn a path up her neck and set fire to her cheeks.

"You put a mighty high price on yourself, Miss O'Shannessy," he said in that same dangerously silken voice. "It remains to be seen if you're worth it."

He bent to grab her arm. She expected his strong fingers to bite into her flesh. Instead his hand was like an iron manacle, his grip relentless, the only pain being in the rub, and that more to her sensibilities than her skin. She was so ashamed, she kept her head bent, a posture almost as foreign to her as being on her knees had been. Irish pride. All her life, it had been her biggest strength, and now it seemed to have completely deserted her.

As Caitlin turned to follow Keegan, her feet got tangled. There was no question of her falling, though. Not with his hand on her arm to catch her. Off balance, she bumped into his shoulder, which was so hard it felt more like rock than flesh and bone.

Oh, God, she almost wished she could fall—and hit her head while she was at it. Unconsciousness at a time like this would be a blessing. But, no. She had to stand there, fully awake and cognizant, while Keegan curtly instructed his men to haul Patrick down. Then, after slanting her another searing glance, he added, "Stand ready to string the little bastard back up if his sister, in true O'Shannessy form, decides not to honor her word."

The implication that there was no honor in her family was almost more than Caitlin's stung pride could take. No matter what her father had done, she was nothing if

not honest and she had never broken her word in her
life. She had no intention of starting now, not because
she felt obligated to deal fairly with a man who clearly
had so little honor himself, but because her brother's life
would be forfeit.

"Boss?" one of the men standing near Patrick's horse
said uncertainly.

His tone drew Caitlin's attention to the group of men
as a whole. Unlike her and Keegan, they stood almost
directly under one of the lanterns, their faces well
illuminated. Upon every countenance she saw either
stunned disbelief or disapproval. Their reactions were
small comfort. Before she had time to completely assimilate them, Keegan released her arm to commandeer one
of the lanterns and then nudged her into a walk ahead of
him down an aisle toward a brace of empty stalls at the
back of the barn.

Feeling like a bit of flotsam carried on a wave, Caitlin
approached a fate that was to her far worse than dying.
What made it even more awful was the man behind her.
His rage was clear in his brisk strides and the jerky
splashes of lantern light on the plank walls.

With each scrape of his right boot heel on the packed
dirt, she wanted to scream. The unmitigated insolence in
the sound was unmistakable. With a numbing sense of
unreality, she concentrated on that uneven rhythm. *Step,
shuffle—step, shuffle.* A slight limp, perhaps? Though it
seemed inconceivable that a man so fierce might have a
physical flaw, she couldn't discard the notion.

The acrid smell of manure and musty hay burning her
nostrils, she peered ahead into the gloom. It was so dark
back there. So horribly dark and forbidding. Keegan had
made his intentions clear, and she had no doubt he was
scoundrel enough to carry through on them. Never in all
her life had she seen such fierce, glittering eyes.

By the time he curled a hand over her shoulder to steer
her into a middle stall, she was trembling violently. If he
sensed it, he gave no indication. She regarded him with
growing apprehension as he hung the lantern on a nail.
No trace of remorse. No hesitancy whatsoever. It made
her wonder if he made a habit of doing things like this.

The lantern hung lower now than it had at the front of the barn, revealing his face in minute detail. A shock of black hair had escaped from beneath his Stetson to trail in a lazy wave over his high forehead. Deep set beneath bold eyebrows, his chocolate brown eyes were lined with thick, sooty lashes. Only a full, sensual mouth saved his chiseled features and square jaw from severity.

Enhancing his dangerous edge, he had a heavy shadow of beard, a straight but slightly off-center nose, and the jagged scar along his left cheekbone, which appeared to be more prominent than his right, indicative of a badly mended break. That explained the twist of his lips when he smiled, she thought dazedly. The nerves and muscles on the left side of his face had apparently been damaged.

Caitlin imagined him brawling in a rowdy saloon and getting his cheekbone shattered by some burly drunkard's fist. Her sympathies all lay with the drunkard.

At the left corner of his mouth, he'd thrust a piece of straw, which he held clenched between strong, white teeth. As a consequence, the right side of his mouth seemed more mobile when he spoke. "Well," he said slowly.

Seeing that piece of straw was nearly her undoing. Not that there was anything particularly sinister about straw; she'd nibbled on a piece herself plenty of times. While watching the sun go down. Or while taking a break out in the fields. But never at a time like this. His doing so was harshly eloquent of his contempt.

When she failed to respond to his drawled prompting, he added, "If you plan to stand there staring at me all night, I have a hanging to supervise, Miss O'Shannessy. The choice is yours."

Caitlin didn't need to be told what he expected of her. She hugged her waist to hide the violent trembling of her hands. "W—would you at least turn out the lamp?"

"I don't think it's too much to ask that I be allowed to see the merchandise."

The merchandise? She squeezed her eyes closed for an instant on a scalding wave of humiliation. "What kind of man are you?"

"The kind with a long memory. Start stripping or

renege on our bargain, I don't give a damn which. But don't test my patience. I can assure you that at this point, I have none."

She saw the truth of that. Indeed, judging by his relentless expression, he would settle for nothing less than complete nudity. With the lamp pulsating brightly a mere two feet away, Caitlin couldn't imagine anything worse.

Why she was incredulous, she didn't know. Except for Patrick and Doc Halloway, No Name's only physician, practically every man she'd ever met, including her father, had been a lowdown skunk. It stood to reason that Keegan would be as well. Of course he wouldn't be satisfied with merely using her. Oh, no. He wanted to degrade her while he was at it.

Looking over his shoulder toward the front of the barn, she could see shadows still dancing in stark relief against the weathered walls. A silhouette of the empty noose swung slowly to and fro. As Keegan had instructed, Patrick had been released.

For an instant, she considered running. But she quickly discarded the idea. It would be a simple thing for him to have his men string her brother back up, and she didn't doubt for a moment that he would do just that.

"Having second thoughts?" he asked, disgust evident in his voice. "I didn't figure an O'Shannessy would keep her word. Like father, like daughter?"

The comparison cut Caitlin to the bone. Keegan turned as if to leave. Her heart went into her throat. "Wait!" She grabbed his sleeve. "Please—I just—don't go yet, please."

He turned back slowly, one dark eyebrow lifted in an unspoken challenge. "Don't play games with me, sweetheart. Trust me when I say I've played with the best of them. You don't stand a prayer."

Caitlin had never hated anyone as much as she did Ace Keegan at that moment. Tears gathered at the back of her eyes. What remained of her pride burned them away. The bastard. She wouldn't give him the satisfaction of seeing her cry.

The smell of hay and horses closed in around her. Determined now to meet his gaze without flinching, she applied herself to the simple task of untying the sash of her wrapper. Only, of course, the task wasn't simple since her fingers had gone numb with terror and her hands were shaking.

As if to better enjoy the display, he nudged his hat farther back and went to stand against the opposite wall. Caitlin almost wished he would move back into the stall doorway. Maybe then she wouldn't be tempted to bolt. But, oh, no. It was almost as if he wanted her to run.

Loosely folding his arms, he crossed his lean legs at the ankles, the toe of one gleaming black boot buried in the straw. With an expression of such bored disinterest that she wondered why he had suggested this proposition in the first place, he awaited the unveiling.

Frustrated by the stubborn knot she'd tied in her sash, she finally had to break eye contact to look down, and even then, her fingers refused to cooperate. She gave the sash a frantic tug.

"Would you like some help?" he asked drily.

Caitlin tried to speak, but her voice threatened to quaver so badly she decided against it. By digging in hard with her fingernails, she was finally able to loosen one loop. Seconds later, the tails of the sash finally slipped apart. Not allowing herself time to think and keeping her eyes averted from his to lessen the shame of it, she shrugged her shoulders and sent the garment sliding down her body toward the dirt.

Now all that remained was the nightgown. With shaking hands, she began unfastening the row of tiny buttons that ran from just under her chin to her midriff. Acutely conscious that Keegan stood there watching her, she tried not to think about the moment when there would be nothing left to shield her from his dark gaze. Tried and failed. Her treacherous mind conjured awful images—of him laying those brown hands on her body, taking her, hurting her. She didn't know which would be worse, the pain or the degradation.

She had no illusions. Life had stripped her of those long ago. Gritting her teeth, still unable to meet his

penetrating gaze, she resolutely worked her way down
the row of buttons. As the last one fell free from its hole,
her heart fell with it. There was nothing to do now but
draw the nightgown off over her head.

For Patrick. She would do it for Patrick. The words
became a litany inside her mind. She crossed her arms
over her body and grabbed handfuls of the unstarched
cotton. Cool air touched her ankles, then her shins. Oh,
God. As the material inched upward toward the apex of
her thighs, she squeezed her eyes closed again. To her
shame, hot tears spilled down her cheeks. She ducked
her head, hoping he wouldn't notice, that God would
grant her at least that much.

With no warning, hard, calloused fingers curled over
her wrists, effectively halting the upward path of her
arms. Startled, she forgot all about hiding her tears and
looked up to find Keegan's dark face hovering only
inches above her own. Every bit as unyielding as his grip,
his coffee-colored gaze held hers. For just an instant, she
thought she glimpsed regret in his expression. Then the
frosty mask fell over his features once again.

His right jaw muscle bunching with what she could
only assume was anger, he said, "This little preview has
been delightful, Miss O'Shannessy, but regretfully, I've
decided to take a raincheck." He gestured toward the
front of the barn. "It occurs to me that my brothers and
three of my hired hands are standing out there, all within
earshot. I think I'd like to wait until we have a bit more
privacy."

Caitlin felt as if the ground had disappeared from
under her feet. His brothers? A rain check? She blinked,
trying to clear the swimming sensation from her head.

Releasing her wrists, Keegan tipped his hat to her, the
hooded expression in his eyes unreadable. Then, without
another word, he turned and exited the stall, leaving her
standing in the flickering lantern light, her hands still
bunched in her nightgown.

Dazed, she listened to the rhythmic shuffle of his
receding footsteps. He definitely had a slight limp, she
decided inanely. As if that mattered. Shock. That was

why her brain seemed incapable of focusing on anything important—why she couldn't seem to gather her composure. Because she was in shock.

Seconds later, she heard Keegan barking orders in front of the barn. There followed the squeak of saddle leather as seven men swung their weight into dangling stirrups and wheeled their horses to depart.

Too stunned to move, she stared at the shadow dance upon the plank walls, slowly assimilating what he'd said, that this ordeal, which might have been finished quickly had he stayed, would now be postponed until it suited him. Meanwhile, she would have to live in dread of seeing him again, never knowing from one moment to the next when he might reappear.

Caitlin couldn't think of anything worse.

Galvanized into motion, she dropped the hem of her gown. "Wait!" She sprang from the stall. "Wait, Mr. Keegan! Please, wait!"

Her cries were still ringing in the air when she heard horses' hooves beating a rapid tattoo of retreat, loudly as they left the barn, gaining momentum as they crossed the yard, then diminishing into the darkness of the night.

2

ONLY A CRAZY MAN WOULD HAVE RIDDEN AT SUCH A breakneck pace over rolling grassland, especially after dark. All it took was one chuckhole to break a horse's leg. In the back of his mind, Ace Keegan knew that. But for the moment, he didn't care. Like a man possessed by demons—or perhaps pursued by them—he spurred his stallion over the uneven ground, hat clenched in one hand, reins in the other, his body angled forward along his mount's neck to attain its greatest speed.

The night curled around him like the seductive arms of a woman, and he longed to lose himself in her. Caressing fingertips of chill wind molded his shirt to his body and threaded through his hair, over his neck, under his collar. He wanted to ride faster—then faster still. To plunge ahead into the darkness. To become separate from himself and a discovery his mind simply could not accept.

But he couldn't escape. Not into the darkness. Not anywhere. A man couldn't run hard enough or long enough or fast enough to escape the truth.

Hauling back on the reins, Ace brought his horse wheeling to a sudden stop. Enraged by the rough treatment, the stallion screamed and reared, striking the air with its front hooves. Using the strength of his arm, the vise of his legs, and the weight of his body as leverage, Ace managed to get the animal under control again, but only just barely.

"Easy, Shakespeare, easy," he said, breathing as hard as if he'd been running himself. He gently stroked the animal's lathered neck. "Easy now, boy. I'm sorry."

Ace truly meant that. Since childhood, he'd never abused a horse or allowed anyone else to do so in his presence. Now, here he was, putting his favorite mount at risk just so he could vent his anger. If he wanted to behave like a maniac, better that he run his fist through a stone wall, or jump off a cliff. At least then the injury would be only to himself. Shakespeare had been unfailingly loyal all his life. He deserved good treatment.

Trying to convey by touch what he couldn't with words, Ace ran his hands over the stallion's powerful neck and shoulders, kneading tense muscles, giving affectionate pats. After a while, the horse nickered softly, a sign of forgiveness Ace knew he didn't have coming.

It seemed to be his night to behave like a bastard, first with Caitlin O'Shannessy and now with Shakespeare. Hauling in a deep breath of air fragrant with the scents of grass, wild flowers, and alfalfa, he rubbed a palm over his face. When his vision cleared, the world looked just as it had a little over an hour ago. The sky was up, the earth was down. Nothing had really changed. And yet it seemed to him that everything had.

Jesus. What had gotten into him back there? For the last three months, ever since he'd begun implementing his long anticipated and meticulously planned revenge against the men who'd murdered his stepfather, he'd been dead certain he held all the cards. He'd planned it all so cleverly, anticipating every eventuality. And then Conor O'Shannessy's daughter had stepped into the light tonight and he'd seen her face clearly for the first time.

With her flashing blue eyes, flame red hair, and delicate features, there was no denying Caitlin O'Shannessy's resemblance to his half-sister Eden. No denying it, no ignoring it, no lying to himself about it. It wasn't just a similarity in their coloring. He might have been able to explain that away. No, this was more than that, a resemblance so remarkable it was stunning. If it hadn't been for the difference in their ages, the two girls might have passed for twins.

Ace felt sick. Physically sick. Caitlin O'Shannessy and Eden Paxton were half-sisters, no question about it, and since he knew damned well they didn't share the same mother, that left only one possible conclusion—that they had the same father, Conor O'Shannessy.

Maybe, way deep down inside, Ace had always suspected the possibility. With her alabaster skin and brilliant red hair, Eden had been so completely different from Dory Paxton's other children, and even from Dory herself. But even if Ace had suspected, he'd never consciously acknowledged it. And little wonder. Just the thought that O'Shannessy's blood flowed in his precious half-sister's veins was so absolutely vile, he could scarcely credit it. His mother had always sworn that Eden's distinctive coloring came from a long deceased great-aunt on her side of the family. In the early years, shortly after Eden's birth, Ace had been too young and naive to question that explanation, and later, when those insidious doubts had tried to slip into his mind, he'd shoved them away. Not Eden. Not his sweet little sister Eden. The mere possibility was incomprehensible.

But now there was no denying it. Not because he was older. Or braver. Or better able to accept it. But because the truth had been shoved down his throat when he clapped eyes on Caitlin O'Shannessy. The night of Joseph's hanging, Conor O'Shannessy had sown his seed, and nine months later, a beautiful girl child had been born, a child Dory Paxton had named Eden in memory of her husband's dream.

Dear God . . . Ace squeezed his eyes closed, trying without success to make his mind go blank, but the image of his mother's dazed eyes as she staggered from the bushes after being used by Conor O'Shannessy grew stronger until her face and Caitlin's merged. That long-ago night, O'Shannessy had destroyed Dory's dignity. Tonight Ace had nearly done the same to Caitlin, a fact that sickened him.

From a distance, he detected the sound of a horse fast approaching and turned to peer through the moon-silvery gloom. After a moment, he recognized his half-brother Joseph on his dun gelding. At a distance of about ten feet, Joseph, hat pulled low over his eyes, blond hair flying in the wind behind him, stood up in the stirrups and hauled back hard on the reins, bringing the gelding to a skidding halt that sent up a cloud of dust.

Using the grip of his thighs, Ace barely managed to keep his seat as Shakespeare pranced in a half-circle around the other horse, tossing his head and blowing loudly through his nostrils.

Swaying agilely in the saddle for a moment to offset his gelding's imbalanced weight, Joseph cried, "What the hell got into you back there, Ace? Have you totally lost your mind?"

That was a good question, and one that Ace wasn't sure he could answer. He shot his younger brother a caustic glance.

Joseph jerked off his hat, swiped his forehead with his shirtsleeve, and crammed the hat back on his head. The dimple in his cheek flashing with every movement of his lips, he cried, "I can't believe you did that! I just plain can't believe you did it."

That made two of them. Ace settled in the saddle,

trying to stay calm. Even though he knew he had it coming, the last thing he needed right now was a dressing down.

"From the very beginning, and at your insistence," Joseph went on, "we all agreed that our quarrel was with the men directly responsible for Pa's death. Nobody innocent was supposed to get hurt."

"Nobody innocent did," Ace shot back. "As bad as it might have looked, Joseph, nothing happened. At least give me credit for that much."

"Nothing happened? How can you say that? Patrick O'Shannessy has been a real bastard, but that didn't give you any call to take it out on his sister." Jabbing a finger to emphasize his point, Joseph added, "You need your ass kicked for this night's work, big brother."

Rage. It reached a flash point within Ace so fast that he had no time to reason his way past it. Luckily it fizzled out just as quickly. A fistfight with Joseph was not the way he wanted to end this. Especially not when he knew damned well he was in the wrong.

He hauled in a deep breath and slowly exhaled. "I'm sorry," he bit out. "I honest to God am, Joseph. It was just—" Ace broke off, searching for some way to explain. "Well, for one thing, I figured she'd hightail it for tall timber the minute she thought her brother was safe. She's not just related to O'Shannessy. She was raised by the son of a bitch. Who would've expected her to keep her end of the bargain?"

"Whether she would've or not is beside the point. You had no call to humiliate her like that."

Ace knew Joseph was absolutely right, but stung pride made him toss back, "Yeah? Well, maybe it was a little harder for me to stay calm. I was there the night Pa died. I saw the whole bloody business, if you'll remember. You didn't come back from the creek until after it was all over."

"That is such bullshit. Any excuse will do, is that it?"

Ace fixed a tortured gaze on his brother. "I'm not trying to excuse my behavior. I went a little crazy there for a minute. I admit it. Let's just thank God it didn't go any further."

"A little crazy? Cheee—rist Almighty! I knew we were gonna have a sham hangin', but for a while there, I thought you were gonna reenact what happened to ma as well!"

"You have to know I wouldn't have gone that far."

Even in the moonlight, the dubious expression on Joseph's face was unmistakable. "I've never seen you act that way." As his anger dissipated, his voice went gravelly. "I didn't know what to do, whether to stand there and let you do it, or whether to try and stop you. At first, I didn't think you could possibly be serious, you know? Then you grabbed a lantern and actually started herding her toward the rear of the barn. You had a look in your eyes I never want to see again."

Ace rubbed a hand over his face. "You did the right thing, Joseph. My good sense won out in the end, and it could've turned nasty if you'd tried to interfere. I'm sorry if I gave you a bad few minutes. When I first realized . . . well, all I could think about was our poor mother and exacting some small measure of revenge."

A tense silence descended, broken only by the occasional stomp of a hoof or the blowing of air through a horse's nostrils. In the distance, Ace could hear a night bird calling forlornly, its cries fading quickly on the wind. In an attempt to calm down, he took a long draught of air, focusing on the myriad scents that assailed him. Was that honeysuckle he smelled? He let his eyes fall closed and concentrated. On the smells. On the sound of his own heartbeat. Breathing in, breathing out. Slow and easy.

He had no idea how much time passed, only that it did, and that with the passing of each second, he felt better. The crushing pain inside his chest ebbed and his thoughts started to feel a little less tangled. Lifting his lashes, he narrowed an eye at his brother, the fact not lost on him that he could have indulged in such introspection with no one else but Joseph. Sometimes his brother seemed to understand him better than he understood himself.

Ace nudged the brim of his hat back and patted his shirt pocket. "I need a smoke."

The corners of Joseph's mouth tightened. Whipcord lean and compact like his father, he wasn't a very large man, but what he lacked in size, he compensated for with sheer grit and orneriness. Ace trusted no other man as much when it came to guarding his back. Joseph would take on a half dozen opponents without thinking twice, and the marvel was, he usually won.

"Smoke, hell," he said. "Like I said, what you really need is a good ass kickin'."

Ace shifted in the saddle. "Yeah? Well, if you plan to do the honors, you'd best pack a lunch."

"Shit." Joseph said the word as though it had two distinct syllables. He drew his Bull Durham pouch and La Croix papers from his shirt pocket and tossed them carelessly to Ace. "The bigger they are, the harder they fall, big brother. If I hit a man and he don't go down, I'll walk around behind him to see what the hell's proppin' him up."

It was a saying Ace had taught Joseph years before to bolster his confidence, and after Joseph's first fistfight, during which he'd sustained two black eyes, a chipped tooth, a cracked rib, and three broken knuckles, the saying had become a joke. The familiarity of it now put them back on safe ground.

After withdrawing a cigarette paper from the packet, Ace creased it and tapped out some tobacco. He retightened the drawstring, then tossed both the pouch and papers back to Joseph. A quick lick and a twist of his fingers later, he had a cigarette. Not as fancy as one of the Cross Cuts he had occasionally enjoyed back home in San Francisco, but it would do.

"Thank you, little brother."

Joseph returned the pouch to his pocket. "Need a match?"

"Your face and the south end of a northbound jack ass?" Ace chuckled at the narrow-eyed glare his brother gave him. "Some people never learn." Shaking his head, he drew a Lucifer from his pocket. "I usually carry a few matches with me. Beats the hell out of rubbing sticks together if I want to build a fire." He struck the match on the seam of his Levis and bent his head to the flame, which he protected from the wind with cupped hands. A second later, he straightened, taking a long, satisfying drag as he waved out the match. After taking two more pulls, he offered the smoke to Joseph.

"Peace?"

Even as he accepted the cigarette, Joseph swept his tawny eyelashes low over his eyes, and a muscle along his jaw began to tick. "You know, Ace, there isn't anything I hold sacred that you didn't teach me to hold sacred, nothing I believe that you didn't teach me to believe, my attitude toward the ladies notwithstandin'. Back there in that barn, it wasn't my rules you were breakin' but your own."

That stung. And yet Ace couldn't blame his brother for saying it. He had broken his own rules, and in doing so, he had betrayed not only his brothers but himself. "Let's just thank God no real harm was done. Nothing happened. I swear it. When I realized she wasn't going to run, I walked out."

"Maybe so, but it still looked bad. You'd better hope nobody in town gets wind of it, or that girl's reputation will be shot, and you won't have anybody to blame but yourself."

Ace bit down hard on his back teeth. It would be a hell of a note if he ended up honor bound to marry Caitlin O'Shannessy to save her reputation. Just the thought was enough to turn his stomach. "Nobody'll get wind of anything, I guarant-ass-tee you that. None of us will say anything, and if any of them do, they're damned fools."

Another brief silence fell between them. Ace finally broke it by saying, "You know what breaks my heart the most? That Ma has lived with the truth all these years, never once asking any of us to share the burden with her. Thinking back on it, I can't recall a single time she even so much as hinted that Eden was in any way less a Paxton than the rest of you."

A blank expression came over Joseph's face. "Less a Paxton?" He left the words hanging, his face slowly registering his incredulity as the truth started to sink home. "What the hell do you mean, less a Paxton?"

Too late, Ace realized that his brother had not seen Caitlin O'Shannessy's face as clearly as he had. When she had moved into the light, her back had been to Joseph, and the rest of the time, it had probably been too shadowy for his brother to tell much.

"Oh, hey, Joseph, I'm sorry. I thought—"

"Son of a bitch!" Joseph pinched the bridge of his nose and squeezed his eyes closed. "Goddamn son of a bitch! You can't be serious. Conor O'Shannessy? That's what you're saying, isn't it?" He dragged in a deep breath. "No, goddammit, not our little sister. I don't believe it. Not Eden. You're wrong."

Ace shifted slightly in the saddle. "Hey, Joseph. I really am sorry. I honestly thought—" He broke off. There was little point in continuing. What he had thought was obvious.

Ace knew that Joseph was feeling just as he had half an hour ago—outraged, stunned, furious. He wished he could diminish those feelings, but knew he couldn't. Joseph would have to work his own way through them.

Ace curled a hand over his brother's shoulder. "Hey, little brother, I know it's tough. But remember this. As hard as it is to accept, nothing's really changed."

Joseph knocked Ace's hand away and, in the process, dealt Ace a stinging blow along the jaw. "Let go of me, goddammit. I don't need or want your mollycoddling."

"Joseph, I know how upset you're feeling. But after you've had a few minutes to think about it, you'll realize it really doesn't matter. Eden's the same little sister we've always loved. Who cares who her father was?"

"I do, damn you! You're saying our sister was spawned by the son of a bitch who hung our pa? Jesus Christ. If it's true, how can you say it doesn't matter?" Joseph pinned Ace with a defiant glare. "As far as that goes, how do you know you're even right? The O'Shannessys aren't the only people in the world who have red hair, you know. Ma's a blonde. So am I. There could be red hair in Ma's family, just like she said. Just because Eden and the O'Shannessy girl have similar coloring, it doesn't mean—"

"It's not just the hair," Ace cut in. "A mirror image, Joseph. Those two girls look enough alike to be twins. Just wait until you get a close look at her. Eden's sturdier of build and taller. But, otherwise, you have to search to find the differences between them."

Joseph closed his eyes again. After a long moment, he heaved an exhausted sigh. "Our poor mother. All these years, keeping it a secret. I'd like to take that bastard apart with my bare hands."

Ace knew the feeling, but before he could say as much, he heard horses approaching. The riders would be his other two half-brothers and the hired hands who had been with him and Joseph over at the O'Shannessy place. Joseph glanced back over his shoulder, his blue eyes narrowed to see. "Are you gonna tell them?"

Ace turned his horse to face the oncoming men. "Let's wait until we get back to the house. I think this should be a family secret, at least until we bring Eden here. Then . . ." He shrugged. "Well, God only knows. I haven't had time to think that far ahead yet. Ma may not even let Eden come now. After all these years, she may not want her to know, and there won't be any way to keep it a secret once she sees Caitlin O'Shannessy."

Turning his attention from Joseph, Ace steeled himself to face his other two brothers. Given that he couldn't provide an explanation in front of the other men for his outrageous behavior, the next few minutes were going to be difficult.

Esa, the youngest of the Paxtons at twenty-three, drew up first. The brim of his hat shadowed his eyes, but Ace could tell by the grim set of the younger man's lips that he heartily disapproved of what had happened back at the barn. The same sentiment was reflected in David's expression when he rode up. The three hired hands weren't quite so easy to read, but even so, Ace could see they were none too pleased.

When all the horses had quieted, Ace nudged his hat back so everyone could see his face clearly. As he spoke, he moved his gaze from man to man, looking each directly in the eye. "I only want to have to say this once, so everybody listen up. I owe you all an apology for what happened back there. I won't go into my reasons. I believe it's enough to say that I went a little crazy there for a minute. I regret that it happened, and I'll be forever ashamed that it did, but unfortunately, some things can't be undone, and this is one of them."

Kurt Bishop, a tall, raw-boned blond, averted his face to spit. When he turned back, he said, "You don't have to explain yourself to me, boss."

"Given the circumstances, I'm afraid I do. There's the matter of the girl and her reputation. I give you my word that when I took her to the back of the barn, absolutely nothing happened between us."

"Hell, we know that." Rob Martin flashed a ruddy-faced grin. He glanced around the circle of riders. "Don't we, boys?" He returned his gaze to Ace. "There's not a man jack among us who'd work for a fellow we thought would shame a woman that way."

"Damn straight," Jim Stevens agreed.

Ace forced a smile. "I appreciate your trust in me. And I'm glad to hear that none of you would want to see a woman shamed, because that's my main concern, the girl's welfare. What I did to Caitlin O'Shannessy tonight was inexcusable. All the poor girl did was try to save her brother's worthless hide, and any consequences she suffers will be entirely my fault."

"We understand," Jim said softly. "No one will hear anything about it from me, boss. You have my word on that."

"Not from me, neither," Rob agreed.

Kurt spat again. "I got no reason to do any talkin', and nobody to tell it to if I did."

Ace hauled in a deep breath, then slowly exhaled. As a general rule, he didn't cotton to making threats, but this was one time when circumstances seemed to justify his doing so. "I want it understood, here and now, that if word of what happened at the O'Shannessy place gets out, the man responsible will answer directly to me. Is that clear? I don't want that girl to be caused so much as one minute of grief as a result of my actions tonight."

"Yessir, boss."

"It's clear as rain to me, boss."

"I got no problem with that."

Satisfied with the responses of his hired hands, Ace forced himself to meet the gaze of each of his brothers. For the first time in his memory, he saw recrimination in their expressions. What hurt most was that he knew he had it coming.

≫ 3

FOR AT LEAST A FULL MINUTE AFTER KEEGAN AND HIS MEN rode out, Caitlin stood in the aisle, so brittle with tension she felt as if a loud sound might make her shatter. Cold. Oh, God, she felt so horribly cold. Her movements stiff, she retrieved her wrapper and slipped it on. The cotton felt icy as she tied the sash. Still cold, she wrapped her arms around her middle and shivered, her mind teetering between the past and the present, old terrors and new. Even though Ace Keegan hadn't actually touched her, she felt violated. And ashamed. It wasn't so much what had actually happened that bothered her, but what she would have allowed to happen if he hadn't decided to walk out. What she would still allow to happen if it came to a choice between sacrificing her honor or her brother's life.

Anything for Patrick. Caitlin closed her eyes on a mounting wave of rage that glowed red against the backs of her eyelids. If not for his drinking like a fish these last three months, Patrick never would have gotten himself into such a pickle.

How dare he put her in such an impossible position? How dare he! She could be as sympathetic as the next person, but enough was enough. Shooting a prize bull?

And taking potshots at Keegan's men? And all because he'd taken a shine to whiskey?

For almost twenty years, their father had made her life a living nightmare. She'd be damned if she would put up with more of the same from her brother. She was older now and not so helpless. Patrick was going to straighten up, or she would know the reason why.

After returning to douse the lantern, Caitlin burst into the alleyway. Ahead of her, the glow of the other lamp beckoned, its pulsating nimbus still throwing a silhouette of the empty noose against the weathered walls. With every step Caitlin took, her stride lengthened and her anger mounted until she was seething.

She found her brother sitting in the feed passage near his horse, where she presumed Keegan's men had dumped him. Beside him, they had left her rifle, the ejected cartridges lying scattered on the ground. Back slumped against the planked partition of a stall, head hanging, Patrick looked so dejected that she was brought up short.

She shoved aside her feelings of pity. That was probably more than half of Patrick's problem, that she had been making excuses for him. Well, not this time. There was no oblivion to be found at the bottom of a whiskey jug, only a wealth of heartache. He couldn't escape the truth by trying to numb himself to it.

She hugged her waist again, so angry she was shaking. Shooting a glance at Hank, who still stood just inside the doorway, she asked, "Are all of them gone?"

Though he was obscured by the shadows, Caitlin could see the elderly man well enough to tell he was leaning toward her, a hand cupped behind one ear. Raising her voice an octave, she repeated herself.

"Oh, yes'm, they're gone." Hank moved into the light, giving Patrick a look that could have pulverized granite. Then he turned a concerned gaze on Caitlin. "Are you okay, honey? Did he—"

"No," she broke in. "I'm fine, Hank. Perfectly fine."

Hank studied her for a long moment, his expression dubious. "I'm sorry I didn't step in, missy. There wasn't much I could do, what with Patrick an inch away from hangin' and all. It seemed smartest to just stand still and keep my mouth shut."

"You did the right thing, Hank. All's well that ends well. We got off lucky."

"No thanks to some I could name." The elderly cowpoke shook his grizzled head. "I reckon it ain't any of my business. In fact, I know it ain't. But I been workin' on this spread for nigh onto twenty-five years, and I'm gonna say it anyhow." He fixed another glare on Patrick. "If you keep on like you are, boy, you're gonna turn out to be one sorry excuse for a man. After seein' what whiskey did to your pappy, a body'd think you'd know better than to make the same mistake. When are you gonna get your head on straight? After it's too late? If I was younger, I'd knock some sense into you, no two ways about it."

"Thank you for coming out to help us, Hank." She glanced back at her brother, who hadn't bothered to acknowledge Hank's comments by so much as lifting his head. "Having you out here made me feel a little less alone."

Uttering those words made Caitlin feel desolate. In the recent past, it had been Patrick who'd always stood at her side, Patrick who had helped her through the rough times. She and Patrick, against their father and the world. What had happened to him that he could sit there now, a pathetic lump of whiskey-fouled flesh who couldn't even stir himself to meet her gaze?

"I wasn't much help," the old man admitted, jerking Caitlin back to the present. "Didn't dare use my equalizer, here"—he patted his rifle—"and my days of fisti-cuffin' are long since over. But I done what I could. Like you say, we was lucky."

Caitlin gave him a shaky smile. "Thank you. And, now, if you'll excuse us? I need to talk with my brother."

Hank nodded his understanding and stepped outside. Caitlin didn't bother to make sure he'd left. She began pacing in a wide circle in front of Patrick.

"So," she said sharply. "You shot Keegan's prize bull,

did you? Brilliant move, Patrick. Let me guess. I'll bet you came up with that fantastic idea *after* you started drinking."

Patrick finally acknowledged her presence by leaning his head back against the wall. Even in the dim light, she could see the glistening trails of tears on his cheeks, and when she looked into his eyes, she forgot whatever else she meant to say.

"Hank's right, you know." He saluted her with his whiskey jug, which he upended to show that it was empty. "I'm a worthless excuse for a man, a worthless excuse for anything."

In Caitlin's memory, she'd never heard her brother's voice sound so hollow, or so hopeless. Beside him, she noticed that the dirt was splotched with telltale wetness where he had poured out the remainder of the liquor.

"I used to look at our da and hate him for being so weak," Patrick whispered in a rough voice. "For loving his whiskey more than he loved you and me. I could never understand the hold it had on him."

What rang loudest to Caitlin was what Patrick had left unsaid, that now whiskey had the same hold on him. The thought wrenched at her. How could it be that in so short a time, her brother had come to this? She stiffened her shoulders against another wave of pity. Feeling sorry for Patrick wasn't going to help him.

"You haven't been drinking long enough to be that far gone, Patrick. You could still quit, if only you'd try." Caitlin knotted her hands into fists, praying to God that what she said was true. "I refuse to listen to any tales of woe. You're the one who decided to take that first drink tonight. Only you. And you're the only person responsible for what came after. Keegan's bull? You had to know he'd come after you for pulling such a stunt. Yet you shot the animal anyway? It was madness. Utter madness."

His blue eyes glistening with tears, his face drawn with regret, he said, "I swear to you, Caitlin, I'll never take another drink. If you'll only just forgive me, I promise you, I won't."

"Where have I heard that before?"

"No, Caitlin . . . I swear to you, this time I really mean it."

As determined as she'd been to give Patrick a tongue lashing he'd never forget, Caitlin realized she was quickly losing a hold on her anger. She looked deeply into her brother's eyes again and saw only heartfelt sincerity there. No lightly made promise this, but a vow. "Oh, Patrick, I believe you do truly mean it."

"I do. I promise you, I truly do." He raised one knee to support his elbow and cupped a hand over his eyes. For a moment, he appeared to be holding his breath, and then he sobbed. "Oh, God, Caitlin. I'm just like Pa. All it takes is a little whiskey, and I'm a stranger, even to myself." He hauled in a jagged breath. "When I realized Keegan meant to take you to the back of the barn, all I could think about was myself, and what would happen to me if you didn't go. I'm sorry. I'm so sorry. Please tell me the bastard didn't hurt you. Please."

Her heart caught at the pain in his voice, and suddenly her one concern was to alleviate it. "No, no. He didn't hurt me. I swear it. I'm okay, Paddy. Honestly, I am."

Some of the tension went out of his body. After a moment, he said, "No thanks to me, just like Hank said. I can't believe I let you go back there with him. I can't believe I did it!"

"Oh, Patrick. It's the whiskey. Don't you see?" Pictures flashed in her mind of all the other crazy, unexplainable things Patrick had done recently. It made her feel as if her brother had left on a prolonged journey and an imposter had taken his place. "It's just the whiskey."

Silence settled between them—an awful silence filled with jittery thoughts of what had just occurred. She listened to the faint sound of the pigs rutting outside in their pen, to the low bawling of the cow in her stall. Anything to avoid thinking about Keegan.

After a long pause, Patrick said, "The danger isn't entirely over, you know."

Caitlin shot an uneasy glance over her shoulder. "What do you mean, not over? Hank said they've all left. We're safe enough—for tonight, at least."

"What'll we do if those men go into town and start shooting their mouths off? If word gets out, your reputation will be destroyed."

Caitlin relaxed slightly. Keeping her reputation intact was not a major concern to her. She was more worried about things like rainchecks and dealing with the very real danger of Ace Keegan's return. Not that she would dare tell Patrick that.

She went to hunker at his side and put her arms around him. "Let's not borrow trouble. Besides, remember me? The nutty sister who loves to bury her nose in a book and dream of faraway places? The one who wants to hare off to San Francisco and attend the opera once a week? If worse comes to worse, a tarnished reputation won't follow me that far."

"If not for me, you wouldn't still be wanting to hare off."

"Don't be silly, Patrick."

"Now that Pa's dead, what other reason is there for you to leave?"

Caitlin didn't know the answer. She only knew she wanted to go. Maybe it was the memories that haunted her here. Or perhaps it was a simple need to wipe her slate clean and start over. Regardless, now was not the time to discuss her reasons. Not when Patrick was drunk. Not when he could seem perfectly lucid one moment, and turn mad as a hatter the next.

"My passion for faraway places has nothing to do with you, boyo. I've been reading about the ballet and opera since I was knee high, and you know it. Why would you think my yearning to experience those things has anything to do with you?"

"Because I just do, that's all."

Caitlin sighed and ruffled his hair, her heart breaking a little at the self-recrimination in his expression. "Patrick, trust me. If anything, you're the one reason I might decide to stay. I love you, silly boy. Don't you know that? I admit, you've been difficult these last few months, and I've wanted to wring your neck more times than I can count. But one rough spot in all the years we've shared is hardly enough reason to make me hate you."

His mouth thinned into a grim line. "You might change your mind when you can't leave because we're making payments to Keegan for that damned bull. Before he left, he told me the only way he'll consider us even is if I pay him five thousand dollars."

Caitlin's stomach tightened. It had taken her five years to save a thousand dollars. "Did he say you could make payments?"

"Monthly." Patrick passed a hand over his eyes again. "Whatever amount I can afford."

Five thousand. The amount was staggering. And in addition to that, Keegan held a raincheck over her head to avail himself of her body. She curled her hands into tight fists. "We'll manage, Patrick. Together. We always have, haven't we?"

Patrick flashed her a glance. "I've really made a mess of things. I can't believe I shot that bull. It seems so crazy now when I—" His voice broke, and he swallowed convulsively. "I gut shot it on purpose," he whispered. "So it would die a horrible death. And then I rode off and left it bawling." He squeezed his eyes shut. "What kind of person does something like that?"

Caitlin had no answers. She wished to God she did. She couldn't imagine the brother she knew doing such a terrible thing. Patrick had always been so gentle—so caring, even with dumb animals.

"It's in my blood," he said in a voice devoid of inflection. "Sometimes I'm so much like him, it scares me to death."

"Oh, Patrick." Caitlin smoothed his hair from his brow. "You're nothing like him. Nothing. Do you understand me? I don't want to hear you say such a thing, not ever again. It's just the whiskey. You get crazy when you drink. If you keep your word and never touch the stuff again, you're going to be fine. Just fine."

With a suddenness that startled her, Patrick grabbed hold of her. Burying his face against her neck, he wept like a child, his entire body heaving. Caitlin had no idea how to ease him, so she just held him. Her heart broke a little at how big he felt in her embrace, how awkward it seemed to gather him close. He was broad across the shoulders, muscular through the arms. It had been a good long while since they'd done more than give each other a quick hug in passing. Her baby brother, whom she'd loved so long and so well, had become a man.

A tormented man.

She had no idea how long they huddled there, only that eventually his sobs subsided and his tears turned to damp streaks of salt on her skin. When he began to lean more heavily against her, she wondered if he'd passed out.

"Patrick?" she whispered.

He stirred slightly. "Don't hate me, Caitlin. I'm sorry I didn't stop you from going back there with him. I was just so scared. I'll never get drunk like this again. I promise I won't. Not ever."

She ran a hand over his hair again and smiled slightly. As frightening as her encounter with Keegan had been, it would be almost worth it if Patrick would stop drinking. For weeks, she'd been racking her brain, trying to think of some way to turn Patrick around. Now, it seemed, her prayers had been answered. In a most unlikely and unpleasant way, to be sure, but having her brother back again was all she truly cared about.

"Come along, boyo. I'm thinking it's time you got to bed. A fine state of affairs it will be if you pass out here in the barn. Come morning, it will be a mite cold, you can bet on that."

Patrick drew away from her and made a gallant effort to stand on his own. Unfortunately, his legs didn't seem to be cooperating. Caitlin looped his arm over her shoulders and strained to stand bearing his weight. After several aborted attempts, they finally managed to gain their feet.

"Holy Mother, Patrick, how much whiskey did you drink?" she asked as they staggered sideways.

"Too much."

She laughed in spite of herself. Too much? Oh, what a silver-tongued devil her brother had become. She tightened her arm around his waist and set off determinedly for the house, taking one step sideways for every two she took forward.

Practice had perfected Caitlin's technique when it came to handling semiconscious drunks. She had long since learned that the most important thing was to get a man bedded down someplace warm so he could sleep it off, be it on the floor or the bed. She had never bothered with stripping off clothes. Removing a man's boots and his gun belt was enough of a struggle, and all that was really necessary.

It took approximately ten minutes to get Patrick into bed and another ten to return to the barn to care for his horse. Only then did she have time to reflect on what had happened between her and Ace Keegan in the horse stall. A raincheck, he'd said. That had to mean he intended to come back.

After assuring herself that Patrick was peacefully asleep, Caitlin returned to bed herself, but sleep eluded her. She couldn't forget the anger she'd seen burning in Keegan's eyes. Should she go to the marshal? The thought was tempting. Then again, what might Keegan do if she reneged on her promise and went for help? After all, unless they sold the ranch, they wouldn't be able to spare much money to make payments to the man, certainly not enough to appease his anger.

She squeezed her eyes closed, her mind filled with images of Patrick out on the range someplace, shot in the back or beaten to death. If Keegan felt she'd tricked him, might he not kill Patrick just as he'd originally planned?

The thought kept Caitlin awake and shivering long into the night. Unless she missed her guess, Keegan would be back, and she would be honor bound to fulfill her part of their bargain. If she refused, her brother's life could be at stake.

BLOWING IN OFF SNOW THAT LAY HIGH IN THE ROCKIES, THE night wind seemed every bit as cold to Ace as it had twenty years ago. Hunching his shoulders against the bite, he listened to the high-pitched wail and recalled how he had once likened it to that of a lonely specter. He guessed some things never changed; only now the ghosts had names, his own among them. For Jamie Keegan, the boy he'd once been, was long since dead.

Tipping his head back, Ace gazed at the network of tree limbs above him. It hardly resembled the towering oak of his nightmares. As oak trees went, this one wasn't all that big, and it certainly wasn't sinister. He couldn't even recall for sure from which of the limbs Joseph had been hung. Of course, over a period of twenty years, the tree had grown and changed. If it hadn't been for other landmarks, Ace wouldn't have been sure this was even the same place.

Ah, but this was it. No mistake about that. Just over the rise to his right was the meandering creek and bathing spot he remembered so well. To his left was the flat area where his stepfather had chosen to make camp that fateful night so many years ago.

For the last three months, ever since his return to No Name, Ace had been coming to this spot in the evening right after the sun went down. He didn't suppose he could say that he actually came to visit with Joseph, for intellectually he knew he couldn't visit a dead man, but emotionally that was his intent. To whisper of his plans. To speak of things deep in his heart. To hope that in some way Joseph knew he was here and that it was only a matter of time until old wrongs would be set aright. As right as Ace could make them, at any rate.

Tonight was the first time Ace had come here feeling any trace of doubt or uncertainty about what he was doing. Tacked to the massive tree trunk beside him, a tattered news clipping rustled in the breeze. He'd taken the clipping from the No Name *Gazette* and hung it here himself, a headline in bold block letters that heralded the financial death of Joseph's murderers. NO NAME FINALLY GETS RAILROAD SPUR. It was the sort of retaliation Joseph would have approved of, a swindling of the swindlers. No violence. Only the predatory and the heartless would get hurt. An ironic twist at the end of the story.

Exposed to the weather as it had been, the clipping was beginning to disintegrate, and much of the ink, diluted by rain, had bled into the bark. To Ace, that seemed fitting, a symbolic missive to the dead, a declaration of his intentions, so to speak. Only now, he felt as if he'd gone back on his word. Someone innocent had been hurt, after all.

Caitlin O'Shannessy . . . God, he couldn't get the image of her face out of his mind. The fear in her eyes. The flaming spots of color that had flagged her otherwise pale cheeks when she'd begun unfastening the buttons of her nightgown. How could he have done such a thing?

With each rise and fall of the wind, the tree limbs above Ace's head whipped and then settled, whipped and then settled, their leaves whispering loudly, then tapering off into a sigh. To Ace, they seemed to be calling Joseph's name, an endless litany in honor of a man whose passing had otherwise gone unmarked. Even the mound of Joseph's grave under the oak tree had been worn away by time, the wooden marker fashioned by a young boy's hands long since lost to the elements. It seemed so sad to Ace—so incredibly sad. This place should have been permanently scarred by what had happened here.

Gazing out over the endless sweep of rolling grassland, he could see, stark against the horizon, the outline of the sprawling log house he and his brothers had begun building three months ago. Except for the interior finish work, the structure was almost completed, nine months ahead of schedule, according to Ace's calculations. Back in San Francisco, he had projected that it would take three months alone just to erect the house, and that hadn't been counting the six to nine months he'd figured it might take to get possession of the land. Patrick O'Shannessy had helped expedite matters by making the mistake of sitting across from Ace in a poker game.

Usually, seeing the house filled Ace with a sense of accomplishment. He was so close to success, damn it. So close. It was too late to start having doubts, too late to call things off. After nearly twenty years of work, he was about to see his stepfather's dream become a reality. The Paxtons would work the land Joseph had died for. They would marry, have children, live and die here. All Ace had to do was see things through to the end.

Until tonight, it had all seemed simple. Now, he realized that the stakes were higher than he'd ever dreamed. How much was his burning hatred for Joseph's killers costing him? Or, perhaps more accurately, how much was he willing to sacrifice for it? When all of this was over, would there be anything decent left within him?

❧ 4

THANKS TO ACE KEEGAN AND HIS MIDNIGHT RAID, CAITLIN felt unaccountably nervous the next morning when she went to fix breakfast. Jumping at her own shadow, her da would have called it. Her cat Lucky gave her a bad turn when he leaped out from under the sink unexpectedly. Then Hank came pounding on the door, the suddenness of his knock startling her yet again. By the time Patrick stumbled into the kitchen for a cup of coffee, she was growing accustomed to having her heart in her throat.

The kitchen was cloaked in predawn shadows, yet Caitlin hesitated to light another lamp. One was aplenty, and really all that they could afford. Lantern fuel cost money, and they had pitifully few pennies to waste.

As if he read her thoughts, Patrick said, "God, Caitlin, I realize you're trying to save money, but do you have to make the coffee this weak? I swear I could make stronger if I tied a bean to a duck's tail and ran downstream to catch a cup of water."

"Oh, now, Patrick," she scolded. "It isn't that weak. Things are lean right now. I've told you that. We have to cut expenses every way that we can, and if that means making weak coffee, so be it. We have to start making payments on that bull now, remember. Where else will we come up with the money if not by economizing?"

Angling her body sideways to keep from getting smoke in her face, Caitlin thrust another length of oak into the fire and replaced the range lid. Inside the stove, the wood ignited quickly, sizzling and crackling like hundreds of muffled firecrackers. Despite everything that had happened last night and might still happen, the sound cheered her. After all, Patrick was unharmed, and for the moment, so was she.

For the moment . . . There was the catch and the main reason she was so jumpy, she guessed. Because she knew Ace Keegan might come back. When was the question.

"Patrick," she said hesitantly, "I've been thinking."

Her brother fixed her with a bleary gaze. "Uh-oh. That's always dangerous."

Caitlin tried to smile, but the attempt went awry. Her insides felt as if they were being fed through a laundry wringer. "This business about the bull and making payments . . ." She caught her lower lip between her teeth. "I know I said we would manage somehow, when we discussed it last night, but the more I think about it, the less certain I am that we actually can. We barely make ends meet now."

Patrick glanced around, as though in frantic search of something. Caitlin knew he was craving a drink, and she felt awful for broaching this subject at a moment when he was so vulnerable. It was just that she didn't see any choice. Keegan was a reality they couldn't ignore, a threat that wouldn't go away.

"We have to manage," her brother said wearily. "We just have to, that's all."

"There is another alternative." Caitlin rubbed her palms on her jeans, a pair of Patrick's hand-me-downs she'd confiscated to wear while working around the ranch. "I know it seems drastic, but we could sell this place." When her brother shot her a horrified look, she held up a staying hand. "Just think about it, Paddy. That's all I'm asking. We could pay Keegan off, and we'd still have plenty of money left over to make a fresh start somewhere else. You and me, in a completely new place. Wouldn't that be grand?"

Patrick's gaze shifted away from her and became fixed. "We can't sell the ranch, Caitlin." His voice sounded oddly scratchy. "I, um, took out a mortgage against it."

Caitlin wasn't sure she'd heard him right. "You what?"

"I invested in some of that railroad spur land," he said softly. "To get the money, I had to mortgage the ranch. If we sold out now, we wouldn't have two nickels to rub together after we paid everyone off."

Caitlin felt a falling sensation that bottomed out with such abruptness her legs jerked. "Railroad spur land?"

She had suspected. Even though she and Patrick had discussed such a move and agreed it was unethical, she had suspected. A dizzy feeling filled her head, and she held onto the counter for support. "Oh, Patrick. I was afraid you might have done something like that, but I figured you probably used the money you stole from me."

"I didn't exactly *steal* it. Borrowed, more like. I'll pay it back. As for using it to invest, it was only a thousand dollars, Caitlin. That much wouldn't have gone far to buy up a lot of land."

"Oh, Patrick, how could you?"

"I was drunk," he said hollowly. "My friends were all talking about what a great opportunity it was. Before I knew it, I was over at Barbary Coast Mortgage signing my name on the bottom line." He gestured feebly with one hand. "I, um, wanted to tell you. Almost did a couple of times. But I knew you'd pitch such a fit, I never got up my nerve."

"Your nerve? And how about the poor dirt farmers whose land you've bought? *That* takes nerve, Patrick, God forgive you." Caitlin thought of the social the church was holding at the end of the month to raise money for those farmers, of all the hours she'd invested in the planning. And now she discovered her brother had mortgaged their ranch to take advantage of their misfortune?

"Those poor people have sweat blood on those parcels of land," she said shakily. "For years. Now, when a railroad company may come along and make all their toil worthwhile by buying their acreages at premium prices, you waltz in for a song and stand to make all the profit?"

Patrick pushed to his feet, his tautly held body swaying slightly from the lingering effects of whiskey. Looking into his eyes, Caitlin knew she should keep her mouth shut, that to anger him right now might be a grave mistake, but her Irish got the best of her.

"Blast you, Patrick! And blast your damnable whiskey! How could you do such a thing when you knew how strongly I felt about it! While you were off signing your name on that bottom line, I was here keeping this place afloat." She held out her hands. "Bloody blisters! Working until I could scarcely walk. And all for what? So you could cheat people?"

Patrick doubled his fists. The wildness she'd come to dread was there in his eyes. "Those farmers were already mortgaged up to their eyebrows because of the drought!" he shot back. "It's not my fault it didn't rain for two goddamned years! They would've lost their shirts, no matter what. Buying their land before they lost it saved them from complete financial ruin!"

"I've already heard all the arguments, thank you very much. Please spare me. The end result is, you'll make money, and those poor people will crawl away with little more than the clothes on their backs. I find that disgusting and indefensible."

His fist still knotted, Patrick jutted out one rigid finger and shook it under her nose. "Shut your mouth!" he bit out. "Or so help me God, I'll shut it for you! You're just a woman. What do you know about business? I did it. It's done. Live with it!"

For the first time, Caitlin felt afraid of her brother. For a terrible moment, she nearly gave way to the habits of a lifetime and backed away from him. Then outrage filled her. "If you're going to hit me, Patrick, do it," she said in a voice pitched to a throbbing whisper. "Just understand that if you do, it will be the one and only time. You aren't our father. You can't make me stay here and suffer your abuse. I'll be gone so fast it will make your head swim."

Seconds passed. She heard the clock ticking. The labored rasp of Patrick's breathing filled the air. He stared at her, his anger a pulsating, suffocating thickness between them. Then he blinked.

"I have never lifted a hand to you in my entire life," he rasped. "How can you think I might now?"

Caitlin brushed his hand away, watched his arm fall limply to his side. "When a man shoves his fist in my face, I tend to anticipate a blow. I wonder why?"

A muscle in Patrick's cheek twitched, and his blue eyes grew suspiciously bright. "I'd never hit you, Caitlin. I'm sorry I mouthed off like I might. It's just—" He spun away and raked a hand through his tousled hair. "My head's splitting, that's all. You yelling feels like a knife slicing through my brains." He planted his hands on his hips, leaned his head back, and took a deep breath. "I'm sorry about mortgaging the ranch. Sorry I invested in the railroad spur land. I know it was wrong. That's why I couldn't bring myself to tell you. Because I knew you'd detest me for it, and I was ashamed."

Caitlin pressed a hand to her turning stomach. Following her brother's example, she took a deep, calming breath. "I don't detest you, Patrick. I'm angry, yes. It was a stupid, thoughtless thing to do. But I don't hate you."

He opened his eyes. The smile he flashed was ill-timed and pathetically shaky. "Wanna haul out the paddle? I'll grab my ankles and take my licks. Just like the old days. Only, please, don't talk about leaving. Okay? I, um . . ." His mouth twisted. "I need you right now, Caitie. I'm never gonna make it without you."

She couldn't remember the last time he'd called her Caitie. A burning sensation washed over her eyes. She stood there, wrestling with her anger and a pain that cut so deep, it hurt to breathe. He had come just that close to striking her. She'd seen it in his eyes.

But he hadn't. That was the important thing, what she should focus on. Their father had never hesitated. If nothing else, this confrontation drove home to her that Patrick was nothing like Conor. No matter what he'd done—no matter what he still might do—there was hope for him. As long as there was hope, she couldn't turn her back on him.

Trying to inject a note of teasing into her tremulous voice, she said, "I only took the paddle to you once, Patrick O'Shannessy, and that was when you nearly blew your head off, playing with Pa's pistol."

"Yeah, well . . . you made that one time stick in my memory."

Unaware until that instant that she'd knotted her hands, Caitlin flexed her fingers. "You never played with guns again."

His gaze clung to hers, his expression aching with regret. "I'll never shake my fist at you again, either."

Caitlin didn't feel herself move. The next thing she knew, she was in her brother's arms, hugging his neck fiercely. "Oh, Patrick, what am I going to do with you?"

"Love me. Just love me, Caitie. Don't give up on me. Please. I'm sorry. I'm so sorry."

Sorry wasn't going to get them out of this fix. Caitlin ran a hand into his hair. She wished he were a little boy again, that she could still try to make everything all right simply by hugging him and telling him it was so.

"The ranch," she whispered. "If it's mortgaged, we can't sell it. And that means even more in payments. What're we going to do?"

He pressed his face against her hair, clung to her. "As much as I hate to say it, I think we better hope and pray that investment I made on the railroad land pays off. If it does, we'll be okay. It's just going to take a few months."

Tightening his arms around her waist, he began to sway with her. She wasn't sure if he was trying to soothe her or himself. "I'm sorry I went against your wishes and made the investment. All I can say in my defense is that I got drunk. I won't again, Caitlin. I need you to believe in me, that's all."

"I do," she whispered. "We'll find a way out of this, Paddy. Somehow. We've been through worse."

They held each other for a long while, remembering those times when all they'd had was their love to get them through. When Caitlin finally drew away, she felt strengthened. There had to be a way to make payments to Keegan and keep abreast of the mortgage installments. Other people had debts, after all, and they seemed to manage. It would mean a lot of hard work, but neither she nor Patrick was a stranger to that.

"Sit down." She patted his arm, then gave it a squeeze. "I'll finish fixing you some breakfast."

Patrick's stride was a little unsteady as he returned to the table. "I'm not sure I can eat."

"You have to try. Otherwise you'll feel sick all day."

As she moved across the kitchen to get the bowl of flapjack batter, Caitlin peeked out the window at the barn. She half expected to see Keegan standing in the doorway. He wasn't, of course. But that didn't make her feel much better.

As she returned to the stove, she glanced back at her brother, who was rubbing his temples, clearly suffering. "I don't want you going off alone for the next few days, Patrick." Batter sizzled as she poured a measure onto the greased griddle. Within moments, the smell of hot flapjacks filled the air. "Please, promise me you won't."

He glanced up at her through splayed fingers. "I won't. You can bet on that, and the same precautions should apply to you. Last night, you got off lucky. If the bastard comes back, he might hold you to that bargain you made with him."

Trapped. That was how she felt. With a lien against the ranch, they couldn't sell the place and leave. *No way out.* During the night and first thing this morning, she'd comforted herself with the thought that she and Patrick could pay Keegan off and skedaddle. No unholy bargain. No moment of reckoning.

Caitlin couldn't quite bring herself to meet Patrick's

gaze for fear he might read more in her eyes than she wanted him to. Last night she had deliberately neglected to tell him anything about Keegan's mention of a raincheck. If Patrick found out, she was afraid he'd go off half cocked and do something incredibly stupid, like challenge Keegan to another gunfight.

Keeping her expression carefully blank, she said, "Oh, I rather doubt he'll be back."

"Nonetheless, sis, I'd appreciate it if you'd be extra careful the next few days. You don't want to be caught off alone, away from the house, any more than I do."

If Keegan did come back, Caitlin prayed she would be alone. God forbid that there should be a confrontation. Patrick wouldn't stand a chance against Keegan, with fists or guns. "I have to cut and bale more grass hay today," she reminded him. "We can't count on this dry weather to hold much longer, and we can't afford to lose any of the crop."

"I'll go out with you then and help."

Sitting with his elbows propped on the scarred mahogany table and his chin cupped in one hand, Patrick looked in no shape to put in a long day of physical labor. His eyes were rimmed with red. His face was pale. With his hair standing on end from sleep and still wearing the clothes he'd had on last night, he looked as if he'd been dragged behind a horse for several miles.

"Are you sure you feel up to working?"

"I'll manage."

"You look like you need"—she nearly said *some hair off the dog that bit you,* but caught herself just in time—"to sleep a few more hours."

"Nah, I'll be fine."

His willingness to help with the heavy work was such a welcome change that Caitlin hated to discourage him.

"Well, I'll certainly appreciate the extra pair of hands," she finally said. "Hank and Shorty do what they can, but there's only so much they're still capable of. That's not to mention I'll enjoy your company. It's been a while since we worked together." She flashed him a smile. "I miss sitting with you in the sunshine, having lunch and talking. I tend not to take as many breaks because it seems so lonely."

"Yeah, well . . . I apologize for that. No more, hm? I'll stay away from the whiskey and start taking care of things around here again like I should. I know it's been hard on you."

Her brother turned a little green when she put two flapjacks on his plate. Smiling sympathetically, she set out the butter and honey, then left him to manage breakfast the best way he could while she went to gather the eggs.

En route to the henhouse, she had to walk directly past the barn. Perhaps it was morbid curiosity, or simply a need to face her demons, but she felt compelled to step inside. The empty noose still hung from the rafter, silent testimony to the tragedy that had almost occurred.

Unable to bear the sight of it, and not wanting Patrick to have to either, Caitlin took the rope down and tossed it in a corner already piled knee-high with junk. Unfortunately, Ace Keegan's presence in the barn wasn't quite so easy to dispel. Everywhere she turned, something reminded her of him.

No stranger to bad memories and how to deal with them, she forced herself to stand in the gloom until her fear receded a bit. Then she closed her eyes, recalling how she and Patrick had played in here on rainy days when they were small, the barn their only refuge because their father was in the house. Playing hide and seek. Swinging from a rope onto a hay pile. Pretending they were the cavalry fighting off make-believe Indians. Good times. Happy memories to help shove away the bad.

As she left the barn, Caitlin scolded herself for having allowed her overactive imagination to run away with her, but even so, her sense of dread wasn't so easily set aside. If she saw a shadow from the corner of her eye, she thought it was Keegan. If she heard a noise, she whirled to look behind her. It was silly. Absolutely silly. And yet she couldn't shake it off.

By the time she got back to the house, her nerves were raw. She hadn't been this jumpy since before her father died.

"You okay?" Patrick asked when she reentered the kitchen.

"I'm fine," she assured him.

Lucky chose that moment to squall like a banshee and come running out from under the stove. Caitlin jumped and cried out, and Patrick came clear up out of his chair.

"That damned cat!" Patrick shook his head. "Under the stove again. One of these times, the poor stupid thing is gonna bake himself well done."

Caitlin knew very well that Lucky wouldn't have run under the stove unless something had frightened him. She gave her brother a long, hard look. There was that glitter in his eyes again. It was like being on a seesaw, up one minute, down the next. She knew his body was starting to scream at him for more whiskey. She could only pray that this time, he wouldn't give in to it.

"It just might help if you wouldn't stomp your boots at the cat, Patrick," she chided gently. "You know how skittish he is."

"That's all I ever do. Just stomp. I don't hurt him any."

"You know how it scares him. Just because you have a headache is no reason to take it out on Lucky."

"He jumped up on the table and tried to eat my breakfast."

"So you scared the sand out of him? You know he isn't right in the head. Why can't you just put him down from the table and leave him alone?"

"I'm sorry!" With a sweep of his hand, he sent his plate skidding across the table. The china came to a precarious stop right at the edge and teetered. "I lost my temper. I apologize. How about giving me a little peace and quiet, huh? My head feels like a splattered pumpkin. "

With that, he stomped loudly from the room.

When her heartbeat had finally returned to normal, Caitlin fished the cat out from under the sink to make sure he was none the worse for having hidden under the stove. His yellow fur felt slightly hot, and when she buried her face against him, the singed smell was unmistakable. Poor fool cat. He didn't have much sense, especially when he got scared.

Not that she was pointing a finger. She had more in common with Lucky than she liked to admit. Hiding from the world out here on the ranch, just as the cat did in his cubbyholes. On the rare occasion when she forced herself to go to town and mingle with people from church, she always held back part of herself. She enjoyed her friend Bess Halloway's company, but even with Bess, she was reserved, afraid of revealing too much.

"Oh, Lucky, my boy. How long will it be before you forget, hm?"

Dumb question. As if she had managed that feat herself? At least she was intelligent enough to understand that Conor O'Shannessy was dead.

Sometimes she'd hear a door slam or a boot scrape someplace in the house and think, just for an instant, that it was her father. Or there would be a loud, unexpected noise, and her knees would go weak with terror. It had to be a hundred times worse for Lucky, who couldn't comprehend that Conor was gone and would never come back.

She dragged in a deep breath and looked around the kitchen, her gaze lingering on the new curtains and rugs she'd made last winter, tangible evidence that her father no longer ruled here with an iron fist. The touches of color, which he never would have allowed, usually cheered her, symbols of her newfound freedom. This morning, however, she didn't feel uplifted. Ace Keegan's visit last night had cast a pall over everything, it seemed.

She glanced at the lard tin on the table, where wilted rose blossoms hung listlessly from their stems. Later today, she promised herself, she'd go out and cut fresh flowers. Seeing them, smelling them, would make her feel better. It always did.

As she rubbed her cheek against Lucky's fur, she found herself looking out the window at the barn. She almost wished Keegan would hurry back and get it over with. Better that than to live in fear day in and day out.

❧ 5

OVER THE NEXT COUPLE OF WEEKS, ACE'S GUILT OVER what he had done to Caitlin O'Shannessy increased. One morning, he found a sealed envelope tacked to the gatepost at the entrance to his ranch, the Paradise. Enclosed, he discovered eight dollars and nine cents, all in loose change, along with a tally, written in a feminine hand, of the amount Patrick O'Shannessy still owed for the bull—precisely four thousand, nine hundred and ninety-one dollars and ninety-one cents.

It was the nine cents she'd included in the envelope that got to him. It told him more than she could possibly know, namely that she'd probably scraped together every spare penny she had to make the payment. *Nine cents.* To Ace, it was a paltry amount, scarcely enough to have bothered with. Yet Caitlin had sent it. Because, to her, nine cents was obviously a lot.

It had been a very long while since Ace had contemplated the buying power of nine pennies. He held the coins on his palm, imagining Caitlin O'Shannessy carefully counting them out and slipping them into the envelope. With them, she could have purchased several bags of penny candy, if she could even afford to indulge herself in that fashion. Or a card of buttons for a new dress. Or a loaf of bread or some potatoes. A lot of money, nine cents, if you had few to spare. Ace could remember a time when he had worked twelve hours for a nickel.

Christ. Those nine pennies made him feel like the world's worst bastard. It wasn't as if he were going to miss the five thousand dollars. He could have lost four times that amount and scarcely noticed the difference in his bank balance. Yet Caitlin O'Shannessy was going to sacrifice and do without to pay it back.

When he'd told Patrick he expected payments to be made on the five thousand he felt was due him, he'd meant for the hardship to be on him, not his sister. And wasn't that just the hell of it? He'd never set out to hurt Caitlin, yet he had.

Even as Ace exhausted himself with the most taxing of ranch work, he couldn't forget the shame and dread he'd seen on her face as she fumbled with the buttons of her night shift. At the very least, he owed her an apology.

But how? And when? He didn't want to scare the girl to death by appearing at her door, not to mention that he'd be running the risk of having an altercation with her brother if he did so. No. He needed to meet her on neutral ground, preferably in a public place so she wouldn't feel so threatened.

"We could have John keep an eye out for us in town," Joseph suggested one afternoon as he and Ace worked together putting in fence posts. "She must go into town sometimes. Most folks make it a habit to do their shopping on a particular day of the week. If John can detect a pattern, then you could be in town on that day and meet up with her, sort of casual like, on the street."

Ace swung the sledge with a little more force. John Parrish was an executive employee of Trans-Con Railway Incorporated, of which Ace was president and principle stockholder. The young man was presently acting as manager of the new No Name branch of Barbary Coast Mortgage, another of Ace's companies. John's purpose there was to assist Ace in the eventual financial ruin of certain investors. Ace felt sure John would happily make inquiries about Caitlin O'Shannessy's shopping habits. But was that wise? Ace didn't want the young man to do anything that might weaken his position as an informant or undermine his position in the community. If he began asking strange questions about Caitlin O'Shannessy, it was bound to raise suspicion.

Ace took another angry swing with the sledge. As the

hammer impacted with the post, Joseph leaped back. Esa and David, who were coming behind them stringing wire, both chuckled.

"Watch out, Joseph. I think he's wishin' that was your head," Esa called.

"And yours might be next if you don't shut your trap," the sandy-haired David warned.

Swiping at his forehead with the sleeve of his shirt, Ace pretended to hear none of this exchange. After the initial discord over his treatment of Caitlin O'Shannessy, his brothers had come to regard Ace's dilemma of how he might apologize to her as highly humorous. Why, Ace didn't have a clue. As far as he could see, there was nothing funny about the situation.

Perhaps it was because none of his brothers had seen Caitlin's face as clearly as he had. It had been a shock to all of them when he'd told them of her relationship to Eden, of course. But nothing was quite as shocking as seeing the resemblance for yourself. More than that, it had driven home to Ace how wrong he'd been to hate Caitlin and Patrick O'Shannessy simply because their father's blood ran in their veins. After all, if he was going to hate them for it, he had to hate Eden for it as well.

Shaking the sting of the hammer blow from his hands, Joseph said, "I was just making a suggestion, Ace. No sense in getting pissed."

Ace hefted the sledge, letting the smooth hickory handle slide through his hands until he got a comfortable swinging grip. "Just hold the damned post, would you? I haven't got all day to fart around out here."

Knees slightly bent, his muscular upper body a full arm's length away, Joseph grasped the post again, his eyes already squinted in anticipation of the next blow. "You just be damned sure you hit what you're aimin' at, big brother."

"Oh, I will," Ace assured him.

When Ace hit the post again, Joseph's entire body jerked with the effort to hold the wood upright. "I don't know why you're so mad. I was just trying to come up with a few helpful ideas to—"

Ace swung the sledge again, cutting him off. "That was not a helpful idea. If you'll remember, none of us are even supposed to know John Parrish."

"Well, I was thinking we could contact him with a note in his mail slot like we do for other things."

"Every time we contact him, we run the risk of someone noticing. I only want to do so when it's absolutely necessary," Ace reminded him. "I'd rather not put all our plans at risk, if it's all the same to you. Not that apologizing to the girl isn't important. It definitely is. But there has to be another way."

Joseph shrugged. "I guess *we* could ask around to see what day she goes to town."

"And then what? It isn't like I have time to sit on the boardwalk in No Name, waiting for her to show. And supposing I did? Out on the street like that, how would I get her to stand still long enough to apologize to her?"

"Maybe we could glue her shoes to the boardwalk," Esa suggested.

"Hell, no. Just toss a lasso over her head and hitch her to a rail until she's heard you out," David called.

Esa laughed. "You ever seen Ace toss a rope? He needs a target big as a barn, and even then he has to stand right on top of it."

Joseph let go of the post and raised his hands. "Okay, you guys, that's enough. It's really not a laughing matter."

"So stop laughing and come up with a suggestion," David challenged.

After checking the post's position with his plumb line, Ace filled the hole full of dirt, packed it, and then kicked the stout length of wood. "She's in tight," he pronounced as he returned the weighted string to his pocket.

Joseph sidled along behind him to the next post that lay waiting. "The way I see it, what you have to do is show the poor girl you aren't a barbarian," he told Ace. "Like maybe present her with flowers or something."

"Ace, packin' flowers on Main Street?" David hooted. "God, let me have my box camera handy when that moment comes."

"He could take her candy," Esa suggested.

"That might work." Joseph turned to look at his oldest brother. "We could spruce you up some. Get rid of the gun, put you in a suit. You'd clean up nice."

"And a bowler hat," Esa added. "One of them checkered ones."

Letting the sledge settle at his feet, Ace folded his hands over the carved end of the handle. "I hope you boys are about finished. I don't mind you laughing at my expense, but what about Caitlin? As it stands, she believes her new neighbors are rapists and killers. Maybe that doesn't bother you, but it does me."

Joseph picked up the post. "So what's your idea? Do you even have one?"

Hefting the sledge for his next swing, Ace stood back while Joseph upended the post into the hole. "Well, no two ways around it, I need to make things right with the girl. I like the idea of a public place. She'd feel safer with people around. But how and when? Near as I can tell, she seldom goes to town."

"She attends the community church. They got one of them there preachers who don't cotton to any one religion," Esa explained. "What's that called?"

"Nondenominational," Ace said, shaking his head. "I swear, boy, you sound like a cracker. Your pa would turn over in his grave if he heard you."

Joseph pressed a hand over his heart. "Well, ain't you some pumpkins. Not all of us got our shine by rubbing elbows with the folks at gambling tables, you know."

Ace gave a loud snort. "I got my shine, as you call it, by listening to our mother and trying to emulate her. You would do well to do the same." He glanced back at Esa. "You're sure Caitlin O'Shannessy attends the community church?"

"Leastways, she used to."

"How do you know that, Esa?" Joseph asked.

"By readin' the paper these last five years."

"The No Name *Gazette*?" Ace asked.

Esa nodded. "While you were following all the important headlines about folks here wantin' a railroad spur,

Eden and Ma was keepin' tabs on the society page. I reckon because they knew they'd move here someday. Anyhow, sometimes Ma would read the articles out loud. About all the dances and socials and such. Who went with who, and what lady wore what. She and Eden have a keen interest in that kind of thing. Anyhow, one of the things I learned by listenin' was that Caitlin O'Shannessy attends community church real regular."

"Will wonders never cease," Joseph inserted. "Our Esa, keepin' tabs on No Name's high society."

Ace sent Joseph a warning glance. To Esa, he said, "Go on."

"Go on with what?" Esa asked.

Striving to keep his patience, Ace said, "Tell me more."

"No more to tell. She goes to church regular like, that's all, and helps with all the ladies' club functions that raise money for the poor."

"There's a social and dance comin' up on Saturday night," David said. "I saw the church poster when I was in town the other day."

"A dance would be perfect," Joseph said. "All joking aside, Ace. She'd have lots of people around to make her feel secure, and you could approach her without raising any notice. Men approach ladies at dances all the time."

"Yeah," Esa agreed. "Even if she doesn't want to dance, it'd give you a chance to tell her you're sorry. At a function like that, it ain't likely her brother would cause any trouble, either."

Ace tried to envision himself attending a small-town social. Not that he was a stranger to dancing. He just hadn't danced with any ladies in a good long while. "I don't know. A church social? I haven't attended something like that in years."

"Better that than to make a fool of yourself tryin' to talk to her out on the street," Joseph observed.

Ace guessed that was true.

"Besides," Joseph went on, "socials aren't really all that churchy."

"Heck, no. To raise money, they gotta charge admis-

sion," David explained. "The public is invited. All kinds
of people go. You see men steppin' out to sneak a swig or
have a smoke. That kind of thing."

Ace glanced down. "I'm a long way from small-town
respectable."

Joseph chuckled. "The roof of the community hall
won't cave in on you, Ace. Trust me."

"I'll go with you," David offered. "I was plannin' on
it, anyway."

"We'll all go," Joseph declared. He flashed Ace a
teasing grin. "This is one social I don't want to miss."

ON SATURDAY NIGHT, CAITLIN FELT UNEASY ABOUT ATTEND-
ing the social. First of all, Ace Keegan might be there,
and she couldn't think of anything worse than running
into him. Secondly, it had been only three weeks since
Patrick had quit drinking, and there would be tempta-
tions galore at a social.

"Patrick," she said as he parked their wagon along the
boardwalk in front of the general store, "I know we've
been over this, but are you sure you're going to be able to
handle this tonight? I really wouldn't mind a quiet
evening at home."

He tied off the reins and set the wagon brake. "You've
been planning to attend this social for over a month, and
you worked all day yesterday helping to get the hall
ready. How do you think I'd feel if I spoiled it for you?"

"There'll be lots of other socials, Paddy. I don't—"

"Exactly," he said with a gentle smile. "Lots of other
socials, and at every single one, there'll be liquor. I can't
spend the rest of my life hiding from it."

"Staying away from liquor for a month or so isn't
exactly what I would term hiding from it for the rest of
your life."

He looked deeply into her eyes. "Caitlin, I know I
haven't given you much cause to have faith in me, but
can't you at least try?"

The plea in his gaze made Caitlin feel ashamed of
herself. "Oh, Patrick, of course I have faith in you. I'm
just worried about you, that's all."

"Well, stop worrying. I'm going to be fine. With someone like you to help me over the rough spots, how can I fail?" He vaulted down from the wagon, then stepped around to the side. "Lord. What all did you bring? Looks like we'll need a small horse to carry it."

"Gertie Howard got sick yesterday. She was supposed to bring a custard. I volunteered to bake one for her." Hoping no one up the street was watching, Caitlin gathered her rose-colored skirts and jumped down beside her brother. It wasn't ladylike, she knew, but it seemed silly to pester Patrick when she was capable of getting down by herself. "It's only three things to carry."

With a wink to let her know he'd only been teasing, he handed her the custard dish, keeping the pan-dowdy and loaf of bread to carry himself. Catching her worried look, he made an exasperated sound under his breath. "Caitlin, would you stop? I'll be fine, I promise. Let's go. I can hear the fiddlers warming up."

As she joined him on the boardwalk, she tucked the custard dish under her arm, moistened her fingertips, and tried to smooth his cowlick. He chuckled and pushed at her hand. "Don't do that. Someone'll see. Next thing I know, you'll be spitting on your fingers and washing my face like you used to when I was little."

"I never!"

He laughed. "You did so. Almost every Sunday on the church steps. I hated it. You got any idea how spit feels on your face after it dries? Kinda like egg whites."

Caitlin flashed him a sidelong glance. "How would you know how egg whites feel on your face after they dry?" Sudden understanding dawned. "Patrick O'Shannessy, don't tell me you tried one of my facial masks?"

"Only once." A flush crept up his neck. "I thought it might help fade my freckles. It seemed to work good on yours." He narrowed an eye. "You tell a single soul, and you're dead."

She giggled, trying to picture her brother with white foam all over his face. "Did you use lemon?"

"Lemon? For what?"

"That's what bleaches the freckles, silly." Unable to

stop herself, she went up on her toes to take another swipe at his hair. "Honestly, Paddy, it's standing straight on end."

"I don't care," he said, batting her hand away. "I like looking rumpled." A twinkle crept into his eyes. "If I listened to you, I'd be so handsome the women wouldn't leave me alone, and then where would I be? Married, most likely, and wouldn't that be a heck of a note? Then I'd have two women trying to straighten my hair all the time."

Caitlin sighed and rolled her eyes. As she fell into step beside him, he ran his fingers through his hair, making deep furrows in the wiry red curls. She itched to fix it, but resisted the urge, concentrating instead on the lovely evening.

It was just turning dark, and on the horizon, a splendorous sunset wreathed the Rockies. The glow washed the weathered clapboard storefronts with pink and reflected off the windows. Above the rooftops, scattered pines rose like royal sentinels, their wind-twisted tops cast in silhouette against a granite sky.

"Looks to be quite a turnout," Patrick commented as they passed several other wagons. "Hope it's not so crowded inside that people can't dance."

"It's so nice tonight, folks may drift outside." She hurried to keep up as they crossed an alley that ran between the buildings. As they stepped up onto the next boardwalk, she said, "Mmm. The smell of that bread is making me hungry."

"It does smell good. So do the apples in this pan-dowdy." He flashed her a grin. "Would you just listen to that fiddle music?" Tucking both the bread and dessert under one arm, he grasped her by the elbow. "Let's pick up our pace."

She gave a breathless laugh. "Who's been looking forward to this social?"

"Guilty as charged. Since I gave up the bottle, I've gone from bein' a gadabout to stayin' at home. I admit, I'm lookin' forward to some socializing."

The community hall, a sprawling log structure, was

located at the end of the street, the last block of which was home to a variety of businesses, including the Silver Spur, the town's only saloon. Caitlin didn't miss the slightly wistful glance Patrick sent toward the drinking establishment as they walked past, and she knew he was wondering how many of his friends were inside. No doubt he missed the comradery.

Catching her worried look, he flashed a strained smile. "I'm fine, Caitlin. Really, I am." His gaze snagged on the dress shop window. "Well, now, would you look at that? If that's not your color blue, I don't know what is."

Caitlin slowed her pace to study the dress on display. "It is pretty, isn't it? A few too many ruffles, though. Don't you think?"

"You could use a few more ruffles. Practically all I see you in nowadays is britches."

"I can't very well do ranch work in a skirt and petticoats."

He steered her around an uneven board in the walkway. "Yeah, well. Now that I'm tending to business like I should, you aren't going to have to do as much of the ranch work, and when our profit margins start to go up, one of the first things I'm gonna do is buy you some dresses just like that one. What do you think of that?"

Caitlin thought of the payment she'd had Hank Simmons deliver to Ace Keegan's ranch a couple of weeks ago. It had been little more than a drop in the bucket. "I think it will be a while before we can afford frivolities, that's what I think," she said.

"Not that long. My investment in the railroad spur land should be paying off soon."

Caitlin preferred not to think about that. Although she'd come to accept it, the fact that Patrick had done such a thing still rankled. She supposed, if she were practical, she would thank her lucky stars. If the investment paid off, as Patrick hoped, the extra money might save their bacon.

"New dresses would be lovely, Patrick, but I can do very well with what I have for a while."

"Very well? You got that gown you're wearing on your

seventeenth birthday. I remember 'cause I worked at the
livery stable mucking out stalls for almost a month to
buy it for you."

Remembering how hard Patrick had worked to buy
her the dress was the final nudge Caitlin needed to set
her bitter feelings aside. Over all, Patrick had been a
wonderful brother. His recent mistakes shouldn't be
allowed to overshadow that.

"And a fine job you did of picking it out," she said,
smoothing the skirt. "After all this time, it's still my
favorite, and it's in amazingly good shape, don't you
think?"

"Not bad, considering the wear it's had. But you've
done a little growing."

"Growing?" Caitlin immediately guessed what he
meant and plucked at her bodice. The neckline had
always been just a trifle more revealing than she considered seemly, and now that her measurements had increased, it was even more so. "Does it look that bad?
Maybe I should go back home and—"

"No, no!" Laughing, he held up a hand. "It looks fine
for now. It's just that you need new dresses, and I'm
looking forward to buying you some, that's all."

The twang of another fiddle drifted through the night,
catching Patrick's attention. He seemed to forget all
about railroad speculation and new dresses as they
covered the last quarter block to the hall. Flashing him
another smile, she said, "Once we get in there, try to
remember you have a sister. I wouldn't mind taking a
few turns on the dance floor."

"Like you won't have plenty of opportunities to
dance."

"You know I don't like to dance with just anybody."

"Yeah? Well, if you weren't so standoffish, you might
be married and have a passel of kids by now. Did you
ever think of that?"

"Dealing with you," she said lightly, "is about all the
frustration I can handle, brother of mine."

Patrick chuckled at the jibe. "I'm not *that* frustrating,
surely."

She pretended to mull that over. "Well, maybe not quite. You come in handy on occasion, especially when I want to dance."

He looped his free arm around her shoulders and gave her a jostling hug. "I'll try to work you in for a number or two, then."

"Only one or two?"

"I'll be busy," he said with a wink. "I have to dance with all the pretty girls, you know. If I leave anyone out, her heart will be broken. It's a terrible responsibility, being such a handsome devil."

Out in front of the hall, wagons were parked helter-skelter. The horses, left to pass the evening in lines and traces, had already hung their heads to snooze. At the back of one wagon, a woman was bent over the tailgate, changing her baby's diaper. Inside the wagon, two toddlers were sprawled on makeshift beds. Recognizing the woman as Mary Baxter, an acquaintance since childhood, Caitlin raised a hand to wave. Evidently Mary didn't see her, for she failed to wave back.

"What's the matter with her?" Patrick asked.

Caitlin shrugged. "She probably didn't recognize me. It is almost dark."

Inside the community hall, the hum of conversation was loud and ceaseless. Caitlin glanced nervously around in search of familiar faces. There was one in particular she hoped she wouldn't see.

Patrick gave their tickets to the door attendant, then turned to hang her cream-colored shawl on a wall hook. "Where do I put this other stuff?" he asked, gesturing at the bread and pan-dowdy he held under an arm.

"We put all the food tables along the back wall."

Strategically placed lanterns bathed the hall in light, but the place was so crowded one could see only a few feet in any direction. Caitlin went up on her toes, trying to look over the top of the crowd to determine the best direction for Patrick to take. Most of the people seemed to be gathered around the dais in the center of the room where the musicians were tuning their instruments.

"Over there," she said, pointing left.

Patrick shouldered his way past a group of men, taking

care that there was room for her to squeeze beside him. All kinds of people were there, from men in suits and women in silk gowns to farming couples in dungarees and calico. Caitlin scanned the room for a tall, ebony-haired man dressed in black and was relieved when she didn't see him. A social was probably too tame for a big-city gambler and gunslinger.

As they passed yet another knot of people, she got the oddest sensation, a prickly feeling at her nape. When she glanced around, everyone whose gaze she encountered looked hurriedly away. She shot a meaningful look at Patrick.

"Do I have a button undone?" she whispered.

He gave her bodice a glance. "No. Is my barn door open?"

She stifled a nervous giggle. "No, so why is everyone staring at us?"

"You got me. I feel like I've grown a third eye in the middle of my forehead."

"Oh, look, Patrick, there's Bess!" Caitlin went up on tiptoe to wave.

Bess Halloway, a slender blond dressed in emerald green, waved back and began working her way through the crowd. "Caitlin!" she cried as she drew near. "I was beginning to think you'd never come. There's something important we need to talk about."

Speaking loudly to be heard over the din, Patrick said, "Talk, talk, talk. I swear, that's the only reason Caitlin gets involved in these fund-raising projects, so she can flap her jaw at you." Flashing Bess a grin, he took the custard dish from Caitlin's arms. "I'll go put this stuff on the table and come right back."

Waving her brother off, Caitlin turned back to Bess, who had the distinction of being her one real friend. Doc Halloway's niece, Bess had been a frequent visitor at his dispensary when she and Caitlin had been younger. Bess had even been present a few times when Caitlin had crept in to seek medical treatment after one of her father's drunken rages. But Bess had proven to be a trustworthy friend, for she'd never breathed a word to anyone of what she knew about Caitlin's home life.

Over the years, Caitlin had come to value her friendship with Bess dearly, something she couldn't say about her guarded relationships with other young women. Bess never pried. She never looked curiously at Caitlin, as if she were trying to see deeper than Caitlin wanted her to see. In short, she was one of those rare individuals who offered friendship and support without condition.

"It's so good to see you," Caitlin told her in all sincerity. "We hardly got to talk yesterday." She glanced around. "Where's that handsome husband of yours?"

"He went up to Denver with his pa on a cattle-buying trip. A last-minute thing. I came with his ma." Bess toyed nervously with a blond curl at her temple, her green eyes dark with worry. "Caitlin, there's a problem."

"Uh-oh," Caitlin said teasingly. "Don't tell me the honeymoon is already over. It's only been—what?—six months."

"Everything is wonderful between Brad and me. This is about something else, Caitlin, and I haven't a clue how to tell you."

"Tell me what?" Again Caitlin got that prickly feeling. She glanced up to find that half the people in the hall seemed to be staring in her direction, some of them whispering behind cupped hands.

Bess tended to be a calm young woman. Caitlin took it as a bad sign when she began wringing her slender hands. "It's Hank. Hank Simmons, your hired man? He's over at the saloon, Caitlin, and drunk as a skunk. From what I understand, he's trying to muster up some volunteers to go with him to teach Ace Keegan some manners."

Caitlin's stomach dropped. "Oh, no."

"I hate to repeat the story that's circulating." Bess touched a fingertip to her mouth, then whispered, "I don't believe a word of it. Not a word. But Hank is telling people that Keegan—well—" She made a frantic little motion with her hand. "That he made you an indecent proposition, and you went along with it to save Patrick. That they were going to hang him, or some fool thing."

Caitlin closed her eyes for a second. When she opened them again, Bess's face had turned crimson. "I detest repeating gossip, especially to the person being talked about. But I felt you needed to know. I'm sorry."

Caitlin shook her head, then cast about for her brother. She had nearly given up when she caught a glimpse of his red hair near the door. He was leaving, she realized, and judging by his expression, he was mad enough to chew nails and spit out screws. He must have already heard the news about Hank and was headed over to the saloon to find him.

The trouble with that was twofold. From the sound of it, Hank had already destroyed her reputation beyond repair, and for another, if he entered the saloon, Patrick would be placing himself directly in temptation's way.

Shaking free of Bess, Caitlin shouldered a path through the crowd, but by the time she got to the door, Patrick was nowhere in sight. The saloon was only about halfway up the block. She guessed her brother had already gone inside.

"You okay?"

Caitlin glanced around to find Bess standing almost on top of her. "Yes, I'm fine. Just a little worried about Patrick. Remember, I told you he quit drinking? Now I think he's gone over to the saloon to find Hank."

"That doesn't necessarily mean he'll have a drink," Bess said reasonably.

Remembering Patrick's plea that she place some faith in him, Caitlin assured herself that Bess was absolutely right. Stepping into the saloon for a minute didn't mean her brother might lose control.

With a sigh, she turned from the door to face the judgmental stares again. It occurred to her that Bess might be wise to make herself scarce. Women were judged by the company they kept, and Caitlin's reputation was in tatters.

Not that Bess would desert her. She was that good a friend, the sort to stand fast through good times and bad. Fishing in her pocket for her watch, Caitlin checked the time. She would give Patrick until nine, she decided. If he didn't make it back within an hour, he probably wasn't coming, and there would be little point in her staying after that.

On a par with Caitlin's somber mood, one of the fiddlers struck a mournful chord. The next instant, boisterous and earsplitting music filled the hall. The sound of the string instruments dug at her temples, and stomping feet sent shudders through the plank floor. Only a short while ago, she had looked forward to the cacophony. Now all she could think about was getting out of there and going home. To the peace, and the quiet, where she needn't worry that a tall, dark-haired gun-slinger might appear at any moment.

🙚 6

OVER THE NEXT FEW MINUTES, CAITLIN BEGAN TO FEEL LIKE a bug impaled on a pin. It was horrible being stared at by so many people. She kept wanting to check to be sure the hem of her skirt hadn't hiked up.

To make matters worse, her rose-colored gown was a trifle tight, just as Patrick had pointed out, and it seemed to be growing smaller by the minute. She was starting to feel like ten pounds of peaches stuffed into a five-pound bag. Social mores dictating, she'd had to wear a corset. A lady simply didn't go around without the proper under-garments. Unfortunately, like the dress she wore, her corset had been purchased five years ago for a far less ample figure. The contraption of whalebone and elastic made her protrude in places she never had in her life, and half the single men in town seemed bent on ogling the display.

"You don't happen to have a handkerchief, do you?" she asked Bess. "To cover my décolletage."

"Don't be silly." To be heard over the din, Bess leaned a little closer. "Half the necklines in here tonight are cut far lower than yours."

"But the women wearing them aren't being stared at by everyone."

"Not everyone is staring at you."

"Name someone who isn't."

Bess nibbled her lip as she scanned the crowd. "Mrs. Etler."

"Mrs. Etler can't see anything beyond the end of her nose."

Bess sighed. "I guess you probably do feel a little conspicuous. Patrick will be back soon. You'll see. He's probably just dealing with Hank."

Dealing with Hank? How, exactly, did one deal with a drunk? Caitlin had been trying for years, and look where it had gotten her. Men. At this point, she wouldn't have given a fig for the whole bunch of them.

Reaching into her pocket, she withdrew her watch to check the time again. Eight-thirty? It seemed to her the minutes were crawling. She glanced over at Bess as she returned the watch to her pocket. "How time does fly when you're having fun."

"Thanks a lot."

Caitlin sighed. "Oh, Bess, you know I didn't mean it that way."

Tapping her toe in time to the music, Bess said, "You could dance, you know. You're getting even more invitations than usual tonight."

"And we both know why." Caitlin wrinkled her nose. "The way some of those men looked at me—" She broke off and shook her head. "I wouldn't dance with one of them if he paid me."

Bess's cheeks flushed. "I never thought about that being the reason." After considering for a moment, she patted Caitlin's arm. "Don't you worry. This too will pass. Rumors always do."

"That's my saying."

"You're rubbing off on me."

At just that moment, a couple swirled past, the young woman caught a bit too closely in her partner's arms, the tops of her stylish kid pumps flashing beneath the hem of her lavender dress. Caitlin couldn't fail to note the furtive way the man ran his hand up the woman's ribs, grazing the underside of her breast.

"Did you see that?" she asked. "Five minutes ago, that same fellow asked me to take a turn with him around the dance floor. Just look what I missed."

"There are a few rapscallions, and I admit, tonight most of them have gravitated toward you. But that doesn't mean every one of them is a rat. If you refuse to dance with anyone, how will you ever find Mr. Right?"

Caitlin and Bess had covered this ground so many times before it had almost become a joke between them. Only tonight, Caitlin didn't feel much like engaging in banter. "Maybe I don't want to find him."

"Come on, Caitlin. If not marriage, what do you plan to do with your life?"

Caitlin arched an eyebrow. "Enjoy it? I know that's a purely scandalous notion for a mere woman to have, but for the second half of my life, I'd really kind of like to do some of the things *I* want to do for a change. That will be out of the question if I'm stupid enough to let some man get me under his thumb again."

Before Bess could reply, a woman nearby said in a stage whisper to her husband, "Caitlin O'Shannessy is here! Can you believe her brass? If I were her, I'd be hiding my head in shame."

Two bright spots of color formed on Bess's cheeks again. She flashed the woman a derisive glance. "Don't pay any attention to her, Caitlin. She's just a mean-hearted old shrew with nothing better to do than pick on other people."

Ignoring the woman was easier said than done, and the worst of it was, Caitlin knew other people were whispering about her as well. She felt like hiding her head, all right. In fact, going home sounded better by the moment.

She was still wrestling with her embarrassment when the fiddlers ceased playing suddenly, and all present turned toward the front of the hall.

Her attention caught by the startled hush that fell over

the crowd, Caitlin's head snapped up. She fixed her gaze in alarmed terror on the lofty, intimidating man dressed all in black who was stepping with deliberate slowness over the threshold. Coming in behind him were three of the men she'd seen in the barn the other night, all of them more slightly built than he, one a blond, the other two with sandy-colored hair.

They were an intimidating lot, well-muscled and exuding an arrogant self-assurance. Each of them wore a gun, but guns were a common sight in No Name and couldn't account for the threatening air that surrounded them.

The doorway was at least fifty feet from Caitlin, but when Ace Keegan came to a halt just inside the room, the crowd parted between them. In deference to the occasion, he had exchanged his black denim shirt for one of black silk, but his attire was otherwise unchanged, his well-worn black denim trousers hugging the powerful lines of his lean thighs, his pearl-handled revolver winking like a mirror in the lamplight.

Like shavings drawn to a magnet, his glittering dark gaze came to rest on her. Panicked, Caitlin grabbed hold of Bess's arm. "I believe we should start mingling," she said with forced gaiety.

Bess threw her a startled look. "It's him! Ace Keegan."

Because Bess had stated the obvious, Caitlin didn't bother to reply. Feeling like a rabbit caught in the open by a hungry hawk, she cast frantically about for an escape route. Ace Keegan. He was here, and he was staring straight at her. Oh, God.

He was every bit as tall and daunting as she remembered. The black silk shirt hugged his broad shoulders and muscular arms, the color complementing the glistening jet of his wavy hair and his darkly bronzed skin. Without his hat to shade his face, he was extraordinarily handsome, the scar along his left cheekbone enhancing his sharply chiseled features.

As he moved a bit farther into the room, he swung around to hang his black Stetson on one of the wall hooks behind him. While his back was turned, Caitlin drew Bess along with her into the encircling crowd. To her dismay, she realized that Bess's dress, a brilliant emerald green, acted as a flag wherever they went.

As Keegan turned back around, he scrutinized the room with piercing brown eyes that seemed to miss nothing. He was obviously looking for her, she realized a little hysterically, her heart kicking so violently against her ribs, she feared she might faint.

"How dare he show up here," Bess whispered. "What with all the talk, that really takes some nerve."

Caitlin thought Ace Keegan would probably dare almost anything. To her relief, she saw his gaze move past where she stood. Then it sliced back, coming to rest on her like a lethally sharp dagger. He began to make his way through the crowd, his gaze still fixed on her. There was no longer a doubt in her mind. He had come here looking for her. Since she'd already made one payment to him for his bull, and well before the designated month had elapsed, she could think of only one other reason why he might wish to speak with her—to make arrangements to collect on his raincheck.

Not here. Caitlin had already made up her mind that she would do whatever she must in order to keep her brother from being hurt. But to have the entire town witness her humiliation . . .

"Your dress," Caitlin whispered. "It's so bright!"

Bess glanced down and understanding dawned in her green eyes. Giving Caitlin a nudge, she said, "Go! I'll find you later."

Caitlin needed no further prompting and once again turned to flee. Only there was nowhere to go. Keegan was blocking the only exit. Thinking fast, she descended upon another group of young women, hoping to melt into their midst. No such luck. The knot of females dispersed like a flock of startled ducks the minute they realized who was standing with them. In a matter of hours, it seemed, Caitlin had gone from being one of the most highly thought of young women in town to a pariah.

The fiddlers began playing another number, and several couples moved to the center of the room to dance, forcing the majority of the crowd to bunch up at the perimeters. Left abandoned near the punch bowl, Caitlin turned to face her pursuer. He was easy to spot as he shoved through the crowd toward her. Her heart caught at the determined expression on his darkly bronzed face.

IT DIDN'T TAKE ANY PARTICULAR GENIUS FOR ACE TO FIGURE out that Caitlin O'Shannessy was doing her damnedest to avoid him. Every time he moved toward her, she darted away into the crowd, the alarmed expression on her face unmistakable. Not wishing to frighten her any more than he already had, he drew to a stop and tried not to stare at her, no easy task.

She wore a rose-colored gown, the low-cut neckline edged in feminine lace, the pleated bodice nipped in at her slender waist to set off her figure to perfection. With her hair brushed to a russet sheen and piled in loose curls atop her head, she was, without question, one of the loveliest women he'd ever seen. She was also the palest, her skin so white he couldn't be sure where she left off and the poster paper behind her started.

Ace couldn't help but want to get this apologizing business over with, but he couldn't ignore the fear in Caitlin O'Shannessy's eyes. The girl seemed terrified, and he supposed she had good reason.

In yet another obvious attempt to avoid him, she went to stand near the punch bowl table. As if she had some sort of communicable disease, the people gathered there for refreshments fell away, leaving her to stand alone, looking wan and forlorn. The anguish on her face made Ace's gut knot and filled him with an awful suspicion.

His temples throbbing in time to the music, he went in search of Joseph, whom he found outdoors with some other ranchers. As inconspicuously as possible, he drew his brother aside. "What the hell's going on with Caitlin O'Shannessy?" he asked. "Everybody at the social seems to be shunning her."

Even in the darkness, Joseph's blue eyes glinted. "Word has leaked about what happened. I was just fixin'

to come tell you. Folks are saying that she—well, you
know—that she traded her favors to you in exchange for
her brother's life."

"Christ." Ace was so furious he wanted to put his fist
through something. "Who talked? I swear to God, before
I fire him, he's going to wish he were dead."

Even as he made that vow, Ace knew that taking his
frustration out on someone else wasn't the answer. The
largest chunk of the blame for Caitlin O'Shannessy's
troubles rested on his shoulders.

Joseph shook his head. "It wasn't one of our men who
opened his yap. It was that old fellow in the barn, the
one she called Hank."

To Ace, that seemed even worse. Poor Caitlin. It
would have been one thing to have had her good name
destroyed by strangers, but to be betrayed by a longtime
employee? He turned back toward the community hall.

"What are you going to do?" Joseph called after him.

Ace never broke stride. Some questions had no simple
answers.

When he reentered the hall, he was sadly amused to
find that Caitlin had worked her way through the crowd
and was about to escape out the front door. The instant
she spotted him, she spun about like a small creature of
prey searching for a bolt-hole. Unfortunately, everywhere she chose to run, people fell away from her as if
she had the plague. One old battleaxe even had the
effrontery to brush at her skirt as Caitlin passed, as if the
girl's touch had soiled it.

Since she obviously realized he wished to speak with
her and was none too thrilled at the prospect, he elected
to put her suffering quickly to an end. He slipped
through the crowd, clamped a hand over her wrist and
spun her toward him. Startled blue eyes looked up at
him from a face so pale her features might have been
carved from alabaster.

"Miss O'Shannessy," he said, trying for a low modula-
tion that wouldn't scare her half to death, "how nice to
see you again."

Her colorless lips quivered as she replied, "Mr.
Keegan."

In that moment, she made Ace think of a frightened child, though the ample curves of her slight frame proclaimed her to be anything but. Her voice was tremulous and barely audible over the buzz of conversation around them. It didn't escape his notice that the pulse in her fragile wrist was leaping wildly under his fingertips. He felt badly about that. But not so badly that he intended to let her go.

He couldn't help but recall how she'd entered the barn the other night, the ominous click of a well-oiled rifle punctuating her forceful demands. Was this even the same girl?

Fiddles whined as the musicians on the dais sought a common note. He could only hope their next number would be slow, something that would allow him to hold her close so they might converse. "May I have this dance?"

Ace expected her to decline. But despite the fear in her eyes, she nodded. Why he felt surprised, he didn't know. From the instant he'd first set eyes on her, this remarkable girl had been doing exactly the opposite of what he expected.

As carefully as he might have handled egg shells, he guided her onto the dance floor, one hand at her wrist, the other settled at the small of her back. A lilting waltz began. When he turned to take her into his arms, her wary expression made him cringe. A head taller than most men, Ace knew he must look huge to someone of her slight stature.

"Caitlin . . ." He searched her gaze. "May I call you Caitlin?"

She shrugged a shoulder, the gesture eloquent. Ace curled a hand over her hip and drew her into the waltz, his guts knotting at how small she felt. Even her hand seemed tiny.

Bending his head to hers, he began by saying, "I am so very sorry about this. Please believe I never meant for things to turn out this way."

No response. Brittle and expressionless, she glided with him across the floor, her motions jerky, her fingertips pressed tautly into his shoulder. An overweight couple bounced by, doing a dance step that looked like a cross between the waltz and a polka. The woman's rump collided with Caitlin's back, knocking her forward. With a startled *umph* of expelled breath, she melted against him for a moment. He couldn't help but notice how nicely she fit or how right she felt, almost as if her soft curves had been molded especially for him.

He shoved the thought aside, more than a little appalled. First, last, and always, this girl was Conor O'Shannessy's daughter. Judging by the way she jerked erect to put some distance between their bodies, the distaste was mutual.

Forcing his thoughts to the matter at hand, he said, "We need to talk."

She gave a stiff nod, the curls at her temple tickling the underside of his jaw. She smelled of soap, sun-dried cotton, and lavender, a scent that was uniquely her own. Innocent. That was how she smelled. Innocent, and incredibly sweet. The kind of girl who tempted a man even as she brought out all his protective instincts. Ace closed his eyes on a wave of regret. He would have killed any man who dared to treat Eden the way he had treated this girl.

"The other night, I . . ."

His voice trailed away. Usually straightforward, he found himself dry-mouthed and feeling awkward. Because of him, her entire life was in a shambles. Somehow, his carefully rehearsed apology no longer seemed enough.

Then, all too soon, the dance ended. Or at least it seemed that way to him. If her relieved expression was any indication, she didn't share the sentiment.

Not relinquishing his hold on her, he said, "The other night, when I was over at your place, I should never have left things unfinished between us like I did. I've regretted it ever since."

Her eyes grew even rounder. "Not here. Please, let's not discuss it here."

If not here, then where? Before Ace could ask that question, she twisted from his grasp and disappeared into the crowd.

"Caitlin, wait!"

She didn't look back, never so much as broke stride. Determined to finish what he had started, he moved after her. Unfortunately, several individuals chose that moment to speak to him, either welcoming him to the community or extending sympathies over the loss of his bull. As politely as he could, Ace extricated himself from each conversation.

Even so, by the time he reached the door and exited the building, Caitlin was nowhere to be seen. Joseph was still standing with the group of ranchers. Ace called to him. "Did you see the O'Shannessy girl come this way?"

Joseph grinned and saluted Ace with a flask of whiskey. Jabbing a thumb toward Main, he said, "Saw a woman run by. Hellbent for breakfast thataway. Can't swear it was Caitlin O'Shannessy, though."

Ace looked up the street just in time to see a wagon careen around the corner and disappear. He suspected the driver of that buckboard was Caitlin.

His first inclination was to rush after her, but he quickly thought better of it. The farther from town he let her get, the more privacy they would have to talk when he finally caught up with her.

She couldn't escape him forever.

❧ 7

"HA! HA!" CAITLIN SLAPPED THE REINS ACROSS PENELope's rump. "Giddyap."

Despite her efforts, the fat old mare lumbered along at the same slow speed. Glancing over her shoulder, Caitlin tried to see if anyone was following. Sadly, she was almost as blind as Mrs. Etler in the dark. If Keegan was pursuing her, she wouldn't see him until he was almost on top of her. A lovely thought.

After several minutes, during which nothing happened, Caitlin relaxed. As slowly as she was driving, Keegan would have caught up with her by now if he were coming. *Thank you, God.* She closed her eyes, letting the rhythmic rattle and shake of the wagon soothe her.

Suddenly, the conveyance lurched and listed heavily to one side. Scrabbling to keep her seat, Caitlin glanced back to see what on earth had happened. Her heart fluttered and seemed to drop to her knees. *Keegan.* He had already jumped from the saddle into her wagon and was tying his horse's reins to her tailgate. The rattle of the wheels must have drowned out the sound of his approach.

"I hope you don't mind," he called politely, "but I really do need to talk to you, and I can't see much point in putting if off until later."

Mind? If she'd had a gun, she would have shot him.

With amazing agility in so large a man, he navigated the length of the lurching wagon and settled onto the seat beside her, a looming shadow dressed all in black. He looked a yard wide across the shoulders and twice that long in the leg. Propping one boot heel on the kick board, he draped an arm over his knee. When he turned to regard her, she noticed that he'd opened the collar of his shirt and rolled his sleeves back over his corded forearms.

Kerwhump!

Caught staring, Caitlin was nearly pitched off the seat by the sudden lurch. She jerked hard to the right on the reins. Penelope snorted at the rough treatment and took a lumbering sidestep, drawing the wagon over another patch of uneven ground. Dust billowed up, stinging Caitlin's nostrils.

"Are you *trying* to hit all those chuckholes?" Keegan asked dryly. "Or does your phenomenal driving skill just come naturally?"

Struggling to keep her seat, Caitlin craned her neck to see the road. Even on a bright night, she had trouble seeing her hand at arm's length, let alone potholes twenty feet ahead of her. "If you don't like my driving, Mr. Keegan, you're welcome to get out at any time."

She immediately regretted those words. An intelligent woman would be doing everything in her power to stay on this man's good side.

"I may bounce out," he said in that same dry tone.

When she glanced back over at him, the shadow of his hat so obscured his face that she could determine very little about his expression. At least she could be thankful he hadn't offered to drive. Her fingers felt frozen around the reins.

With her free hand, she drew her shawl more closely around her and asked, "What is it you wish to speak with me about?"

As if she didn't know.

His firm mouth quirking at one corner, he said, "Now there's a question."

What kind of response was that? A tense silence settled between them, broken only by the rhythmic creaking of the wagon and the steady *cloppety-clop* of the horses' hooves. The silence wore on Caitlin's nerves.

He plucked a match from his breast pocket and clasped it between his teeth. Then, shifting position, he braced his arms at his sides, propped his opposite boot on the kick board and sat forward, his hands gripping the seat. Though she knew she had to be misreading him, he looked almost as nervous as she felt—as if he wanted to say something and was having trouble getting it out.

If that wasn't absurd. Ace Keegan, nervous? Somehow, she doubted it.

With burning eyes, she stared out into the darkness. Though she couldn't see much, she knew the terrain from here to the ranch by heart. To the east were endless stretches of green plains. To the west was hilly shrub land where dense thickets of glossy-leafed oak were interspersed with occasional clusters of dull-leafed mahogany. In short, nothingness. Miles and miles of it in all directions.

She looked back over her shoulder. The dim glow of No Name's lights had already vanished. She was alone with him. Completely and utterly alone. On Saturday nights, Shorty, their other hired hand, always went into town with Hank. That meant no one would be at the ranch when they got there. Absolutely no one.

Caitlin had never felt quite so helpless. To protect her brother, she had struck a bargain with this man. If she reneged, Patrick could end up dead. She couldn't take that chance. That being the case, it only made sense to get this distasteful business over with quickly.

Quickly—that was the key word. Hopefully, Keegan would cooperate. A few minutes. That was all it would take. A few awful minutes.

Panic fluttered in her stomach. She quickly squelched it. Nothing could be as bad as she was imagining. Besides, experience had taught her that no matter how unbearable a situation might seem, it always passed and things eventually got better. Sometimes, that was all a person had to cling to, the knowledge that tomorrow would come.

The important thing—the only important thing, for now—was to keep Keegan happy so he wouldn't retaliate against her brother.

Just as Caitlin reached that determination, the man shifted on the wagon seat and bumped her shoulder with his arm. She felt as though she'd collided with a mountain of solid rock, not a reassuring feeling, given the situation.

His mouth tightening around the match he held between his teeth, he nudged up the brim of his hat to regard her. Fleetingly, she wondered if the reason he seemed to have a penchant for holding something between his teeth was to camouflage the paralysis in his cheek.

Then his gaze caught hers and all thought of his cheek fled her mind. The color of coffee and lined with long, thick lashes, his eyes made her skin tingle wherever they touched.

In that whiskey and smoke voice she remembered so well, he said, "It's one hell of a situation we've got here, isn't it?"

Caitlin couldn't have agreed more, though why he

should complain, she didn't know. She was the one in a fix. "Yes."

Just then, the wagon hit another pothole, pitching her sideways against him. He huffed softly at the impact, whether with laughter or from getting the breath knocked out of him, she wasn't sure. Encircling her waist with a strong arm, he drew her against his side. She flinched when she felt his large hand claim a resting place just above her right hip.

"Sorry," he said. "On a stiffly sprung wagon seat like this, a little gal like you should avoid the chuckholes or put some rocks in her drawers for ballast."

She cast him such a startled look that Ace went back over what he'd just said. Rocks in her drawers? A suave talker, he definitely wasn't. *Christ.* He'd followed her out here to apologize. So why didn't he just do it and get the hell out of here?

"Caitlin . . ." Even in the moonlight, he couldn't miss the tension in her slender body or deny that he was the cause of it. An awful, suffocating sensation lodged in his throat. "Caitlin, I—"

Whatever Ace intended to say, it fled his mind. Never in his life had he seen such eyes. Huge and luminously blue, they revealed her every emotion. How could a man look into eyes like that and tell a woman he was sorry for having destroyed her life? Essentially, that was what he was doing, offering her a crumb when he owed her the whole loaf.

In the distance, he saw the O'Shannessy spread rising against the horizon. House, barn, a few ramshackle outbuildings. Even the moonlight wasn't kind enough to make the place look like much. From gossip his brothers had heard in town, he knew Caitlin had been doing most of the work around the place since her brother had taken to the bottle. Try as he might, Ace couldn't imagine her having the strength to push a plow or run a hay baler. What troubled him even more was that she'd found it necessary to try.

As Caitlin drove the wagon up in front of the barn, he glanced around the dark service yard. As he'd noted the last time he visited, junk was strung from hell to breakfast. Rusted old balers. Broken wagon wheels. A cylinder washing machine someone had used for target practice. There was even a Studebaker road cart with a cracked axle, its one-person seat cocked at an angle. Other stuff sat in the shadows of the barn, too indistinct to make out.

After tying off the reins and setting the brake, she twisted from his grasp and, snatching up her skirts, vaulted from the wagon, as agile and surefooted as a boy. Feeling big and cumbersome, Ace jumped down beside her.

She stepped around him to unhitch the horse. "I'll only be a minute," she said in a tight little voice. "Then we can—" She broke off and threw him a look. "First, I'd like to take care of Penelope, if you don't mind."

"Here, let me get that," he said, brushing her hands aside.

To say she stepped back to allow him better access to the traces was an understatement. Leaped was more like it.

He was glad for the busywork of unhitching the horse and was pleased she didn't demur about letting him help. Until he decided what to do about her, he didn't want to leave, and he was quickly running out of excuses to stay.

After he released the old mare from the traces, the animal was so eager to reach her stall he wasn't sure who was leading who on the way into the barn. "Which space is hers?" he called.

Lantern light flared, then bobbed toward him. "The second one on the right." There was an unmistakable note of hesitation in her voice. "Mr. Keegan, I am perfectly capable of taking care of my own horse."

"What kind of a gentleman would I be if I let you do the heavy work?"

The look she gave him said more clearly than words that she'd never thought of him as a gentleman.

He glanced back to see that she was still holding the lantern high. As he looked around the shadowy barn, it struck him like a fist between the eyes exactly where he was. The place rang with accusations, all directed at him.

"I'll get her grain and water." After hanging the lantern from a hook out in the alley, she stood fidgeting at the entrance to the stall. "A quick rubdown will do, Mr. Keegan. I'll curry her in the morning."

Ace had a feeling the girl's sole aim was to hurry him on his way. He wished he could oblige her.

After snubbing the horse, he grabbed an old rag from the dividing rail between the stalls and looked toward the back of the barn where he and Caitlin had stood the other night. Even now, with the memory so clear, he couldn't quite believe it was he who had done such a thing. A quick glance at Caitlin's pale face told him she was remembering, too.

Ace made fast work of rubbing down the mare so they could get out of there. Caitlin saw to measuring the feed and hauling over fresh water.

"Shall I douse the light?" he asked when she stepped into the passage and closed the stall gate.

Instead of replying, she rose on tiptoe to lower the lantern wick herself. Darkness swept over them. Ace paused a moment to let his eyes adjust. When he could see once more, he said, "Well, I guess that's that."

He turned to see Caitlin still standing beneath the extinguished lantern, one hand splayed on the stall gate, her other extended in front of her. Recalling the incredibly rough wagon ride she'd just treated him to, he couldn't help but grin.

"Caitlin, are you night blind?"

"Not at all," she said a little too quickly, then took a couple of hesitant steps. "It's just so dark in here. Don't tell me you can see?"

"I won't say I can see good enough to count your freckles, but I can see."

"I don't have freckles." She moved farther forward, patting the air before her as she went. "I hate it in here at night," she said, her voice ringing with tension. "Why on earth don't they build barns with more windows?"

The barn was so tumbledown and had so many cracks, there was plenty of moonlight for most people to see by.

"Here, let me help you," he said and grasped her elbow. She jumped as if he'd stuck her with a pin. "Whoa . . . I just"—he steered her around a galvanized tub—"mean to lend you a hand, that's all."

"I'm perfectly capable of walking by myself," she assured him, waving her other arm rather wildly in front of her.

"I can see you are," he replied in a voice thick with suppressed laughter.

"Well, then?"

He tugged on her arm slightly so she'd miss stumbling over a shovel blade. "Well, then, what?"

"Well, then"—the exaggerated patience in her voice made it sound as if she were addressing an imbecile—"why don't you turn loose of me?"

Ace was tempted. Six inches to her right was a manure gutter. "We're almost there," he assured her.

"Almost where?"

He thrust his free hand directly in front of her nose. She never so much as blinked. Another smile warmed his chest. The barn entrance ahead of them was at least twelve feet wide, and moonlight poured through the opening in generous measure. "To the doors, Caitlin. Can't you see them?"

"Of course I can."

As they came up on the entrance, he did as she'd suggested and released her. Cast adrift, she stumbled and swung around, her eyes wide and staring, her slender hand groping. "Where are you?" she asked faintly.

"Right here."

She jerked and pressed a hand over her heart. "Dear heavens!"

A man seldom given to spontaneous laughter, Ace was surprised to hear himself chuckle. Not feigned laughter, but a genuine, straight-from-the-belly chuckle. "Sorry, I didn't mean to give you a start."

Grasping her by the elbow again, he guided her the

few remaining steps outdoors. She gave an audible sigh of relief. "Light. Thank goodness."

He settled his hands on his hips, acutely conscious of the fact that she sidled away the instant he released her. "Well . . ." He left the word hanging, not entirely sure what to say. He only knew he didn't want to leave without settling matters between them. "Caitlin, about the other night."

"Yes?" she said, her voice quavery.

"I hope you'll excuse me for hemming and hawing, but the truth is, I'm really not sure how we should proceed from here."

"You aren't?" she asked, sounding mildly horrified.

Ace wondered if, maybe, she was hoping for a proposal of marriage. He couldn't blame her, if that was the case. He just wasn't sure how he felt about it. He scratched beside his nose. "It's not exactly your usual situation."

"No. It certainly—isn't."

Marriage. The word hung in his mind like a six-shooter with the hammer cocked. If a proposal was what she was angling for, he wished she'd just come straight out with it. Was that why she was so palpably nervous? Because she saw no other way out, and she wasn't sure how he would react? Ace had to admit, his first inclination was to run like hell. On the other hand, he wasn't sure he could and still like himself. Not if that was what she wanted.

"I, um . . ." He sniffed and cleared his throat. "Look, Caitlin. Let's be up front with each other, all right? No matter how we circle it, you're going to be the one who suffers the most from this. A man . . . well, it isn't so difficult for a man. You know what I mean?"

She looked as if she might faint.

"Are you all right?"

She gave a slight nod. "I—yes, I'm all right."

Ace's nose felt as if it were about to itch off. He scratched again, searching for words. "Well, anyway . . ." He scuffed a boot, glanced around the yard, then brought his gaze back to her. "I guess maybe what

I'm trying to say is, since you're the one who'll suffer most, maybe you should be the one to call the shots. What would you like to see us do?"

She gulped, the sound a hollow plunk at the base of her throat. "Mr. Keegan, I really haven't much experience with situations like this."

He puffed air into his cheeks, then slowly exhaled through his clenched teeth. "Yeah, well . . . that's two of us. I don't want to make myself sound bad, but the truth is, I've steered clear of respectable women for this very reason."

Her pupils dilated until her eyes looked nearly black. "I do believe I'd like to make one request."

Ace almost dropped to his knees and gave thanks. Anything, just to have all the decision-making off his shoulders. "What's that?" he asked eagerly.

"I really do think I'd like to go inside."

He took a moment to circle that. "Inside?"

"The house," she elaborated. "It, um, seems like the, um . . . logical place for us to continue with this— conversation. More comfortable, at least."

As uneasy as she had been about entering the stall with him a few minutes ago, he couldn't imagine her wanting to go in the house to discuss things, but who was he to argue? With a shrug, he said, "Suits me, I guess."

Looking none too thrilled at the prospect, she gestured for him to follow. En route, she said, "Will your horse be all right tied to the wagon? We can water him, if you'd like."

As nervous as she obviously was, her concern for his horse's welfare told him more about her than she could possibly know. "I watered him back in town. He should be fine for a few minutes."

All he wanted was to make amends and get the hell out of there, not that he dared say as much. How to make amends, that was the question. So far, the woman was proving to be as hard to pin down as a politician.

From the looks of the ranch, she and her brother could have used some extra money. Only, if he made an offer like that, how would she feel about taking it? His aim here was to mend fences, not offend her even more.

As Caitlin approached the front porch, Ace found himself hot-footing it along behind her, half-afraid she might trip over something. "Careful," he warned as she gathered her skirts to scale the first step.

At the sound of his voice so close behind her, she jumped. Not wishing to make her feel uncomfortable, he fell back a little.

"I have some freshly baked sugar cookies," she informed him in that same tremulous voice. As she gained the top step, she asked, "Would you, um, mind if we had tea and cookies first?"

First? That struck him as an odd request. As if they couldn't talk and sip tea at the same time? "No, I don't mind."

Following in her wake, Ace felt some of the planks in the steps give with his weight, cementing his suspicion that the place was about to fall down around her ears. He reached to help her with the lock. The knob turned easily, and the door swung open with a ghostly whine. He stepped aside for her to enter. She shivered slightly as she moved over the threshold.

"If you'll wait just a moment, I'll light a lamp," she told him.

Ace nearly offered to do it for her. He was able to see, after all. But something about the way she held her shoulders forestalled him.

Skirts rustling, she moved in a direct line to the hall table, where she groped for the lamp and removed its chimney. He heard the stick matches shivering in their box. Then, with a rasp of sulphur against glass paper, yellow flame leaped and then flickered. Warding off drafts with a cupped palm, she touched the fire to the lamp wick. With a hiss, the kerosene-soaked canvas caught, blazing white, then diminished to a mellow gold. Leaning sideways to avoid the fumes, she quickly replaced the smoke-streaked chimney.

"There," she said, brushing her hands clean. "Isn't that better?"

Ace moved farther inside and pushed the door closed behind him.

ACE HADN'T EXPECTED THE O'SHANNESSY HOUSE TO BE quite so shabby. Bare plank floors that hadn't seen a coat of varnish in years. Paint on the walls dingy with age. It was obvious the moment he stepped inside that little coin had been spared for maintenance.

Despite that, he saw evidence aplenty that Caitlin had tried to fix the place up. In front of the door lay a colorful braided rug, the scraps of interwoven material as yet unfaded. Indeed, the cloth in the rug was in far better shape than that in her dress, which was worn at the cuffs and elbows.

"Very pretty," he said, gesturing at the rug, feeling intensely awkward. "Wish I had a few over at my place. The floors are still bare as bones."

She rubbed her palms on her skirt. "The dry goods store had a sale on remnants last year. In the winter when it snows, I go crazy if my hands are idle."

Ace glanced about, noting that most of the wall hangings had been crafted by a feminine hand as well— an oval piece of needlepoint that read "God Bless Our Home," a cluster of dried flowers under glass. Nothing that had cost much money, but pretty, all the same. Beneath the lantern lay a tatted doily that, judging by its yellowness, he guessed her mother might have made.

A wave of sadness swamped Ace. Though he couldn't have explained why, he suspected this barren foyer was a reflection of what Caitlin's life had been like—a girl grabbing for beauty wherever she could find it.

Above the hall table, illuminated by a fan of gold from the lamp, hung a portrait of Conor O'Shannessy and a petite woman Ace guessed was his wife. Ace hung his hat on a crudely fashioned coat tree near the door where Caitlin had draped her shawl. Then, ignoring the fact that she nervously evaded him in a swirl of skirts, he stepped closer to the picture.

Given Caitlin's striking resemblance to Eden, she had obviously gotten her looks from her father's side of the family, but she had just as obviously inherited her diminutive size from her mother. The woman beside Conor O'Shannessy was a tiny little thing, not just slightly built, but fragilely so.

Conor O'Shannessy . . . Ace stared at the man's hated visage until his eyes burned. Then, with a concentrated effort, he looked away. Tonight, the old hatreds had to be set aside. This girl had had nothing to do with the atrocities committed against his parents.

His attention shifted to a framed photograph of Caitlin and Patrick below the one of their parents. He guessed Caitlin had been about ten when the likeness was taken, Patrick about eight. Even as a child, she had looked out at the world with a wary gaze, her expression guarded, her posture conveying a fierce protectiveness of her brother.

"Your mother, I take it?" He turned to regard her. "I wondered where you got that fragile build of yours. Now I know."

She straightened her shoulders, and her chin came up a notch. "I'm stronger than I look, Mr. Keegan."

Ace guessed she'd had to be. Since Patrick had taken to the bottle a few months back, she'd been doing the work of a man around this place. The thought made his guts clench. Somehow, her fierce pride made her seem all the smaller and more delicate, not the effect she was aiming for, he felt sure.

Dropping his gaze to her work roughened hands, he found himself thinking things that should have been downright alarming to a confirmed bachelor. Was he losing his mind? He didn't owe Caitlin O'Shannessy his whole goddamned life served up on a platter to make amends.

"Your mother passed away when you were very small, didn't she?"

She fastened a puzzled gaze on him. "Yes, when I was two. How did you know?"

"Just a guess." Ace could only wonder how much easier her life might have been if her mother hadn't died when she was so terribly young. "It must have been hard on you, losing her when you were so little."

"I survived."

She had survived a lot of things, Ace suspected. But that didn't mean it had been easy. That peculiar tightness came back into his throat as he watched the expressions that crossed her face. It was anyone's guess what hardships she had endured. One had only to see the shadows in her lovely eyes to know that she had suffered.

Clearly not needing or wanting his sympathy, she picked up the lantern. Ace followed her and the dancing play of light down a long hallway to a closed door that he assumed led to the kitchen. Even though he hung back by several feet, Caitlin kept glancing nervously over her shoulder at him. As if he might jump her from behind? As galling as that was, Ace didn't suppose he could blame her.

Like the front of the house, the kitchen bore signs that Caitlin O'Shannessy had learned to make do with very little. Utilitarian with its unpainted plank floors and walls, the room had nevertheless been made to look cheerful with yellow gingham curtains hung over the window and open cupboards. Colorful braided rugs lay scattered across the floor, an occasional scrap of yellow in the weave. Even the scarred plank table had been lent a touch of elegance by an embroidered dresser scarf and a dented old lard tin filled with wild roses, the hue of the blossoms an almost exact match for Caitlin's dress.

It was the kind of kitchen that invited a man to sit down and warm himself by the fire. The colorful rugs and potholders, the crisply starched curtains. Little touches from loving hands that told him a great deal about the girl who had put them there. The newness of the cloth told him another story, that Caitlin had done the decorating recently, probably after her father's death.

Not wanting to crowd his nervous hostess, Ace leaned a shoulder against the door frame. Uncertain what to do with his hands and wanting to appear as unthreatening as possible, he finally hooked his thumbs over his gun belt.

"You must have a domestic bent." He inclined his head at the dresser scarf. "Your handiwork, I take it. Or does Patrick wield a needle and thread when he isn't off slaughtering the neighbors' livestock?"

Crimson flagged her delicately hollowed cheeks. "You have a very bad impression of my brother, I'm afraid. Believe it or not, he has shot only one bull in his lifetime, and that was yours."

She set the lantern on a shelf near the cookstove and grabbed up another box of matches to advance on a swing bracket lamp along the adjoining wall. Judging by her expression, Ace wasn't sure if she meant to light the damned thing or dismantle it. He bit back a smile, pleased to see she had a little spunk. After being around his sister Eden, who thought nothing of going toe-to-toe with him, Ace wasn't sure how to deal with Caitlin, who jumped every time he made an unexpected move.

Caitlin and Eden . . . As uncannily alike as the two girls were, Ace reluctantly had to admit that Caitlin was lovelier. Compared to Caitlin, Eden lost radiance, like a painting that had begun to fade. Eden's hair wasn't as deep an auburn, nor were her features as delicately etched or her skin as flawless. As for her eyes? Well, no two ways about it, Ace had never looked into more beautiful eyes than Caitlin's. The color of a summer sky, they were so deep and clear a man could get lost in them.

With a start, he realized he was doing just that. Judging by Caitlin's expression, she had said something and was expecting a response.

"Beg pardon?"

She waved a hand toward the table. "I said, please have a seat and make yourself comfortable."

She returned the box of matches to the shelf and stepped over to the wood box. While she stoked the fire in the belly of the range, Ace lowered himself onto a straight-backed chair. Like the porch and the barn, it was in sore need of repair, wobbling and groaning under his weight.

Ever conscious of her nervousness, which made him feel like a mouse at a quilting bee, he glanced around. While he'd been woolgathering, she'd lit three wall lamps. He felt badly about that, for he had a feeling lantern fuel was an expense she could ill afford. The glow of light created a golden nimbus around her fiery hair.

"It won't take a minute to get some water boiling for our tea," she said over her shoulder. "The water in the reservoir is already piping hot."

Fixing his gaze on her slender back and the feminine flare of her hips, he settled carefully back in his seat. With a little luck, the chair wouldn't collapse under him. "There isn't any big rush as far as I'm concerned. I have all night."

Hands poised in the act of dipping water from the range reservoir into a copper tea kettle, she once again threw him a startled glance. Going back over what he'd said, Ace rushed to add, "Not that I plan to stay that long."

The angry spots of color that had dotted her cheeks a moment ago drained away, leaving her face drawn and bloodless. Ace studied her with a troubled frown, wondering why she had invited him in if he made her so nervous.

She slid the tea kettle to the back of the stove, then stepped to the cupboard to get some china. While she fussed with the cups and saucers, Ace found himself being accosted by a huge yellow tabby. The cat leaped from under the table onto his knee, then dug in with all its claws to hold its perch. Not overly fond of cats, Ace was none too pleased to play pincushion. His enthusiasm took another dive when he noticed the yellow hair already clinging to his black clothes.

After giving the cat an obligatory scratch behind its

ears, he gathered it up and gave it a little toss. To his horror, the overweight feline hit the floor belly first with a soft thud. For a frozen instant, Ace just stared. He'd never seen a cat land spread-eagle before.

"Well, damn."

"Oh!" Caitlin cried. Giving Ace an accusing look, she flew across the kitchen in a swirl of rose-colored skirts. The cat chose that moment to let loose with a pitiful meow.

"Lucky, my poor, sweet baby. What did that big, mean man do to you?"

"All I did was put him down."

He may as well have not spoken. Caitlin crouched to gather the squalling cat into her arms. "Oh, dumpling."

The cat was a dumpling, all right. Or, more precisely, a huge, boneless lump of flesh and fur. He eyed the creature with amazement and distaste, feeling guilty for having hurt it. "All I did was put him down. Honestly. I thought all cats landed on their feet."

Hugging the cat close and caressing the top of its head with her cheek, she fixed him with that same accusing gaze. "Not all cats. Lucky is tetched. Surely you could see that."

Tetched? Ace's gaze shot back to the cat. Now that he thought about it, the poor thing did have a funny look about the eyes. An unfocused, daft sort of look. "What exactly do you mean by tetched?"

"He got his head banged when he was little," she explained. "Afterward, he was never quite the same."

So the cat was brain damaged. In Ace's opinion, it might have been kinder to put the animal down, but he refrained from saying so. Caitlin clearly loved her pet.

Ace smiled slightly as he watched her set the cat gently on the floor. It took Lucky a moment to get his balance. Caitlin gave him a pat on his fanny to send him on his way, then pushed to her feet as the feline waddled off. "I didn't mean to snap at you. I suppose tetched cats are something of a rarity."

"You could say that. I apologize for hurting him. I didn't mean to."

"I should have been keeping a closer eye out. He isn't

very smart, I'm afraid." She brushed her hands clean. "If something frightens him, he's just as likely as not to hide under the stove when there's a roaring fire in the box."

Ace glanced at the stove. "Surely he comes out when it starts to feel hot?"

"No. He doesn't seem to realize it's the stove making him feel uncomfortable." Flicking cat hair from her bodice, she moved back across the kitchen. "I keep a broom handy, just in case."

"I've heard of people and animals without enough sense to come in out of the cold, but never the reverse." Just the thought of a poor, stupid animal hiding under a stove until it caught fire prompted him to say, "Has it occurred to you that you may not be doing Lucky a kindness?"

"How so?" Her eyes reflected her incredulity as his meaning sank in. "You can't mean you think I should"—her gaze flicked to the gun on his hip—"put him to sleep?"

The expression on her face told Ace that he'd just cemented all her worst opinions of him. Why that bothered him, he didn't know. But it did. Thinking fast, he said, "No, I meant—well, I was just thinking that it might be better if you took measures to see he never came into the kitchen. What if he gets under the stove sometime when you're not around?"

"He doesn't go under there unless someone scares him, I told you."

To be precise, she had said "something" not "someone," but Ace was too busy wondering who had frightened the poor cat to point out the difference. Not Caitlin, certainly. That left only Patrick or one of their hired men.

After working the pump to rinse her hands, Caitlin gathered up the china. As she moved toward the table with her burden, she trembled so badly the dainty little cups did a perilous jig upon their fluted saucers. So much for his quick thinking. Now, in addition to gunslinger and gambler, he had another count against him, cat killer.

He eased forward on the chair, elbows braced on his knees, hands clasped. "Caitlin, it really isn't necessary for you to go to all this trouble. I don't actually even want a cup of tea. Wouldn't it be better if we—"

"Oh, surely you'll have some tea first!" Setting the cups and saucers on the table with a loud clatter, she fixed a pleading gaze on him.

Ace sighed. "Caitlin, I—"

Cutting him off, she rushed on to say, "Neither one of us stayed for the buffet at the social. I'm absolutely famished. Aren't you?"

She whirled away to advance on another cupboard. A second later, she returned to the table with a covered plate. Whipping away the checkered towel, she presented him with a golden mound of sugar cookies.

"They're not exactly what you could call hot from the oven, but I did make them only this afternoon."

At just that moment, the teapot whistled. The shrill sound startled her so that she leaped and sent the pile of baked goods sliding off the plate. Ace forgot all about the weak chair joints and lunged forward to make a wild grab. Cookies went everywhere—over the table and the floor as well.

Caitlin stood in the middle of the mess, her white-knuckled hand still clasping the plate, her mouth quivering, eyes welling. Seeing her tears was the killing blow. Ace sensed she wasn't the type to cry easily, and probably never in front of anyone. That was made obvious by the frantic way she kept blinking to dry her eyes.

"Caitlin, sweetheart, please, don't cry. I swear to God, I'd rather you took a horsewhip to me."

Setting aside the cookies he'd caught, he pushed up from the chair and took the plate before she dropped it. Then he started picking up the cookies that had fallen on the floor. Her fear of him was so intense it seemed almost palpable—a cold, thick, electrical feeling in the air. To know that he had caused it—that he deserved it—made him feel sort of sick.

"I never intended to hang him, you know," he heard himself say. "The rope was ringed and would have snapped when his weight hit the end. I just meant to teach him a lesson." He glanced up, saw the incredulity reflected in her gaze, and said, "Where's the goddamned rope? I'll happily prove it to you."

She retreated a step, her face so pale it frightened him. "In the b—barn someplace."

"Remind me to find it before I leave so I can show it to you." Bending forward on one knee, Ace gathered more cookies. Tossing them onto the table, he said, "As for my behavior toward you, Caitlin, I have no excuse. For reasons it's probably best I don't get into, I went a little crazy for a while. All I could think about was getting revenge. Your father wasn't around to take the brunt of it, so I took it out on you."

His voice was gravelly with regret. Pushing to his feet, he stepped to the stove to take the whistling tea kettle off the heat. Then, moving back to Caitlin, he said, "That's no excuse, I know, but I swear to you, I never would have gone through with it. The truth is, I figured you were just like your father and brother, that promises meant nothing to you and that you'd run the first chance you got."

He glimpsed a flash of anger in her eyes at the slur he had cast upon the menfolks in her family. Since he couldn't in good conscience retract the statement or apologize for it, he rushed on to say, "When I started to realize you had no intention of running, that you meant to keep your word—well, to my shame, I didn't realize that until it was too late."

The incredulity in her gaze remained, only now Ace sensed it was for an entirely different reason. "Does this"—she moistened her lips—"mean you're releasing me from our bargain?"

"What?"

Mouth atremble, she waved a hand. "Does this mean—you know, the raincheck?—does this mean that you and I aren't going to—that you don't . . ." Her voice trailed away. "Are you releasing me from our bargain?"

It hit him then, like a fist between the eyes. Dear God. No wonder she'd been so nervous all evening. For the past three weeks, while he'd been trying to think of some way to apologize, she'd been waiting for him to appear on her doorstep, to collect on that stupid raincheck.

Ace's first reaction was anger that she would think him capable of being so slimy. Then he realized that he'd led her to believe exactly that. Amazement edged away his anger as he digested what all this meant, that she had invited him in here tonight with every intention of honoring her word. God only knew why. When a woman was being victimized by a man, especially in such a way that it might compromise her virtue, no one expected her to deal fairly with him.

All the same, he couldn't help but admire her for it. Caitlin O'Shannessy was as different from her father and brother as she could possibly be. Unfortunately, in his blind obsession with revenge, he had ruined any chance she might have had for a normal life, a fate that she was far from deserving.

Staring up at him in obvious disbelief, she gave a shaky little laugh. "You don't—you didn't come here to—you don't expect me to—" She broke off, clearly too embarrassed to continue.

"No," Ace assured her. "No, Caitlin, I don't. All I wanted was to apologize and make amends somehow." He sighed and ran a hand over his hair. "I guess I've done a damned poor job of it, haven't I?"

She touched her fingertips to her lips and squeezed her eyes closed, clearly so relieved she was nearly weak with it. When she looked at him again, some of the color had returned to her cheeks. "Amends," she repeated faintly. "I see."

Only, of course, she didn't see. She didn't see at all. How could she? Ace sat back down on the wobbly chair, braced an elbow on the table, and splayed a hand over his face. "Caitlin, I swear to you, I had no idea that was what you were thinking." An awful—and undeniably inappropriate—urge to laugh came over him. *Do you mind if we have tea first?* "Ah, Caitlin. I'm so sorry."

Sounding almost giddy, she said, "It's all right. Truly."

As he lowered his hand and focused on her sweet face,

Ace knew he was lost. He couldn't just apologize and leave. Maybe Southern gentlemen were a dying breed, but Joseph Paxton's values were still strong within him. A man didn't destroy a girl's reputation and then abandon her to deal with the consequences. Especially not when the young woman was someone like Caitlin. She deserved better, no question about it, and by God, she was going to get it.

"Caitlin, the more I think about this mess, the more convinced I become that the only solution is for you to marry me."

"What?" She made tight little fists on her skirt. "What did you say?"

For the second time in a very short while, Ace had cause to wish he were a little more silver-tongued. Perversely, her appalled expression only made him all the more determined. "You heard me. I think you should marry me. It's the only solution that makes any sense. My actions the other night were inexcusable, and the backlash is going to affect you for years."

Splaying a hand over her heart, she stared at him in horrified silence, not moving, not even seeming to breathe. "Are you out of your mind?"

Possibly. Hell, probably. "It's not such a crazy idea if you think about it."

She fell back a step. "I'm not marrying anyone, not to mend my reputation or for any other reason."

"Now, Caitlin . . ."

"No!" She held up a hand. "As for the backlash?" She shook her head. "I don't intend to stay in No Name long enough for that to matter."

He bent to retrieve a cookie he'd missed on the floor. "Oh? And just where are you going?"

"San Francisco, I think."

Convinced he couldn't possibly have heard her right, he said, "Say what?"

"San Francisco. As soon as Patrick gets the ranch back on its feet and can pay back the money he—um— borrowed from my savings last month, I intend to leave for San Francisco."

"San Francisco?" he repeated stupidly.

"Yes. I had nearly a thousand dollars saved. That should be plenty to hold me over until I can get settled and find employment."

He hadn't missed the way she'd stumbled over the word "borrowed" a moment ago, which led him to suspect that good old Patrick had stolen the money from her savings. As much as Ace abhorred thievery, he couldn't help but think that, in this instance, Patrick had done Caitlin a service. A young woman alone in one of the most dangerous cities on the West Coast?

"You can't be serious. San Francisco? You'd be penniless and destitute within a week of your arrival."

Ace refrained from adding that there was only one type of employment a young woman could find quickly in San Francisco. Judging by Caitlin's pallor at the mention of marriage, he seriously doubted she was cut out for that particular line of work, though God knew she'd been blessed with all the right equipment for it.

Taking a quick assessment of that equipment and imagining some lowlife scoundrel putting his filthy hands on her, Ace decided that, come hell or high water, he wasn't about to let this girl take off anywhere alone. In her naivete, maybe she didn't understand how cutthroat men could be, but Ace did. The waterfront in San Francisco was where he'd learned to play cards and handle a gun—a place where predator preyed upon predator and only the strong survived.

As if she guessed his thoughts, she said, "I am not a child, Mr. Keegan. I'm perfectly capable of looking after myself, I assure you."

Ace agreed with her wholeheartedly on one point; she definitely was not a child. Unfortunately, it was her maturity, or perhaps a better word might have been "ripeness," that made her so vulnerable.

Before he could think of a way he might successfully argue his point without embarrassing her, a hoarse shout from outside broke his train of thought.

"Keegan! Goddamn you, get out here!"

Her eyes going wide with alarm, Caitlin pressed a hand to her throat. "Oh, no! It's Patrick!"

She whirled and fled from the kitchen, Ace right on

her heels. At the front door, she swept the window curtain aside to peer out. Bending to look out over her shoulder, Ace saw Patrick O'Shannessy standing in the moonlit front yard, feet spread, six-shooter drawn.

"Christ! The crazy kid. As if he can go up against me with a gun?"

"Oh, my God . . ."

Not liking the way O'Shannessy was waving his weapon, Ace seized her by the shoulders. "Caitlin, I want you to go back to the kitchen. I'll handle this."

She jerked free of his grasp. "I'm not going anywhere! That's my brother out there. Do you think I'm going to hide in the kitchen and let you shoot him?"

Ace could hope. "You're the one who's liable to get shot." He grabbed her by the arms and spun her around, putting himself between her and the door. "Now, dammit, do what I say. Go to the kitchen. The way he's swinging that gun, it's liable to go off accidentally."

"Keegan!" Patrick yelled. "Get out here, you no good son of a bitch! You can't dishonor my sister and get away with it!"

"Oh, God, he's drunk!"

"Drunk and very dangerous. Go to the kitchen."

With a broken sob, she grabbed fistfuls of his shirt. "Swear to me you won't shoot him!"

"Caitlin, he's got a gun. If he starts firing, what choice will I have?"

"But you can't shoot him! He's drunk. He doesn't know what he's doing! Promise me you won't shoot him."

Her panicked expression made him wish he could make her that promise. Unfortunately, he wasn't quite that gallant. "Drunk or not, those are real bullets he's got in that six-shooter. I'll try not to kill him, but that's the best I can offer."

"Keegan!" The sharp report of a rock striking the door punctuated the summons, making Ace jump nearly out of his skin. "Get out here, I said. You've ruined my sister's reputation, you hear me? Everybody in town is talking about her. By followin' her home tonight, you've made things even worse!"

"I hear you!" Ace called back. "Put that gun back in its holster, Patrick. Let's talk calmly about this. There's no point in anyone getting hurt. Your sister is in here, don't forget. You fire that gun, and she could be the one you hit!"

"That's right, she is in there, you rotten, miserable lowlife. I caught you red-handed, didn't I? Maybe you can get away with compromising some other man's sister, but not mine. You understand?"

Caitlin released the front of Ace's shirt and pressed the back of her wrist to her forehead. "Oh, dear Lord. Oh, my God . . ."

Ace swept aside the door curtain again. Patrick was still swinging the gun around and staggering to keep his balance. Drunk didn't describe his condition.

"You think 'cause you're fast with that gun you can do whatever you want?" he cried. "Well, come out here, you arrogant asshole. I'll show you different. You'll either make an honest woman of my sister, or I'll blow your goddamned brains out!"

Ace was about to tell Patrick O'Shannessy he might die trying when it suddenly occurred to him exactly what the younger man had said. Fate, he realized, had just dealt him the proverbial royal flush. He arched an eyebrow at Caitlin. "Did you hear that? Even drunk, your brother seems to have better sense than you do."

Her expression totally bewildered, she said, "Pardon?"

Looking down at her pale face, Ace wished there were another way. But there wasn't. Someday, she would be able to see that. "Unless I misunderstand him, Patrick is giving me a choice. I can either marry you or get my brains blown out."

Her eyes went wide. "You can't be serious."

"Oh, I'm serious, all right."

So fast he scarcely saw her move, she grabbed fistfuls of his shirt again. He had a feeling she had nearly gone for his throat. "Don't you even think it! Do you understand me? I won't be blackmailed into marrying you or anyone else."

His chest aching with regret, not for what he was

about to do, but for the manner in which he meant to accomplish it, Ace nonetheless managed to smile. The way he saw it, there were no choices. Not for either of them. The sooner she accepted that, the better off she would be.

"Would you rather I shot him?"

❧ 9

OVER THE COURSE OF THE NEXT HOUR, CAITLIN FELT AS IF she were sliding down a steep slope of solid ice on well-waxed runners. No matter what she said or how loudly she said it, Patrick just kept waving his gun and threatening to shoot Ace Keegan if he refused to make an honest woman of her. Since Keegan didn't seem opposed to doing exactly that, Caitlin was the only one who objected when Patrick escorted them to town at gunpoint.

"A shotgun wedding, Patrick? This is madness, absolute madness," she said as Keegan brought the wagon to a halt out in front of Abraham Guthrie's house at the edge of town. No lights shone in the windows of the small, clapboard dwelling. "Look! You see? The poor people are already in bed! Surely you don't mean to wake them up. Let's just wait and see Mr. Guthrie in the morning at his office."

Patrick drew his horse up beside them. "Tomorrow's Sunday. Besides, he's the justice of the peace. He's used to people wakin' him up."

Caitlin doubted that. "Paddy, please. Can't we wait until morning? You may see all of this differently once you've slept on it." Once he sobered up was more like it, but she hesitated to say as much for fear he'd become even more obstinate.

"How could I possibly see it different?" Patrick demanded, still so intoxicated he slurred his consonants.

"Never let it be said that Patrick O'Shannessy is a coward. If a man dishonors my sister, he'll either do right by her or die for his trouble. Nobody can say otherwise."

Caitlin's patience snapped. "This isn't about what your friends may say about you, Patrick. It's about my life, which is going to be destroyed if you go through with this! Can't you understand that?"

Still seated on his horse, Patrick squinted down at her along the bridge of his nose. "Don't you worry, Caitlin. I'll see to it the son of a bitch makes things right. Your life won't be destroyed, not if I have anything to say about it."

Caitlin's heart sank. In the past, she'd had similar exchanges with her father. Unreasoning anger, mindless retaliation. She knew it was hopeless. Quite simply, Patrick didn't hear her. Not really. When he got like this, mere words couldn't penetrate the whiskey haze. She wasn't sure what would.

"Give it up, Caitlin," Keegan said as he leaned forward to set the wagon brake and tie the reins.

"I can't give it up! According to you, our father killed yours. You despise us and everything we stand for. Why would you even contemplate marrying me? Unless, of course, you have an ulterior motive?"

"I do not despise you. And even if I did, what kind of ulterior motive could I possibly have?"

An awful squeezing sensation seized hold of her throat. "Having an O'Shannessy at your mercy, possibly?"

He gave a startled bark of laughter. "At my mercy? I realize marriage isn't high on your list, but let's not get carried away."

To her, this was no joking matter, but a nightmare that had somehow commandeered reality. Her father had been dead a little less than a year. She'd only just begun to get a taste of freedom and experience life without constant fear hanging over her like a dark cloud. Now this man meant to make her his chattel? No matter how people tried to pretty it up with romantic notions, Caitlin knew marriage was little more than a contractual union in which the man was granted authoritarian rule and the woman was indentured for a lifetime. She wanted no part of it, especially not with someone who reviled the very blood that flowed in her veins.

"It isn't funny!" she cried shakily. "Of course, it's easy for *you* to laugh. You're the man."

"And how, exactly, does that signify?" He searched her gaze for what seemed an endless moment. Then, in an intimately low voice, he said, "Caitlin, maybe we need to discuss this."

Discuss it? They could talk all night, and she would never change her mind. She quickly averted her face. "As if anything I say matters?"

Evidently she had him there, for he made no rejoinder. Not that it surprised her. If either man had been taking her protests seriously, she wouldn't be here. Wasn't that always the way of it? Men making the decisions, and women being forced to live with them.

At the thought, a fresh wave of panic threatened to crash over her. Marriage? She couldn't believe such an awful thing was happening. For the moment, to prevent an altercation between Keegan and her brother, she had no choice except to cooperate. But what about later? Unlike the bargain she and Keegan had struck that night in the barn, this was no stopgap measure. A marriage would be permanent unless she could convince Keegan to have it annulled.

Patrick, who for reasons beyond her, still seemed to think he had complete control of the situation, brandished his revolver and slid down off his rented horse. Watching him, Caitlin couldn't help but consider running. Away into the darkness. Away from the insanity. If her brother ended up getting hurt, it wouldn't be her fault.

She dug her nails hard into the wooden wagon seat, trying to shove back the memories. Of Patrick, at seven . . . pummeling Conor with his small fists, trying to make him stop hitting her. Of Patrick, at twelve . . . helping her to pack and run away from home, only to get the whipping of his life when well-meaning neighbors found the two of them walking along the road and fetched them back to their father. Of Patrick, at sixteen

. . . spending a year's savings, which he'd earned cleaning horse stalls, to consult a lawyer in a futile attempt to get her legally emancipated from their father's custody. Of Patrick, at eighteen . . . leaping from bed in the dead of night to cook Conor a predawn breakfast, knowing beforehand that he would end up taking a beating in her stead before he got the food on the table.

How could she forget those times? More to the point, how could she abandon the brother who had, until only recently, loved her better than he loved himself?

After staggering about to regain his balance, Patrick led the horse to the porch post. "Get down from there, Keegan. It's time to pay the piper."

Apparently oblivious to Patrick's threatening gestures, Keegan eyed the ramshackle house. "You say this fellow Guthrie is a justice of the peace? That looks like a goat on the porch."

"You don't like goats, or what?" Patrick asked.

Caitlin squinted through the dimness. Sure enough, there was a white blur on Guthrie's front porch that seemed to be moving. As she watched, the animal jumped through the rails and fled. "Patrick, for heaven's sake, the least you can do is take us to the preacher!"

"Preacher's at the social. Roundin' him up'd take all night."

"What's this fellow do for a living, anyway?" Keegan asked. "Besides being a justice of the peace, I mean."

With as little inflection in her voice as possible, Caitlin replied, "Back in No Name's gold rush days, he was the assayer. Since we obviously don't have much need of one anymore, he became a justice of the peace. He sells goat's milk to supplement his income."

Keegan pushed up from the seat, placed a hand on the sideboard, and vaulted down from the wagon. Before Caitlin could react, he turned, caught her at the waist, and swept her to the ground to stand next to him. As she caught her balance, she gave him a nervous appraisal. Not that his strength came as any great surprise. The man had a musculature to rival that of a stevedore.

As though he sensed her assessment of him, he turned toward her. To her dismay, their gazes locked, and for a long, endless second, she was helpless to look away. The smells of tobacco smoke, leather, and man blended with the faint odor of horses to curl around her.

"Caitlin," he said softly. "About those ulterior motives you suspect me of having. Despite what you may think, I—"

"Come on, Keegan. Dawdling ain't gonna save your ass."

Keegan sighed. "Your brother would try the patience of a saint."

His expression was so disgruntled that for a moment, Caitlin was able to see some humor in the situation. Patrick, who was so drunk he could barely stand up, threatening a man who could probably shoot the berries off a juniper tree at a hundred paces? It was ludicrous.

That thought brought Caitlin full circle back to her reason for being there, to save her brother's hide. For the last three months, that had been the way of it, Patrick getting himself into impossible situations and her bailing him out.

On the way up the steps, Patrick staggered sideways and nearly fell off the porch. As fervently as Caitlin had been hoping he might pass out, she didn't want him to take a five-foot dive into the bushes and break his neck. "Patrick, for heaven's sake, be careful!"

Somehow her brother managed to catch his balance, cross the porch, and rap on the door with the butt of his gun. "Guthrie!" he yelled. "Get your ass out of bed. We got a wedding for you to—" He broke off and threw a bleary-eyed grin over his shoulder. "Does he witness the weddin' or perform it?"

Caitlin saw lantern light flicker inside the house. "What earthly difference does it make?"

Patrick shrugged and started pounding on the door again. "I don't reckon it does, long as it's legal."

Abraham Guthrie chose that exact moment to throw open his door, nearly getting smacked in the nose with Patrick's gun butt in the process. "Good evenin', Abe," Patrick said drunkenly.

Guthrie reared back. "Jumpin' Jehoshaphats!" Clad only in a striped nightshirt and nightcap, he looked ill-prepared to officiate at a wedding. "What the devil is the trouble, boy? You're makin' enough noise to wake snakes."

Patrick gestured with his revolver toward Caitlin and Ace. "My sister has been compromised by that no-account scoundrel, and I am insisting, at gunpoint, that the son of a bitch do right by her."

"You want your sister to marry a no-account scoundrel?" A thin, bony legged little man, Guthrie swatted the tassel of his nightcap from over his eye and held the lantern higher to give Patrick a closer study. "I should've guessed it. You've been snortin' the old orchard."

"I'm sober enough to know he's gotta marry my sister. If he doesn't, I'm gonna blow his goddamned brains out."

"I see." Guthrie sighed and changed hands with the lamp to peer out at Caitlin and Ace. "Evenin', Miss Caitlin, Mr. Keegan. Looks like you two are in one tarnation fix." Stifling a yawn, he cast Patrick a thoughtful look, then winked and said, "One dollar, regular rates, two for my special version, if you get my drift."

Caitlin's heart leaped with hope. Patrick was so drunk, he'd never know the difference if Guthrie performed a sham ceremony. "Oh, Mr. Guthrie, that would be absolutely wonder—"

"We're not interested in your special version," Keegan interjected. "Miss Caitlin has done me the great honor of agreeing to become my wife."

Caitlin shot him a glare. "I haven't willingly agreed to anything."

"Did I say 'willingly'?"

She gathered up her skirts and started up the steps. "As for our not being interested in his 'special' version, speak for yourself."

"I always do," he assured her in an amused voice that further infuriated her.

Guthrie motioned all of them inside. "Well, if you're wantin' the regular version, I best roust my missus and mother-in-law out of bed to stand as your witnesses."

"You really don't need—"

His dark eyes twinkling with suppressed laughter, Keegan cut her off again. "Please, do wake them. Without witnesses, the ceremony won't be legal, and we can't have that."

Limping on gnarly feet, the elderly man ushered them into his parlor, a dingy little room, everything in it, from furniture to wallpaper, yellowed with age and tobacco smoke. "Don't usually marry folks here at the house, but when I do, the missus likes me to use the parlor, it bein' the fanciest room and all."

Before he left them, Guthrie lit a lamp on the fireplace mantel. Feeling chilled and missing her shawl, Caitlin rubbed her arms. Patrick went to lean against a wall, his gun still clasped in one hand, his heavy-lidded gaze fixed malevolently on Keegan. In Caitlin's opinion, her brother looked about ready to pass out. Unfortunately, close didn't count.

His right boot heel scuffling with every other step, Keegan went over to the coat tree to hang up his Stetson. Despite the slight limp, he managed to be intimidating. While his back was turned, Caitlin couldn't help but notice the breadth of his shoulders. Even in the loose-fitting shirt, the muscular swells across his back and through his arms were plainly visible. She gulped and looked away.

Married. The word kept going off in her mind like a rifle shot. Oh, God. This couldn't really be happening. Yet it was. And unless Patrick passed out within the next few minutes, she didn't see any way out. The instant she refused to cooperate, Patrick would feel honor bound to shoot Keegan. In that event, Keegan would shoot back, and that would be the end of the story.

"Well, now." As he reentered the room, Guthrie dragged a suspender strap up over his shoulder. He had exchanged his nightshirt and cap for rumpled brown trousers and a partially buttoned white shirt. He wore fur-lined house slippers on his otherwise bare feet. "I reckon we might as well get started."

Tossing another look at her brother, Caitlin said, "We're in no hurry."

Her overly cheerful tone brought Keegan's head around. He, too, glanced at Patrick. The twinkle of laughter crept into his eyes again, making Caitlin want to kick him. "I'm sure Mr. Guthrie and his family would like to conclude the ceremony as quickly as possible, sweetheart, so they can return to bed." He cocked a jagged eyebrow. "Unless, of course, you had some reason to delay?"

She wasn't about to dignify that with an answer.

Two elderly women followed Guthrie into the parlor. Caitlin recognized one as his wife Florrie and guessed the other was his mother-in-law. Both ladies wore blue nightgowns and wrappers that had been cut from the same bolt of cotton. Their gray hair hung down their frail backs in braids gone fuzzy from sleep.

Pushing a wing-backed chair out of the way, Guthrie grabbed a black book from the mantel and beckoned Ace and Caitlin to stand in front of him. Meanwhile, his wife made busy opening a mahogany secretary that stood in the corner and laying out papers on the drop-down leaf. The couple had clearly been officiating at weddings for a number of years and had the procedure down pat.

Her shoulder bumping Keegan's hard arm, Caitlin walked over to face the unlikely-looking justice of the peace. Unfortunately, it didn't matter what Guthrie looked like, only that he was empowered by the state of Colorado to perform marriages. Her stomach felt as if she'd eaten some of those newfangled Mexican jumping beans she'd seen yesterday at the general store.

A lifetime as Ace Keegan's wife . . . The thought came unbidden into her mind, then refused to leave. Oh, God. Claustrophobic and breathless, she glanced frantically around the room, her one clear thought to escape. As if he sensed her rising panic, Keegan curled a large hand around hers, the grip of his fingers unbreakable.

Sweat broke out on Caitlin's face. A loud humming vibrated against her eardrums. For an awful moment, she thought she might faint. But, of course, she didn't. Fainting would have been too easy.

As if from a great distance, she heard Guthrie intoning

the nuptials. The words made no sense. Numbly, she responded when bidden. Just as numbly, she heard Keegan say, "I do," in a low, steady voice.

A nightmare. She was having a nightmare. One of those particularly awful ones, where nothing made sense. That was why she yearned to run and couldn't. Why her brain refused to function.

Suddenly, the fog of unreality parted, and for a moment, everything went sharp with clarity. His expression solemn, Keegan turned toward her. His dark eyes holding hers, he removed an onyx and diamond ring from his little finger and slipped it onto her left hand.

"I know it's too large," he said in that gruffly tender voice she was already coming to despise. "I'll buy you another as soon as I can."

Not if Caitlin had anything to say about it. Pray God, before he had a chance to visit the jeweler, this marriage would be nothing but a memory. An annulment. Once Patrick passed out, she would convince Keegan to give her an annulment. That was her only hope.

Muttering something about the state of Colorado and the power vested in him, Guthrie concluded the brief ceremony with "I now pronounce you man and wife. Mr. Keegan, you may kiss your bride."

An awful feeling of weakness attacked Caitlin's legs as she looked up at Ace Keegan's darkly burnished face. Amber lamplight glistened in his wavy black hair and gilded his strong features, enhancing the muscular hollow along his jaw and the bold thrust of his bladelike nose. Black, winged eyebrows lifted as he gave her a slow perusal with twinkling brown eyes, the color of which made her think of mulled burgundy spiced heavily with cinnamon.

He grasped her chin. The hand that bracketed her jaw was warm and incredibly hard, the fingertips slightly calloused. With firm but gentle pressure, he tipped her head back. Caitlin wanted to close her eyes, needed to, but for the life of her, she couldn't. She held her breath as he bent his dark head to hers.

She expected wet, slippery lips. She got moist velvet.

She expected teeth to grind against hers. She got a featherlike caress so fleeting she couldn't be certain it even happened. Surely this wasn't all there was to it?

She blinked and almost lost her balance when he released her. He caught her from falling with a proprietorial hand on her arm.

Proprietorial. Now there was a word to keep a woman awake nights. It was also one Caitlin couldn't chase from her thoughts as he turned her toward the secretary where Guthrie was filling out the marriage documents. There was an unmistakable difference in the way Keegan touched her now.

The words had been said. The unthinkable had occurred. She belonged to him.

As though privy to her thoughts, he smiled, took her hand again, and gave it a hard squeeze. "Sweetheart, you're like ice."

Sweetheart? The word burned into her like a brand. She was shaking. Shaking uncontrollably. With a little jerk, she tried to free her hand, but he kept a firm grip and guided her the remainder of the way to the secretary.

Caitlin bent to sign her name on the indicated line, knowing as she did that she might be signing away the rest of her life. What if this man refused to get an annulment? Ace Keegan's property, to have and to hold and to do with as he pleased, until the day she died. The thought was so unsettling, she almost forgot how to spell her last name. Now, of course, it wasn't her last name anymore. Might never be again.

When she finished, Keegan took the pen from her numb fingers and bent to sign his name as well, not with shaky hesitancy as she had, but with a bold flourish.

Guthrie's wife and mother-in-law twittered and gushed as they bent to add their names to the documents. "Oh," Mrs. Guthrie said in a dreamy voice, "you do make such a lovely couple." She stepped forward to hug Caitlin. "My dear, dear girl. I wish you all the happiness." For Caitlin's ears alone, she whispered, "You've landed yourself a very handsome fish, young lady."

Throwing a quick glance at Keegan, Caitlin had to admit that was true; he was handsome. But, then, so was the occasional killer stallion. Big, dark, powerful, and intimidating. From a safe distance, he was fascinating to watch, the play of muscle in his body harmony in motion. But no woman in her right mind would want to get too close.

Keegan chose that moment to curl a hard arm around her waist, his large, heavy hand coming to rest above her left hip. Caitlin couldn't help but grow tense. At her reaction, his grip tightened slightly.

Mrs. Guthrie had it all backward, Caitlin thought a little hysterically. Keegan wasn't the one caught on a hook; Caitlin was. What was even worse, she had the awful feeling he was slowly reeling in the line, that at any moment, he'd throw his net. The thought made her feel slightly sick.

Caitlin glanced at Patrick, who at last count had been standing sentinel over them. Her heart sank when she saw that he'd slid down the wall and was now sitting slumped on the floor, the gun dangling harmlessly from one limp hand.

She whirled back toward the secretary. "Wait! I've changed my mind."

She descended on the drop leaf. Just as her fingers grasped the corner of one marriage document, a large brown hand slapped down in the center of it. She jumped with a start, then rounded on her new husband.

"Patrick's passed out! Don't you see? We don't have to go through with this!"

"It's already done, honey. There's no turning back."

"But I only—" She touched a hand to her throat. "To keep Patrick from getting hurt! That was the only reason I did it. Now he's unconscious and—" Her gaze clung to his. "Please, why can't we call it off?"

"It's too late." He glanced at Guthrie. "I'm right about that, aren't I? It's legal and binding. Correct?"

Guthrie threw up his hands. "I offered to perform a fake one. If that was what you wanted, Miss Caitlin, you should've said so."

"I did say so."

Nudging her aside, Keegan picked up one copy of the marriage document. After folding it in half and then into quarters, he slipped it into his shirt pocket. With a tolerant smile that made her want to grind her teeth, he said to Guthrie, "What we have here is a classic case of bridal jitters."

Caitlin gave an outraged gasp. "Bridal jitters, my foot. I've changed my mind! I don't want to marry you."

Flashing a grin, Keegan withdrew a money clip from his trousers pocket, peeled off a ten-dollar bill, and handed it to the older man. "Keep the extra." At Guthrie's surprised look, he smiled. "By way of appreciation. I'm sorry we dragged all of you out of bed." He turned a warm gaze on Mrs. Guthrie, then took her hand. "It was a pleasure making your acquaintance, madam. I hope we encounter one another again soon."

The older woman blushed. "Likewise, I'm sure."

So furious she couldn't have spoken if she tried, Caitlin drew away, mildly surprised he allowed her even that much. The yellowed roses in Mrs. Guthrie's wallpaper swam in her peripheral vision, and the rank smell of stale cigar smoke in the room seemed suddenly overwhelming.

Stay calm, she lectured herself. Keegan will be reasonable once you have a chance to talk to him. And even if he isn't, it won't be the end of the world. You can probably get an annulment without his cooperation, after all. It will only be a simple matter of getting away from him long enough to start the proceedings.

Getting away. The words had a familiar ring. The same refrain, a different man. She'd been unable to escape her father. Pray God that Ace Keegan didn't prove to have so long a reach.

"Well," Keegan said, "I suppose we should get your brother out of here. These good people would probably like to go back to bed."

He fetched his hat from the coat tree, set it on his head at a jaunty angle, and went to collect Patrick. Feeling oddly numb, Caitlin followed him.

Glancing back, he said, "Would you mind getting the door for me?"

After stuffing Patrick's revolver under his belt, he hefted the younger man up off the floor and slung him over his shoulder. Left with no choice that she could see, Caitlin hurried ahead of him. As she swung the door wide, the Guthries began issuing the obligatory congratulations.

"I only hope you two are as happy as we have been," Mr. Guthrie said.

"Thirty-seven years," Florrie said proudly. "I've never regretted a moment."

Just the thought of being married to Ace Keegan for thirty-seven years was almost enough to send Caitlin into apoplexy. Stepping across the threshold, she said, "Please, don't bother to see us out. We've already intruded on your sleep."

"It was our pleasure. Goodnight, now!" Florrie called.

Relieved to be away from them, Caitlin drew the door closed. Keegan made his way across the porch and down the steps, his footsteps resounding on the weathered wood.

Hurrying to catch up with him, she cried, "Mr. Keegan, we need to talk."

"Will the wagon do?"

Having no clue what he meant, Caitlin drew to a stop. "The wagon?"

"Your brother," he said patiently. "Should I put him in the wagon?"

"Oh!" She passed a hand over her eyes. "Yes, the wagon." Hauling in a deep, ragged breath, she nodded. "Yes, that would be simplest, I guess. Once I get him home, I'll just pull the wagon into the barn and cover him with blankets."

He gave her an odd look. "He can sleep it off perfectly well right here."

"Here? But he'll freeze!"

"Not likely." Caitlin winced when Patrick was dumped unceremoniously onto the wagon bed with little or no regard for his lolling head. After returning the younger man's gun to its holster, Keegan directed another meaningful look at her. "Alcohol doesn't freeze, you know."

"That is not funny."

"Who's joking?"

"I can't leave him here." The moon came out from behind a cloud, revealing the harshness of Keegan's expression. Caitlin wasn't at all sure she liked the look in his eye. "I have to take him home. I—well, that's all there is to it."

Jamming hard fists on his hips, he sighed and lifted a dark eyebrow. "Caitlin, I know you'd prefer not to be reminded, but you're a married woman now. Your place is at the Paradise with me, and that's where you're going. Patrick got himself into this mess. He can get himself out."

Caitlin didn't know which point to address first, the fact that he considered this to be a genuine marriage, or that he was insisting she leave Patrick in the wagon all night. In the end, the habits of a lifetime prevailed. "But he's unconscious!"

"Maybe he'll think twice before he starts guzzling whiskey the next time. Regardless, he isn't your responsibility anymore."

Not her responsibility? This was her little brother, whom she'd loved and protected since infancy. "He *is* my responsibility! Who are you to say he isn't?"

"Your husband." With that, he turned to untether his stallion from the tailgate of the wagon. "Trust me, honey. He'll be just fine. I admit, it's a chilly night. But we haven't had frost on the ground for weeks."

"You are my husband only by the loosest definition of the word."

He glanced at her over his shoulder. "I guess it all depends on how you look at it."

Caitlin noticed the rented gelding Patrick had tethered to the porch post, and seized upon the excuse to stall for time. "Surely you don't intend to leave that poor beast and Penelope here until morning without food or water."

"If I don't, Patrick will come to in the morning and

not know where I put them. They'll make out fine for a few hours. Penelope's been fed, and the rental horse probably was as well."

The well-muscled black stallion snorted and nudged Keegan's shoulder affectionately. After giving the animal a quick scratch behind the ears, he turned back to Caitlin. Before she guessed what he meant to do, he grabbed her by the waist and lifted her into the saddle. Her flared skirt and petticoat hiked clear to her knees, revealing her bloomers.

"What are you doing?"

"Putting you on my horse."

"No, I mean—" Caitlin took a deep, calming breath. "Mr. Keegan, we absolutely must talk."

"About what?"

"About this sham of a marriage!"

"Sweetheart, I hate to tell you this, but this marriage isn't a sham."

So furious she forgot to be intimidated, she leaned down so their faces were mere inches apart. "You are being deliberately obtuse!"

He smiled up at her. "Ob what?"

"Obtuse! And, please, don't insult my intelligence by pretending you don't know what that means." She jerked angrily at her dress. "This is an outrage." She made an attempt to stick her foot in the left stirrup and swing down, but the confines of her bell-shaped skirt wouldn't allow that much freedom of motion. "A lady doesn't ride astride in a dress! Get me down from here this instant."

"Everybody in town is over at the social. Who's going to see?"

"You!"

Shoving his hat back to regard the display, he seemed to consider the point. "That's true enough, I guess. But where's the problem? I'm not complaining, and since I'm your lawful husband, you shouldn't be either."

"I want down from here right this—"

He effectively cut her off by grasping the saddle horn and thrusting a booted foot into the stirrup.

"What are you—?"

Once again, he cut her short by swinging up a leg and settling into the saddle behind her. The hard juncture of his thighs shoved her high on the pommel. Grasping the reins in his left hand, he encircled her waist with his other arm—an extremely hard arm—and drew her firmly back against him.

"Mr. Keegan?"

Ignoring her, he nudged the horse into a brisk walk.

"Mr. Keegan!"

He finally relented with, "What?"

"We have to talk. Please, stop the horse!"

"We can talk while we ride," he replied calmly. "We need to hurry and get out of town. Your drawers are shining, remember?"

Right then, the least of Caitlin's concerns were her bloomers. She grasped his broad wrist, trying without success to pry his hand off her midriff. "Mr. Keegan, please."

He tightened his hold on her. "That hand's not going anywhere, Caitlin. Try to relax, hm? I'd move it. But sure as the world, if I did, Shakespeare would take it into his head to buck."

That she should be so lucky. As for her relaxing, how on earth could he possibly expect anything of the sort? There wasn't enough space between their bodies to insert a sheet of parchment. With exaggerated patience, she said, "You have to listen to me."

"Honey, I have been listening. It's just that you haven't said a damn thing that makes sense."

Taking another deep breath, Caitlin gathered all her courage. Then, not allowing herself a second to agonize over what she was about to do, she blurted, "This marriage is totally unnecessary."

To her dismay, she saw they were riding past the farrier's, one of the last businesses they would pass before reaching the north end of town. There would be nothing but open country from that point westward. "I'm sorry for not telling you sooner, but I didn't dare. Not as long as Patrick was drunk out of his mind and still conscious. I was afraid the two of you would get into a fight and you'd shoot him." She glanced uneasily over her shoulder at him. "Anyway, better late than never, right? I'm telling you now. You needn't feel obligated to marry me."

"Really?"

His sarcastic tone set her teeth on edge. "Yes, really." Her next words didn't come easily, but desperation drove her. "I'm not the virginal young lady you believe me to be. I was compromised by another man years ago."

She expected him to jerk back hard on the reins and stop the horse. Instead, he kept right on riding.

"Mr. Keegan?"

"Hmm?"

"Didn't you hear me?"

"Yes, Caitlin, I heard you."

"Well, then?" She twisted around to look at him again. "I realize you're probably a little angry. And, honestly, I don't blame you. But if you'll just stop and think about it, you'll realize I couldn't possibly have divulged the information earlier. This way, no one got hurt, and even though we went through the motions of getting married, no lasting harm has been done. Come morning, we can have the marriage annulled. Patrick will have sobered up by then, and I'll be able to reason with him. No offense to you, but if he were sober, you'd be the last person on earth he'd ever choose as my husband."

Letting the reins slip through the fingers of his left hand to give himself the necessary slack, Keegan reached up to push his hat back. Relentless dark eyes impaled her. "Did you love him?"

"Patrick?"

"No, not Patrick. The man."

"What—? Oh, *that* man. No, of course, I didn't love him. What has love to do with it? The important thing— the only important thing—is that there isn't any need for you to feel responsible for me. Though it isn't common knowledge, any chance I may have once had to make a good marriage was destroyed long ago."

"I see."

Now that he knew, Caitlin waited patiently for him to turn the horse back toward town. Instead he kept heading west. She twisted in the saddle again. "Mr. Keegan, where do you think you're going?"

That infernal eyebrow of his shot up again. "I thought you'd probably like a few changes of clothes. I'm taking you by your former home to collect them, along with any personal things you'd like to take with you to the Paradise."

Convinced he couldn't possibly have understood her, Caitlin slowly and succinctly said, "Mr. Keegan, didn't you hear what I said? I . . . am . . . not . . . a . . . virgin. I was already ruined before you ever met me."

His firm mouth tipped into a disarmingly crooked grin. "I'm not exactly uncharted territory myself. If you can accept my past, I reckon I can accept yours."

10

TWO HOURS LATER, CAITLIN'S CLOTHING AND CHERISHED personal possessions had been stowed away in two satchels, the handles of which were tied together with rope so they could ride saddlebags fashion over the rump of Ace's horse.

Up ahead, Ace saw his ranch rising in silhouette against the moonlit horizon. The sprawling log house stood on a rise, holding court over a newly constructed barn and several outbuildings. This being a Saturday night, his brothers and all the other workers except Mike, the elderly stable hand, were still in town. In Ace's opinion, that was just as well.

Until tonight, Ace had believed his mother and sister would be the first women to live at the Paradise. For an instant, his thoughts drifted to them. He should write to his mother at the first opportunity to inform her of his marriage and to tell her he had discovered the truth about his half-sister Eden's parentage. The catch might be in finding a private moment to do so. He couldn't take a chance that Caitlin might see the letter. Eventually, when she'd grown to trust him a little, he would have to tell her that Conor had sired another daughter. But now was definitely not a good time to open that particular can of worms. She already suspected that his motives for marrying her stemmed from hatred. If she learned the truth about Eden, it would only add fuel to the fire.

Keeping secrets from his wife was no way to start a marriage, and Ace knew it. For the moment, though, he had more immediate concerns. Her brittle tension worried him most of all. This being their wedding night, he had to decide fast how he meant to proceed from here.

Given the circumstances, Ace was willing to wait on consummating the marriage—if waiting would be easiest for Caitlin. The question was, would it be? On the one hand, she scarcely knew him and could definitely use some time to adjust. On the other, there was the possibility that waiting would only prolong her agony. How did a man best handle a situation like this?

On the tail of that thought, another struck Ace. The longer he waited, the longer Caitlin would be able to get that annulment. If it came to a choice between consummating the marriage or letting her take off for San Francisco alone, he'd have her in bed so fast her head would spin.

Ace decided to play it by ear. God knew it would be no great hardship if he had to make love to the girl. He recalled how she had felt in his arms on the dance floor, how incredibly right, as if her slender shape had been molded just for him. A woman who felt that good had to have passion smoldering within her somewhere.

The thought left Ace burning low in his guts. As he drew the horse to a halt in front of the house, he said a little more abruptly than he intended, "Well, this is it."

Beginning to feel disgruntled by her wariness, Ace swung down from the horse.

After pulling her bags from Shakespeare's rump and

dumping them on the porch, he reached up to help her down. He saw her hesitate before putting her hands on his shoulders.

"Caitlin, try to relax," he said as he swung her to the ground. "It's going to be all right, sweetheart. Honestly."

Judging by her pallor, Ace didn't think she believed that. No matter how either of them circled it, this marriage gave him certain inalienable rights. If he chose to exercise them, there wouldn't be a whole hell of a lot she could do about it.

After wrapping Shakespeare's reins loosely around the saddle horn, he slapped the stallion on the rump to send him on his way to the stable. To forewarn Mike that the horse was coming, Ace pressed a thumb and forefinger against his teeth and whistled shrilly. Within seconds, Mike signaled back.

"My stable man," he explained to his bride, who had given a noticeable start when he whistled. "He'll rub Shakespeare down and give him his grain."

Fishing under the fringe of her shawl, he grasped her by the elbow and guided her up onto the newly constructed porch, the floor of which was made of planed boards, the framework of sapling pine. The sharp scent of the newly sawed wood filled the chill night air.

Before opening the door, he paused to regard her. Still as pale as milk, her small face glowed up at him in the filtered moonlight, her wide, wary eyes filled with unvoiced questions. Now was definitely not a good time to carry her over the threshold.

Resisting the urge to capture her face between his hands and spout foolish promises, he thrust open the door and stepped aside for her to enter.

Clasping her hands over the tails of the shawl at her waist, she moved hesitantly forward, her eyes huge as she tried to see through the darkness. With a touch at her back, he urged her farther forward so he could close the door.

Blackness swooped down over them. Ace waited only long enough for his eyes to adjust, then moved to the table in the center of the room where a lantern was kept.

Groping for a match in his shirt pocket, he said, "Stand tight. I'll have some light in here in two shakes."

Striking the Lucifer on the side seam of his denim pants, he set flame to the raised lantern wick. The lamp huffed, and golden light flared, flickering over the log walls. As he replaced the fluted glass chimney, he scanned the room, trying to see it as she must. To put it mildly, the house needed a feminine touch. Log walls, plank floors, no knickknacks or doodads. Despite the gleam of varnish, a step up from what she was accustomed to, it wasn't the kind of place a woman was likely to find appealing. Someday it would be a pretty and welcoming home, if all went as planned, but for now, it was rather austere, and even that was being kind.

"We're still doing the finish carpentry," he explained. "And I'm afraid we weren't expecting any company when we left earlier so I hope you'll excuse the mess." He grabbed a shirt from off the table and tossed it in a corner. "My brother Esa thinks the dressing room is wherever he happens to be standing." He rapped his knuckles on the plank table. "We don't have much furniture yet. Just the essentials, and that homemade." Picking up the lamp, he said, "Come on. I'll show you around."

She moved toward him with about as much enthusiasm as she might have shown for a tooth extraction. He flashed what he hoped was a halfway normal-looking smile. He'd just used the last match in his pocket and tossed it somewhere on the table. Without something clenched between his teeth, he tended to look as if he were leering when he grinned.

"This is the main living area," he said, indicating the large, open-beamed room in which they stood. "I wanted it big so everyone in the family could gather in here. We hauled all the rock for the fireplace in from Golden Creek. You'll notice it's veined with fool's gold. I thought it was kind of pretty. Shines like a son of a— well, really bright—when there's a fire in the grate."

Rubbing one moist palm on his trousers, Ace cleared his throat, wondering why he was so nervous. Pointing to a wide archway, he added, "Right through there is the kitchen." Pressing a hand to the small of her back, he guided her forward. As if she couldn't tell it was a kitchen. God, he was rambling like an idiot. Hoping there might be a certain humor in his pointing out the obvious, he inclined his head and added, "That monstrous thing is our cookstove. There along the side wall is the kitchen piano. Like most folks, we keep all kinds of staples in it, sugar, flour, salt, cornmeal—" He broke off and tapped a toe. "Beneath us, we have a solid pine floor." He jabbed a thumb upward and winked. "That's the ceiling. How'm I doing so far?"

The corners of her mouth curved up slightly. It wasn't exactly what he would call a smile, but he'd take what he could get. Where his hand pressed against her back, he could still feel her trembling. *Christ.* He was starting to feel a little shaky himself.

Guiding her back to the main living area, he said, "To our left is the parlor and the study, neither of which is finished yet. There'll be another fireplace in each, and I'd like to build floor-to-ceiling bookshelves in the study. I'm an incurable book hound."

He thought he glimpsed a spark of interest in her eyes. "Do you like to read, Caitlin?"

"Mmm."

Ace ground his teeth. *Mmm?* The girl wasn't helping him out much here. He cast another glance around the room, which seemed to look emptier by the second. "We'll ship all the furnishings in, of course. I hope you like to decorate. As you can see, there will be a lot of that to do." Holding the lantern high to illuminate the way, he turned her toward the rear of the house. "Back here are the bedrooms. Five, for starters. That should be plenty, though. My brothers will probably build their own places when they start their families, and my little sister Eden is already engaged to be married next June. That'll leave just me and my mother. And now you, of course." Ace nearly added, "And our children," but caught himself. "That's assuming that you like my mother and don't mind having her around."

"You have a mother and a sister?"

She sounded so amazed that he found himself smiling again. "No, actually, I hatched out under a cabbage leaf."

She gave a startled laugh. The sound was so welcome that, for the second time that evening, he nearly dropped to his knees and gave thanks.

"I'm sorry," she said softly. "I meant no offense. It's just that it's hard to picture a man like you with—well, with a mother."

"A man like me?" Ace wasn't sure he liked the sound of that. "What kind of a man do you think I am, exactly?"

She looked flustered by the question. "Well . . . a gambler." Her gaze dropped to his gun. "And a—a shootist."

"A shootist?" Ace chuckled in spite of himself. He'd been called a lot of things, but never quite so politely. "A gunslinger, you mean."

"Yes," she admitted, "a gunslinger."

"Which equates to scoundrel and killer?"

Her eyes widened. "I, um . . ."

"Do you know the main reason I've found it necessary to be so fast with a gun, Caitlin?"

She shook her head.

"Because I never draw unless another man goes for his gun first."

"I've offended you." She looked honestly distressed, whether it was because she was afraid she'd hurt his feelings or because she feared some sort of retaliation, he didn't know. "I'm sorry."

"No need. I'm not offended, just clarifying things. I won't lie to you and say I've never shot a man. But I'm not the cold-blooded killer my reputation paints me to be, either. I sure as hell haven't ever taken any pleasure from it."

Their shadows, cast every which way by the shifting lantern light, leaped over the pine walls as they moved farther down the hall. He stopped to throw open one door. "Just to give you an idea of the size of the bedrooms. The master bedroom, which is quite a bit larger, is the only one finished so far. It's at the back of

the house." He drew her along to another doorway.
"This is my pride and joy. Or at least it will be when it's
done, a full-fledged water closet. I put the windmill up
last month and got the pipe all in. We're hoping to get
the plumbing in working order sometime next week.
You'll have running water, gravity-fed from the attic,
just like they do in the city."

He nudged her farther along to the back bedroom.
After opening the door, he handed her the lamp. "Wait
here just a second," he said and left her standing at the
doorway. "I'll light this lantern in here for you. Then I'll
bring in your bags and get a fire started. I imagine you're
cold and exhausted."

"A little cold," she admitted, tugging her shawl more
closely around her shoulders. Holding the lantern aloft,
she darted a nervous gaze around the room, her cheeks
turning a pretty pink as she took in the adjoining
dressing room and the colorful quilt his mother had
made for the bed. "But I'm not at all tired."

Ace knew damned well that had to be a lie. After the
evening she'd just been through, she had to be so
exhausted she could scarcely see. She had obviously
concluded, and correctly, that with only one finished
bedroom in the house, the two of them would have to
share a bed.

Under any other circumstances, Ace would have sym-
pathized and done everything in his power to make the
situation more palatable for her. After all, the girl had
been thrust into a marriage against her will with a
virtual stranger. No matter how kind or understanding
he tried to be, the situation was bound to be difficult.

Unfortunately, the long and the short of it was that
fate had not dealt them another set of circumstances,
and while he was prepared to cut her a wide berth, he
wasn't of a mind to sleep in the barn or on the floor in
another room. No matter how you cut it, that was no
way to begin a marriage.

As if she read his thoughts, she pressed a hand to her
waist, cast about the room as though searching for
words, and finally said, "Mr. Keegan, I, um, have a
request to make."

Ace knew what was coming. He pretended to be preoccupied with the lamp.

"Since there are several bedrooms—" She broke off and let the words hang between them. "Well . . . you know. Could you—that is, would you consider . . ." Her voice trailed away.

Ace met her worried gaze. "We are legally married, Caitlin," he reminded her gently. "No matter what arrangement we may make between ourselves, for appearances, it's pretty much a given that we have to share a bedroom. If we sleep apart, there's bound to be speculation. I think there's talk aplenty circulating about us already, don't you?"

"Your own brothers would spread gossip about you?"

"I do have hired hands around the place. They would get wind of our sleeping arrangements sooner or later."

"But surely you intend to give me some time to get to know you."

Ace resisted the urge to walk back over to her. As forlorn as she looked and as badly in need of comfort as he sensed she was, he knew she wouldn't welcome any attempt on his part to provide it. "What better way to get acquainted than by sharing a bed?"

Clearly at a loss, she curled her slender fingers so tightly around the base of the lantern that her knuckles turned white. "I see."

Only, of course, she didn't see. Not at all. Right now, she clearly viewed him as a heartless monster. The quavery faintness of her voice nearly made him relent. Only the shadows in her eyes forestalled him. No simple case of nervous jitters, this, but a deep-rooted, bone-shaking fear. In his experience fears, great or small, were always best dealt with head on. She had to learn to trust him sometime, and sleeping with him would be a damned good way to start.

The light from the lamp etched her delicate features in shadow, casting them into sharp relief against the pale planes of her face. For an instant, she looked almost skeletal, a lifeless caricature instead of a flesh-and-blood woman.

"Caitlin," he said softly, "I have no intention of hurting you. If you can believe nothing else I say to you, please try to trust in that."

Her mouth quivered as she replied, "My worry is that you may have an entirely different definition of the word 'hurt,' Mr. Keegan."

"I'll tell you what," he said, striving for a friendly, matter-of-fact manner. "Let's take things one step at a time, hm? Even the worst situation looks a little less daunting after a good night's sleep."

She didn't appear to be reassured. He finished lighting the lamp on the bedside table, then rejoined her in the doorway to reclaim the other lantern.

Inclining his head at the bed, he said, "Why don't you go ahead and make yourself comfortable while I bring in your bags and start a fire?"

Judging by the look she gave him, you would have thought he'd just invited her to jump into a pit of vipers.

 11

AWAY . . . THE INSTANT CAITLIN WAS LEFT ALONE, THAT was all she could think about, getting away. Beyond that, nothing mattered. Not how she would get back to town without a horse. Not how she planned to find her way in the dark. Not how she hoped to reclaim her possessions. Nothing mattered but putting as much distance between herself and Ace Keegan as she possibly could.

So he wanted her to trust him, did he? Every time Caitlin thought about what he'd said, she nearly burst into hysterical laughter. What better way to become acquainted than by sharing a bed? Just who did he think he was kidding? She wasn't quite that naive, thank you very much. She knew all she needed to know about him, or for that matter, any man. In short, she didn't trust

Ace Keegan any farther than she could throw him, which wasn't darned far. As for his not hurting her? She'd believe that when she saw it.

After bringing her satchels to the bedroom, Keegan had excused himself to go outside and fetch in some firewood from the woodpile she'd seen out front. She could hear him there now, the logs going *kerchunk* as he gathered an armload. At any moment, he would return, and then her chance to run would be gone. She had to act fast.

Leaving her satchels where he'd set them on the colorfully draped bed, she hurried from the well-lit bedroom. After easing the door closed behind her, she moved down the shadowy hallway, her gaze fixed anxiously on the golden glow of lantern light ahead of her. Oh, please, God. All she needed was a couple of minutes. Just a couple of minutes, and she'd be out of there.

With a little luck, Keegan would see the closed bedroom door when he came back inside and think she was changing into her nightclothes. If he was a gentleman about it and decided to allow her a bit of privacy, that would buy her a few minutes. Not that she was foolish enough to believe he was a gentleman—or anything close to it. But maybe—pray God—he would be on his best behavior for a while—the better to trick her into trusting him.

Earlier, when he'd shown her the house, she'd seen a back door leading off the kitchen. If she left that way, he wouldn't see her from out front. If things went well, she would be a mile away before he realized she was gone. He would find it difficult to track her until daylight, and by the time he found her tomorrow, she would already have annulment proceedings well under way.

A sudden thump brought her advance down the hallway to a halt. She couldn't be sure where the sound had originated. She held her breath, her gaze fixed on the living room ahead of her. From her vantage point, all she could see was the table and the fireplace beyond it. Surely, if Keegan had entered the room, she would at least see his shadow.

After what seemed like an eternity of waiting, she

moved forward a step, then hesitated, half-expecting him to walk into her field of vision. When nothing happened, she took several more steps. The table was only a few feet away, but it seemed like a mile.

To her intense relief, there was no one in the main living area. She guessed that Keegan had decided to haul several armloads of wood up to the porch before coming back in to build a fire. Good.

Hesitating only long enough to take a steadying breath, she raced for the kitchen. The smell of beans and cornbread surrounded her as she drew near the stove. She imagined him and his brothers spooning up bowls of beans before leaving for the social. Soon, they would return, and she wouldn't have a prayer of slipping away without one of them noticing. At the thought, a clammy sweat broke out all over her body. Oh, God.

Beckoning to her like a beacon, the new brass doorknob on the back door reflected light from the lantern. She didn't slow her pace until her hand closed over it. Then, with a hard twist, she discovered the door had been locked shut.

Frantic, her fingers clumsy with urgency, she struggled to draw back the bolt. At any given second, Keegan could come back inside. Tarnation! With a frustrated sob, Caitlin jerked on the bolt with all her strength. With a suddenness that startled her, the metal bar finally pulled free of its niche.

So relieved she nearly wept, she flung the door wide. Her breath caught on a strangled cry the instant she stepped outside. *No porch.* That was the only thought her brain had time to assimilate. Then she was falling. Though she tried desperately to stifle it, a scream tore from her throat.

ACE HAD JUST GATHERED A THIRD ARMLOAD OF WOOD WHEN he heard a strangled cry. It might have been a cougar. Sometimes big mountain cats sounded very much like a woman screaming. But he'd never heard one sound quite like that.

Concerned, he dropped the armload of wood and hurried around the side of the house. To his amazement, he found his bride lying just below the back door, her crumpled form illuminated by a shaft of light spilling from the house. Even in the shadows, he could see her mouth working for air like that of a landed fish.

Ace ran toward her. In preparation for deep winter snowfall, he'd built the house on a high foundation, so she had fallen no short distance. Because a porch hadn't been built yet, he'd bolted the back door as a safety measure. Night blind as she was, Caitlin clearly hadn't seen the extreme drop before she stepped outside.

"Dear God, Caitlin. Are you all right?"

Of course, she wasn't all right. Any idiot could have determined that. She'd obviously been attempting an escape and would have been long gone if she hadn't taken such a nasty fall.

His heart caught with fear as he dropped to one knee beside her. She lay amid the scraps of lumber like a broken doll, eyes bugging, mouth agape. By the way her chest kept catching, he deduced she'd gotten the wind knocked out of her.

"Easy, sweetheart. Easy. Just try to relax."

Ace pressed a hand to her midriff, felt the whalebone of her corset, and bit back a curse. He eased an arm under her shoulders and carefully lifted her to a sitting position. Her body convulsed with her futile efforts to breathe.

"Easy, honey. It'll come. Just don't fight it. The wind is knocked out of you, that's all."

Even as he spoke, Ace was casting a frightened glance over her. Her dress was ripped at the shoulder, and he could see scraped flesh beneath the rent. At best, she was bound to be bruised up. At worst—God, he hated to think. And like a damned fool, he was moving her around. What if she had a broken arm or leg? Or, God forbid, a cracked rib. He might puncture one of her lungs.

Usually level-headed in a crisis, Ace was a stranger to the panic that surged through him. With three rough-and-tumble younger brothers, he'd been called upon to play nursemaid more times than he could count. Caitlin wasn't one of his brothers, though. She wasn't even as sturdily built as his little sister Eden. The thought of her falling such a distance and landing in a heap of jagged wood made him feel sick.

Hands shaking, he kneaded her thin arms. Twigs. Brittle little twigs. He'd never felt an elbow with so many bones. Relief flowed through him when he discovered nothing broken.

Her lungs whistled as she grabbed unsuccessfully for breath. With a sweep of his arm, he cleared away some of the boards and eased her gently back. "Just relax," he urged her softly. "Easy does it. It'll come, honey. Just relax."

Having had the breath knocked out of him more than once, Ace knew that relaxing was easier said than done. When a person couldn't breathe, it was instinctive to panic and fight for oxygen. Unfortunately, he also knew that as long as she struggled, her lungs would probably refuse to work.

Fairly certain, after a cursory examination, that she had no fractures in her upper torso, he put his hands to work massaging her shoulders and arms, hoping to help her go limp. Even at that, it seemed like an eternity before he finally felt her chest expand.

Unaware that he'd been holding his own breath, Ace hauled in a draught of air with her. "There's a good girl. Easy, now. Take it slow."

Her lungs whistled and caught again. Then, after only a moment, she was able to take another deep breath. The tension immediately eased from her narrow shoulders where his hands were clenched. *Damn it.* Tomorrow the poor girl would probably have bruises all over her from the grip of his fingers.

"Another breath," he coaxed. "Slow and easy. Just let your body take over." He watched anxiously as she struggled to make her lungs function properly again. "That's the way."

She shuddered. Was she relieved because she could finally breathe or revolted because he was touching her? Clamping a small hand over her ribs, she passed the next several seconds just working her lungs.

Ace sat back on his heels to give her space, which he sensed she needed almost desperately. Guilt began to rack him. This was entirely his fault. He'd known when he left her alone that she was feeling trapped. If he had been using his head, he wouldn't have given her any opportunity to run.

"No porch," she finally managed to croak.

He glanced at the yawning doorway above them. Six feet up, if it was an inch. Damn it all to hell. Taking his cue from her, he concentrated on breathing. To calm himself. To chase away the sensation of weakness that had attacked his legs. At some point tonight his feelings for this girl had gotten into an impossible tangle. The emotions that churned within him were as bewildering as they were difficult to identify. He only knew that seeing her lying there had scared the bejesus out of him.

Rubbing a calloused palm over his face, he blinked and refocused. Then he leaned over her. "Let's assess the damage, shall we?"

She made an inarticulate sound as he ran his hands up under her skirt. He realized it wasn't exactly the best thing to do. But how else was he to see if she'd broken a leg? Like most women, she was draped in so many layers, he had no hope of telling much until he'd dispensed with some of them.

His fingertips skimmed a fragile ankle sheathed in a ribbed cotton stocking, then a shapely calf encased in a cotton bloomer. A dimpled knee. A silken thigh. When he ran his hand past the layers of cotton to the slit in her drawers, she jumped like a terrified rabbit with one hind foot caught in a trap. His guts knotted.

"Easy, honey. It's okay." Assured that her left leg was reasonably intact, Ace turned his attention to her right one. As he gently prodded the network of bones in her small foot, he added, "Holler if anything hurts." He planted a hand on her chest when she tried to sit upright. "Goddammit, Caitlin, hold still. You could have a broken rib."

"I don't," she protested weakly. When his hand curled over her knee, she jerked again. "Mr. Keegan!"

"I said hold still." Running his hand up her thigh, he methodically embedded his fingers into her satiny flesh, searching for any abnormalities in her femur. To his relief, the bone felt unbroken. When his knuckles grazed a soft thatch of curls, it was his turn to jerk. He got his hand out from under her skirt in short order, the backs of his fingers burning as if he'd touched a hot coal.

"Well," he said in an oddly scratchy voice, "no bones seem to be broken. Not from the waist down, at any rate."

She shoved his hand from her chest and pushed up on her elbows. "No bones are broken anywhere."

It was his fear that she might not know if a bone was broken. With severe injury, shock often set in. "You're lucky you didn't break your silly little neck." It occurred to him he hadn't checked her there. When he reached to do so, she moved sideways and batted with a hand to stop his groping. "Caitlin, for God's sake."

"Would you please get your hands off of me?" she said shrilly. "I'm fine, I said."

That remained to be seen. "Let's get you in the house."

Not giving her time to protest, Ace ran one hand under her knees and caught her around the shoulders with his other arm. He was a little surprised at how easily he was able to push to his feet bearing her weight. As he jostled her in his embrace to get a secure hold, he made a mental note that his first order of business as her husband would be to put some meat on her bones.

"I can walk, Mr. Keegan! Please, put me down."

"I'll put you down when I'm damned good and ready, and not before." He struck off for the front door. "Dammit, stop wiggling. Do you want me to drop you?"

That got her attention. She stopped squirming, at any rate, although she seemed to be in a quandary about where to put her arms. One around his neck would have better facilitated him, but she seemed loath to touch him. Not entirely sure what possessed him, he pretended to lose his grip on her. At the downward plunge, she squeaked and grabbed hold of him around the neck.

Eating up the distance with long strides, he gained the porch and took the steps two at a time, the planks resounding with each impact of his boots. Bending at the knees, he managed to work the doorknob with one hand. As the latch released, he gave the solid oak panel a kick and sent it crashing open.

He made a beeline for the table and deposited her gently on one end in a sitting position. Her small feet sought purchase on the bench. Immediately she bent forward to pull her skirt down and arrange the folds primly around her ankles. It irritated the hell out of him that she seemed more concerned with modesty than the extent of her injuries.

He clenched his teeth to keep from cursing. Now that he had good light, he could see blood oozing from a cut at her temple. Her shoulder wasn't in much better shape, and there was a rent in her skirt that indicated she had probably sustained cuts on her hip as well.

"Jesus H. Christ."

He stepped around the end of the table to survey her back. Her rose-colored dress was splotched here and there with crimson. The goddamned nails had stabbed her. Silently vowing to take a strip out of Esa's hide for not hammering down all the points as he'd been told to do, Ace reached to lift Caitlin's curly red hair so he might better assess the damage. She wasn't going to bleed to death, that was the best he could say. Luckily, the nails were all newly purchased and hadn't been exposed to the elements long enough to rust.

Bracing himself for the battle that was sure to come, he left her to lock both the doors and draw the makeshift curtains over the front windows. Just in case his brothers came home early, he didn't want any of them looking in until this bit of business was concluded. As he walked back by the table en route to the kitchen, he noted that Caitlin was busily trying to repair the damage to her dress, apparently concerned that her shoulder was exposed.

He clenched his teeth again, with steely determination. Whether she liked it or not, a whole lot more than her shoulder was about to be uncovered. He wasn't about to lose her to a nasty infection just to spare her a few minutes of embarrassment.

He rummaged about in the kitchen cupboards until he found the whiskey and some clean rags. She eyed him askance as he returned to her. Avoiding her wary gaze, he set the jug and rags on the table behind her, then drew his knife from the scabbard on his belt. Not hesitating long enough for her to guess what he meant to do, he slashed the back of her gown from neckline to waist.

"What are you—!" She gasped and grabbed frantically to hold up her dress. "Mr. Keegan!"

Ace curled his fingers over the top edge of her corset and hauled her back toward him. "Be still, Caitlin. I don't want to cut you." He inserted the blade under the edge of her chemise and tightly laced corset, whereupon he began sawing downward. She screeched as the whalebone and cloth gave way with a popping sound. "I said be still. This is no time for nonsense."

"But—what do you think you're—oh, my God!"

"You have cuts all over you," he told her in the same gruff tone as he pushed the stays and cotton aside to survey her bare back. He slipped his knife into its scabbard. In her present frame of mind, he was afraid she'd plunge it right through his heart if he laid it where she could get her hands on it. "Someone has to clean these so you don't get an infection, and since you can't, I'm elected."

"But my clothes. You've ruined them!"

"I'll replace every stitch."

In truth, Ace would have preferred letting her remove the clothing herself, but given her wariness of him, he figured there was about as much chance of that as a blizzard in hell.

When he touched her skin, she flinched and reared away from him. Clamping a hand over her uninjured shoulder, he drew her back again.

"Caitlin," he said more gently, "you're apparently mistaking my intentions. I'm not going to force myself on you. I give you my word."

"You aren't?"

No longer afraid she might be seriously injured, Ace bit back a grin at the incredulity in her voice. Uncorking the whiskey jug and grabbing the rag, he said, "I rarely lose control of my baser urges over a woman who is streaming blood. Call me squeamish if you like, but the sight dampens my ardor."

"Oh."

That one little word, uttered with ill-concealed dubiousness, made him smile again. For the second time that night, Ace had cause to wonder what it was about this slip of a girl that made him feel so . . . He wasn't exactly sure how she made him feel. Sort of warm inside, he guessed.

"You needn't sound so disappointed. Without the blood, I'm sure yours is a very lovely back. Under other circumstances, I would undoubtedly be overcome."

She threw him a glance filled with equal parts puzzlement and wariness. Ace deduced by the look that he wasn't behaving quite as monstrously as she had expected. That conclusion led him to wonder just what manner of men the girl had known in her lifetime. Degenerates, evidently. No stranger to depravity, growing up as he had on the San Francisco waterfront, Ace knew the world was filled with all manner of scoundrels. He just found it difficult to fathom how any man who called himself a man could look into Caitlin's luminous blue eyes and still bring himself to hurt her.

Since he knew it was unlikely that he could continue to conceal the disfiguring paralysis at the left side of his mouth, he abandoned the attempt and allowed himself to flash her what he hoped was a reassuring smile. Her gaze immediately shifted to his lips.

His guts tied into knots again. His smile was grotesque, he knew. Even so, he couldn't very well go around with a matchstick between his teeth constantly to camouflage the flaw.

Dragging his gaze from hers, he concentrated on dabbing at a puncture wound. She hissed air through her teeth at the sudden sting of alcohol.

"I'm sorry. I know it hurts like the devil." He swallowed and glanced up again. She was craning her neck to look back, her small face a pale oval above the torn dress. "I'm sure you're wondering what happened to my face," he said with a nonchalance he was far from feeling, "so I'll put your curiosity to rest. When I was a boy, I was struck with a rifle butt. The blow laid my cheek open, shattered the bone, and damaged some of the nerves. My cheek and the left corner of my mouth are paralyzed."

Even as rattled as she was, Caitlin couldn't mistake the pain and humiliation she heard in his voice, and for a moment, she forgot everything but that. He obviously thought she found him ugly, which was about as far from the truth as he could get. In her estimation, the scar along his cheekbone lent his dark, chisled features a rugged appeal, and his crooked grin was extremely attractive.

Staring up at him, she found it difficult to believe that women didn't make fools of themselves over him on a fairly regular basis. His smile was enough to make even her feel frittery, and that was saying something.

Her gaze drifted from the thick, glistening black waves of hair that fell over his forehead to his bladelike nose, high cheekbones, full mouth, and the stubborn thrust of his square jaw. He had skin the color of strong coffee lightened with cream. Where his collar fell away at his throat, she could see a furring of black hair that she suspected fanned downward over his muscular chest. The rolled back sleeves of his black shirt revealed tanned wrists and forearms that were roped with steely tendons and lined with popping veins.

As if he felt her staring, he glanced up again and their gazes locked, his almost challenging. Not quite able to believe her eyes, Caitlin watched a flush creep up his neck. He truly was embarrassed about his face. The realization made her view him in a different light, if not as someone she could like, at least as someone with feelings.

Without taking the time to consider the ramifications, she heard herself say, "You have a very nice smile, Mr.

Keegan, and anyone who told you that scar on your cheek makes you less than attractive was either blind or jealous."

Even as she spoke, Caitlin wished she could call back the words. She had to be mad to make a friendly overture, especially one that might lead him to believe she found him attractive. Her biggest downfall, that—feeling sorry for anyone or anything that was helpless or in pain, including her retarded cat Lucky and the hapless insects she carried from the house to set free.

The flush on his neck deepened and spread to his face. Lowering long, dark lashes that Caitlin and most of her female friends would have happily killed for, he pretended to be completely absorbed in cleaning the scratches on her back. "Is that a compliment, Mrs. Keegan?"

His use of her married name had the effect of a fist in the stomach. When her lungs finally began to work properly again, she hauled in a quavery breath. "No, Mr. Keegan, I was simply stating a fact. I'm sure many women find you extremely handsome."

"But not you, of course."

His lashes lifted, and his twinkling brown eyes held hers for several endless seconds. She felt like a bug pinned to velvet.

"No, not me," she said thinly. "It's nothing personal, just that I—" She broke off, not certain what she'd meant to say.

"Just that you what?" He returned his attention to her back, setting another scratch on fire with alcohol. "I have a feeling you don't care overmuch for men."

"Not especially," she admitted.

His gaze flicked back to hers. "I guess it will be my job to change your mind about that, at least as it pertains to me. Otherwise this marriage of ours will be a difficult row to hoe."

"Which leads me back to my request for an annulment. It would save us both a lot of trouble if you'd put a stop to this travesty before it's too late."

His mouth quirked at one corner. "I don't run from

trouble, especially not when it comes wrapped in such a pretty package." His dark eyes met hers again. "As for an annulment, perhaps it's a subject we should discuss in more depth. I had you pegged as a woman who stood behind her word."

"I do."

The instant she spoke, Caitlin saw a gleam of satisfaction enter his eyes. She realized almost instantly that she'd been had.

"If that's so, then how could you possibly try to run off in the dead of night?" he challenged. "Correct me if I'm wrong, but I thought I heard you vow to love, honor, and obey me until death do us part."

"I had no choice. It was that or see my brother shot."

"The why and wherefore don't matter. What does is that you gave me your word, and now you'd break it without batting an eye. As I recall, your sire didn't honor his word, either. Like father, like daughter?"

"That isn't true." The heat of anger raced up her neck. She made tight fists in her skirt, striving to regain control. A smart woman didn't argue with a man, especially not when he outweighed her by a hundred pounds, nearly every ounce of which appeared to be muscle. She'd learned that the hard way. "There are extenuating circumstances, and you know it!"

"To hell with the circumstances," he shot back. "You made vows to me before God, and if you're truly a woman of your word, you'll live up to them."

Caitlin felt her pulse pounding behind her eyes. It was as if he'd stripped away the layers and seen deeply inside of her, as if he'd watched and waited to find the one bit of leverage he could wield against her. *Her word.* To her, it was everything. For years, she'd seen her father lie and cheat and steal. To her shame, she'd always felt his lack of character was a reflection on her and her brother. To combat that, she'd made a vow long ago. A far more important vow than the ones she'd made to Ace Keegan. To be nothing like Conor O'Shannessy, not in thought, word, or deed. Somehow this man had sensed that, and now he was using it against her.

Mingled with her rage was an awful helplessness, for

Caitlin realized he had maneuvered her into a trap of her own making, one far more confining than any he could have sprung himself.

Though she knew it wasn't wise, and anticipating a good cuffing the instant the words passed her lips, she said, "You, sir, are a manipulative bastard."

Braced for a blow, Caitlin was amazed when all he did was throw back his dark head and laugh. The sound was a deep, rich rumble of sound that took her completely off guard. What he found so funny, she didn't know.

"You're probably right," he said as his mirth subsided. His expression gave no indication that he bore her any animosity for having spoken her mind. "I'm also the luckiest bastard you'll probably ever meet." He gave her a slow wink that made her heart lurch. "Just look at the reward I get for my efforts, a lovely wife."

"Are you that desperate?"

He shrugged, the gesture conveying that no matter how she viewed the situation, he was pleased with its outcome and wasn't about to change his mind. "The way I see it, I've been dealt a few incredibly lucky hands in my time, but this one beats them all. As much as I regret my behavior toward you a few weeks back, I can't feel sorry for the way things have turned out. The idea of being married is starting to grow on me, I guess."

"This isn't a game, Mr. Keegan. I'm not the ante in a poker game."

Setting aside the whiskey and cloth, he straightened and chucked her under the chin. "Oh, yes, Mrs. Keegan, it is a game. For very high stakes. And I'm winning." He bent again to examine the scrape on her shoulder. As he peeled away the cloth, he whistled through his teeth. "When you take a tumble, you don't do it halfway, do you?"

Caitlin was so upset, she felt separated from the pain. "Don't change the subject. You're twisting things to make me feel obligated to stay here."

He arched a dark eyebrow. "Is it working?"

It was, and they both knew it. She glanced quickly away before he could read the truth in her eyes. "You're not being fair."

"That's why I'm so successful at gambling. I cheat."

Her stomach lurched at the lighthearted way he said it. He clearly had no conscience to which she might appeal. "Please, try to understand. I cannot stay here."

"Oh, but you can, and what's more, you will," he replied with absolute certainty. "You gave me your word, and I intend to hold you to it."

With a sudden jerk, he pulled the material of her dress farther down her arm. When she gave a reflexive leap, he slanted her a mocking glance. "Relax, Caitlin. For the moment, at least, you're perfectly safe."

She doubted that. She hadn't been truly safe since the first moment she clapped eyes on him, and if she stayed here, she'd never be safe again. Nonetheless, he'd maneuvered her into a corner. If she ran off, she would be breaking her word. Not just her word to him, but, as he'd so cleverly pointed out, her word to God.

✷ 12

AFTER TENDING TO MOST OF CAITLIN'S ABRASIONS, ACE gave her the rag and whiskey and sent her to the bedroom where she could clean the scrape on her hip and change into her nightgown in private. Positive thinking, the latter. When his bride emerged from the bedroom, she was fully clothed in a faded blue muslin dress with a button-up collar and long sleeves. Since it was already after midnight, he didn't take that as an encouraging sign.

Not that he'd had high hopes. Intimacy of any kind, emotional or physical, was clearly not in the cards. Unless, of course, after thinking things over, he decided that forcing the issue would be best. Prolonging her misery might be more a cruelty than a kindness.

In an attempt to help her relax, he decided to make a batch of hot cocoa. Warm milk was believed by most ladies to have tranquilizing properties. Ace didn't harken much to the practice himself, preferring a belt of strong whiskey on the rare occasion he felt the need. But whiskey didn't seem quite the thing to offer Caitlin. If she was privy to the wiles of men, she might think he was trying to ply her with liquor.

After building fires in both the fireplace and the cookstove, he chipped off some sugar from the sugar cone into a pan, mashed it into fine granules with a spoon and then began mixing in the cocoa, ever conscious that Caitlin sat at the table watching him. The silence seemed deafening. As he drew a pitcher of cool milk from the ice box, he decided to make an attempt at small talk.

"Luckily, I went into town to buy a stove and ice box a few days back. Only picked up one block of ice, but now that we have a lady in the house, I'll arrange for regular deliveries."

"I can get along perfectly well without a continuous supply of ice, Mr. Keegan. I know it's expensive."

At least she no longer seemed inclined to argue with him about whether or not she'd be staying at the Paradise. That had to be a sign of progress.

Ace slanted her a look over his shoulder as he bent to rearrange the stove wood with a poker. Her faded blue gown was obviously one she'd made to wear around the house, its dimensions ample enough to accommodate an uncorseted waist, the sleeves slim and cuffed widely at the wrists, with no lace or other impractical trim to get in the way while she worked. Even so, the garment was threadbare, eloquent testimony to the fact that she was accustomed to doing without.

He suspected that had been the case for most of her life. Conor O'Shannessy had been a self-centered, meanhearted bastard with no regard for women. Definitely not the kind of man to put his daughter's needs high on his list of priorities.

Not wishing to sound like a braggart, yet wanting to

relieve Caitlin's mind about his finances, Ace said, "A few blocks of ice a week won't deplete my savings, Caitlin. I'm not what you would term fantastically wealthy, I don't suppose, but I am well set."

"From gambling?"

She said "gambling" as if it were a filthy word. Ace arched an eyebrow at her. "From making a few sound investments." With a little more force than he intended, he closed the stove door. "I seem to have a knack for it."

"What kind of investments?"

Ace nearly said railroads but managed to bite back the word. If she discovered he was behind the rumors about the railroad spur being built between No Name and Denver, all his carefully laid plans of revenge would go up in smoke. "In transportation, mainly. I've lived in San Francisco for nearly twenty years. In that fair city, wealthy people aren't content to go about in wagons and modest buggies." That much wasn't a lie. "I decided that investing in more modern means of conveyance might prove profitable, and I was right."

"How lucky for you."

The disdain in her voice was unmistakable. Ace nearly told her that luck had had nothing to do with his becoming financially well set. He had clawed his way up from penury as a youth by sweeping the spittle-smeared floors of waterfront saloons. The long hours had been horrible, the abuse he had suffered at the hands of the intoxicated patrons even worse. He'd eventually turned to gambling as an easier way to make money, and he would be the first to admit his success at cards had been largely due to sleight of hand.

But he'd been selective in his victims. He had never fleeced anyone who wouldn't have done the same to him or someone else. He wasn't particularly proud of that, but then he wasn't exactly ashamed of it, either. He'd grown to manhood in a cutthroat world in which he had learned to live by his wits, to guard his back, and to make a profit instead of being bilked. No great disgrace in that.

"Yes, I guess I was lucky," he said. Luckier than most waterfront waifs, at any rate. "Thus my nickname, Ace."

He moved the pot of flavored milk onto the heat and

turned his attention to stirring the mixture so it wouldn't scorch. When the edges of the milk began to bubble, he filled two mugs and removed the pot to the warming shelf.

"I hope you like hot cocoa," he said as he bypassed the benches at the table in favor of a seat on the hearth. Extending one of the mugs toward her, he suggested in as kindly a voice as he could muster, "Move over here beside me, honey, where it's warm. Summertime or no, this house is chilly at night. Until I came back here, I'd forgotten how cool Rocky Mountain evenings are."

She rubbed her arms as she moved from the table toward the fire. Looking up at her, Ace decided he could have done far worse for himself. Even in a ragged, ill-fitting dress, Caitlin managed to be beautiful, particularly so in firelight. Her hair glistened like liquid fire where the amber light struck it, and her delicate features looked as if they'd been cast in gilded ivory. His fingertips ached to trace the fragile curve of her jaw. Her skin, he knew, was silken, wonderfully warm, and lightly scented with lavender.

The sporting women he'd kept company with on rare occasions during his adult life had usually worn so much perfume the smell had been nearly overwhelming. Not that there was any comparison between Caitlin and a sporting woman. This girl was a lady from the tips of her toes to the top of her head.

Hoping she might feel more at ease if she could keep a little distance between them, he indicated a small stool before the hearth that he'd fashioned from scrap wood a few days earlier. "Take a load off your feet. I promise, I don't bite."

His gaze shifted to her bodice as she perched gingerly on the stool. Like the rose-colored gown she'd worn earlier, this dress had been fashioned for a less ample bosom.

He was pleased that she'd chosen not to wear stays this time. Fashion be damned. He hoped the corset he'd destroyed was the only one she owned. In his opinion, the contraptions were torturous inventions and bad for women's health. If God had meant for a female's internal organs to be squeezed into her chest cavity, he would have made her that way. That was not to mention the fact that a man liked to feel flesh when he touched a woman, not cloth and rigid whalebone.

When the stool rocked slightly under her weight, Caitlin jerked to catch her balance. Ace flashed a sheepish grin. "Sorry about that. I tried my damnedest to get the legs even, but the more I sawed, the worse it got. A carpenter, I'm not. Let's just hope the house doesn't fold in the first high wind."

She threw an anxious glance at the walls, then at the fireplace. "Everything looks solid enough."

He handed her a mug of cocoa, then took a slow sip of his own. "Trust me, the only thing plumb around here is my patience—as in plumb gone."

She gave a startled little laugh. Ace decided he could live with hearing that sound for the next fifty years. It reminded him of chiming crystal, light and airy and incredibly sweet. He wished she'd relax and let herself laugh more often. Maybe in time.

The damned stool rocked under her again, causing her to shoot him a questioning look. "Surely you aren't that bad a carpenter."

"If you spill anything on the kitchen counters, it will run downhill." He winked at her. "A crooked house built by a crooked man. Luckily the worst of the actual construction is over. No matter how I try, I hit my thumbs more than I do the nails. After all of this"—he gestured at the newly raised house around them—"the only thing I've managed to improve upon with practice is my ability to turn the air blue."

"If you have to nail anything else, maybe I can help. I'm fairly good with a hammer."

"Does that mean I should guard my back?"

She gave another startled laugh. Then she glanced quickly away, as if she feared what he might see in her expression. "Hopefully you won't give me cause to bean you, Mr. Keegan."

"I'll probably give you cause about a dozen times a day, as will my brothers. Without Ma here to keep after us, we've all become Yahoos." He didn't miss the tension that drew her small features suddenly taut. He hadn't meant for her to take him literally. "Harmless Yahoos, of course. As rough as our manners have gotten, you have nothing to fear from any of us. Just the opposite, in fact. My brothers and I watch out for our own, and now that you're my wife, that includes you."

Her gaze lifted to his. Huge, distrustful blue eyes. Ace could have strangled Conor O'Shannessy if the bastard hadn't already been dead. He felt only marginally less violent when he thought of her brother. This young woman had been treated badly, no doubt about it.

His thoughts turned to his half-sister, Eden, who had grown up in the midst of four rough-mannered young men. Impulsive and lighthearted, she thought nothing of approaching an unfamiliar male and striking up a conversation, after which she proceeded to talk his hind leg off, much to Ace's dismay. The girl had never known a stranger, and probably never would. Luckily, she had four older brothers to look out for her, one of whom had a fearsome reputation with a gun. No male on the prowl had ever dared to take advantage of her.

Caitlin had had no protectors. Just the opposite. Gazing into her eyes, Ace recalled having glimpsed that same expression in his own eyes years ago when he'd seen his reflection in a mirror. He knew from personal experience that only the most cruel of betrayals could cause such shadows. He also knew how hard it was to regain one's ability to trust. He still hadn't quite mastered the art, and he had a feeling Caitlin had suffered at others' hands even more greatly than he had. It was one thing to be betrayed by strangers and quite another to be betrayed by one's own father and brother.

Lowering his gaze to his mug, he was stricken with the enormity of the task he'd taken on by marrying this girl. She needed help. The kind of help he wasn't even certain he was capable of giving. It was going to take one hell of a lot of patience to bring her around.

When he tackled a job, he liked fast results. It wasn't in his nature to stand around waiting for things to happen. Over the last twenty years, his sense of urgency had proved to be his worst enemy. More than once he

had rammed his fist against a wall, enraged because he'd
been unable to exact revenge against Joseph's killers
immediately, frustrated because his only guarantee of
success lay in the waiting and careful planning. Now,
here he was, married to someone who wore wariness like
a cloak.

When he heard her delicately slurp the last dregs of
hot cocoa from her cup, he finished off his own with
three large gulps. Extending a hand, he said, "Here, let
me get us each some more. On a cool night like this, hot
cocoa has a way of warming the bones, doesn't it?"

As she handed over her mug, she carefully avoided
touching her fingertips to his. Ace bit down hard on his
back teeth as he pushed up.

When he returned from the kitchen with their refilled
mugs, he couldn't help noticing the way she sat with her
shoulders hunched and her arms hugging her waist. The
posture screamed, "Don't touch me."

Ace wasn't sure which was worse, drinking bucketfuls
of hot cocoa when he yearned for a jigger of good Irish
whiskey or trying to make small talk with a nervous
bride. Fifteen minutes later, neither endeavor was one
he cared to repeat.

After pouring them each a third cup of cocoa, he
resumed his seat on the stone hearth and lifted his mug
to her in a mock toast. With wry amusement, he said,
"To marital bliss."

Caitlin did not drink to the toast. Indeed, Ace thought
it fair to say she nearly ran screaming from the house. So
much for a note of levity.

Sitting on the roughly hewn tripod in the flickering
firelight, she was impossibly beautiful. The bits of hair
that had escaped the bunch of loose curls atop her head
looked as though they'd been artfully arranged to best
enhance her loveliness, wispy curls framing her small
face, longer ones lying in shimmering splendor along the
graceful slope of her neck.

Feeling unaccountably nervous, an affliction that
seemed to grow worse by the moment, he glanced
around the room, searching desperately for something,
anything, as a topic of conversation. There was nothing.

He set his mug on the hearth and rubbed his hands over the denim that sheathed his legs. Then he lifted the mug again, gave it a turn, and proceeded to sit staring at it as if he'd never seen a cup before. Much more of this, and he'd be the one who ran screaming from the house.

He glanced over at Caitlin. She too seemed unaccountably interested in the conformation of a coffee mug. She was also absently toying with the onyx and diamond pinkie ring he'd slipped onto her finger, twisting it round and round, running her thumb over the upraised stone. Her eyelids were beginning to droop.

With a yawn and stretch to emphasize his point, he said, "It's getting late. I suppose we should probably be thinking about bed."

In the silence, his voice rang out like a rifle shot. Caitlin jerked and came wide awake, fastening huge blue eyes on him. Ace might have laughed, but at the moment, it didn't seem all that funny. The poor girl was miserable.

Regardless, he was tuckered. As frightened as she obviously was of going to bed, he couldn't pander to her all night. They both needed at least a few hours' sleep.

He shoved up from the hearth. "I'm beat." Gesturing toward the hallway, he said, "Why don't you go in while I bank the fire? I'm sure you could use a few minutes of privacy."

She threw a glance of sheer dread at the shadowy hallway. "Oh . . . yes." She touched a hand to her slender throat and gulped. "I, um . . . privacy, yes. Thank you."

She pushed slowly to her feet. Pretending a nonchalance he was far from feeling, Ace leaned a shoulder against the rock face of the fireplace and watched her walk to the bedroom. Every step she took appeared to be an effort.

He sighed and rubbed a hand over his face, half tempted to give in and let her have the bed to herself. But, no. The sooner she became accustomed to being physically close with him, the sooner he could make love to her. And the sooner he could make love to her, the sooner this agony of tension would be over.

13

AFTER BANKING THE FIRE, ACE GAVE CAITLIN AN ADDITIONal five minutes to prepare for bed. Then, turning out the lantern, he made his way down the dark hallway toward the slit of light shining under the bedroom door.

He found his bride standing before the window, which he'd cracked open that morning and forgotten to close. He guessed he'd been so wrapped up in his concern for Caitlin earlier that he hadn't noticed it. Her small hands clasping the top window rail, she turned slightly.

The faint smell of lavender wafted to his nostrils. Pushing the door closed, he paused a moment to savor the sweetness. He had been to bed with countless women, but this would be the first time he'd ever spent the night with one. The occasion was especially momentous because Caitlin was a lady, exactly the kind of female he'd made it a point to avoid. A decent woman usually expected a marriage proposal from a man who dallied with her.

As Ace moved toward Caitlin, it occurred to him that he'd probably spend nearly every night for the rest of his life with her. Caitlin, with her glorious red hair and ivory skin. Only a crazy man would object to such a forecast.

Clad in a voluminous white nightgown, she looked small, defenseless, and too nervous for his peace of mind. The folds of cotton seemed to swallow her. Dainty feet peeked out from beneath the gown's hem, her heels a rose-petal pink. Used to his own raw-boned feet, he was fascinated by her spindly little toes.

She was shivering again, he realized, as he drew up behind her. He reached past her to draw the window

closed. Within seconds, he realized why she was standing there, shaking like a leaf in front of the upraised
glass. The damned window was stuck.

"I, um, tried to open it earlier. It wouldn't budge."

Ace recalled her headlong dive from the back doorway
and arched an eyebrow. "You tried to go out the
window?"

"I couldn't fit."

Nudging her out of the way, he put some muscle into
trying to move the double-hung frame. With a grating
sound and a loud thunk, it finally gave way and fell
closed.

"My talents definitely don't lie in carpentry," he said
drily. "There isn't a window or door in the place that
doesn't tend to stick."

His talents evidently didn't lie in seduction, either, if
the wide-eyed gaze she trained on him was any indication. "Have you tried soap?"

"Soap?"

"You rub a door or window with soap where it sticks,
and it usually solves the problem. If you have a bar, I'll
happily fix this one."

Ace had a feeling she'd happily do anything to avoid
going to bed. "In the morning, maybe."

Lightly grasping her by the shoulders, he turned her
toward the bed. She moved ahead of him like a con-
demned person about to be executed. When her knees
encountered the mattress, her whole body jerked.
Though he tried not to, Ace felt sorry for her. After
living his entire adult life as a bachelor, crawling into
bed with a stranger of the opposite sex had become old
hat to him. Such was definitely not the case for her.

Resigned, he leaned around her to drag the quilt and
sheets back, then gave her a nudge. With unmistakable
reluctance, she crawled in and curled into a shivering
little ball on the far side of the mattress. Ace covered her
with the quilt, then bent to turn down the lamp.

In the sudden darkness, he crossed to the other side of
the bed, unstrapping his gun belt en route. As was his
habit, he hung the weapon over the bedstead, just in case

he needed it quickly during the night. Next, he removed his trouser belt, which he folded and laid on a chair. He sat on the edge of the bed to remove his boots. As he peeled off his socks, he could have sworn he heard Caitlin's heart pounding.

With a sigh, he abandoned all thought of sleeping in the nude and settled for removing only his shirt, which he tossed in the general direction of his belt. As he slid under the covers, he felt the bed shaking. The sensation put him in mind of the time he'd awakened in the middle of the night to a San Francisco earth tremor.

Jesus H. Christ. These weren't just little shakes, but violent jerks that seemed to seize her whole body. He lay staring at her slender back, wondering what the hell he ought to do.

"Caitlin?"

"Wh—what?"

To be sure he wasn't imagining things, he curled a hand over her waist. Sure enough, she was quaking like a dry autumn leaf in a high wind. Ace was about to say as much when she sat bolt upright in the bed.

"I can't d-do th-this," she said shrilly. "I'm s-sorry. I just can't."

He pushed up beside her. In the moonlight, she looked ethereal—a fragile angel with one hand pressed over her heart, the other clutching her throat. "You can't do what?" he asked stupidly, playing for time.

"This!" Her voice went high-pitched. Waving a hand at the bed, she said, "I just can't. Promises or n-no, I can't."

The hysteria in her voice told Ace more than she could know. He sensed panic wasn't long in coming, and he knew he had no one to blame but himself. Instead of pussyfooting around her all evening and dragging out the misery, he should have insisted they go to bed an hour ago. Now her nerves were strung so taut, she could scarcely think, let alone reason her way through it. "Caitlin, sweetheart, come here." Ace slipped an arm around her waist, pulling her down and slightly beneath him as he lowered himself back onto the mattress. She gave a startled squeak, but before she could physically react, he used his forearm to anchor her, his hand to capture her wrists. "Easy, now. It's all right."

She bucked sharply with her hips. "L-let g-go of me! Please!" She punctuated the words with a low sob. "Don't hurt me. Please, don't. I w-won't fight y-you. I sw-swear it. Just, please, don't hurt me."

Half sick with regret, Ace angled a knee across her thighs, more to keep her from throwing off the covers than to hold her down. The warmth from the fire out front did little to take the chill off the bedroom, and with her already shaking as she was, he was afraid to expose her to the night air. "I'm not going to hurt you, honey. I promise. Calm down, hmm?"

"I—I'm calm. Just, please, turn loose. I can't br-breathe."

"Sure you can. You're talking, aren't you? You can't talk without breathing." He brought her hands to his mouth and trailed his lips over her tightly clenched knuckles. "Just calm down," he repeated firmly, huffing his breath against her icy skin in an attempt to warm her. "Take a deep breath. Come on. There's a good girl. Now, one more."

At the tail end of a shuddering breath, she said, "I don't want to be married. I never w-wanted to be."

"I know. Unfortunately, life has a way of throwing loops at the best of us sometimes." Knowing that she'd been around a number of cattle, he didn't feel it necessary to explain that analogy. She'd probably tossed her fair share of lassos. He ran a massaging hand up her side. "We'll work our way through this, Caitlin. You'll see. It won't seem quite so bad once the idea of being married starts to grow on you."

Releasing her wrists and drawing his leg off hers, he rolled onto his side and drew her close, pillowing her head on his arm. Their faces mere inches apart, he searched her frightened gaze, wondering what exactly had happened to her that she would be so terrified. He didn't believe the word "compromised" drew an accurate picture. Anger welled within him.

She splayed her hands on his chest, whether to cling to him for comfort or to hold him at bay, he wasn't sure, and he guessed she probably wasn't either. Her palms were so cold they seemed to burn his skin, her fingertips like ice shards digging in.

"Mr. Keegan?"

Ace ran his hand up her side and over her hair. As he'd noticed earlier, it was coarser than most women's and far curlier. He liked the way it felt. He traced the hollow of her cheek with the back of a knuckle, his throat going tight with an emotion he didn't wish to name. Only one thing seemed certain to him in that moment, that he wouldn't force this girl to do anything. Hers wasn't a simple fear, but sheer terror.

"Mr. Keegan?" she said again.

"What?" he asked gruffly.

In the filtered moonlight, her huge, luminous eyes clung to his, imploring, beseeching. After several long seconds, she whispered raggedly, "Why me? If you wanted to get married, why did you pick on me?"

Ace nearly reminded her he hadn't been given much choice in the matter, that fate had done the choosing for both of them. But that didn't seem a very smart thing to say, especially not to his wife on their wedding night. "Some things are just meant to be," he whispered. "I think this is one of them."

As he said the words, Ace realized he truly meant them. His body still absorbing the residual shudders that wracked her fragile frame, he gazed down at her small face and knew with absolute certainty, which had nothing to do with reason and everything to do with instinct, that fate had led him in a circle back to this place, that for reasons neither of them could conceive she was supposed to be lying here in his arms.

For a hero, he had a few too many rough edges, and he'd be the first to admit it. But in a way, maybe that qualified him for the role more than anyone else. Given his reputation with a gun and his tendency to be an ornery son of a bitch when he got crossed, no one would dare try to hurt her again. That was a step up from the situation she'd been in a few hours ago, vulnerable to any Jack who cared to do her dirty, her spoiled brother at the head of the line.

"Caitlin, sweetheart, listen to me."

Ace hadn't a clue what he meant to say, only that he ached for her. It was a terrible thing to feel so afraid. He knew because he'd been there. Even now, at a weight of well over two hundred pounds and with plenty of muscle to defend himself, he could still remember the sick fright he'd felt as a boy when he'd been helpless against grown men.

Trapped in a female body, Caitlin would always be at a disadvantage when pitted against a man. She undoubtedly feared that if she let down her guard, even for an instant, someone would harm her.

"I'm not going to hurt you," he promised huskily. "I'll even go a step farther and not touch you. Not anywhere personal, at any rate. How does that sound? For tonight. A period of grace, so to speak. Would you like that?"

She nodded, but her expression told him she wasn't sure she believed him. Ace sighed and shifted his weight to get more comfortable. At his movement, her whole body snapped taut. She wasn't going to relax, he realized. He could talk himself blue, promise her the moon, and nothing he said or did was going to ease her mind. Lying within the circle of his arms, she felt so small and frighteningly brittle. He was almost afraid to tighten his hold for fear he might hurt her.

Her features were drawn with the ravages of exhaustion. Yet he doubted she would get much sleep, possibly not any at all, unless he thought of some way to reassure her.

Not sure what possessed him—even as he released her and swung from the bed, he questioned his sanity—he strode across the shadowy bedroom to the chair. Grabbing up his belt, he removed his knife and scabbard. As he walked back to the bed, he extended the weapon to her. When she made no move to take it, he realized she couldn't see what he held.

"Here," he said gruffly as he bent to put the leather-sheathed blade into her hands. "It's my knife. I sharpened it myself to shave my whiskers. I already unfastened the strap that holds it in the scabbard, so you can pull it out easily."

"Your knife?" she repeated in a bewildered voice.

As he slipped back into the bed beside her, Ace couldn't help but wonder if he'd live to laugh about this madness later. "Yes, my knife. I, um, thought it might make you feel a little safer."

"Safer?" she echoed.

Ace couldn't help but smile. "Yes, safer. If I try to hurt you, you have my permission to slit my throat. All I ask is that you don't go for the belly. A gut wound is a slow death, and I'd prefer to die quickly—if it's all the same to you."

He settled in beside her, his head resting on the pillow next to hers, their noses almost touching. She clutched the sheathed knife in both hands, the blade nestled between her breasts. "Are you crazy?"

"Probably."

"Why would you—I mean—" She glanced downward. "This is a real knife. You used it to cut my dress."

"Which probably dulled the blade a little, so be sure to put some muscle behind it if you decide to use it. Like I said, I want to die quick."

He heard her gulp. The sound caught at his heart. "I—I couldn't stab you, Mr. Keegan."

"That's good to know. By the same token, I don't make a habit of forcing myself on women. Call me lazy, but for some reason, it just never struck me as being worth all the effort." Her incredulous expression made his grin broaden. "I do, however, have my quirks. One of them is to get at least a little sleep every night. I don't function very well without it. I thought maybe both of us could get some shut-eye if you felt a little more relaxed about being in bed with me."

"What if the knife comes out of the scabbard and one of us rolls on it?"

"I doubt that will happen. It has a fairly long blade, and it's buried to the hilt inside the leather." He could think of something else he wished were buried to the hilt. Fat chance of that.

She tucked in her chin to regard the weapon she held to her chest. Ace wasn't sure what he expected, only that it wasn't the sob that tore from her throat. He bent his head to try to see her face, an impossible feat given her tousled hair.

"Caitlin, what's wrong?" He'd meant to reassure her by giving her the knife, not to upset her even more. "Caitlin?"

"It's n-nothing," she managed in a squeaky voice. "It's just th-that I didn't expect—" Her voice broke, and she shuddered.

Ace closed his eyes and pressed his cheek to the top of her curly head. With a heavy sigh, he said, "You didn't expect what, sweetheart? For me to give you the knife? It's a small thing and worthwhile if it makes you feel better."

She gave her head a shake. "To under-understand. I d-didn't expect you to understand. About h-how I feel."

He had a hunch this girl had rarely been understood or had her feelings taken into consideration. "It seems simple enough to me. It's not like you got out of bed this morning expecting to get married tonight. My being a stranger makes it even worse. I don't blame you a bit for feeling a little frightened." A little frightened? A master at understatement, that was he. He curled a hand over hers where they were knotted around the knife handle. "I just hoped you'd feel a little safer if you had some way to defend yourself, that's all."

Another sob worked its way up from her chest. "You could t-take it away. If I tried to use it, y-you could take it away from me, lickety-split."

Ace had never been much of a hand at lying. Even so, he decided to give it his best. "Honey, I wouldn't stand a chance. I'll bet you're mighty fast with those small hands. A man my size tends to be slow at—" He nearly said *slow at the draw* but caught himself just in time. "To move. We tend to be slow to move."

She raised her face to regard him with eyes gone silvery with tears. If Ace had been fully clothed and standing erect, he felt pretty sure he would have melted and run into his boots. This girl had wormed her way straight into his heart. If things continued at this rate, he doubted he'd know which way was up by this time tomorrow.

"From what I've heard, you're quicker than greased lightning with those hands of yours," she informed him in a thin voice. "You're just saying that to make me feel better."

Ace knew when it was time to fold. "Is it working?"

She stared up at him for several deafeningly quiet seconds. "Yes, I think maybe it is."

He reached to smooth a curl from her cheek, then settled his hand on her hair. Her skull felt incredibly small in the cup of his palm, driving home to him how vulnerable she must feel. His throat went tight. "That's all that matters, Caitlin, that you feel better. As for my taking the knife away, why would I bother to give it to you if that was my plan? There's always the chance you're faster than I think. If I had mischief in mind, I could end up with my throat slit."

She sniffed and bent her head to dry her cheek on the shoulder of her nightgown. The wonderfully clean smell of sun-dried cotton wafted to his nostrils. When she looked back up at him, he thought some of the fear had slipped from her eyes. "Thank you," she said so softly he nearly didn't catch the words.

"You're welcome." He touched his thumb lightly to the small gash at her temple. It was good to feel at least some of the tension ease from her body. For a stupid man, he had his moments. Now, just as long as she didn't get spooked. . . . He shoved the thought from his mind. He doubted that even terrified she had it in her to knife a man. "Now, can we try to get some sleep?"

She nestled the knife more snugly between her breasts and nodded. Ace watched as her eyelids drifted slowly closed. For several seconds, he scarcely breathed for fear of startling her. Then he forced his own eyes closed. He was exhausted, no two ways about it. Tomorrow would be a long day.

Against his eyelids, he saw her face, so pale and drawn.

Where the crook of his arm pressed against her shoulder, he could still feel her shivering slightly. They had a long way to go, the two of them, but this was a start. Once this first night was behind them, she'd surely begin to realize he didn't mean to ravish her, and would start to relax a little in his company.

He tried to think of something they might do together tomorrow, some unthreatening activity she might enjoy that would allow her to get to know him a little better. The idea of going for a picnic along the creek leaped to mind. He envisioned the creek bank, bathed in sunshine, the two of them sharing a meal on a blanket, Caitlin's hair glinting like melted copper.

Yes, a picnic might be just the thing.

CAITLIN LAY BESIDE HER NEW HUSBAND, SO TENSE SHE WAS almost afraid to breathe for fear of waking him. In his sleep, he moved his hand from her hair to her shoulder, his thumb and long fingers curling warmly over her arm. Her every instinct screamed at her to draw away, to escape the bed, to huddle in some dark corner where she would be safe. Remaining still was one of the hardest things she'd ever done.

Gradually, though, the heat of his body began to envelop her, radiating warmth that seemed to reach clear to her bones. If she left the bed, she'd be freezing within minutes.

His even breathing stirred a tendril of hair at her temple and sent it tumbling over one eye. Each time he expelled a breath, the flyaway hair tickled her eyelashes. She blinked. She wrinkled her forehead and wiggled her eyebrows. Nothing helped. Within minutes, she could stand the tickling no longer. Very carefully, so as not to waken him, she reached up to brush the hair from her eye. At the movement of her arm, slight though it was, he mumbled something unintelligible and slipped his hand from her shoulder to her waist.

Caitlin gulped and held her breath. As though he was unaccustomed to finding a woman's body beneath his hand, he kneaded slightly with his fingertips, learning

the shape of her even as he slept. Her pent-up breath
rushed out when he trailed his palm over her hip and
gave it a gentle squeeze.

Soon, though, he grew still again, his hand limp,
heavy, and wonderfully warm. She clutched the knife
more closely and smiled, remembering how gruff he'd
sounded as he handed it to her. Empty gesture though it
was, not many men would have bothered to make it. The
fact that he had meant more to her than she could say.

Caitlin lifted her gaze to his dark face, which hovered
just inches from her own. Even in slumber, he looked
dangerous. Nonetheless, she felt oddly safe now that
he'd gone to sleep. For tonight, at least, he clearly meant
her no harm. He was touching her, yes, but not in an
improper way. And as crazy as it was, the way he
touched her made her feel sort of cherished. Silly, that.
But it was how she felt, even so.

She shifted her gaze to his shoulder and upper arm,
which were bathed in silvery moonlight, the thick pads
of muscle clearly defined. Calling to mind how her father
and brother had looked without their shirts, she was
fascinated in spite of herself. Ace Keegan wasn't just a
big man, he was also incredibly strong, putting her in
mind of the Grecian sculptures she'd seen in picture
books. A lump rose in her throat. With such physical
power, he could have had his way with her without even
working up a sweat. And what had he done instead?
He'd given her his knife and touched her with tender-
ness.

Tears sprang unbidden to her eyes. The next instant
she felt a ripping sensation in her chest as a sob worked
free. She was so awfully, horribly tired. All evening long,
from the very first moment he had mentioned the word
"marriage," she'd been expecting him to conclude the
evening by raping her. She felt as if she'd been shoved off
a cliff and saved at the last second—by her most feared
enemy. Why that made her need to cry, she didn't know.
But it did. And despite her fear of waking him, the need
seemed bigger than she was.

When her shoulders jerked with another sob, he
stirred in his sleep, running his hand from her hip to her

back. She held her breath, trying to be still and quiet. When her breath finally broke free, it did so in a loud, wet-sounding gush. She felt his body stiffen with sudden awareness.

"Caitlin?"

"I'm sorry."

He rubbed his hand up and down her spine. "Sweetheart, what's wrong?"

To Caitlin's absolute horror, he applied pressure between her shoulder blades with that huge hand of his, forcing her forward until she was flattened against his chest and firmly anchored there by his arm. The knife scabbard poked uncomfortably at her ribs. Her face found a nesting place in the hollow of his shoulder, and she knew he must feel her wet tears. He probably felt her breasts against him as well. And her thighs. She certainly felt every inch of him. The hard planes of his body seared through his denim trousers and her cotton garments, making her skin feel afire wherever they touched.

"Honey, it's all right. Shhh. It's going to be all right."

She didn't see how anything was going to be truly all right, ever again. Though it didn't seem possible, he drew her even closer and tightened his arm around her body. For an instant, she felt almost frantic to get away. But then the heat of him surrounded her, and his strength started to seem soothing rather than threatening. What little resistance remained in her body ebbed away in a rush, leaving her exhausted and limp.

"Don't cry." His voice was deep and wonderfully husky, the expulsion of his breath tickling her ear. "Please, don't cry. I'd rather you took that knife to me."

The sincerity in his voice meant more to Caitlin than the actual words. How long had it been since anyone had cared about her tears?

She sobbed again, trying to stifle the sound against his shoulder. No luck. Her trapped breath made a squeaking sound midway up her chest.

"Well, hell . . ." He jostled her closer, in what she perceived as a clumsy hug intended to comfort her, and oddly, it did. "Cry, then, sweetheart. Go ahead and get it out."

She needed no encouragement. It was embarrassing to have her emotions stripped so bare in front of him. Humiliating to have lost control. But she couldn't help herself. The suffocating ache was tearing at her chest, and she could no more hold it back than she could stop breathing. She cried until her throat felt raw, until her eyes felt as if the wind had blown sand into them, until she had no more tears left to shed. And then she simply lay there, too weary to move, safely enveloped by the hard heat of his body.

When silence fell over them, Caitlin expected him to say something, perhaps even to berate her. Instead he continued to hold her. After a while, she realized rather dimly that his every caress was cautious, that he was keeping his hands in unthreatening places, never once taking advantage of her vulnerability. She wanted to thank him for that, but she was too exhausted, too drained.

Tomorrow. I'll thank him tomorrow. It was the last conscious thought she had before sleep stole over her like a black blanket.

14

THE NEXT MORNING, ACE JERKED AWAKE TO THE SOUND OF someone shouting out in the yard. Consciousness brought with it surprises, not the least of which was that Caitlin had wrapped herself around him like a baby opossum, her body warm and enticingly soft. Sometime in the night, her gown had ridden up—or, God forbid, he'd shoved it up—and in his sleep, he had placed a hand on her thigh.

He rubbed his fingers across the cotton bloomers that encased her shapely leg. They were more a tease than actual protection, open at the seam from knee to crotch.

Bless her heart. He supposed wearing them to bed had made her feel a little safer, so he would refrain from teasing her about it. But he smiled all the same, wondering if she'd worn her chemise to bed as well.

In response to the shout that had awakened him, he heard his brothers' voices chiming in, laced with anger. It sounded as if a hell of a fight was about to erupt.

None too pleased about having to leave his cuddly wife and the warm bed, Ace groaned and pushed up on one elbow. He was tempted to stay put. His brothers were perfectly capable of handling any kind of trouble that came calling.

And wasn't that just the problem? Joseph didn't take shit from anybody, especially not on his home turf, and the younger boys tended to take their cues from him. Ace groaned again. Would the day ever come when he ceased to feel responsible for his siblings? He guessed not.

His sudden movements startled Caitlin awake. She scrambled to pull her nightgown down, then froze mid-motion, her blue eyes going wide with alarm as her sleepy gaze fell on him.

"Good morning," he said in a voice still scratchy from sleep. "Fancy meeting you here."

She sat bolt upright. "What—? How did—?" She gave the rumpled quilt a couple of pats, as if she'd lost something in the folds. Ace remembered giving her his knife and bit back another smile. In her sleep, at least, she was a trusting little soul. She blinked and rubbed her eye sockets with her fists. "Holy mother and all the saints."

He grinned and tossed back the covers. "Good morning to you, too."

Another shout came from outside, followed by "Get out here, you yellow-bellied son of bitch! Face me like a man!"

Since his brothers were already outside, it didn't take a wagonload of brains for Ace to determine that he was the "yellow-bellied son of a bitch" being summoned. Of course, it also helped that he now recognized the voice.

Patrick O'Shannessy, in high dudgeon. Wonderful. Just the way he wanted to start his first day of married life, having words with his new brother-in-law.

"Oh, God! That's Patrick!" Caitlin cried.

Ace rolled out of bed and started to get dressed. This marriage was already off to a rotten start. The last thing he needed was for Joseph to make matters worse by beating the snot out of Caitlin's only brother. After putting on one boot and partially shoving a foot into the other one, he hopped in the general direction of his shirt.

Behind him, Caitlin leaped from the bed and began flitting about, first in one direction, then another. As he shoved his arm down a sleeve, he glanced back at her. Clad in the white nightgown, with only part of her hair still caught up in the topknot of curls, she reminded him of a frantic little white hen with a floppy red comb, the roomy sleeves of her gown fluttering around her like wings.

"Caitlin, what are you doing?"

Her face creased and splotched with crimson where it had rested against the pillow, she came spinning to a stop and stared at him, eyes not quite focused. "That's Patrick out there," she said weakly.

Fortunately, Ace could come wide awake from a deep sleep almost instantly. That did not appear to be the case with Caitlin. She was clearly befuddled and struggling to orient herself. No small wonder, he supposed, given her sudden change in circumstance.

"Get out here, Keegan!" Patrick yelled again. "My quarrel isn't with your brothers, goddammit!"

Not bothering to button his shirt, Ace stepped around Caitlin to grab his gun belt from the bedstead.

"Oh, God, he must be drunk!" she cried.

Ace didn't think so. As outraged as Patrick sounded, he seemed to be enunciating his words with no difficulty. Last night, he hadn't been able to say shit without farting.

Caitlin fastened a horrified gaze on Ace as he quickly buckled his gun belt and bent to tie down the holster. "Wh-what are you doing? Why the gun? Don't hurt him. Please, Ace, don't hurt him."

It was the first time she'd called him by his first name. He glanced up at her. "I have no intention of hurting him, sweetheart. He's your brother." He flashed her a reassuring smile. "Don't look so worried. I can be quite the diplomat when I try to be. He'll calm down."

She clamped her hands over the lopsided lump of flyaway curls atop her head. "Oh, God! You don't know him. He's crazy when he gets like this."

Grasping her shoulders, he bent slightly to look directly into her eyes. "Caitlin, I promise you, I won't lift a hand to him." Releasing her, he chucked her lightly under the chin. "I realize you don't know your way around the kitchen, but do you think you could put on some coffee?"

She looked at him as if he'd lost his mind. "Coffee?"

"He is my brother-in-law. Once I get him calmed down, I'll invite him in. It's going to be okay. Trust me."

Trying to project a good deal more self-confidence than he actually felt, Ace exited the bedroom. Once in the hall, he picked up his pace and said a quick prayer that Joseph, who hadn't yet been informed of Ace's marriage, wouldn't kick the shit out of Patrick before he could get out there. For Caitlin's sake, he and his brothers were going to have to get along with the little bastard.

Ace's worst fears were realized when he threw open the front door. Patrick stood in the yard, his legs spread, his shooting hand hovering over his gun. Even though his hat was sitting crooked on his head and his clothes were disheveled, he didn't appear to be all that drunk. A little, maybe. With the O'Shannessys, that seemed to be all it took, one or two belts of whiskey. Add a dash of temper, give it a stir, and you had crazy mad, all wrapped up in a dangerous package.

"Patrick," Ace said with an inclination of his head as he stepped out onto the porch. Closing the door firmly behind him, he added, "Good to see you."

From the corners of his eyes, Ace saw his brothers circling, Joseph to his right, Esa to the rear, and David to the left. Their stances indicated that they were not only ready for trouble, but almost eager for it. The redheaded youth had done everything, short of committing murder, to earn that regard.

Under other circumstances, Ace might have let his brothers have a go at Patrick. He definitely had it coming. Caitlin's becoming a member of the family made that impossible. Bygones had to be bygones, now and forever, amen.

Out near the barn Ace could see his hired hands standing in a bunch, their gazes fixed on O'Shannessy. As much as Ace hated to have his dirty laundry aired in front of them, he guessed there was no help for it.

"What do you mean, it's good to see me?" Patrick cried. "You rotten, no-good son of a bitch. Where is she, Keegan? I want her out here so I can talk to her. Right now. You understand? Don't think you can keep her away from me. So help me, God, I'll kill you first."

Ace had a feeling Patrick was more pissed off at himself than at anyone else. He had drunk himself stupid last night and forced his sister to marry a man he despised. That couldn't be a very pleasant memory to wake up to.

"If you're referring to my wife," Ace replied evenly, "she's inside making us all some coffee. We'd be honored if you would come in and join us. Fact is, if you don't have any pressing engagements, you're welcome to stay for breakfast."

Patrick took a threatening step forward. Until that moment, Ace had left his brothers to draw their own conclusions. Now he saw them making a slow advance, each of them plainly prepared to fill O'Shannessy with lead if it became necessary. They were rumpled from sleep and sporting bits of hay from their makeshift beds in the barn. But looks could be deceiving. Ace had taught each of them how to handle himself in a fight, be it with fists or six-shooters, and, even if he did say so himself, he'd been a damn fine teacher. In defense of one of their own, the Paxton boys would fight fair and square—or mean and dirty. Whatever it took to get the job done, that was their motto.

Ace held up a staying hand. Whether he liked Patrick O'Shannessy or not, the man was Caitlin's brother and she loved him. If it came to a physical confrontation, Ace would take care of it himself.

"You get my sister out here! I was out of my head last night. Didn't realize what I was doing. You're the last man on earth I want her with. I'm taking her home."

Ace placed his hands on his hips. "Caitlin isn't a piece of baggage to be bandied about. I admit, you were drunk last night, and if you say you didn't know what you were doing, I won't argue the point. But that doesn't change what happened, does it? It's a little late now to start having second thoughts."

"You bastard! If you touched her . . ." Patrick knotted his shooting hand into a tight fist, then slowly extended and flexed his fingers.

"I wouldn't do that if I were you," Ace said softly.

Behind him, Ace heard the front door crash open. Before he could react, Caitlin dashed past him and down the steps. Still clad only in her nightgown and whatever undergarments were concealed beneath it, she placed herself squarely in Patrick's line of fire. "Don't be stupid, Patrick. Do you want to get yourself killed?"

"Get out of my way!" Patrick's voice shook with fury. "I mean it, Caitlin."

Signaling for his brothers to stay back, Ace moved slowly down the steps. Damn it to hell. If lead started flying, Caitlin would be the first to take a bullet.

The thought made Ace feel weak at the knees. He had to do something. The problem was, what. As Caitlin had pointed out, Patrick was crazy when he got like this. He didn't have sense enough to consider the consequences of his actions; he just reacted and cried over the spilled milk later.

As Ace drew up behind Caitlin, he grasped her gently by the arm. A bullet. Sweet Jesus. He'd seen the damage a slug could do when it impacted flesh and bone. Caitlin didn't have enough extra meat on her to survive such an injury.

"Sweetheart, I think you'd better go back in the

house," Ace said in a voice rough with fear. It had been a long time since the prospect of gunfire had made him quake in his boots. He didn't like the feeling. It was one thing to risk death for himself, and quite another to have his wife standing in the line of fire.

The depth of feeling Ace was beginning to have for this girl was driven home as he stood behind her, helpless to protect her. If anything happened to her, he'd never forgive himself.

"Let Patrick and I work this out between ourselves, Caitlin. It'll be all right, I promise."

She looked back at him, her eyes filled with distrust. "If I go back in the house, you'll end up shooting him. I just know it!"

"I give you my word that I won't hurt him."

She jerked her arm free. "Right. And if he draws on you? I suppose you're just going to stand there and let him kill you."

Ace turned his gaze back to Patrick. Standing in such close proximity to the younger man, he was almost overcome by the sour stench of whiskey. "We're both grown men. Aren't we, Patrick? I'm sure we can settle this by talking it out."

"Go in the house and get your things, Caitlin. We're leaving."

To Ace's surprise, Caitlin made no move to obey her brother. Instead she squared her shoulders and raised her chin. "I can't do that," she pronounced in a tremulous voice. "I spoke marriage vows. I never break my word, you know that."

"What do you mean, vows? Have you lost your mind? Staying with him would be crazy. He despises us and everything we stand for. He'll make every day of your life a misery."

Caitlin stiffened. Her brother's predictions had clearly struck home. "Yes, well, perhaps you should have thought of that last night, Patrick, before you went off half-cocked and forced me to marry him. Now it's done." She hesitated for a second that seemed to last an eternity. When she resumed speaking, there was no doubt in Ace's mind that every word cost her dearly. "What God has joined together, let no man put asunder."

A fiery glint entered Patrick's blue eyes. He stared at his sister as if he'd never seen her before. A muscle along his jaw twitched as he clenched and unclenched his teeth. "You slept with him? That's what you're saying, isn't it? The marriage is consummated. You played the whore for him!"

For an instant, Ace thought Caitlin would deny the accusation. In the end, she faced him in silence. A silence that clearly damned her in his eyes. Ace's heart broke for her. Misguided or not, she obviously adored her brother. He knew it had to be killing her to see the contempt in his expression.

Patrick went ruddy with anger. Jabbing a finger toward Ace, he said, "Ever since that bastard came back to No Name, he's been telling anyone willing to listen that our father was a crook and a cold-blooded murderer, goddammit. He spits on the O'Shannessy name and everything it stands for. And you played the whore for him?"

Where Ace came from, calling a lady a whore went beyond the pale. He knotted his hands into aching fists, every muscle in his body tight with the yearning to pound the words back down Patrick's throat. For Caitlin's sake, he held himself in check. Barely. Patrick O'Shannessy needed to be taught a few manners. No question about it. But not in front of his sister.

So outraged he was almost shouting, every inflection of his voice dripping with contempt, Patrick said, "Dear God, how could you?"

Before Ace could guess the younger man's intent, Patrick drew back his arm and backhanded Caitlin across the cheek. At the force of the blow, she reeled into Ace's chest. He was so taken by surprise, he had to scramble to keep her from falling. The instant he felt her catch her balance, he set her gently aside.

Rage rolled over him in molten waves. Without conscious thought, he reacted instinctively, and with all his strength. The next thing he knew, Patrick hit the dirt, dust billowing around him. In two strides, Ace stood over him, his fist aching where it had connected with the younger man's mouth.

"Get up, you miserable son of a bitch. Let's see how tough you are with someone who can fight back!"

"No!" Caitlin threw herself forward to cling to Ace's arm. "No, please! He's drunk!"

"Drunk, my ass. That's no excuse!" Ace jerked his arm free and grabbed Patrick by the front of his shirt. Scarcely feeling the younger man's weight, he hauled him to his feet, drew back his fist, and hit him again. Caitlin shrieked. This time, Patrick staggered backward under the blow, but managed to stay standing.

"Feel good, asshole?" Ace advanced on him as he spoke. "Not much fun to be on the receiving end, is it?"

"Stop it! Please, stop it!"

The panic in Caitlin's voice brought Ace back to his senses. He halted mid-stride toward Patrick and lowered his arms. He'd gotten his message across. There was no point in driving it into the ground, not at Caitlin's expense.

Patrick touched the back of his hand to his mouth, then stared down at the blood that came away on his skin. He blinked and shook his head. Caitlin ran over to him, hands hovering, face pale.

"Oh, God, Patrick. Are you all right?" She threw an accusing look at Ace. "How could you? So much for your promise not to lift a hand to him!"

After swallowing and hauling in a deep breath, Ace finally felt calm enough to reply, "He hit you, dammit!"

"And so you took it upon yourself to hit him? At least he's drunk. You're not!"

Ace happily could have remedied that. "No man strikes a woman in front of me and gets away with it."

"He didn't really hurt me! I've survived far worse, believe me!"

Ace's gaze shot to the red mark along her cheekbone. By this time tomorrow, she'd be sporting a God-awful bruise on her beautiful face. Yet she claimed Patrick hadn't hurt her? What, exactly, did she call it? The son of a bitch had knocked her clear off her feet. Rage welled up in him again. In some distant corner of his mind Ace knew that he should keep his mouth shut, but God help him, he couldn't. No woman should have to take the abuse of a man's fists, especially not someone as fragilely built as Caitlin.

He narrowed his eyes at Patrick. "Get off my land, you rotten little bastard. The only reason you're so determined to keep your sister at home is because, without her, you won't have any means of keeping yourself in drinking money."

Caitlin clamped a hand over her chest, as if his words were knives being driven straight into her heart. Ace didn't care. Protecting her was all that mattered to him right then, and keeping her away from Patrick had to be a good step in that direction.

"If I see you around here again," he bit out, "I'll stomp the ever-loving shit right out of you. Do you understand me, Patrick? Get off my land, and stay off."

Patrick spat blood. "Come with me, Caitlin. You don't have to stay here."

"She sure as hell does!" Temper was doing Ace's talking for him now. He knew it, but he had crossed over the line. "She's my wife, in case you've forgotten. By law, she belongs with me. At least here, no one will knock the shit out of her."

"Right!" Patrick sneered the word. "Conor O'Shannessy's daughter, and you'll treat her like a regular little princess, won't you?" He shot a look at Caitlin. "This is your last chance, sis. Get your things."

"We're married!" she cried. "I can't just walk away from that. I gave my word, Patrick. Maybe that doesn't mean much to you, but it does to me."

"Your word? Jesus, Caitlin, use your head. I don't care if you slept with him. Short of having you examined by a doctor, he can't very well prove it, can he? We'll have the marriage annulled!"

"No," she said thinly. "I made promises, and unless he releases me from them, I won't break them."

At any other time, Ace might have felt a stab of guilt for holding promises over the girl's head that she hadn't wanted to make. Coming on the heels of Patrick's mistreatment of her, though, he didn't have it in him to feel so much as a trace of remorse. "It'll be a cold day in hell before I release you from your marriage vows," he said succinctly. To Patrick, he added, "Now get on your horse before I decide to finish what I started. Nothing would please me more."

As her brother turned to walk away, Caitlin wrung her hands, her expression one of such torment that Ace reached out to grasp her shoulder. As if his touch were the most vile thing she'd ever encountered, she tried to twist away from him. He clamped down hard to maintain his grip. "He's not badly hurt," he bit out. "Just let him go."

"He's my brother!"

"He's an abusive bastard, that's what he is."

Her blue eyes lifted imploringly to his. "If not for the drink, he never would have hit me. I know you're angry, but, please, don't let him leave thinking he can't ever come back. Please!"

Ace had a feeling that "if not for the drink" was Patrick's favorite song. In Ace's books, that was no excuse, and as far as he was concerned, Caitlin would be better off if she never saw the asshole again.

With one last look toward Caitlin, Patrick headed for his horse. As he saddled up, he cried, "Stay then! Just remember, you've made your bed. The first time he decides to take his temper out on you, don't come running to me. As his wife, you're his property. If you choose to stay here, my hands will be tied."

He sat on his pinto as though waiting for Caitlin's response. She made none. Only Ace, who felt her shaking, knew what the silence was costing her. He had won, after all, he realized. She was his wife, for better or worse.

As her brother rode from sight, she turned woodenly toward him. Her eyes huge splashes of blue in a face gone tight with pain, she said, "How can you possibly believe we can build any kind of life together? You've just driven a wedge between me and the only person in this entire world that I love!"

She jerked away from him and fled into the house. Ace was left standing there, the morning wind feathering through his hair, its cool caress helping to clear his mind and enabling him to take a step back from the emotions that were roiling within him.

The only person in this entire world that I love. Ace closed his eyes. *How can you possibly believe we can build any kind of life together?* They obviously couldn't. He had driven a wedge between her and her brother, and whether it made any sense to him, she would mourn the loss until he rectified matters.

Just the thought of having to apologize to Patrick O'Shannessy made Ace's guts churn. The bastard didn't have an apology coming, goddammit, and snowballs would melt in hell before Ace gave him one.

Even as that vow took shape in his mind, Ace scoffed at himself. He was new at this marriage business, but even so, one lesson had already been driven home to him. He could no more ignore the pleading look in Caitlin's big blue eyes than he could stop breathing. Ever since meeting the girl, he'd been in way over his head and barely managing to tread water. He'd probably find himself hotfooting it over to the O'Shannessy place to apologize to Patrick before the sun went down.

Struggling to keep his emotions from showing on his face, Ace turned to confront his brothers. His gaze went first to Joseph. Blond hair trailing in the wind, whipcord-lean body a slow harmony of motion, Joseph came to brace a boot on the bottom step of the porch. After regarding Ace for several long seconds, he bent to spit, then gave his head a bewildered shake.

"Do you ever do anything the normal way, big brother? The last I knew, you were a confirmed bachelor. How the hell did you end up married?"

As quickly as he could, his thoughts mostly with Caitlin, Ace gave his brothers a quick accounting of the previous night's events. "The long and short of it is," he concluded, "you have a new sister." He looked each of his brothers in the eye. "As you witnessed, hers has not been an easy life. I'd appreciate it if you'd all walk a wide circle around her for a while. Give her time to get to know you before you scare her to death by being your usual obnoxious selves."

"Our obnoxious selves?" Esa rolled his eyes. "Like we've ever been anything but gentlemen around a lady."

Ace thought that was a slight overstatement, but he refrained from saying so. Lowering his voice so Caitlin wouldn't hear, he replied, "It doesn't take a genius to realize Caitlin has probably been mistreated more times than not, and that's putting it mildly. I'm serious, Esa. Be on your best behavior."

Joseph cocked an eyebrow and pursed his full lips. "Why'd you let the bastard walk away? He belted her a good one, for Christ's sake. If it had been up to me, he would have left here ass up over the back of his horse!"

Ace sighed. "She loves her brother, Joseph. The fact that he doesn't deserve it is beside the point. He needs his butt kicked. I don't deny that. But I couldn't bring myself to hurt her that way."

Joseph snorted, clearly disgusted. "The miserable little turd better watch his step. If I ever run into him when she's not around, I'll beat the holy shit out of him."

"No," Ace said softly, "you won't. I want your word on it."

Joseph's blue eyes went narrow with anger. "You're kidding, right?"

Ace hooked a thumb toward the house. "That girl in there is part of our family now. Whether we like him or not, that makes her brother a part of it, too."

"I'll be damned! Patrick O'Shannessy? He isn't any kin of mine!" Joseph glanced at his younger brothers. "Don't just stand there with your tongues stuck to the roof of your mouths. Tell him I'm right!"

David cleared his throat. "She's upset about Ace smacking him, Joseph. We ain't none of us gonna be too popular with her if we treat her brother bad."

"Conor O'Shannessy killed our pa!" Joseph fastened a

fiery gaze on Ace. "Just 'cause you've turned traitor doesn't mean I have to. I'll accept the girl into the family because you married her, but not her goddamned brother. He's been a pimple on my ass ever since we got here. Just think of everything he's done!"

Ace met Joseph's unflinching gaze. He knew what he had to say, but his throat felt paralyzed as he forced out the words. "I'm not going to defend Patrick O'Shannessy. He's a miserable little shit, and we all know it. But now that I'm married to Caitlin, that's beside the point. It's your choice, little brother. If you can't honor my wife by showing the proper respect for her next of kin, then pack your things and ride out."

"What? You saying you want me to leave? I don't believe I'm hearing this!"

"Believe it. I won't stand for that girl in there being put through any more heartache. If that means kissing her brother's ass, then pucker up or saddle up."

Joseph rammed his fists on his lean hips and kicked viciously at the dirt. "If this ain't a hell of a note, I don't know what is!"

"It is kinda harsh, Ace," Esa put in softly. "Give us some time to get used to the idea, why don't you, before givin' us ultimatums."

"I don't have that luxury. This marriage changes things. It has to. This family has never stood divided, and it's not going to start now. Patrick O'Shannessy just became my brother-in-law. Someday he'll be the uncle of my children. All the bellyaching in the world won't change that, so get used to it."

Joseph gave another disgusted snort. "Seems to me you aren't practicing what you preach. Excuse me for pointing it out, but as I recall, you just ordered the son of a bitch off our place and told him never to come back."

Ace hauled in a bracing breath. "Yeah, well, I was dead wrong to do that."

A twinkle of amusement edged the anger out of Joseph's blue eyes. "Can I take that to mean you're gonna eat crow to Patrick O'Shannessy?"

Ace swallowed, hard. "You can."

Joseph chuckled. "Well, hell . . . That makes it mighty difficult for me to saddle up and ride out, big brother. Ace Keegan, puckering up to kiss Patrick O'Shannessy's ass? That's a show I definitely don't wanna miss."

❧ 15

EATING CROW. AS THE MORNING WORE ON, ACE FOUND himself contemplating the prospect with growing dread. After getting dressed, Caitlin slipped outside while breakfast was being prepared, thereby managing to avoid meeting any of his brothers or joining them at the table. When the meal was finally finished and the dishes were all washed, Ace went to peer out the front windows in search of her. He wasn't concerned that she'd try to run off again, not after seeing her stand up to Patrick as she had, but underscoring his newfound confidence was a gnawing uneasiness. To a girl made timid of men by what he suspected had been a lifetime of abuse, he and his brothers probably seemed like a pretty frightening bunch.

He was relieved when he sighted a flash of blue just inside the yawning doorway of the newly erected barn. Cloaked in shadow, Caitlin's form was indistinct. It took Ace several seconds to determine that she was hunkered down with her hand outstretched. He pressed closer to the glass, trying to make out what she was doing. A moment later, he saw one of the barnyard cats come tearing out the doorway, evidently terrified by Caitlin's overture of friendliness.

The feline's terror didn't surprise Ace. Both of the cats had been raised in the No Name livery stable and were impossibly wild. Joseph had brought them home to control the mice.

Pushing to her feet, Caitlin gazed after the tabby, her

posture dejected. Watching her, it occurred to Ace that his bride had more in common with that pathetic, terrified cat than she probably realized.

"Maybe she thought we'd toss her on the breakfast table and dig in like she was our main course," Joseph said from behind Ace. To punctuate the comment, Joseph whistled air through his teeth. "You've got your work cut out with that one."

There was no arguing that, so Ace said nothing. Joseph came to stand beside him, the concern in his blue eyes outshining the bitterness as he watched Caitlin through the glass. "She sure does put you in mind of Eden, doesn't she?"

The observation made Ace realize that he'd ceased to notice the similarities between the two women. "Once you get to know her a little, she doesn't look as much like Eden as she seems to at first."

"That's usually the way of it, even with identical twins. The difference in personalities, I guess." Joseph scuffed the sole of his boot over the newly varnished floorboards. It was a habit of his, scuffing his boots, especially when he was upset. The scuffing usually turned to kicking when his temper got the best of him. "Do you think maybe it would help if I shaved?"

Ace slanted his brother a knowing look. Under that outer layer of bluster and orneriness, Joseph had a soft heart. It was one of the things Ace most admired about him. Joseph tried to hide it, but every now and then, his sensitivity peeked through. "You might look a little less intimidating if you scraped off the stubble."

Joseph rubbed his jaw, his fingers making a raspy sound against blond whiskers. "Do I look intimidating?"

To compensate for his lack of stature, Joseph had had a chip on his shoulder all his life. Ace knew damned well he'd worked hard to acquire that lean and mean look of his. "Does a badger have teeth?"

Joseph chuckled. "I reckon I'd best shave then. Maybe if all of us follow your example and get slicked up, she'll relax a little."

Ace doubted it, but anything was worth a try. He also appreciated the thought. Joseph's gaze returned to the girl out in the barnyard for a moment. When he looked back at Ace, there was a question in his eyes. "Did everything go okay with her last night?"

Ace nearly told his brother that was none of his goddamned business, but he caught himself. Joseph wasn't asking because he hoped to hear any juicy details. The concern in his expression was proof of that.

Suddenly, it all seemed overwhelming to Ace. His problems last night with Caitlin, then the nasty scene with her brother this morning. He supposed there were some things he would never be able to share with his brother. On the other hand, what had happened thus far wasn't really of an intimate nature, and it just might help if he could talk it out. Joseph had a good head on his shoulders.

"She was as nervous as a whore in church and came to bed damned near fully clothed under her nightgown," Ace said gruffly. "I'm surprised she didn't wear her shoes. Before she could relax enough to go to sleep, I had to give her a weapon to defend herself. Does that answer your question?"

"A weapon?"

"My knife. I told her she had my permission to slit my throat if I hurt her."

"Jesus H. Christ."

Ace heaved a sigh. "Yeah. My sentiments exactly."

Joseph dug at the floor with his boot heel. "That was a damned fool thing to do, Ace. What if she'd gotten spooked and taken you up on it?"

Ace gave his brother a lazy look. "I'd have taken the knife away from her. What d'you think?" He glanced downward. "Would you stop that? You're going to scar up the goddamned floor."

Joseph stomped his boot on the floorboards as if the very force of the gesture would anchor his foot to the spot. "Sorry."

"Sorry won't varnish the floor again."

Joseph glanced at the slightly crooked window frame. "I hate to tell you this, but sorry became my middle name when we started building this place."

Right now, Ace felt as if his whole life was a little off plumb. He leaned a shoulder against the window frame. "If you were me, Joseph, how would you go about handling her?"

Joseph rubbed his jaw again. "I've never consorted much with skittish females."

"Me, neither."

"Well, big brother, you've got yourself hogtied to one now." Joseph shook his head. "If I were you, I'd break her to ride real slow and gentle, kinda like you would a skittish mare. I'd say she's had some mighty rough handling."

"Break her to ride? Jesus, Joseph. If you don't clean up that mouth of yours, the first thing Ma'll do when she gets here is shove a bar of soap in it."

"She'll have to catch me first."

Imagining his mother lighting out after Joseph brought a smile to Ace's lips. "I sure wish she was here right now. She'd hug that girl up and have her set to rights in no time." Unfortunately, Ace didn't plan to send for his mother or sister for months yet. Not until things in No Name had reached their inevitable boil and then started to simmer down. Things could get nasty when he started foreclosures. "Maybe I should pack Caitlin up and send her to San Francisco. She's dreamed of living there, you know. From what I gather, she would probably already be gone if Patrick hadn't swiped her savings."

Joseph pursed his full lips. "He sure is a little bastard, isn't he?"

"Whiskey does that to some men."

"Excuses are like assholes. Everybody has one. Just because you're drunk is no reason to smack a woman."

Ace agreed. Wholeheartedly. Unfortunately, what he thought didn't count for much. It was Caitlin's thoughts and feelings he had to deal with.

"If you send her to Ma, you'll just be postponing trouble," Joseph observed drily. "You're the one who's going to have to sleep with her."

"Is sex all you ever think about?"

Joseph narrowed one eye. "Not all, no. But it'd be fair to say it occupies a good share of my thoughts most of the time. How about you?"

"Right now, I'd be satisfied if that girl out there just felt comfortable enough to sit down and have breakfast with me."

Joseph grinned again. "You're as sorry a liar as you are a carpenter. Just do me one favor?"

Feeling disgruntled, Ace snapped, "What?"

"Hide that knife of yours before you go dipping for honey. I'd hate like hell to find you in bed some morning with your throat slit. Who'd give me hell all the time if you weren't around?"

"You've been such a help, Joseph, I don't know how to thank you."

Joseph tossed a shank of blond hair out of his eyes. "You bit off this particular chunk of trouble, big brother. Now it's up to you to figure out how to chew it. Me? I'm happy with the occasional jug of good whiskey and five dollars' worth of a sporting woman's company. No fuss, no muss, that's my motto."

Until last night, it had been Ace's motto as well. "A man's got to settle down sometime."

"Yeah? Well, go to it then." Joseph cast a final glance out the window. "Looks to me like you're going to have to do some mighty fancy footwork before you do much settling."

THOUGHTS OF THE KNIFE HE'D LENT CAITLIN STILL FRESH IN his mind after talking with Joseph, Ace searched the master bedroom for the weapon before he went outside to fetch his wife. The knife had been a gift from his stepfather when he was just a boy, and he felt undressed without it riding on his hip.

He found the bedroom surprisingly tidy, the bed already made, Caitlin's empty satchels in one corner. As he searched for his knife, he stumbled across some of her things in his bureau drawers and in the dressing room closet, yet another sign that she had decided to stay at the Paradise.

Oddly, the knife was nowhere to be found. Feeling like

a thief rifling through her personal things, Ace checked between the layers of Caitlin's folded underthings, which she'd stowed in a bottom drawer. *Nothing.* He allowed his hand to linger a moment on a dingy, nearly worn out pair of pantalets. The scent of her drifted up from the cotton, sunshine and lavender and innocence, all blended irresistibly together. He shoved the drawer closed, wishing it were as easy to put a lid on his male yearnings.

He turned to survey the room with a thoughtful frown. Where would she have put his knife? Unless she had it with her, which seemed highly unlikely, it had to be here somewhere. His gaze came to rest on her satchels. Maybe they weren't empty, after all.

His guess proved to be correct. She'd left some of her personal possessions in the first satchel he opened—a small daguerreotype of her mother, a framed photograph of her brother, a few books, one about New York City, another about San Francisco, complete with pictures of places of interest. The pages were especially dog-eared in the sections about libraries, museums, and the performing arts. A slight smile touched his mouth. His wife seemed to have a yearning for culture and beauty, which he seriously doubted had been fulfilled by living near No Name.

Recalling her former home, with its cheerful gingham curtains, rag rugs, and cross-stitched wall hangings, he decided Caitlin had been trying to make a silk purse out of a sow's ear for most of her life. Roses in a dented lard tin. Picture books of faraway places, telling about operas and ballets, famous plays and exquisite symphonies. *Wishes and dreams.* Aside from the pretty little things she'd created herself, wishes and dreams had been all she'd ever had.

Ace's hands froze when he opened the other bag, for it was filled with pieces of Caitlin. He could think of no other way to describe the contents, little mementos she'd saved, each telling its own story.

He found a childishly scrawled note from someone named Bess that read, *I'm sorry about your rist, Caitlin. I hope it is beter and that he does not get mad at you like that agin.* After carefully refolding the scrap of tablet paper and putting it back, Ace drew out a small rag doll. It had obviously been crafted by a little girl's hands and been very well loved—a pathetic-looking thing with a crooked smile and button eyes that didn't match, the sparse crop of hair made from thick tufts of orange rug yarn faded with age. Its calico dress was a crookedly sewn rectangle with clumsily attached sleeves, one of which was longer than the other.

Ace had no doubt that Caitlin had made the doll for herself when she was very small. His heart broke a little as he turned it over in his hands. He couldn't help but compare this doll with the beautiful ones Eden had played with as a child. Dolls that Ace had bought her— for her birthdays or Christmas. Was this all that Caitlin had had by way of a doll—one she'd made from rags? Surely not.

He opened the bag more widely, carefully replacing the rag doll inside. His gaze was immediately caught by a small porcelain face lying in the jumble of items. Believing he'd found another doll, a store-bought one this time, he picked it up, only to discover that the doll head had been separated from its body. It had also been shattered and carefully glued back together.

He fished through the satchel for the rest of the doll, locating its parts, piece by piece. As he laid them all out on the floor, his skin turned icy.

The doll had been savagely ripped apart.

Ace stared down at the pieces. No child could have done damage like this. The doll's cloth body had been completely dismembered, and with such violent force that chunks of its torso had been ripped away.

A scalding sensation washed over his eyes. He returned the dismembered doll to the satchel. Without Caitlin's confiding in him, he might never know the full story behind the doll's destruction, but he could certainly guess. *Her father.* Ace curled his hands into tight fists.

Such savagery . . .

It was frightening and chillingly significant. Ace could only wonder what kind of childhood the girl must have had.

As he started to close the satchel, his gaze was caught by a worn, leather-bound book, on the front of which was scrolled in gold, *My Daily Diary*. Never in all his life had he wanted to pick something up so badly. He curled his fingers over it, then stopped himself. Caitlin would undoubtedly perceive his snooping as an invasion of her privacy, which it undeniably was. If he wanted to know more about her, he should be up front about it and simply ask. Learning a person's deepest secrets by reading her diary was underhanded. If he wanted her to trust him, he had to earn it.

On the other hand, he doubted Caitlin was going to reveal much about herself willingly, and certainly not any time soon. He'd be able to help her far more quickly if he were armed with more knowledge.

He picked up the book, hefted it in his hand. It fell open where a faded red ribbon separated the pages. The entry was dated March 12, 1879. She would have been fifteen, maybe sixteen, at the time. It read, *I'm not going to write in this diary again. A diary is a record of life so one doesn't forget the day-to-day things that happen. I have decided I don't want to remember. In fact, I pray I will forget.*

Nothing more. Ace flipped through the remaining pages. They were all blank. He turned toward the front of the book, glimpsing the awkward handwriting of a young girl in various stages of development. He wanted to lock the door and read every word, which would take hours. What had happened in March of 1879 that had made his wife abandon her lifelong practice of writing in her diary? Would the earlier entries enlighten him?

Pa has been gone for three whole days. This morning, Patrick sneaked into town and sold his pocket knife to buy sugar and corn syrup. To celebrate my birthday, we made a cake and had a taffy pull. It was so much fun. In another section, he glimpsed the words, *Patrick worked at the livery to buy me yardage to make a dress.* Ace flipped through several more pages. *Patrick is having difficulty chewing, so I'm grinding his food. Bless his heart. I think Pa may have cracked his jaw. Will he never learn not to interfere when Pa gets in a temper? It only makes things worse.*

A door slammed someplace in the house. Ace nearly jumped out of his skin. He dropped the diary back into the satchel as though the touch burned him. Then he shot to his feet. He didn't believe in reading another person's mail, for Christ's sake, let alone a diary. Caitlin had recorded her innermost thoughts on those pages, and he had no right to pry.

Turning resolutely away, Ace forced himself back to his original quest to locate his knife. He finally found it tucked under the bed pillow.

As he left the bedroom, he hauled in a deep, cleansing breath, relieved that the slamming of a door had startled him. He and Caitlin had enough barriers between them without his adding a guilty conscience to the list.

ACE FOUND CAITLIN OUT AT THE HORSE CORRAL. HE SMILED slightly as he approached her from behind. While he could stand with his arms folded over the top rail, she was barely tall enough to see over the fence. She'd compensated for her lack of height by stepping onto the bottom rung.

When he drew up beside her and draped his arms over the rail beside hers, she gave such a start she nearly lost her footing. That she spooked so easily troubled him. What had happened to her that she would be so terrified of men? Remembering the dismembered and crushed doll, he wondered if Conor O'Shannessy had ever attacked his daughter with the same feral anger. Judging by her timidity, Ace feared the answer was yes. *Will Patrick never learn not to interfere when Pa is in a temper?*

He was tempted to return to the house and lock himself in the study with that diary until he'd read it from beginning to end. How could he help this girl if he didn't understand her? Right now, he had little to go on but supposition.

I'm sorry about your rist, the little girl named Bess had written. The remainder of the note left Ace with little doubt that Conor had flown into a rage and injured Caitlin. The question was, how badly? Had her wrist been merely sprained, or had it been broken? Had Conor pushed the girl, causing her to fall? Or, as Patrick had done that morning, had he struck her with such force that he had knocked her off her feet?

The questions burned within Ace, and he felt he needed answers. Should he abandon the convictions of a lifetime and read that diary? She might never forgive him if he did.

There had to be another way to get her to open up and talk about herself. He guessed he would have to play it by ear, just as he had last night. If he saw an opening, he'd take it. Otherwise, he'd simply have to bide his time.

After regaining her balance on the fence rung, she glanced down at the leather scabbard that once again rode at his hip. Come bedtime, Ace promised himself he'd give the knife back to her if she still needed it.

Pretending not to notice her preoccupation with the weapon, he gazed out across the ranch. Rolling green grassland stretched endlessly from the corral toward the foothills. In the foreground, he could see Kurt Bishop and Rob Martin, two of his hired men, opening irrigation gates. On the horizon, the craggy peaks of the Rocky Mountains were outlined magnificently against the slate-blue sky.

Occasionally, he heard cattle bawling in the distance, the sound rather forlorn. Luckily, the majority of his stock could fend for themselves at this time of year on the fenced summer grazing land. Come winter, he'd have to supplement their feed, but for now, most of the seasonal work had already been done.

Joseph and his younger brothers had tended to the barnyard animals this morning before coming in for breakfast. Ace had things he should be doing, of course. On a ranch like this, that was usually the case. But there was nothing all that pressing. He could devote the next day or two to Caitlin without feeling guilty about it, and make up for the lost time later. He had hoped to take her for a picnic along the creek this afternoon, but now, thanks to Patrick, there was something else he had to do instead.

On a sudden gust of breeze, the rank smell of the barnyard drifted to him. When he'd first come here, he had found the odor extremely offensive, but now he realized he'd grown to like it. Earthy and soothing, that was how it smelled. He found the stench preferable to that of unwashed bodies crowded into the inadequate confines of a waterfront saloon, at any rate.

Nope. He didn't miss the jarring notes of a barroom piano or the constant chink of whiskey jugs tipped against tumblers. Sequined dresses. Exposed bosoms. The cloying scent of heavy perfume. All of that had been in another world, one that he'd left behind with no regret.

Now, here he stood, a timid young lady at his side. No more gilded mirrors reflecting hardened faces. No more crass innuendos. No more erotic sexual foreplay with rouged prostitutes who meant nothing to him. Just a girl who put him in mind of an angel, with the breeze seeming to sing a lullaby as it toyed with her hair.

A sense of rightness settled over him. A feeling of peace.

He inclined his head at the black stallion that circled the enclosure, glossy mane flying, head and tail held high. "He's a beaut, isn't he?"

For a long moment, she said nothing. When she finally spoke, it was to ask, "Why did you name him Shakespeare?"

Ace nearly said "Damned if I know," but then thought better of it. He couldn't expect this young woman to reveal her secrets to him if he kept parts of himself back from her. Still, the words didn't come easily. Some things never did.

"Because of his glossy black coat. When my stepfather died, my ma gave me his collection of Shakespeare's work, each volume bound in glossy black leather. When this horse was born, the first thing I thought of when I clapped eyes on him was my pa's books." Ace cleared his throat and ran the back of his hand over his mouth. As he settled into position again, he laughed softly. "Kind of a dumb reason for naming a horse, I guess, but there you have it."

He felt her gaze on his face. The sensation made his nose start to itch. He sniffed and glanced down at her. Her large blue eyes were filled with unvoiced questions. "What?" he said softly.

Her mouth twisted into a sad little smile that seemed oddly lopsided. Ace realized that the bruise along her cheekbone probably made it painful to move the right side of her face. "You loved your stepfather very much, didn't you?" she said.

"Yes, I loved him," Ace admitted. "In some ways, as much or more than I love my mother." Memories rolled over him. "He was an extraordinary man. My own father was killed breaking a horse when I was just a baby. Joseph Paxton took me under his wing and loved me like his own. I was never once made to feel I was less his son than his own boys. Being loved like that is something you never forget, or stop feeling grateful for."

A lengthy silence fell between them. Caitlin seemed preoccupied with watching the horse. At last, she looked up at him.

"I'm very sorry he died the way he did. My father— well, if he did the terrible thing you say, I'm very, very sorry."

Ace couldn't fail to notice the shadows in her eyes. "It all happened a long time ago. At the time, you were probably only knee-high to a grasshopper. You had no control over your father's actions, and you needn't apologize for them."

She turned her wrists to stare down at her palms. "He wasn't a very nice man, my father. He loved his whiskey, and when he drank, it made him crazy just like it does Patrick. After my mother died, he drank most of the time. Keeping himself in whiskey was expensive. There were times—" She broke off and swallowed, her tension at odds with the matter-of-fact tone of her voice. "There were times when he'd do almost anything to get the money he needed to buy a jug. If he swindled your stepfather, I'm sure that was why."

When she lifted her gaze to his again, her expression was carefully blank. He searched her face, trying to glean something from the set of her mouth, the look in her eyes. Sometimes she was very good at hiding her feelings. At others, her face was like an open book.

As if his regard made her nervous, she fluttered a hand and said, "Enough of that. One should never speak ill of the dead. He had his faults, my father. But now he's gone, and I try to remember the good times."

Ace wondered if this girl could even comprehend what good times were really like. *To celebrate my birthday, we made a cake and had a taffy pull. It was so much fun.* Most young girls would have felt they hadn't had a birthday celebration at all. Yet Caitlin had recorded that afternoon in her diary as if it had been a memorable occasion.

As he gazed down at her pinched expression, he vowed that as her husband, he would dedicate his life to filling her days with laughter. There would undoubtedly be bad times ahead of them. And sorrow. That was the natural way of things. But if he had his druthers, there'd be no more of either than he could help.

"Caitlin, about this morning."

She shot him a wary glance, her eyes going dark with emotions he couldn't define.

He coughed and ran a hand over his hair. "I, um . . . I've done a lot of thinking about what happened, and I've decided I owe you an apology."

She looked at him as if he'd just told her pigs could fly. An incredulous, fragile sort of look that said, "You're pulling my leg, right?" He had a strong urge to slip an arm around her shoulders and give her a hug. Anything to wipe that disbelieving expression off her face.

Instead he smiled slightly. "Hasn't a man ever apologized to you before?"

"Patrick," she replied softly.

Patrick again. After glimpsing some of her diary passages, Ace was better able to understand her devotion to her brother. But after seeing Patrick strike her, it still didn't sit well. The youth had obviously changed, and for the worse. Ace hauled in a deep breath. "I'm very sorry I broke my word to you, Caitlin. It's not a very good way to start a marriage, making you promises and then breaking them before the hour is out. I feel really bad about it."

She shrugged one shoulder, the gesture conveying that she had never really expected him to keep his word.

Her offhanded attitude made Ace feel more guilty than if she'd ranted and raved. It drove home to him that she wasn't feeling disillusioned by his actions, because she had no illusions—and no grand notions. People were never going to disappoint her. Not if she never allowed herself to believe in them.

An enigma, that was Caitlin. A girl who would go to any length to stand behind her word, even if it meant staying married to a man she didn't love. Yet she didn't seem to expect him or anyone else to abide by the same moral precepts.

He had originally come out here to tell her he meant to go see Patrick this afternoon and to try to justify why he'd nearly knocked the young man's teeth down his throat. Instead, he heard himself say, "A promise should be kept, no matter what, Caitlin. If a man doesn't stand behind his word, he isn't much of a man."

Under the circumstances, it was about the stupidest thing he'd ever said. He may as well have asked for a little more rope so he could hang himself.

She fastened a bewildered gaze on him. Not that he blamed her for feeling bewildered. What the hell was he saying? That he wasn't much of a man?

He rubbed a hand over his face and blinked. The situation hadn't much improved when his vision cleared. This girl had kept her word to him, at great cost to herself, and he'd broken his to her. No matter what his reasons, he felt like a shit.

"I, um . . ." It was his turn to stand with his palms turned up. Tracing the lines there with his gaze, he wondered which was his wisdom line and decided he probably didn't have one. "I've never been a great one for expressing myself," he told her ruefully. "After you've been around me a while, you'll learn I think tact is something little boys put on chairs for the teacher to sit on."

He paused a moment, waiting for her to laugh. *Nothing.* So much for a touch of levity.

"The only way I know to say things is pretty much straight out, Caitlin. I'm really sorry for breaking my promise to you. But sometimes things happen that make it difficult to keep your word. When Patrick hit you, I saw red and just reacted."

He glanced down and saw that she was raking her fingernails over her palms. There was anger in her. A great deal of anger. Yet her expression revealed not a trace of it. He wondered how it felt to be that furious and not feel free to vent it. The concept of holding one's feelings back was completely foreign to him.

In his family, everyone expressed themselves, sometimes loudly, sometimes destructively, always honestly. He remembered Joseph and Eden getting into it one night over whose turn it was to clean the kitchen. By argument's end, they'd broken every dish in the cupboard. It had cost Joseph fourteen dollars to replace all the china, and Eden had had to make his bed for six months to reimburse him for her half of the damages. To this day, whenever a loud argument broke out, his mother would cry, "Not my crystal! I don't care about the rest, but don't you dare touch my crystal!"

Anger. In the Paxton household, it was as common as eggs and bacon for breakfast. You got mad. You yelled and pitched an unholy fit. Then it was over. In contrast, Caitlin seemed to think expressing her feelings was some kind of sin. Either that or she was afraid to. Neither sat very well with him.

Ace didn't know what possessed him, but the question sprang to his lips before he could swallow it back. "Do you want to hit me, Caitlin?"

She flashed him a startled look. "Of course not."

"You're very angry."

For a moment, he thought she would deny it. Then her mouth twisted tight at the corners. "Yes."

"With me?"

Her mouth tightened even more.

"It's all right to admit you're mad at me," he assured her. "The sky isn't going to fall on you."

She flashed him another disbelieving glance that spoke volumes, but said nothing.

Ace knew on some level he probably shouldn't press her. But he felt compelled to get his point across. "I asked you a question, Caitlin, and I'd like an answer," he said, his tone a little more stern than he intended. "Are you angry with me?"

She stopped raking her nails over her palms and made trembling fists. "Yes!"

The admission was more a hiss than a word, its sibilance hanging in the air. After making the confession, she went rigid and withdrew from him a little, as if she expected him to smack her. In fact, she seemed braced for it.

"Is that all?" he asked her softly. "Just 'yes'? If you're mad at me, Caitlin, let fly. Give me a dressing down. Scream at me. Knock me up alongside the head. I'd rather that than for you to just stand there. At least then it'll be out in the open, and we can finish it."

"Finish it?" she echoed in a high-pitched voice.

Judging by the way her voice shook, he'd almost pushed her beyond caution. Instinctively, he gave her another nudge by saying, "Yes, finish it. I'm a firm believer in clearing the air. Otherwise, misunderstandings fester and cause far more heartache than they ever would otherwise. Talking things out may not solve everything, but it can go a long way toward calming the waters."

"This can't ever be finished. Not until you bury me. Until death do us part, remember? Between you and Patrick, I've been put in a position that will *never* be finished!"

Ace avoided her gaze, afraid she'd see too much reflected in his eyes. He had her talking, at least. That had to be a good start. Now, if he could just keep prodding her. It wasn't a particularly admirable way to go about things, but he'd take what he could get. "So you're angry with Patrick, too?"

"With both of you." Her whole body was beginning to shake. "He got drunk and crazy, and you took advantage of it, the two of you railroading me into a marriage I abhor! Then this morning, he came staggering over here, all in a huff, as if it's entirely *my* fault? To add insult to injury, he slapped me. My own brother! And then you jump in and beat him up? You're both acting like barbarians, and I'm trapped in the middle!"

Ace tightened his grip on the fence rail. *Slap* wasn't the word to describe the blow Patrick had dealt her, but he guessed now wasn't a good time to split hairs. "Are you angry because he slapped you?"

She looked at him as if he were an imbecile. "Of *course* I'm angry. If I *liked* being slapped, Mr. Keegan, I would have found myself a husband years ago to do the honors."

She started to push down from the fence. Ace snaked out a hand and grabbed her arm. "Oh, no, you don't. Rule number one in this marriage, no storming off in the middle of an argument. We're going to settle this."

She clenched her teeth and tried to wrench free of his grasp. "Settle it, finish it! How can you possibly believe either is possible? As for your rule, I'm not storming off. I'm simply ending a conversation that's going nowhere."

Taking care not to bruise her, Ace maintained his grip on her arm. "If you dislike being hit," he asked in a low voice, "why have you stayed there and taken it?"

Her eyes went wide and filled with sparkling tears. She tried to jerk her arm free again. Ace could see he'd touched a real sore spot. Her indignation was almost palpable as she twisted to escape him.

Though she'd said nothing, his question had been answered with far more eloquence than she probably realized. "So you did try to leave?"

One of her feet slipped off the fence rung. She scrambled for purchase, then threw him a hate-filled glance. Her mouth thinned into an uncompromising line.

"What happened?" he asked gently. "Tell me, Caitlin."

"The same thing that would happen if I tried to leave here. People fetched me home, or he came after me. The end was always the same."

"People took you home to your brother?"

There was that look again, as if he didn't have brains enough to fill a thimble. "Not to my brother! To my father. Patrick was always with me."

"With you? Trying to run away, you mean?"

The fight went out of her, and her expression became closed again. Ace had an unholy urge to shake her. *Secrets.* Her eyes were dark with them. Secrets he sensed she would never willingly divulge. He would have to pry them out of her, one by one, like rusty nails out of seasoned oak.

"Caitlin, how can I help you if you won't talk to me?"

"Help me?"

Ace could have bitten his tongue. He hadn't meant to say that. "We're married. Somehow we have to make it work. We can't do that if you erect a wall between us."

Her expression remained shuttered. "Making this marriage work is your problem. If you're beginning to realize what a stupid move it was, I'm perfectly willing to rectify the situation by getting an annulment."

"No annulment."

She averted her face and dragged in a quavery breath. "You'll undoubtedly change your mind, probably after it's too late. Then where will I be?"

She said it with such certainty. Ace leaned around slightly, trying to see her expression. "Why on earth do you think I'll change my mind?"

She flashed him another bitter glance. "The merchandise, remember? You haven't seen it yet."

The words were like a slap. He remembered saying them to her that first night in her barn. An insult calculated to shame and intimidate. He relaxed his grip on her elbow slightly. It was all the opportunity she needed. With a violent twist of her body, she leaped off the fence and tripped away from him in a tangle of skirts. He watched her go for a second. Then he struck off after her.

As he rounded the corner of the barn, he saw her disappear into the building. It occurred to him she had no place to run. His brothers were in the house, so she couldn't seek sanctuary there. The realization drove home to him how trapped she must be feeling.

Ace leaned against the barn door, his shoulder smarting where a bent nail in the crossbuck poked him. He ran a hand over his face again. Why he indulged in the habit of trying to blink away his frustration, he didn't know. It never seemed to help.

The merchandise. There was nothing quite like having your stupidity thrown back in your teeth. He'd forgotten all about saying that to her. She obviously hadn't. He guessed because the words had hurt—maybe more deeply than he'd ever dreamed. *You place a very high price on yourself, Miss O'Shannessy. It remains to be seen if you're worth it.*

He closed his eyes, feeling slightly sick. Maybe it was just the opposite. Maybe she didn't place much value on herself at all. *The merchandise.* Thinking back on it, that was one of the cruelest, rottenest things he'd ever said to anyone. And it was only one in a long list of mean shots he'd taken at Caitlin in the short time he'd known her.

Like father, like daughter? He'd raised that question so glibly last night, recognizing her weakness and capitalizing on it. Using it against her to keep her at the Paradise. Why did he never stop to think that where there was weakness, there might also be pain? Maybe a pain that ran too deep for tears.

He recalled all she'd done since he'd known her. Scraping together eight dollars and nine cents, payment made well in advance of the stipulated month. Her willingness to sacrifice herself to save Patrick. Her decision to stay at the Paradise because he'd taunted her about keeping her word. Everything the girl had done screamed that she was trying to prove something to herself, and maybe to everyone else. It didn't take a genius to figure out what that something was—that she was nothing like her bastard of a father.

Her reasons didn't really matter. What did was that

he'd recognized the weakness and used it against her. Thoughtlessly. Heartlessly. Winning the game had been all that counted to him.

As a gambler, it was a talent he had, reading other people. Reading. Gauging. Moving in for the kill. He was so damned good at it. So well practiced, it came second nature. Only this wasn't a game. And Caitlin wasn't a pot of money. She was a person with feelings, and to suit his own ends, he'd trampled all over them.

Did she feel below standard? Did she truly believe that once he began to peel away her layers and saw who she really was, he wouldn't want to be married to her anymore? *Crazy, so crazy.* She was a beautiful girl. With that flaming red hair, those lovely blue eyes and creamy skin, she was probably the most striking young woman for a radius of a hundred miles. What man in his right mind wouldn't want her?

Yet she felt flawed. He'd seen it in her eyes.

Why, that was the question. Was it merely because of the kind of man her father had been? Or something more? March 12, 1879. From that day on, Caitlin had stopped making entries in her diary. *I pray I can forget.* Something had happened to her. Something so terrible she'd tried to wipe it from her memory.

As her husband, it was up to him to find out what. He had a bad feeling that might be easier said than done.

 16

THE LOFT WAS WONDERFULLY DARK AND QUIET. CAITLIN huddled in the back corner, legs drawn to her chest, forehead pressed against her bent knees. All she wanted was to be left alone. Just for a few minutes. Until she could gather her composure. Until her anger ebbed. Until her stomach stopped roiling.

Ace had been goading her, deliberately trying to make her furious. In retrospect, she saw that. Only the realization came a little late. She'd revealed too much to him. Would have revealed more if she hadn't gotten away.

She dug in hard at her knees with her fingernails, enraged at herself and at him. *Stupid.* She felt so stupid. Like a chess piece. He'd skillfully maneuvered her around the board, until he had her just where he wanted her.

She *never* volunteered to talk about her father. Not about the beatings. Not about her and Patrick's futile attempts to run away. She'd never even discussed it much with Bess or Doc Halloway, who, aside from her brother, were her very best friends in the whole world. Trying to talk about it was like pouring alcohol on a wound.

That was how she felt now, as if her skin were raw with abrasions and Ace Keegan had slopped whiskey all over her. She felt as if she might get sick, her belly twisting and cramping, a hot acidic sensation at the back of her throat that wouldn't go away.

Why have you stayed there and taken it?

He was just like everyone else. No one but Patrick had ever understood what it was like to live with someone like their father. Other people didn't have an inkling. Maybe because they didn't really want to. It had been easier to turn their heads, to tell themselves things weren't really all that bad out at the O'Shannessy place.

All children tried to run away sometimes, they'd told themselves. All children hated their parents sometimes. All children got it into their heads at some point that they were sorely mistreated. By lying to themselves, the people of No Name had avoided feeling guilty.

If Conor said his boy had tripped over a shovel and bruised his cheek, then that was what had happened. If Conor said his girl had fallen off a fence and broken her wrist, who were they to question him?

No one had had the guts to stand up to Conor O'Shannessy. That was the truth of it. A whole town full of cowards.

Was she angry? Ace had asked her.

How on earth did he think she felt? The word "angry" didn't come close to describing it. She doubted there was a word that could. From birth, she'd been imprisoned with a monster as her warden, and she'd been unable to seek help for fear of his retaliation. In the early years, before she'd begun to realize that people preferred to ignore her plight, she couldn't count the times she'd looked into the eyes of an adult, silently pleading for rescue.

She had soon learned there were few heroes in the world. As a child, she'd wished on stars. *I wish I may, I wish I might, have this wish I wish tonight.* And her wish had always been for a hero. A man who would step forward out of the crowd. Someone big and strong, who'd fight for her and Patrick. Someone who'd steal them away. Someone kind and wonderful, with a big deep laugh, who gave hugs and read stories and bought sugar to make candy. Someone who would hit her and Patrick only when they were naughty, not when they were trying their hardest to be good.

Instead of getting her wish, her pleading looks had been all but ignored. The owner of the general store had given her candy and patted her on the head. The man at the livery had let her feed his horses apples. The proprietor of the dry goods store had given her a porcelain-faced doll, then later, scraps of calico to make a rag doll because her father had flown into a rage and torn the first doll apart. No one was going to spoil Conor O'Shannessy's children by giving them highfalutin' gifts they didn't deserve.

Only one man in town had ever stepped forward and offered to help her, and that had been Doc Halloway, a little man with the heart of a hero and the body of a plump, oversized elf. She'd been afraid to accept Doc's offer of help, afraid that her father might hurt him if he tried to interfere.

All the other men who might have been able to hold their own against Conor had been kind as they sent her on her way. All of them had turned their heads or pretended not to see. Until finally, she stopped looking into their eyes. Stopping wishing and hoping. Not because she no longer yearned to escape, but because she came to realize that big, strong men seldom spent much time worrying about others. They were too concerned with their own wants and needs, many of which they satisfied at the expense of people weaker than themselves.

Was she angry? Oh, yes, she was angry. A burning kind of anger she'd long since tamped down and buried inside herself because it was useless to expend energy on it. Besides, she was tired. Awfully, horribly tired.

Twenty-two years. And now her brother was following in their father's footsteps. She felt so helpless. Helpless to save him. Helpless to save herself. All her life, she'd felt like a fly on tacky paper, frantically trying to get free. And then, just when she'd finally escaped her father's dominion, Ace Keegan had come along, and here she was, trapped again.

She wanted to hate him. Wanted to with all her heart. But he kept her so off balance by being kind, she couldn't hold fast to the emotion. Giving her a knife last night. Telling her he was sorry a few minutes ago. He could be relentless and ruthless. But just when she began to despise him for it, he changed tactics.

He was very good at playing games. And that's all this was to him, a game. He'd admitted as much. *I'm winning.* He studied her all the time just as he might an opponent over a poker table, watching her expressions, searching her gaze with eyes that saw too much. He made her feel naked. And powerless.

What did he want with her? That was what troubled her most. Why would a man as handsome as he force a woman to marry him? She couldn't believe he was that lonely, or that desperate. He wanted her to believe he felt responsible for her, that because he'd destroyed her reputation he felt obligated to marry her. Only she couldn't quite credit that. No one but Doc and Bess and Patrick had ever cared what happened to her before, so why should he? He scarcely knew her, and he knew next to nothing about her past.

Did he really expect her to believe he was that much

better a person than everyone else in No Name? That he had only altruistic reasons for making her his wife? Most people didn't do things for someone else, at great cost to themselves, unless there was something in it for them. He had to have an ulterior motive. No man would just up and marry a woman he barely knew out of the goodness of his heart.

A sudden creak of wood brought Caitlin's head up. She cocked her head to listen. Below the loft, chickens pecked the dirt, clucking among themselves. Occasionally, a horse kicked the wall of its stall.

Creak. Her gaze shot to the loft ladder. She held her breath, waiting, hoping no one was climbing up it. At the other side of the loft, she'd seen blankets and pillows. Ace's brothers slept up here. With her luck, it would be one of them, coming up for a mid-morning snooze.

A dark hand appeared over the highest ladder rung. Then a black head of hair. *Ace.* He braced the heel of a hand on the wood and vaulted over the half-wall with such power and grace it made her heart skitter. When his boots bottomed out in the loose hay, he caught his balance, then swung his ebony head around, his gaze routing through the dimness. When he spotted her, he grew still, his eyes moving slowly over her, seeming to miss nothing.

"I thought you were probably up here."

He started toward her, his gait lurching as his feet found the solid surface of bales one moment, loose hay the next. The powerful muscles in his legs bunched with every movement, drawing his black denim pants taut over his thighs. His upper body was just as impressive, shoulders and arms flexing under his black shirt as he swung for balance.

To her relief, he didn't join her in the corner, but chose instead to sit on a stair-step stack of bales, hands braced on the compressed hay, long legs extended and slightly bent, the toes of his gleaming black boots turned inward for leverage.

He had positioned himself between her and the ladder.

Caitlin hugged her knees more tightly, afraid of him as she'd never been of any other man. He had so much power over her. *Her husband.* If he chose to throw her down in the hay—to tear her clothes off and roughly take her—no one would stop him. Indeed, no one would even raise an eyebrow. She was his wife, his property. He could do what he liked with her, and for as long as he wished.

He was staring at her again. He made her feel like a difficult mathematical equation he was trying to decipher.

"The train kind of got off its tracks out there by the corral," he said huskily. "I originally followed you out here to apologize and tell you I intend to go see Patrick this afternoon."

"Patrick?"

He scrubbed the back of his hand over his mouth. "I stepped out of line this morning, telling him he couldn't come around. I won't apologize for hitting him. But I will retract what I said about his not being welcome here. He's your brother, and you love him. If you want to see him, that's your right, and I've got no business making it difficult for you."

He was doing it again, being kind. Caitlin stared at him, so filled with gladness she nearly leaped up and hugged him. Instinctive wariness held her rooted. He made her feel as if she were treading over ice, and that if she let him, he'd lure her onto a thin spot.

"Thank you."

The words sounded toneless and hollow, not at all filled with gratitude. She supposed she was being unforgivably rude. It was a generous gesture on his part. But she couldn't bring herself to lower her defenses. He was a trickster, this man, a calculating, manipulative trickster. He did nothing off the cuff, and if she let herself trust him, she would end up paying dearly for it.

She forced her mind back to the subject at hand. The thought of him and Patrick having another confrontation made her stomach twist. The cramp knifed from her navel to her groin, an awful, ripping sensation that made her grit her teeth. She was beginning to wonder if she wasn't coming down with something. And wouldn't that be a fine kettle of fish, sick in bed with only Ace Keegan to play nursemaid? Just the possibility made her stomach hurt worse.

"What if Patrick is still drunk when you go over there?" she asked.

"What if he is?"

"He might try to pick a fight with you."

Ace moved his hands on the hay bale. "I've never walked away from a challenge in my life, Caitlin. But for you, I will. I promised you this morning that I won't lift a hand against your brother. Unless he hits you again or somehow threatens my life, I won't break my word to you again."

Caitlin wanted to believe him. Oh, God, how she wanted to believe. Experience told her not to be a fool. He'd broken his word once, without batting an eye. He would again. It didn't matter that Patrick had deserved the licking. If she were honest, she had to admit she'd wanted to light into him herself. But, then, she hadn't sworn not to. Ace had. And he'd broken that promise without one second's hesitation.

"What if—" Acid rolled up her throat, forcing her to swallow. "What if he pulls a gun on you? You could end up killing him. I'm not sure your going over there is a good idea, as much as I appreciate the offer."

"I'm good with a gun, Caitlin."

"I realize that, which is why I'm worried."

"I didn't get my reputation slapping leather without knowing how to place my bullets. If Patrick draws on me, I won't kill him. You have my word on it."

She wasn't willing to bet her brother's life on Ace Keegan's word. "I'd really rather—"

"Caitlin, you're just going to have to trust me," he cut in. "I can handle your brother. We have enough problems without borrowing trouble, and talking about Patrick isn't the only reason I came up here."

She hated to ask what his other reason was. Given his kindness last night, she supposed it was silly to think he might have joined her in the loft with nefarious plans in mind. But, then, men had been kind to her before. She'd learned the hard way just how treacherous some members of the opposite sex could be, smiling one moment, driving the knife between your ribs the next. Oh, yes, she knew . . .

He puffed air into his cheeks. "I came up here to talk to you about a couple of other things. First off, to apologize again. I'm sorry our conversation got off track out there. I meant to calm the waters. Then the first thing I knew, we were quarreling."

That he would sit there and apologize for something he'd done deliberately caused a sudden whirlpool of rage to surge in Caitlin's stomach, its heat mixing with the acid as it came up her throat. She was fed up with him toying with her. Frightened by it. A person couldn't have her wits about her every single second.

"You goaded me into quarreling with you." She kept her voice carefully calm. "You were trying to dig information out of me."

She expected him to deny it. Instead he chuckled, a deep, warm sound that curled around her. "I must be losing my touch. Was I that transparent?"

"Maybe I'm just smarter than your average victim."

"Victim?" He shook his head, his grin turning wry. "That's an odd choice of words, Caitlin."

"Is it?"

"You're still upset with me."

She refused to dignify that with a reply. He went back to studying her, his dark gaze giving hers no quarter. After what seemed an interminably long while, he apparently grew bored with the pastime and shifted his attention to her body. With her knees drawn up, she knew he couldn't see much, but he made her feel as if he could. She curled her toes inside her shoes.

"I'll tell you what," he said, the sudden sound of his voice making her jump. His gaze drifted slowly back to her face. "I'll stop playing games and come straight out with it. How does that sound?"

"Straight out with what?" Her voice sounded tinny.

"Questions." His eyes locked with hers again. "And understand before I ask them that I want answers. Honest ones."

Caitlin's face felt stiff. She thought of Patrick and the egg-white facial mask, and the next thing she knew her eyes were stinging with tears. She determinedly blinked them away. "You can't force me to answer questions I don't want to answer, Mr. Keegan."

"So we're back to 'Mr. Keegan,' are we?"

He laughed again, soundlessly, the slight shake of his shoulders and chest the only sign of his mirth. Then his mouth twisted down at the corner as a smile flitted across his lips. A crooked smile. A smile that, despite the disfiguring scar on his cheek, managed to charm and disarm. She wondered if he'd practiced it in front of a mirror. He bent his head for a moment, moving his boots back and forth as though to check the shine.

"As for my not being able to force you to answer my questions, you're dead wrong. I have a couple of trump cards up my sleeve, and they're whoppers. My advice to you is to fold before I play them."

Caitlin pressed her back more firmly against the wall. "Are you threatening me?"

"More or less." Even in the dimness, his eyes twinkled when he looked back up at her. "But my intentions are good."

She wanted to jerk her gaze from his but found she couldn't. "What exactly are you threatening me with?"

"You're my wife. Go figure."

Her knees were going to break. She tried to loosen her arms from around them, but her body seemed frozen in that one position.

He shifted his feet again. "The way I see it, Caitlin, I don't have a lot of choices. I married you, and somehow or other, I'm determined to make the marriage work. Somewhere along the line, that means no secrets can remain between us. It also means that, sooner or later, I'll want to make love to you. I've already gathered that the thought of my doing so is a little less than appealing to you. Fact is, I'd say you're terrified."

She said nothing, just stared at him with her heart knocking around in her throat.

"Since I'm your husband now with certain inalienable rights, I think it'd be a real smart move if you told me why you're so afraid. Otherwise, I'm left guessing. That puts me at a hell of a disadvantage, and it isn't really fair to you. If there's a problem, I need to know it. Do you understand what I'm saying to you?"

Her lips had stuck together, and her tongue felt glued to the roof of her mouth. When she said nothing, he heaved a tired-sounding sigh.

"You're not helping me out much here."

"I think," she said shakily, "that you're giving me an ultimatum."

He folded his arms, the fingers of one hand thrumming on his shirt sleeve. His patience was obviously growing thin. "I prefer to think of it as giving you a chance to avoid unnecessary heartache. I'm not an unreasonable man. If you're frightened and you have good reason to be, then it's time to acknowledge the corn. If not, I will assume I'm dealing with an ordinary case of bridal jitters and proceed accordingly."

"In other words, either I tell you whatever it is you're wanting to know, or you'll force your attentions on me?"

He held her gaze. "Force. That's a real favorite word of yours, isn't it? You used it just a second ago, too." He regarded her thoughtfully. "I have a hunch there's another word bouncing around inside your head right now. A real similar one." He paused, as though for emphasis, then said very softly, "I think that word is rape."

Caitlin had a sudden and painful urge to vomit. Her stomach twisted, then lurched upward. The knifing cramps that followed would have bent her double if she hadn't already been in that position.

"Last night you told me you were compromised years back. I don't think 'compromised' was exactly the right word. Was it?"

She clamped a hand over her mouth and squeezed her eyes closed. While she battled with the spasms attacking her stomach, he sat there, watching and waiting.

"Caitlin . . ." He said her name gently, making it sound like a caress. "Don't misunderstand me. I'm not asking for a detailed account. Just a simple yes or no. I'll even settle for a nod or shake of your head. If something like that happened to you, honey, you have to tell me. It isn't the kind of secret a woman should keep from her husband."

With a lurch, she twisted onto her knees and bent forward. "I'm going to be sick."

For just a second, Ace thought she was faking. Then he saw her retch, the veins along her throat distending, her face contorting. He came up off the bale so fast it made him dizzy. As he slogged toward her through the hay, several thoughts raced through his mind, the first that he had an answer to his question, the last that he was the stupidest son of a bitch who had ever walked.

He'd expected his frontal attack to upset her. But nothing like this.

She retched again, the sound making his throat crawl. She didn't seem to be getting anything up.

Dry heaves. He'd had them a few times, and he knew how they hurt. Only in his case, they'd been just reward. He'd always been drinking when he'd suffered such attacks. Caitlin hadn't touched a drop of liquor.

Concern filled him. He dropped to one knee beside her and looped an arm around her waist. "Jesus H. Christ."

She batted weakly at his arm. "G-go away. Don't w-watch me!"

She followed the plea with another mewling sound that nearly made him lose his own breakfast. He'd been there a few too many times not to feel waves of sympathetic nausea. He gulped and fixed his gaze on the back of her head, trying a little frantically to think about something else. It was a trick he'd learned to combat his weak stomach years ago when his brothers got sick, getting his mind off the vomiting and onto something pleasant.

Only with Caitlin the method didn't work. Every time she retched, he felt it clear to his toes. The noises had that tearing, ripping kind of edge, and she seemed so fragile. He couldn't help but worry she was going to hurt herself. Along the side of her neck, he could see the veins popping out. It felt as if every muscle in her body was straining.

Thinking back, he knew she hadn't had supper last night, and she'd skipped breakfast. Now it was mid-morning. If she'd had an early lunch yesterday, that meant she hadn't eaten in twenty-four hours. On top of that, she'd been tied into nervous knots ever since he cornered her at the social last night. Little wonder her stomach was rebelling.

He heard her gulping convulsively and dragging in deep breaths. He knew she was trying to regain control. Only with dry heaves, it was seldom quite that easy. Soon, he could almost feel her exhaustion.

Worry for her helped him ward off his own nausea. Cupping a hand over her brow, he supported her head and took more of her weight against him. When the retching finally subsided, he twisted, putting his back to the wall and sitting in the hay so he could draw her onto his lap. Though she tried, she was too weak to resist. When she ceased struggling, she did so with a defeated sob, turning her face against his shoulder.

He curled his arms around her and rested his cheek atop her head. She was crying, softly, heartbrokenly.

Impatience. All his life, it had been the bane of his existence. He wanted everything accomplished yester-day, if not sooner. He'd never been able to stand cooling his heels. It was that way with work, that way with play, that way with revenge. And now he was behaving the same damned way with this girl, charging in, not think-ing first. They'd been married roughly twelve hours, and already he was trying to pry secrets out of her and make her trust him. She needed time, dammit. Any idiot should have been able to see that.

Back home in San Francisco, pianos had skirts, for Christ's sake, not for decoration, but because revealing the piano legs was considered to be risque. People referred to trousers as inexpressibles, and called their asses "sit-down-upons." Respectable women pretended not to have legs or arms, referring to them instead as appendages or limbs. Their breasts and private places were touched by their husbands only in the dark of night behind locked bedroom doors, never to be mentioned in the light of day.

Ace knew all that. He did have a mother and sister, after all, both of whom were models of ladylike behavior. Neither of them would say "shit" if they had a mouthful, and he doubted they'd scream "rape" even if they were being attacked.

That was the way it was in polite society. Things weren't quite so straight-laced around No Name, but close. Yet he had confronted Caitlin, expecting her to not only say the word "rape" but to discuss the experience with him? He had to be out of his goddamned mind.

Part of the problem was that he hadn't lived at home in years. Rooms above saloons. Suites in fancy hotels. He'd been rubbing elbows with sporting women for so long, he'd evidently forgotten how to treat a real lady. A gentleman didn't give ultimatums, and he sure as hell didn't try to engage a female in conversations about indecent topics, rape being high on the list.

"I'm sorry," she whispered against his shirt.

Ace closed his eyes. "No, sweetheart, I'm the one who's sorry. I shouldn't have brought up the subject."

He felt her body grow tense, felt her hands tighten into fists on his shirt. "No, please. I'd like to answer your question. I—I don't want—you to proceed accordingly."

For a moment, Ace couldn't figure out what the hell she meant. Then he remembered saying that if she didn't acknowledge the corn, he'd assume hers was a mere case of ordinary bridal jitters and proceed accordingly. He nearly groaned at the memory, and on the tail end of that urge came another, even stronger one to go get Joseph and have him take over. For all his brother's rough edges, he'd probably handle this girl with a hell of a lot more finesse than Ace was. Joseph hadn't spent quite so much time in saloons and gambling houses.

Only, of course, that wasn't an option. As Joseph had pointed out earlier, Ace had bitten this off, and now he had to chew it. Besides, just the thought of another man holding her like this made Ace feel a little green around the edges. She was *his* wife, *his* responsibility. He'd deal with her. Somehow. He just had to rearrange his thinking a little, that was all. Wipe the last twenty years out of his mind. Clean up his mouth. Acquire some manners. Start remembering he was dealing with a lady and not a whore.

Jesus. The poor girl was in for some rough road.

Ace tightened his hand in her hair. "Caitlin, I'm not going to proceed with anything, okay? Just forget I said that."

"You aren't?"

The hopeful note in her voice set off warning bells. He opened one eye. "Not directly, no."

The tension didn't ease from her body. In fact, she seemed to grow more rigid. "What does that mean?"

He had no idea. "That there's nothing for you to worry about right now."

She wriggled to sit erect and fastened bone-melting blue eyes on his. "But what about later?" Her stomach rumbled, and she gulped, slipping a hand between them to press it against her waist. "I really think I'd better ans—"

"Honey, you already did."

"I did?" She looked totally perplexed. "I don't remem—"

"Trust me," he said huskily. "I have my answer. Now let's just drop the subject, all right?" Her stomach chose that moment to growl once more. "If we don't, you're liable to start puking again. It's nerves making you feel sick, I think. That and not eating for so long."

Puking. Now there was a word. Yet another to strike from his vocabulary. His mother referred to vomiting as "purging" or "tossing up." He felt pretty sure the word "puke" had never passed her lips.

Suddenly Ace felt exhausted. A bone-deep kind of exhaustion. He leaned his head against the wall, absently rubbing a hand up and down Caitlin's arm. "Just relax for a few minutes," he told her softly. "Let your stomach settle down. Then we'll go and get some food into you. I made you up a plate and set it on the warmer."

"I'm really not hungry."

"You are and just don't know it. We've got cool milk in the icebox. Wouldn't a big, tall glass taste good?"

"No."

"Sure it will."

He drew her back against him and pressed her head to his shoulder. He definitely liked the way she felt in his arms. She squirmed, trying to get comfortable. The friction caused some interesting changes to occur inside his trousers, namely an erection the size of a log. He hoped to God she couldn't feel it.

There was no God in heaven. She suddenly stopped breathing and went unnaturally still. Ace mentally ticked off the seconds. When ten had passed, he opened his other eye. "Caitlin?"

"What?"

Her voice sounded as thin as parchment paper, and she didn't so much as twitch. She may as well not have bothered. The warm pressure of her rump against him was enough. He willed his body to behave itself, but that particular part had never seemed to be connected to his brain.

"Don't be afraid," he said in a thick voice that made him want to kick himself. "I'm not going to hurt you."

"W-would you mind if I moved?"

Ace nearly said no. Then he thought better of it. If he made her sit tight, she'd learn an important lesson, that he didn't let his baser urges control him. Hardly ever, anyway.

"No, I don't mind." He let his arms fall away, resisting the urge to shove her off his lap. A man with a will of iron, that was he. "Scoot."

She didn't need to be told twice. He doubted she could have moved faster if he'd yelled, "Fire!"

He drew up a knee as she slid off his lap, the better to hide the bulge in his trousers. He tried to ignore the fact that his shaft was nearly bent double by the change of position. She went back to where she'd been sitting before, bracing her back against the wall. Her eyes regarded him with wary alertness.

Ace rubbed a hand over his face. Blinked. Hauled in a deep breath. When the ritual was over, he draped his arm over his upraised knee. Blinked again. *Christ.* Now he knew why Scotsmen wore kilts.

Silence settled between them. The kind of silence that made a man sweat. He listened to the chickens clucking below the loft. One hen had a strident, shrill cluck that made him seriously consider having chicken for supper. Wringing a neck right then sounded diverting. Nice and violent.

Rape. He wondered who the bastard was who had done such a thing to her. Did he still live around No Name? Ace was dying to ask. It was a question he absolutely would not allow to pass his lips. No more pushing. He had to give the girl some room to breathe. *Patience.* It was a virtue. One he needed to cultivate.

"Who was the son of a bitch?"

Caitlin blinked in startlement. "Pardon?"

Ace clenched his teeth. He felt his right cheek start to twitch. "Is he still around these parts?"

"Wh-why?"

He knotted and relaxed his fist. "I'd like to pay him a social call."

"A social call?"

Ace regarded her in stony silence. He could tell straight off he wasn't going to take to gentlemanly behavior like a duck to water. "I want to pound his face in. Introduce his tonsils to his asshole. Make him wish his mother had been a nun."

Her eyes went wide. "Oh."

"Well?"

She bent her head and began picking at something on her skirt. "I don't want to talk about it," she said shakily. "Please don't make me. You said no details."

He had said that. "I'm not asking for details, just the son of a bitch's name."

"I can't talk about it," she said, her voice going shrill.

"That's all I'll ever ask. Just give me his goddamned name."

She clamped a hand over her face. "You promised!"

Ace tossed his head back and nearly cracked his skull when it impacted against a log. He bit down so hard on his back teeth he almost broke a molar. "I'm sorry," he finally said after several long, throbbing seconds. He was definitely going to kill that stupid chicken. "I did say I wouldn't ask for details."

Silence again. He hated it when she stopped breathing like that. It made him wonder if she'd gotten so scared she'd died on him, or something.

"Just one question." He slanted her a look. "Did the bastard pay for what he did? Or did he waltz off scot-free?"

She gave what sounded like a tortured little laugh behind her hand. "Oh, yes, he paid."

Ace relaxed slightly. "Good."

She made to response to that. "You're not feeling sick again, are you?"

She took a while to answer. "Only a little queasy."

"Milk might help."

She drew her hand from over her eyes, but kept her gaze carefully averted from his. "I'd really rather not." She toyed with a clump of straw beside her. Silence again. The smell of the hay seemed to be bothering her. She kept rubbing her nose. Or maybe it was just a nervous gesture. "Now that you, um, know . . ." Her voice trailed away, and she sneaked a glance at him. "Do you feel differently about getting an annulment?"

That was a loaded question. He couldn't tell by her expression if she was hoping he'd say yes or no. "I'm not giving you an annulment, Caitlin, so get it straight out of your head."

"Not even now?"

He narrowed an eye at her. He was thirty years old, and he'd never known a woman yet whose mental functions didn't bewilder him. "Now? Why would I?"

"Well, because . . ." She left that hanging. Toyed nervously with the straw. Nearly rubbed her nose off. Then she waved a limp hand, the gesture conveying there were a number of things she wanted to say that she couldn't quite bring herself to articulate. "I wasn't honest with you last night. Being compromised isn't exactly the same thing as—" She broke off and tossed a handful of hay away from her. "You know."

It hit Ace then. She truly did feel soiled, just as he'd suspected. In their society, rape indelibly marked a woman for the rest of her life. She was never again considered to be quite up to snuff. Respectable men usually chose chaste virgins as their brides, or equally respectable widows, or compromised young women who'd emerged from the experience with their reputations unscathed.

A lump rose in his throat. Gazing at her averted face, he thought he'd never seen such a sweet countenance. Auburn lashes cast shadows on her pale skin, which was absolutely flawless except for the bruise along her cheekbone. A small, delicately shaped nose. A full, rosy mouth made for kissing. A pointy chin that she somehow managed to make look stubborn. She wore her hair in a braided coronet that might have been severe on any other woman, but on her, it looked delightfully mussed, with coppery tendrils escaping everywhere.

She was beautiful . . . And in his books, innocent. Endearingly so. Slender with small breasts and a fashionably tiny waist. One look at her, and a man knew she was uncharted territory. She may have been raped, but she'd never been loved. There was a hell of a difference. Ace yearned to tell her he felt lucky to have landed her, but now didn't seem an appropriate moment, and he doubted she'd believe him, anyway.

"I don't want an annulment, Caitlin."

She sneaked another glance at him. "Are you sure? It won't make me feel bad or anything."

Ace nearly chuckled at that. She'd more likely to leap for joy, even if, deep down, his rejection hurt. He had a hunch she had long since grown accustomed to feeling inadequate, that considering herself to be a rotten apple in the barrel was something she'd learned to live with, just as he'd learned to live with a limp and a messed-up face. You never forgot your flaws; you just worked your way around them and tried not to feel hurt when other people found you lacking.

"I'm absolutely positive I don't want an annulment," he told her gently, "now and forever, amen."

She plucked up some more hay, studying the strands with fierce concentration. "Now that—" She paused to drag in a tremulous breath. "Now that you know, can I safely assume you plan to give me some time?"

The quavery note in her voice told him just how important his answer was. "How much time are we talking about? A few days, a few weeks?"

"A year would be nice."

He did laugh then. "Caitlin, physical intimacy is a mighty important part of marriage. A whole year?"

"Six months?"

He tried to imagine walking around with a throbbing erection bent double in his trousers for six months. "I don't think so."

"Three, then."

He raised his other leg and rested his loosely folded arms on his knees. "How about if we take it a day at a time?"

She turned the full effect of those blue eyes on him. He had already learned his lesson on that front and looked away. "A day at a time?" she said thinly. "With me never knowing from one minute to the next when you might decide to—" She broke off and made a small sound of frustration. "At least give me a designated amount of time so I can relax between now and then."

He forced himself to meet her gaze, steeling himself, determined not to give way. "There's no reason you can't relax on a day-to-day basis, Caitlin. Making love is nothing to dread, you know."

"No, I don't know."

"Well, take my word for it. I make no claims to be the greatest lover who ever walked, but I do know my way around a woman's body. I can't promise you falling stars and bells ringing in your ears like my sister reads about in her dime novels. But I can guarantee you it will be at least passably nice."

"Passably nice? What exactly does that mean? Somewhere between bearable and downright awful?"

He chuckled again. He couldn't help himself. She looked so stricken, as if having him touch her would be the most dreadful thing she could imagine. "What's your favorite treat?" he asked softly. "Your very favorite."

"Why? What does that—?"

"Just answer the question."

"Chocolate candy," she said without hesitation.

He made a mental note of that so he could get her some the next time he went to town. "Mediocre sex with me will be every bit as good as chocolate candy. And that's if things don't go very well. Good sex will be like—" He hesitated, then smiled. "Imagine sinking neck deep in a whole tub of melted chocolate and being able to eat until it comes out your ears. That's what making love can be like. Better than anything you can dream of."

She was looking at him as if he were crazy.

His amusement faded. "I mean it, Caitlin. Why would I lie to you? The first time I touch you, you'll find out for yourself. Right?"

"You're a man."

"The last time I checked, yes."

Her eyes went suddenly stormy. "You're making fun of me and deliberately missing the point. I realize men like it. That doesn't mean women do. They just endure it. Once they're married, they aren't given any choice. Their only consolation is that it's the only way to have babies."

"Who told you that?"

"That it's the only way to have babies?"

"No, of course not. Who told you women just endure it?"

"No one. I've simply observed and reached my own conclusions."

"Wrong conclusions. If women were as unenthusiastic as all that, the world's population would be drastically diminished."

"So you say."

"And one day I'll prove it to you. Until then, there's little point in dreading something that will be very nice when it happens."

He heard her stomach growl again and pushed to his feet. Stepping over to her, he extended a hand. "Come on, Mrs. Keegan. Let's get you in the house and feed you before you get sick again."

"I'm not hungry."

"Caitlin . . ."

"Well, I'm not! I guess I should know if I feel like eating."

He wiggled his fingers. "Your choice. You can walk to the house, or I can carry you ass up over my shoulder with your bloomers shining."

"I don't want to go in there."

"Why?"

"Because all your brothers are in there, and they hate me."

"Hate you? What the hell makes you think that?"

"Simply put, my last name is O'Shannessy."

"Not any more, it isn't. You're a Keegan, and you're part of this family. They're all pacing the floor, nervous as cats in a roomful of rockers, waiting to meet you. They're afraid you won't like *them,* Caitlin, not the other way around."

Panic welled in her eyes. "I saw all of them last night at the social, and again this morning. They look mean."

"Well, they're not. Come into the house. Meet them. Let them prove it to you."

"I'd really rather just sit here for a while."

He shifted his weight onto one foot and regarded her with a raised eyebrow. "Has anyone ever told you you're a tiny bit stubborn?"

"I'm not stubborn. I just don't feel like eating."

"And argumentative?"

"My stomach is still turning."

"Which is due, in large amount, to the fact that you haven't put any food in it for twenty-four hours."

"I'll eat later."

"You'll eat now. Even a few bites will help." He waggled his fingers again to draw her attention back to his extended hand. "Are you really bent on showing your bloomers to everyone on the place? I've got three hired hands out there who'll probably enjoy the show. And then, of course, there's my brothers. You wanna sell tickets?"

17

THE LAST THING CAITLIN WANTED TO DO WAS GO BACK inside the house. But being towed along beside Ace Keegan was rather like being caught by a whirlwind. The grip of his hand was so strong, his momentum so resolute, that every time she tried to balk, she found herself pulled forward onto her toes.

The Paxton brothers sat around the plank table. Two of them had short, sandy-colored hair. The third had shoulder-length blond hair as straight as a bullet. Unlike Ace, they had blue eyes. They were small men compared to their older half brother, their frames compact and whipcord lean. At Caitlin's entrance, they all shot up from their seats.

Unwilling to approach them alone, Caitlin waited just inside the doorway for Ace to step in behind her. She heard the door close. Then his large hand settled warmly at the small of her back to urge her forward. She couldn't drag her gaze away from the three young men. They stared back at her as if they'd never seen a female before.

After giving his pant leg a shake, the blond raked his fingers through his hair and shrugged his shoulders to straighten his blue chambray work shirt. Giving him a

quick appraisal, Caitlin decided he was the most intimidating of the three, despite the fact that he was the
shortest. For what he lacked in height, he made up for in
muscle. Well-developed shoulders rippled beneath his
shirt, his every movement stressing the seams. His faded
blue denim trousers skimmed the powerful contours of
his legs. The gun belt he wore strapped around his
narrow hips looked as though it belonged there, a lethal
appendage of his body.

"Caitlin, I'd like you to meet my brother, Joseph."

The blond took two long strides toward her, his
brown, calloused hand outstretched to her in welcome.
Caitlin rubbed her palm on her skirt, then clumsily
shook hands with him. "Hello," she said in a twangy
voice that sounded as if it came from the bottom of a tin
can. "I'm pleased to meet you."

A deep dimple, much like the one Ace sported, flashed
in Joseph's cheek as his full lips lifted in a smile. He had
an arresting face, she decided, a curious blend of boyish
cuteness and hard-edged masculinity, his full mouth
almost feminine yet manly in its firmness, his jawline
square and sharply defined with a ridge of muscle. He
had beautiful blue eyes that managed to twinkle with
friendliness and make one feel nervous at the same time.
An unflinching gaze, the kind she imagined would come
in handy during a poker game or a gunfight, revealing
little, yet missing nothing.

"The pleasure is all mine," he finally said, his voice
laced with amusement.

With a start, Caitlin realized he was still gripping her
hand and that he could undoubtedly feel how badly she
was shaking. She no sooner registered that and started to
blush than he released his hold on her.

"And this is David," Ace said, turning her slightly to
face the other two young men.

The taller one stepped forward. His hand felt hot and
damp as it closed around hers. "Ma'am." He bobbed his
head, then proceeded to jerk her arm up and down as
though he were working a pump handle. "Good to make
your acquaintance."

"Likewise." Caitlin noticed a small rent in the shoulder seam of his red plaid shirt. It occurred to her that it would be her responsibility to do the mending around here once she got settled in.

"And this is Esa," Ace finished.

Esa grinned and took her hand the instant David let go of it. "I only got one question, and if your answer is yes, I know I'm going to love you. Can you cook?"

The sound of deep masculine laughter bounced off the log walls for several seconds. When the sound died down, Caitlin said, "I've never won any blue ribbons, but I can find my way around a kitchen well enough."

Esa winked at Ace. "It's a unanimous vote then. She's a keeper."

Caitlin found herself smiling. She instantly liked the youngest Paxton. Despite the fact that he wore a gun on his hip and could undoubtedly use it, he had a certain gentleness about him. When he grinned, it was nearly impossible not to respond in kind. She guessed him to be about her age, possibly a shade older. Even so, he was irresistibly boyish, the only one of the bunch she didn't find frightening.

"I'd already decided she's a keeper," Ace said with a chuckle, "so I'm glad you like her."

Joseph rested his hands on his hips and scuffed the sole of his boot on the floor. With one eye slightly narrowed, he rested his startling blue gaze on her face for a moment. "You're gonna have a shiner, girl. Looks to me like I ought to scrape a spud and make you a poultice."

Caitlin touched her cheek. "Oh, no. Please don't bother. It's nothing, really."

"No bother." He hooked the toe of his boot around the crossbuck leg of the bench he'd been sitting on to draw it farther out from the table. "Take a load off. I just made fresh coffee."

"That sounds nice." Caitlin took the seat he had provided. "Thank you."

"Honey, are you sure you wouldn't rather have milk?" Ace asked her.

The smell of the coffee was making her mouth water. At home, she never made it strong enough for there to be a rich aroma. "No, coffee will be fine."

He swung a leg over the bench to sit beside her. The two younger men resumed their seats across from them. Acutely aware of her husband's hard, muscular arm brushing against her shoulder, Caitlin folded her hands in her lap and dug into her skin with her fingernails. They were all staring at her, she realized with a sick sensation at the pit of her stomach. As the seconds wore on, she became increasingly nervous.

From the adjoining kitchen, Joseph hollered, "You want cream?"

The cow at home had stopped giving rich milk over a year ago, and Caitlin hadn't been able to spare any cream for her coffee since. Making cheese and butter had taken precedence. She leaned forward slightly. "Yes, please."

"So . . ." David smiled across at her. "How's married life treating you so far?" He no sooner finished speaking than he jerked and said, "Ouch! What'd you do that for, Ace?"

Ace made no reply. Caitlin glanced up at his dark profile. Unless she missed her guess, he'd just kicked his brother.

"All I said was—"

"Just drink your coffee," Ace cut in.

Looking disgruntled, David picked up his mug and took a loud slurp.

"And mind your manners," Ace added.

David took his second sip of coffee more quietly. He met Caitlin's gaze over the rim of his cup and winked at her. She bent her head to hide another smile. Just then, Joseph returned from the kitchen carrying a plate and two steaming mugs of coffee. After plopping the plate down next to her elbow, he set the coffee with cream before Caitlin and handed the other cup to Ace. Grabbing up his own abandoned mug, he stepped around to take a seat at the other side of the table with his younger brothers. It wasn't until he sat down that she noticed he held a potato in the crook of one arm. After setting aside his mug, he drew his knife from its scabbard, cut the potato in half, and began scraping one exposed center with the knife blade, forming pulp.

Caitlin cupped her mug in her hands and took a slow sip of coffee. The steam was wonderfully warm on her cool cheeks, and she closed her eyes for a moment, savoring both the smell and the rich taste. It had been so long since she'd had good strong coffee lightened with cream that she had nearly forgotten how delicious it tasted. She wished with all her heart that Patrick were here to enjoy it with her.

Her stomach picked that moment to growl. To cover the sound, she quickly said, "This is lovely, Joseph. Thank you."

His dimple deepened again as he flashed her a grin. "You're very welcome." He shot a look at Ace. "How's yours, big brother?"

Caitlin glanced up to discover that Ace had been staring down at her. He'd obviously been too preoccupied to try his coffee and was embarrassed to have been caught gaping. He looked a little flustered for a moment, then narrowed an eye at Joseph. Caitlin didn't miss the silent message that passed between them, Joseph's expression jocular, Ace's dark and threatening. To Caitlin's surprise, the younger and more slightly built man didn't seem to be intimidated. He was still grinning as he leaned sideways to hand her the potato mash.

"Press that against your cheek. It'll take the soreness out," he told her.

Feeling silly, Caitlin did as he instructed. How she was supposed to drink her coffee, eat the plate of flapjacks and eggs Ace had saved for her, and still manage to hold the potato against her cheek, she didn't know. Perhaps it was just as well. She was so nervous, her stomach threatened to turn inside out again if she tried to put anything more than coffee on it.

To her amazement, the poultice soothed the burning sensation along her cheekbone after only a few seconds. "Thank you," she murmured. "This feels wonderful."

Joseph chuckled. "You're welcome." He glanced over his shoulder. "Am I starting to hear an echo in here?" He returned his gaze to Caitlin. "Not that I have anything against being polite, mind you, but are 'please' and 'thank you' all the words you know, or what?"

Esa sputtered and nearly choked on a mouthful of coffee. Ace's expression turned even darker. David suddenly became unaccountably interested in the shape of his cup handle.

"I, um . . ." Caitlin met her new brother-in-law's twinkling gaze. "I'd be happy to engage in a conversation, Joseph, if one of you will be so kind as to pick a subject."

"How about cattle?" Joseph grinned at Ace. "We're in the business now, you know."

"Yes, I know," Caitlin replied.

"The problem is, we don't know shit about cows."

"Watch your language," Ace inserted.

Joseph's smile widened. "Excuse me. We don't know diddly about cows." He arched a blond eyebrow at his older brother. "Better?"

Ace glanced at Esa. "Be sure to put soap on our supply list, Esa. When Ma gets here, we'll be needing a goodly amount."

Caitlin had washed out Patrick's mouth enough times when he was little to realize Ace had just issued a subtle threat. "What would you like to know about cattle?" she asked.

Joseph considered the question for a moment. "One thing I've been puzzling over is how a cattleman can look at a cow, then do a little figuring on a tablet and come up with its weight, almost to the pound."

Caitlin took another sip of coffee. "It's simple, actually. There's a formula."

The teasing twinkle disappeared from Joseph's eyes, replaced by serious interest. "What kind of formula?"

Caitlin felt Ace staring at her as well. From the corner of her eye, he looked impossibly large sitting beside her, the breadth of his shoulders dwarfing her own. Setting down her mug, she said, "Length and circumference, applied to a formula. It really is quite simple. It's most accurate if you take the cow's measurements, but even without a tape, you can make an educated guess and come close."

"Go on," Joseph urged.

She felt four pairs of eyes fixed raptly on her. "If you have paper and pencil, it would be easiest to just show you."

Joseph pushed up from the table and disappeared behind her into the room Ace had identified last night as the unfinished study. He returned seconds later with paper and pencil, which he slapped down on the table in front of her. Setting aside the potato poultice, Caitlin took up the pencil and angled the paper so she could write on it.

"Let's say you estimate a cow's heart girth at seventy-six inches and its body length at sixty-six inches. You multiply seventy-six by seventy-six, then multiply that amount by the body length, and divide that total by three hundred." She did some quick figuring. "The cow would weigh approximately twelve hundred and seventy pounds."

She shoved the paper across the table to Joseph. He studied it for a moment, then said, "Well, I'll be a son of a bitch. That is easy."

"Jesus H. Christ, Joseph. I said watch your language. She's going to think you were raised in a barn." The words had no sooner passed Ace's lips than a flush started to creep up his neck. He slanted Caitlin an apologetic glance. "I'm sorry, Caitlin. Please excuse my brother and me." He cleared his throat. "We seem to have a problem keeping our mouths clean."

Caitlin couldn't help but smile again. With a start, she realized that somewhere along the way, she'd begun to relax. She was a long way from feeling entirely comfortable in the company of these men, but she had to admit, they were all far nicer than she'd expected.

After the formula for estimating cattle weight had been passed around and duly studied by each of the men, the conversation turned to other cattle-raising concerns, such as proper feeding, winter and summer grazing practices, what caused and how to treat colic or scours, and how to save calves with pneumonia. Caitlin had never had her brain picked by members of the opposite sex. In her experience, the male gender tended to regard a woman's knowledge as worthless.

"Having you around is going to be a blessing," Joseph concluded. "We lost three calves last week. None of us knew for sure what the hell was wrong with them. We just stood around with our thumbs up our—"

"Joseph!" Ace cut in.

Joseph folded the paper Caitlin had done her figuring on and stuck it in his shirt pocket. "As I was saying, we just stood around, scratching our heads, and watched the poor things die. A man at the feed store said they had scours and gave me a long rubber hose to siphon broth and gelatin into them." He held up his hands. "I swear to God, that hose was this long. If I'd done what he told me and shoved it down one of their throats, it would have come clear out the south end."

Caitlin gave a startled laugh. "You have to measure from a certain point along the rib cage to tell how far to push the hose," she explained. "It's that long so you can reach the second stomach of any size calf."

Joseph made a mock toast to her with his mug. "Like I said, having you around is going to be a blessing. Next time we come up with a sick calf, we'll let you shove the hose down its throat and out its ass." He gave a low laugh. "Ace got it in about a foot before he got squeamish. I refused to even try. Here I thought that having to castrate the poor things was bad. The next thing we know, some damned fool is telling us to ream them out."

Ace shook his head and slid his coffee cup to the center of the table. "I give up, Joseph. You're hopeless."

"What'd I say now?"

Ace just chuckled and pushed up from the table. "Never mind." Settling a hand on Caitlin's shoulder, he said, "Excuse me, Caitlin. If I plan to pay your brother a visit this afternoon, I'd best get a stew on for lunch. While I'm doing that, I'd like you to choke down at least a few bites of your breakfast."

He spoke kindly, but there was no mistaking that it

was an order, just the same. Since her father's death, Caitlin had grown accustomed to making her own decisions, following her own rules. She resented being told what to do by another man, especially since she'd sworn to herself she'd never kowtow to anyone again.

Now that she was married, that vow took second seat to the ones she'd made to God and her new husband. There was no question that she'd do whatever Ace Keegan told her to do. She didn't have the courage to do otherwise. Years of groveling around her father had taught her that much. If it came to a choice between obeying an order or getting cuffed, she always took the path of least resistance. Always would.

She reached for the plate, hating herself for her cowardice, yet unable to help herself. She would eat, even if it made her sick to do so. It was a small thing, filling her mouth with flapjacks gone soggy with butter and honey. Unfortunately, the next time he demanded something from her, it wasn't likely to be so simple for her to oblige.

Even through her dress, her husband's touch made her skin tingle. He had a large, heavy hand, the grip of his long fingers incredibly strong. He wasn't hurting her, but she knew that, with very little effort, he could increase the pressure. There was a nerve right under the shoulder and along the outer edge of the collarbone where the vicious grip of a man's fingers could inflict paralyzing agony. Ace's fingertips rested directly over the spot, gently, almost caressingly, his strength restrained. The threat was there, nonetheless.

She tried to imagine those hands sliding over her body and started to dread the coming night. Sooner or later, he would insist she do her wifely duty. When he did, she wasn't sure she could submissively lie there and allow him the liberties he would want to take.

A mouthful of flapjack hung up in her throat. For a horrifying moment, she thought she might gag. Her shoulders jerked convulsively in her attempt to hold it back. Ace's hand tightened slightly on her shoulder.

"Honey, are you all right?"

The gagging sensation faded as she gulped determinedly to get the food down. Nodding, she forked another piece of flapjack and stuck it in her mouth. Groveling. She was so very good at it. As in all endeavors, one could attain perfection with practice.

✣ 18

CAITLIN'S HEART LEAPED INTO HER THROAT WHEN SHE turned from the cookstove and saw Ace standing in the kitchen archway with her cat clutched to his chest. The entire time he had been gone, she'd been worried about how his talk with Patrick would go. It had been her intent to quiz him relentlessly as soon as he got home, to make certain her brother was still in one piece. Now all thought of Patrick fled her mind.

"Lucky," she whispered. "You brought Lucky?"

Ace hefted the cat in his muscular arms. "He kept telling me he was hungry. I didn't have the heart to leave him, and I figured if you knew he wasn't being fed, you'd probably rather have him here."

Nothing could have been farther from the truth. Better that Lucky miss a few meals than to be thrust into what she felt certain would be an unfriendly environment here. The front of Ace's dark clothing was already covered with yellow hair, which she didn't take as a very good omen. Poor Lucky managed to be a pest even when on his best behavior.

Glancing up into Ace's twinkling brown eyes, she could see that he was hoping she would be pleased that he'd brought the cat back with him. She was anything but. Even after getting kicked innumerable times by her father, the poor cat still hadn't learned to stay out of the way. Around here, there would be four men to dodge.

Caitlin felt sickened at the thought of what might

happen to Lucky if he dared to pull any of his naughty tricks in Ace's house. He would very likely get knocked clear into next week by an angry male fist. Caitlin wasn't sure Lucky could survive such mistreatment. Not to mention that it would break her heart.

"Lucky," she said again. Stepping quickly forward, she wrested the plump cat from Ace's arms and cuddled him to her cheek. Flyaway hair drifted up from his fluffy yellow coat to tickle her nose. It was a hopeless situation. Within a day, her poor little kitty would be taking the brunt of four male tempers. She just knew it. "Oh, Lucky."

Caitlin closed her eyes. As much as she would have loved having her cat with her, she knew he would be better off at home. If Patrick kept drinking, he might scare the sand out of Lucky, but he'd never actually hurt him. "I know you meant well, Ace, but you really shouldn't have brought him here. He's not like most cats. I'm afraid he won't adjust well to a strange environment."

She lifted her lashes to discover that Ace was regarding her cat thoughtfully. "He doesn't strike me as the highly nervous type," he said with a crooked grin that flashed the deep dimple in his cheek. "I thought he'd raise holy hell when I climbed on my horse, but he handled the ride like a veteran. If he can take something like that in stride, surely he'll settle in here all right."

That was the entire problem; Lucky didn't have sense enough to be scared when he ought to be, and he was too stupid to learn from experience.

"You don't understand," she said shakily. "He isn't very well behaved, and because of his head injury, he isn't trainable. He may, um . . . " She sought her new husband's gaze. "What if he jumps up on the counter and tries to eat the meat laid out for supper, or something?"

Ace arched an eyebrow. "I guess someone will have to move him down."

Caitlin searched his gaze. "It will make you angry, surely."

He shrugged. "Maybe. If I get riled, I'll survive it. He's your pet, and this is your home now, Caitlin. We'll all have to make some adjustments, that's all."

"At home, he has a crate of dirt in my bedroom to potty in. I don't let him go outdoors much for fear he'll get hurt."

"I'll take a look in the barn. I think we have a couple of empty crates out there."

Caitlin hugged the cat more tightly to her chest. "I'd really prefer you just take him home. He's familiar with everything there, and I think he'll be far happier."

"Not without you, he won't." Ace gave the cat a measuring glance and smiled slightly again. "No offense intended, but it's obvious by his girth that he's accustomed to being fed well and frequently. That will no longer be the case if you leave him in Patrick's care. When I got over there, your brother's horse was still saddled and wandering loose in the barn. Hadn't been fed or watered. Didn't even get a good rubdown after being ridden hard. I found Patrick passed out in one of the stalls. Is that what you want for Lucky, to be neglected and left to starve while your brother is off somewhere, drinking himself into a stupor?"

Caitlin could think of no response. Of course that wasn't what she wanted for Lucky. It was just that his staying with Patrick seemed the lesser of two evils.

Ace caught her chin on the edge of his hand and lifted her face for his perusal. His smile deepened, revealing straight white teeth. "Let's give him a chance to see how he gets along," he said in a low, sonorous voice. "If he doesn't settle in, I can always take him back to Patrick. Right?"

That settled, at least to his satisfaction, he turned toward the stove. Caitlin fixed a worried gaze on his broad back. "If Patrick was passed out, I guess you didn't get to talk to him."

"Nope. I decided to leave him a note on the kitchen table."

"What did you say? In the note, I mean."

Grabbing a potholder, Ace glanced back over his

shoulder at her. "That, for your sake, he and I need to mend our differences, and that he has a standing invitation to visit you here any time he likes. I signed off by adding that I hoped he'd make it a point to drop by soon."

Caitlin's throat felt unaccountably dry. She swallowed and drew in a deep breath. "Thank you, Ace. I know you don't think very highly of him."

"Not so. He's your brother, and that makes him a very important person, in my estimation." He turned his attention back to the stove. "Whatever you have in that pot sure does smell good."

Preoccupied with other concerns, Caitlin gazed blankly at the cooking range. It took her a moment to recall what she'd been preparing for supper. "It's, um, sauerbraten. Esa brought in a roast from the smokehouse. I thought you all might enjoy having something a little different tonight. I got the recipe from Romilda Eisenbein, the lady who has the German restaurant on Main Street. She made sauerbraten for one of our church potlucks a few months back, and it was so delicious that—" She realized she was rambling and broke off. "I hope you don't mind my experimenting."

"Mind?" The warm twinkle in his eyes became more pronounced. "We haven't had a decent meal around here in so long we'll probably be worshipping at your feet before the week is out. I'm just sorry you ended up doing kitchen duty your first day here. Where the hell are my brothers?"

"David and Esa rode out to check on a calf they thought was looking peaked yesterday, and Joseph said he had chores to do. He took the milk bucket, so I assume he's out milking the cow."

Glancing past her out the window above the sink, Ace said, "I guess it is getting to be about that time." He lifted the lid of the pot and sniffed the rising steam. "Mmm, that does smell good." He rolled back his shirt sleeves and stepped over to the water pump. As he worked the handle, he asked, "What can I do to help?"

In truth, Caitlin preferred to be left alone. The

thought of rubbing elbows with him for another hour while she finished fixing supper wasn't highly appealing. As kitchens went, this one was large and roomy, but with Ace in here with her, it seemed a lot smaller than before. "I'm sure you have better things to do than cook."

"Not a damned thing," he assured her. "My brothers can handle the chores for a few days. You and I have been married less than twenty-four hours, remember. I feel bad enough that you didn't get to have a nice wedding or a traditional honeymoon. It seems that the least I can do is take some time off so the two of us can get to know each other a little better."

Caitlin yearned to say, "Don't do me any favors." Instead, she caught the inside of her cheek between her teeth and kept her mouth shut.

Grabbing a towel off the hook beside the window, he quickly dried his hands, then used the damp linen to brush off his shirt and trousers. When his clothing was finally somewhat divested of cat hair, he tossed the towel into a corner and turned to regard her with his unsettling dark eyes. "Now, what can I do to help with this wonderful supper you're fixing?"

With a reluctance she had difficulty concealing, Caitlin bent to put Lucky down. The instant the cat's feet touched the floor, he waddled off to explore. She gazed after him, still gnawing on her cheek.

"Sweetheart, would you relax?" Ace said softly. "There's nothing he can hurt in here."

"He may potty on the floor if he doesn't have a box of dirt."

Ace bent forward and planted a kiss on her forehead. Startled, Caitlin reared back. When their gazes met, he gave her a mischievous wink. "If he makes a mess, I've got nearly a whole case of toilet paper in the water closet I ordered from Montgomery Ward and Company. We'll just clean it up, all right? These floors have three coats of varnish on them. They can take a little abuse without being permanently damaged, believe me. I'll have Joseph get you a crate full of dirt as soon as he comes in from the barn."

Dubious, Caitlin watched him step over to lift the lid off the roasting pot again. Leaning low, he hauled in another deep breath of the rising steam. "Lord, honey, that does smell divine. What're we going to fix to go with it?"

Caitlin was tempted to tell him the roast would never get tender if he kept letting the steam escape, but she didn't have the gumption. "I, um . . ." She gestured toward the pantry off the kitchen. "I saw some potatoes and turnips in there. I thought I'd peel some of those."

"How about a tin of corn to go with them," he suggested, rubbing his hands together.

With four men to feed, she doubted one small tin of corn would stretch. "Have you plenty?"

"One thing I don't dare run low on around here is canned foods. We've got a garden planted out beside the barn, but it won't start producing for a couple of months yet." He stepped into the large pantry and took three tins of corn from a shelf. Glancing back at her, he said, "Any time you need anything for the house or yourself, don't be shy. Esa keeps a list hanging here just inside the door. Make a note of anything you need or want, and I'll be sure to get it the next time I go to town."

Before he exited the pantry, he winked at her and stopped to jot something on the list. A few minutes later, Caitlin couldn't resist stepping over to see what he'd written. Her heart caught when she read the words.

A tub full of chocolate for Caitlin.

BY THE TIME CAITLIN GOT SUPPER ON THE TABLE, HER nerves were completely frazzled. Living up to her prediction, Lucky relieved himself in one corner of the living room shortly after she turned him loose, and despite her protests, Ace fetched toilet paper to clean up the mess himself. Fully expecting him to get angry and turn on the poor cat at any moment, Caitlin hovered at his elbow, determined to protect her pet if necessary, yet quailing at the thought of standing up to her new husband if he flew into a sudden rage. Ace Keegan was intimidating enough when his mood was mild.

As soon as Joseph returned to the house, Ace requested that he go back outdoors to find a crate and fill it with dirt for Lucky. Joseph did so, but only after he cursed to turn the air blue. Cats, he contended, had never been meant to stay indoors. According to him, there was nearly four hundred acres of dirt outside for Lucky to piss in. That being the case, it made no sense to bring a box full of dirt into the house.

After some discussion, during which Caitlin had difficulty making herself heard over the loud and angry discourse of the two men, the cat box was positioned in one corner of the master bedroom. Joseph direly predicted that the box would start to stink the instant Lucky began to use it.

As it turned out, getting Lucky to use the box turned out to be the greatest problem. Immediately after the crate was put in the bedroom, Caitlin carried her pet to that corner and showed him the dirt, after which Lucky promptly forgot its location and relieved himself in the corner of the living room again. To Caitlin's surprise, instead of getting angry, Ace suggested the box be moved to accommodate the cat, instead of the other way around. Joseph made no secret of the fact that he was none too pleased with the arrangement. A cat toilet in the living room? Everyone who walked in the door would be bound to smell it.

Caitlin was nearly in tears by the time she finally put supper on the table. After saying a cursory and appallingly insincere blessing, the four males heaped their plates and began shoveling. Hoping that the meal might mollify her disgruntled brothers-in-law, Caitlin's heart sank when Esa spat out his first mouthful of supper.

"Don't eat the meat," he announced. "Something's wrong with it."

Everyone at the table froze in varying positions, Joseph with his cheek bulging, David with a forkful of roast halfway to his lips, and Ace with his coffee mug suspended in midair.

"It's sauerbraten," Caitlin explained in a voice gone thin with nervousness.

"I knew it," Esa said, scrubbing his lips clean with the sleeve of his shirt. "I wonder what made it go sour?"

"Vinegar," Ace put in. "There's nothing wrong with the meat, Esa. It's a special German dish Caitlin made for us."

Joseph gulped down his unchewed mouthful. "You mean she took a perfectly good roast and made it sour like this on purpose?"

Caitlin had to admit the meat was a little more tart than Romilda's had been. She glanced around the table to find that Ace's brothers were all regarding her as if she were out of her mind. Contrary to Ace's prediction, they were a long way from worshipping at her feet. She bent her head over her plate and forked a slice of turnip into her mouth as an awful silence descended.

Finally she heard the sound of silver scraping china again. When she glanced back up, Ace's three brothers were all busily applying themselves to the meal, their expressions glum. So much for pleasing them with something different for supper.

Joseph was determinedly chewing his third bite of roast when Lucky leaped onto the table and proceeded to stroll the length of it, stopping at each dish to sniff the contents. Caitlin, sitting to Ace's right, was so horrified she couldn't move, and everyone else seemed to be equally dumbfounded. Only Lucky seemed oblivious to the tension, unable to grasp in his dimwitted brain that he might be placing himself in serious peril. When the cat happened upon the roast, he greedily attacked, displaying none of the men's distaste for the sour taste.

Ace was the first to finally react. He shot to his feet, leaned forward, and hooked a large hand under the cat's rotund middle. Caitlin, caught in a tangle of skirt and bench legs, nearly lost her balance when she leaped up.

Grabbing Ace's arm, she cried, "Don't hurt him. Please, don't. He hasn't any idea he's doing something wrong!"

Keeping a firm grip on the cat, Ace nestled him in the crook of one arm. "I have no intention of hurting him, honey."

Ace directed a glance at his youngest brother. "Esa, cut off Lucky's end of the roast, would you, please? I'll go get him a bowl."

When Ace struck off for the kitchen with the cat still tucked under his arm, Caitlin ran after him, convinced he would wring Lucky's neck the minute he was out of her sight. Instead, he went directly to the cupboard, fetched a bowl, and nearly ran over her when he turned around. Caitlin fell back, once again nearly losing her balance.

"Sweetheart, would you relax?" he said softly. "No one is going to hurt the goddamned cat, I promise you."

That he was now referring to Lucky as "the goddamned cat" did little to ease Caitlin's mind.

"He meant no harm," she hastened to explain. "Honestly, he didn't. Ever since my father threw him against a wall, he's been dimwitted. He doesn't mean to do bad things. He just doesn't understand that they're wrong."

Ace turned the cat slightly to gaze into its badly crossed eyes. "Against a wall?"

Caitlin gulped. She hadn't meant to divulge that bit of information. She felt a scalding heat inch up her neck. "I tried to stop my father from hurting him. Really, I did. But he was drunk, and when I—" She broke off and wrung her hands. "He was so angry with Lucky, there was just no stopping him."

Ace's heart caught at the expression in Caitlin's blue eyes. She wasn't just embarrassed to admit what had happened to Lucky, but ashamed. As if she were somehow to blame. He tried to imagine her going toe-to-toe with Conor O'Shannessy when he was in a drunken rage. The top of her head barely cleared Ace's shoulder. He doubted she weighed a hundred and ten pounds, soaking wet. That she had tried to interfere with her father to protect a cat was beyond his comprehension. That she felt ashamed for having failed was even more befuddling.

"Caitlin, you aren't responsible for Lucky's retardedness."

"Yes."

That one word, uttered so faintly, made Ace ache for her.

"No," he said. "Nothing your father ever did was in any way your fault. Not his treatment of Lucky or anything else."

Ignoring the silent plea in her eyes, Ace kept hold of the cat. As difficult as it might be for her, she had to learn that he wasn't of her father's ilk. Lucky would not be thrown against a wall in this household, no matter what he did. Unfortunately, the only way Caitlin would ever be convinced of that was from experience.

Acutely aware of her trailing in his footsteps, Ace returned to the supper table and extended the bowl to Esa so he might transfer the ruined portion of roast onto it. Lucky, purring loudly, happily began to eat the minute Ace lowered him and his purloined supper to the floor. Resuming his seat at the head of the table, Ace pretended not to notice that Caitlin stood at his elbow, apparently ready to grab her cat and bolt. Giving each of his brothers a silent glare that spoke volumes, he picked up his fork.

For what seemed like an endless moment, Joseph sat staring down at the cat, his expression filled with distaste. Only when he finally began to eat again did Caitlin sit back down. It wasn't long before Ace noticed that his wife wasn't touching her food. He considered insisting she eat because he didn't want her to get sick again, then he decided she'd be better off left alone. Hopefully, she would begin to relax around him and his brothers soon. Time enough then to get some meat on her bones.

BEDTIME. WITH BUILDING DREAD, CAITLIN HAD ANTICIPATED its coming all day. By the time Ace's brothers retired to the barn that night and Ace began turning out the lanterns, she was a bundle of raw nerves. Last night, her husband had refrained from exercising his conjugal rights. She didn't expect him to be so generous again. *A day at a time,* he'd said. This was night number two.

Scurrying ahead of him to the bedroom, Caitlin made short work of dressing for bed, convinced that he would barge in on her at any moment and catch her half clothed. She was more than a little relieved when that did not prove to be the case. Climbing quickly into bed, she huddled in a ball and drew the quilt to her chin. Maybe, just maybe, he would leave her alone if she pretended to be asleep.

She had no sooner squeezed her eyes closed than a light knock came at the door. Startled, she lifted her lashes. Another light rap of male knuckles against wood made her start. She gnawed her lower lip. If she called out for him to enter, he would know she wasn't asleep.

Rolling over, Caitlin put her back to the door and jerked the quilt over her head. Tap, tap. She flinched with each report. Finally, the door creaked open.

"Caitlin, are you decent?"

She clenched her teeth, almost afraid to breathe. She heard the light thump of his footsteps as he crossed the room, the sole of one boot shuffling softly over the floorboards. The next second, his weight depressed the outer edge of the mattress and the support ropes groaned. She listened to the sounds he made as he divested himself of his clothing. Boots thumped. Cloth rustled. His holster thudded against the wood as he slung his gun belt over the bedpost.

Her eyes flew open when she heard pocket change chinking. Had he taken off his trousers? Her heart kicked violently against her ribs. The next instant, cool air struck her backside as he lifted the covers to slide in next to her. The mattress bucked under her as he bounced around to get comfortable, his greater weight forming a depression that threatened to swallow her. Caitlin squeezed her eyes closed again. Making fists in the sheet and the ticking beneath, she strained not to roll toward him.

The effort proved absolutely futile. A hard, muscular arm hooked her around the waist. A broad, well-padded chest pressed hotly against her back. The quilt drew away from her face, and the heavy blackness that pressed against her eyelids told her he had doused the light. She tried to ignore the various parts of his body as they connected with hers. Thighs roped with steely tendons. Wide, bony knees. A hairy shin bone brushing against the heel of her foot. Oh, God.

She assured herself that, short of rape itself, this would

be the worst of it. He couldn't possibly subject her to any more indignities than he already was. And then he settled a large hand over her midriff, his long, blunt fingers nestling familiarly against the underside of her right breast. His touch seared through her chemise and nightgown as though they didn't exist. Despite her resolve to pretend she was sleeping, she jerked. She couldn't help it. To be touched there . . . well, it was so unnerving, she simply couldn't control her reaction.

"You're awake," he murmured against her nape, his breath tickling the fine hair there. "I figured you probably were."

"Mmm," was her response.

He settled his hand more snugly beneath her breast, nearly making her heart stop. Memories flashed through her mind—of how it felt to be held down by someone stronger than she, how terrifying it had been to be explored by rough hands, helpless to stop the pain, suffering humiliation beyond bearing. There would be little she could do to protect herself, not against strength such as Ace Keegan's. A lump of dread rose in her throat.

"Why didn't you answer when I knocked?"

Surely he already knew the answer. If she tried to concoct a lie, he would see right through it. "I, um . . ." She couldn't stand his touch. Grabbing his hand, she dug in with all five fingernails. "I was hoping—maybe—that you wouldn't—well, you know—if I was asleep."

He shifted his weight. To her dismay, he managed to hunch his broad shoulders around her, cocooning the back of her torso in a blanket of warm, resilient flesh that reminded her of velvet over steel. "I see."

She waited for him to say more. When nothing else seemed forthcoming, she lay in an agony of waiting. He suddenly wiggled his trapped fingers. "You're cutting off the circulation."

She relaxed her hold on his hand a little, pleasantly surprised when he didn't move it. She swallowed. She hoped he couldn't feel her shaking. Fat chance. He hadn't left enough space between their bodies for a flea to wiggle.

"Caitlin . . ."

"Wh-what?"

He lay silent for a moment. Then he rubbed his nose against her hair, which, for hurry's sake, she'd left braided in a coronet atop her head. So much for its usual hundred strokes.

"Correct me if I'm wrong, but are you under the gross misconception that you are controlling my hand by hanging onto it like that?"

She realized she was squeezing the life out of his fingers again. Forcing herself to once again relax her grip, she replied in a humiliatingly squeaky voice, "Of course not."

"Good," he murmured against her nape, his escaping breath raising goose bumps on her skin. "Because the truth is, if I wanted to touch your breast, you wouldn't have a snowball's chance in hell of stopping me."

The words hung between them like icicles from eaves. Caitlin's mouth felt as dry as jerky. "Are you g-going to?"

"Am I going to what?"

"T-touch me there."

"Not unless you'd like me to."

She stifled an hysterical urge to laugh, the sensation quickly becoming an ache inside her chest. "Like you to?" she finally managed to say.

She felt his shoulders jerk. On the tail end of a low chuckle, he said, "I assure you, Caitlin, it will happen one day. Up to your neck in melted chocolate, remember? I can be an irresistible fellow when I set my mind to it."

He said nothing more. Just held her close, his body warming hers. After a few minutes, Caitlin heard his breathing deepen and grow raspy.

Was he asleep? She couldn't believe it. Yet when she moved his hand, it was limp. He was asleep. Sound asleep. She nearly wept with relief.

For a long while, she lay rigid, half afraid to so much as wiggle a toe. Then she finally started to relax. Moonlight slanted through the window, gathering like pools of silver on the rumpled quilt. Caitlin gazed at it for a long while.

It was a very long time before she drifted into slumber.

❧ 19

Ace AWOKE TO A HEAVY, BREATHLESS FEELING AND A tickling sensation under his nose. Cracking open one eye, he discovered that a cat was standing on his chest, its golden rump mere inches from his face, the tip of its tail occasionally flicking his nostrils.

Lucky. Ace gave the cat a gentle nudge to get its posterior out of his face, whereupon four feet, weighed down by what felt like a hundred pounds, went tromping down his belly. Claws dug in, prickling his skin with every gut-jarring step. Only then did Ace realize he'd shoved off the quilt during the night and lay covered by only the thin cotton of his underdrawers and the linen sheet.

Like most men, when Ace first woke up of a morning, he usually had an erection. Today was no exception, the only difference being that this time Lucky had a front row seat for the performance. When the sheet began to wiggle, as sheets tend to do at such a time, the cat launched itself forward and brutally attacked.

"Jesus H. Christ!" Ace grabbed his crotch, pitched sideways, and hit the floor on all fours. "Son of a bitch!"

"What?" Caitlin bounded from the bed, bloomers flashing beneath the uplifted hem of her nightgown. She whirled to search the room, then turned back to him, clearly bewildered. "What! What is it?"

"That goddamned cat!" Ace clenched his teeth. "He attacked me!"

When Ace straightened with both hands thrust between his thighs, her eyes went as round as supper plates. Her horrified gaze dropped. "Oh, Ace, I'm so sorry. Did he hurt you?" She glanced frantically around the room again, this time in search of her cat. "I'm sure he didn't mean any harm. I wiggle the tip of my finger under the sheet for him sometimes. He must have thought——" She jerked her gaze back to his lower portions. "Oh, my. He must have thought you were playing mouse."

Playing mouse? Ace set his teeth. Mice were pathetic, inconsequential little creatures.

The door crashed open, and Joseph ran in. He came reeling to a stop, holding his gun in one hand, looking ready to start shooting at anything that moved. After glancing around the room, he fixed a questioning gaze on Ace. "What the hell happened? Where is the son of a bitch?"

Caitlin threw herself between Joseph and the bed. "I won't let you shoot him. You'll have to shoot me first!"

Bewildered, Joseph glanced past her. "He's hiding under the bed? The miserable coward."

Ace was slowly beginning to realize that his manhood was still intact. Feeling foolish, he jerked his hands from between his thighs and sat back on his heels, acutely aware that his wife was staring at his brother as if he'd sprouted horns and a third eye.

"It isn't Patrick, Joseph. The cat attacked me, that's all."

"The cat?" Joseph repeated incredulously. "You scared the living shit right out of me! I thought O'Shannessy had sneaked in here."

"I'm sorry. Lucky took me by surprise, that's all. I hollered without thinking."

Caitlin wrung her hands. "He didn't mean to hurt anyone. Truly, he didn't. I'm sure he thought Ace was playing mouse with him. Lucky and I do that a lot."

Joseph shot a glance in the general direction of Ace's lap. His entire face turned an amazing shade of crimson. He slowly holstered his gun. "I see," he said in an oddly tight voice.

"I'm all right," Ace managed to say in equally strained tones. "I think so, anyway."

From the corner of his eye, he saw a streak of yellow shoot from under the bed and disappear out the bedroom doorway. Lucky was smarter than Caitlin thought. He knew enough to run like hell.

Ace pushed to his feet and raked his fingers through his hair. "Go on. Get out of here," he told his brother. "We'll be out as soon as we get dressed."

When Joseph had exited the room and closed the door behind him, Ace went to take his wife by her shoulders. She looked adorable in her rumpled nightgown, her hair straggling in unruly bunches of curls to her shoulders. "I'm sorry for roaring that way. I kind of—" He broke off, his gaze fixed on her flushed face. Unless he missed his guess, she was trying her damnedest not to laugh. "Is something funny, Mrs. Keegan?"

She gave her head a brisk shake, curls bobbing. "Not at all," she said thinly. "I hope that, um, Lucky didn't do you any permanent damage?"

"Is that a hopeful note I hear in your voice?"

A high-pitched giggle escaped her. She clamped a hand over her mouth, her eyes wide above her tightly clenched fingers.

"You know," he told her in a teasingly gruff tone, "laughing at me under the present circumstances probably isn't the smartest move you've ever made."

Her mirth instantly evaporated. The delightful twinkle in her eyes vanished, replaced by a sudden darkness that reminded him of storm clouds drifting across a summer sky. Ace wanted to kick himself for spoiling the moment.

Brushing her hand aside, he caught hold of her small chin and lifted her face. "Honey, I'm teasing you."

"You are?"

Ace yearned to kiss the suddenly tremulous corners of her mouth. "Of course, I am. It didn't seem all that funny when it happened, but I have to admit it does in retrospect."

He bent to press a light kiss to her forehead. "Get dressed, Mrs. Keegan. I think I smell breakfast cooking.

Joseph's eggs are bad enough when they're piping hot. We probably won't be able to choke them down if we let them get cold."

Turning away from her, Ace grabbed his trousers from the chair. To his consternation, the black cloth was covered with yellow cat hair, irrefutable evidence that Lucky had slept on his clothes most of the night. Biting back a curse, he gave his pants a shake and batted at them with his hand. Hair flew, tickling his nostrils.

Caitlin scurried to the dressing room, which didn't yet have a door. From the corner of his eye, Ace saw her peek around the wall at him, then she disappeared from sight. Judging by the sounds that drifted out, Ace guessed she was pouring water from the pitcher into the wash basin. Surprised that she trusted him enough to dare wash up before donning her clothing, he shot an amazed look at the yawning doorway.

He froze with one foot stuffed into a trouser leg. The mirror. Special ordered from Montgomery Ward and Company, it was a full-length dressing mirror, positioned handily beside the closet. Unbeknownst to Caitlin, who stood at an angle across from it, she was reflected in the glass from head to toe.

Ace knew he should look away. He *tried* to look away, but his baser instincts were momentarily in full reign. His wife had stripped off her soiled chemise, which according to his calculations, she'd been wearing for three days running, to change into a fresh one. Before donning it, she was bathing her upper torso with a moist cloth. Clearly in a hurry for fear that he might intrude upon her privacy, she took rough swipes at her armpits and jiggled her breasts up and down with jerky scrubbing motions.

Ace had seen his share of breasts. Maybe more than his fair share. But never a set as lovely as hers. Shaped like succulent little melons, they were flawless ivory veined faintly with blue, their crests an incredibly delicate rose that put him in mind of cream pinkened slightly with strawberry juice. Stimulated by the brisk rubbing, the tips had sprung to a tantalizing erectness that made his mouth salivate.

He forced his gaze away, ashamed of himself for breaking her trust. Someday—soon, he hoped—she'd stand before him in all her naked splendor. When she did, he could look his fill. And touch her. And taste the sweetness of her. But not until she came to him willingly.

His manhood throbbing, Ace jerked his trousers on.

WHEN CAITLIN EMERGED FROM THE BEDROOM A WHILE later, she found all the men in her new family, including her husband, gathered around the breakfast table. Ace's black shirt was still lightly covered with cat hair. Beside Joseph on the bench, Lucky sat preening, an empty bowl beside him. Esa, his mouth edged in white, plunked his milk glass down on the table.

"Your cat likes hot sauce on his scrambled eggs. Can you believe it?"

What Caitlin had difficulty believing was that their seating arrangements had evidently been changed to make room for Lucky on the bench. As she circled behind Ace, who sat at the head of the table, she cast Joseph a bewildered look.

He flashed her a broad grin and winked. "Anybody who manages to get Ace by the balls is my friend for life."

Ace threw his napkin down in the middle of his half finished plate of food. "Jesus H. Christ, Joseph, I can't believe the things that come out of your mouth."

David and Esa both snickered. Caitlin flipped around and went into the kitchen. It was that or burst out laughing. So far, Ace had been a good sport about Lucky's attack on his unmentionable parts, but his magnanimous attitude might go the way of the wind if he became the target of too much teasing. For Lucky's sake, she hoped the incident would soon be forgotten.

"Just help yourself," Joseph called to her. "Everything's in skillets on the stove." In a lower voice she could only assume she wasn't meant to hear, he added jokingly, "Hopefully no mouse will jump out from under the stove at her. Not without Lucky in there to protect her. Dangerous little buggers, those mice."

Caitlin heard a bench scrape the floor. She had just

lifted the lid off the skillet of scrambled eggs when Ace walked up behind her, and settled his large hands warmly on her waist. She gave a startled squeak and nearly dropped her plate. He chuckled and bent to nibble her ear.

After what seemed an unbearably long while, he finally ceased the nibbling and said in a throbbing whisper, "After a meal, a man always likes a little dessert, you know. There's nothing I'd rather have than a taste of you."

Caitlin stood stock still. Her new husband clearly saw her as a delectable dish he meant to sample. Her only question was, how long might he wait before digging in?

Nuzzling the curve of her neck, which set nerve-endings to tingling that she hadn't realized she possessed, he murmured, "God, you do smell sweet."

"You must be afflicted with a chronic case of catarrh. In truth, I'm in desperate need of a bath."

"I'll bring in the tub. The boys'll be out most of the morning doing chores."

The boys weren't Caitlin's main concern. Evading her husband's searching mouth, she gave him a look over her shoulder. His dark face, illuminated on one side by a shaft of sunlight coming through the window, was so handsome her heart caught. Pitch black hair trailed in loose waves over his high forehead. A burnished glint defined the slightly crooked bridge of his nose. His eyes were the color of hot fudge, and his full yet firm lips shimmered like silk.

"Where will you be this morning?" she asked weakly.

"Where do you want me to be?"

"Long gone."

His broad shoulders shook with laughter. "Damn. I was hoping you might ask me to wash your back."

"Don't you have a back scrubber?"

He held up a brown palm. "See all those calluses? They work great."

Her heart skittering at the thought, Caitlin turned back to the stove and began dishing herself some eggs. She stopped after a moment, staring at the gigantic portion she'd plopped on the plate.

"Nervous?" he asked softly.

She sniffed and slid some of the eggs back into the skillet. "Should I be?"

He gave her neck another nuzzle, then left the kitchen without answering. A second later, she heard the front door open and close. She finished dishing up her breakfast and took her plate to the table. She was just sitting down when she heard the door open again. She glanced up to see Ace reenter the house carrying a huge galvanized bathtub. He winked at her over the rim as he made his way toward the kitchen.

"It ain't Saturday," Esa said in a complaining voice. "Don't tell me we all gotta take baths again."

"Only Caitlin," Ace called as he plunked the tub down on the floor in plain view of everyone in the adjoining room. "I promised her you boys would all make yourselves scarce until lunch."

David leaned forward and whispered conspiratorially, "Be sure to wash your ears good, Caitlin. Ace always checks."

"Fingernails, too," Joseph said with a grin.

Caitlin managed a strained smile.

BEFORE STRIPPING DOWN TO IMMERSE HERSELF IN THE TUB OF piping-hot water, Caitlin locked all the doors—an effort in futility if Ace had keys, which she felt certain he must—and drew shut the front window curtains, which proved to be crookedly cut strips of old sheeting pinned haphazardly over a wooden dowel. The unhemmed panels served the purpose of protecting her privacy, nonetheless, which was more than she could say for the kitchen window, which the men had left bare.

She undressed with the harried swiftness of an actress peeling off a costume backstage between acts. Into the tub she went, the thought never far from her mind that unseen eyes might be watching her. At every little noise, she jumped with a start. What if Ace walked in?

Just the thought of being caught naked and defenseless in the tub set her heart to thudding. Quickly dunking herself, Caitlin set to work scrubbing her hair, making

short work of the job for fear the door might bang open
at any moment. So, he thought his calloused palm would
make an ideal back scrubber, did he? Not on her life.

Wincing when her fingertips accidentally connected
with the gash at her temple, Caitlin recalled her ungainly
exit through the back door the other night. Gingerly, she
touched the scrape on her shoulder, pleased to feel that
the sores there were healing over quite nicely. The
deeper ones on her hip and back were still a little tender,
but not uncomfortably so. Ace's insistence that the
abrasions be disinfected had saved her from getting any
inflammation.

A slight frown pleated Caitlin's brow. What with all
her injuries, the bruise on her cheek notwithstanding, it
was no wonder Ace wasn't sneaking in here to catch her
at her bath. In fact, now that she thought about it, that
was probably why he hadn't yet insisted she submit to
him in the marriage bed. He was squeamish. He'd
admitted as much himself. If blood dampened his ardor,
scabs and bruises undoubtedly did as well.

Suddenly Caitlin didn't feel quite so pleased that all
her injuries were healing quickly. In her present circumstances, the unsightly sores might be all that was saving
her.

Despite the steaming hot water that lapped over her
skin, Caitlin shivered. Last night, Ace had completely
surprised her by doing nothing, but would he be so kind
again tonight?

Like poisonous spiders scrambling from a dark corner,
awful memories assailed her, just as they had last night.
Propping an elbow on the edge of the tub, Caitlin
pressed a wet hand over her face and sobbed. She would
never forget that night. Never, not as long as she lived.
Even more frightening, she might endure worse treatment at Ace Keegan's hands. He was a far larger man
than her rapist had been, and much stronger as well.

She remembered all the times he had touched her, the
latent strength in his hands. He could easily hold both
her wrists in one of those hands, leaving the other free to
take liberties. Just that quickly, and she could be pinned
beneath him, as defenseless as a child.

Suddenly the constant tension she'd been under the last two days seemed overwhelming. Another sob tore up her throat. She wouldn't trust him, she promised herself. All his niceness had to be an act. Sooner or later, his true colors would start to show.

✖ 20

DETERMINED TO FOLLOW THROUGH ON THE PROMISE TO herself that she would never trust Ace, Caitlin allowed nothing he did to alter her low opinion of him. When night after night passed without his forcing her to submit to him in the marriage bed, she told herself he was only waiting to spring his trap. Once he realized his ploys to gain her favor would never work, he'd turn on her just as she'd expected him to from the very beginning.

When Lucky had survived several days in the Keegan household without sustaining a serious injury, Caitlin convinced herself the cat simply hadn't done anything awful enough yet to get anyone riled. Sooner or later, poor Lucky would make one of the men explode, and then it would be left to her to protect her pet from serious, if not fatal, harm.

In Caitlin's mind, the passing days became a blur, one giving way to another, and then another, until a week had elapsed. Deep down, in a place she didn't want to explore and refused to acknowledge, she began to develop a bone-shaking fear, not that she or Lucky might come to a disastrous end at Ace Keegan's hands, but that they wouldn't.

Ace loved to laugh, deep, rich, soul-warming laughter. Sometimes when he wrapped his strong arms around her in a bear hug and refused to let go, she felt as if all the wishes she'd once made as a frightened little girl were finally coming true. A big strong man who would step forward from the crowd and fight for her. *I'd like to pay him a social call. Introduce his tonsils to his asshole. Make him wish his mother had been a nun.* Someone who would buy sugar once in a while for candy. *A tub full of chocolate for Caitlin.* He hadn't brought her a whole tub full, of course, but he had given her a huge box filled with layers of dipped chocolate candy. And there was always plenty of sugar in the house for any sweet she wished to make.

I wish I may, I wish I might.

He seemed to find the strangest things funny. One morning, when he went to find his Stetson, it was to discover that Lucky had used the inverted hat for a potty box. When he strode from the bedroom to inform Caitlin of her cat's latest shenanigan, she fully expected him to fly into a rage. Instead, he said, "Well, at least now Joseph won't be exaggerating when he calls me a shit head." With that, he burst into uproarious laughter that didn't cease until he was holding his sides and tears were streaming down his cheeks. Luckily, he had a spare hat.

Under such circumstances, it wasn't easy for Caitlin to cling to her old convictions. Piece by piece, Ace was chipping away at her fear of him. Day by day, she became less uneasy in his presence. The change ate at her. Terrified her. If he didn't stop this infernal make-believe soon, she might find herself doing something truly stupid—like falling in love with him. In doing so, she would be thumbing her nose at every lesson life had ever taught her.

Only a fool turned her back on reality and invested her heart in fairy tales. Heroes were few and far between. She'd learned that as a little girl, and unless she'd missed some earth-shaking event, human nature hadn't changed all that much since then. Most men didn't charge into women's lives on glistening black steeds to rescue them. They did use force of arm to get what they wanted, and then used their authority as males to keep it. Women accepted what they got dished out to them.

If she allowed Ace Keegan to convince her that there were such things as heroes and miracles and magic, then she deserved any heartache he slung at her.

Oh, no . . . Not her. She was too smart for that. Never her.

After Caitlin had been there a week, construction on the house resumed. "Finish work," Ace called it. Caitlin soon began to think of it as "cussed work," for it seemed to her that Ace and his brothers spent more time cussing than anything else. Not a man among them was very adept with hammer and nails, and they were even less impressive with a saw.

Since Caitlin had come to accept the fact that she was doomed to remain at the Paradise and would consequently have to live with her husband and his brothers' failures, she did the only thing a woman could do under the circumstances; she decided to help.

One afternoon, while looking over Ace's shoulder as he tried to construct a vanity table for the water closet, Caitlin said, "That isn't how you cut a forty-five degree angle."

Four pairs of eyes turned on her, none of them friendly. Around nails he held clenched between his teeth, Ace said, "Oh, really? Pray, tell me how you cut one."

"Well, a miter would help."

Joseph, who was kneeling in the opposite corner making hash of a length of mopboard, tossed down his handsaw. "If a miter is a little person who stands around with her thumb up her nose, telling everyone else what they're doing wrong, we already have one."

Sensing that none of the men were in the best of moods, Caitlin made ready to retreat, but Ace interjected, "Oh, no, you don't. You opened the can of worms. What the hell is a miter?"

Caitlin inched toward the door, the smell of sawdust stinging her nostrils. "It's, um, nothing that important. I didn't mean to criticize your work." She glanced around at the horrific mess. "You're doing—a wonderful job here. Truly."

"Caitlin . . ." Ace's voice held a note of warning.

"We're not idiots. We know how things are supposed to fit together. We just can't seem to—" He threw down his hammer. "What the hell is a miter?"

She wrung her hands. "Well, I suppose I could make you one. It's a gadget you use for cutting. It has guides for your boards and grooves in which to make your cuts. It simplifies angular sawing tremendously."

"I'll be damned," David said. "I knew there had to be an easy way to make these cuts. No wonder we're botching everything."

From then on, Caitlin became a member of the work crew. Aside from the occasional outburst of profanity when one of the men pulverized a thumb with a hammer, she rather enjoyed the experience. With her assistance, the water closet was completed in record time, the only snag being that after Ace installed the inside plumbing from the attic to the water closet, water refused to flow through the pipes.

Everyone stood expectantly over the lovely new bathtub that had just arrived from Montgomery Ward and Company, their ears straining for any sound that might possibly be a gurgle of water.

"If this isn't a fine how-do-you-do," Ace bit out. "I can't believe I spent all that money—I even built a gas water heater, for Christ's sake!—and now the damned plumbing won't work."

Joseph gave vent by kicking a leg of the tub. "Why that surprises you, I don't know. Name me one thing in this goddamned house that worked the first time around. Remember the chimney?"

"Shut up!"

Joseph winked at Caitlin. "With the first light rain, the mortar dissolved. We woke up in the morning to a mushy rock pile."

Ace shot him a glare. "It's fine now, isn't it?" He followed his brother's example and kicked the bathtub. "I'll get the damned plumbing to work."

"One of us could use the tub for a bed," Esa said with a chuckle. "At this rate, it'll be a year before we get the bedrooms finished."

"I said shut up!" Ace ground out between partially

clenched teeth. His eyes fairly glittered as he glanced at each of them, Caitlin included. "Now is no time to joke."

Lucky chose that moment to waddle into the room. He headed straight for Ace's black pant legs, whereupon he began to rub and arch his back, depositing a goodly amount of hair on the jet denim. Ace stared down at him as if he were contemplating murder. Caitlin jumped forward to pick up her cat. Ace shot out a hand to grasp her shoulder.

"Leave him be. He's fine."

"But he's getting hair all over—"

"I can see that," he said in a more mellow tone. He bent to scoop Lucky up in a large hand. With a twist of his wrist, he put the cat nose-to-nose with him. "You and I have an understanding, don't we, Lucky?" Ace glanced at Caitlin. "He sheds and I wear it."

Caitlin hugged her waist, her gaze fixed on her hapless kitty. Lucky looked around at everyone with badly crossed eyes. Joseph chuckled.

"That has got to be the dumbest-looking animal I've ever seen."

"No look to it," Esa inserted. "He *is* dumb."

"He can't help it," Caitlin said. "His brains got rattled."

"What brains?" Joseph asked.

Ace drew the cat to his chest and began scratching him behind the ears. Returning his gaze to the unproductive waterspout, he said, "Right now, I'm not sure I could compare my intelligence with Lucky's and notice a measurable difference. Goddamned bathtub, anyway. It should work. The windmill pumps the water up to the attic, and force of gravity is supposed to bring the water down."

"Maybe you misread the book," Joseph suggested.

Ace shot him a warning look. "I'm not illiterate, Joseph. I followed the directions exactly."

Caitlin gathered her courage. "I'm just venturing a guess, but I think the lack of water is probably due to an unconnected section of pipe somewhere between here and the cistern. If they're not all level . . ." She let her voice trail away and lifted her hands. "Well, as you know, water runs downhill. If there's a low section, it'll pool there and possibly leak. If the ground gets soft and there's enough pressure, the pipe joints could separate."

"Are you suggesting we dig up all that pipe?" Ace asked in an ominous tone.

"It was just a thought." She shrugged. "You could probably just look for damp earth, and start digging there. I doubt you'd have to uncover all the pipe."

Fifteen minutes later, the men were unearthing pipe. It wasn't long before they found an underground leak in the joints where the soil had become saturated and allowed the junction to settle and become disconnected.

"You probably should have lined your ditch with gravel," Caitlin pointed out.

Ace narrowed an eye at her. "Are you saying we need to dig it all back up and redo it?"

Caitlin stared down at the unearthed section of ditch for a long moment. "Heavens, no."

The following morning, Ace went to town for a wagonload of gravel. When he returned to the house, he plopped two white boxes on the table and insisted Caitlin open them. Inside she found three new dresses, one of which was the lovely blue one that she and Patrick had admired in the dress shop window. Beneath the dresses were several undergarments, four new chemises, two pairs of lace garters, three new sets of bloomers, two petticoats, and a half-dozen pairs of silk hosiery.

It had been so long since she'd gotten any new clothes, her hands trembled when she touched the garments. She'd never owned silk stockings in her life. "Ace, you shouldn't have," she said in awe. "You must have spent a small fortune."

"It'll be worth it to see you in that pretty blue dress," he said offhandedly. "Why don't you go try it on?"

"Oh, no, I couldn't. It should be saved for special occasions. For going to church or into town shopping. That sort of thing. I'd ruin it wearing it at home."

Caitlin gathered up her new clothing and spirited it away to the bedroom where she hung each dress carefully on a hanger and covered the lot with a sheet so it wouldn't gather dust. When she returned to the front of the house, there was another package on the table, this one a large lumpy one wrapped in brown paper.

Ace was standing between the kitchen and the living room, leaning against the archway. He held a steaming cup of coffee in one hand. "I forgot it in the wagon. It's for you. Open it."

Caitlin couldn't imagine what else he might have gotten her. Frankly, she found his generosity a little overwhelming. When a man gave a woman gifts, he usually expected something in return.

Hands shaking, she carefully untied the string and peeled away the paper. Inside was a myriad collection of yard goods. Scads of yellow gingham, just like she'd gotten on sale last winter for curtains. There were smaller amounts of other yardage, the colors similar to those she'd used in her braided rugs and potholders.

"You had everything fixed so pretty at the other place," he said gruffly. "I thought maybe this might seem more like home to you if you had curtains and rugs and stuff, like over there."

Tears pricked Caitlin's eyelids as she lifted the folded yardage to look at all the colors he'd chosen. He'd remembered nearly every hue in her rag rugs. He'd also gotten her embroidery thread, needles, a pattern book, hoops and cloth on which to do cross-stitch. She lifted her gaze to his.

"Jesus. Don't cry," he said.

He sounded as if it would be a disaster if she shed one tear. "Thank you, Ace." Caitlin carefully folded the paper back around the dry goods and retied the string. "In my idle time, I'll enjoy keeping busy making things to brighten it up around here."

"Caitlin, what's wrong?"

She blinked and forced a smile. "Nothing. This was very—thoughtful. Thank you."

She was lying. Everything was wrong. He'd remembered every detail about the things she'd made and bought all her favorite colors. No one, not even Patrick, had ever paid that much attention to what she liked. Patrick had bought her things. Lovely things. Sometimes, he'd worked weeks to get them. But he'd chosen items that he liked, never once stopping to think that she might have preferred a green dress instead of pink, or checks instead of polka dots. She had appreciated the gifts no less. It was just that no one had ever before tried so hard to get her what *she* liked.

It was a little thing. A silly, unimportant thing. Only it wasn't unimportant to her. Or silly. Ace made her feel . . . special, that was how he made her feel. And it scared her to death. She felt as if he were dangling all her wishes and dreams before her. All she had to do was reach out and grab them. Only to do that, she would be stepping into his arms.

That night after supper, Ace invited her on a moonlight walk. A little nervous because they were so seldom alone except at night when they went to bed, Caitlin nearly jumped out of her skin when he seized hold of her left hand and drew her to a stop. For a long moment, he just looked down at her, his eyes glowing speculatively. Then he glanced at the onyx and diamond ring on her finger.

"I've been wanting to take my ring back," he said huskily.

"Oh." Caitlin reached to remove the piece of jewelry. "By all means. It's lovely. But it's rather large, and I worry about losing it."

He stopped her from removing the ring from her finger. "Allow me."

With a slight smile, he slipped the ring from her hand, then bent to kiss the backs of her knuckles. "There. That's much better."

Caitlin's eyes widened when she saw that he had replaced his ring with another, a very large, sparkling diamond. She blinked, absolutely certain she couldn't be seeing what she thought she was seeing. "Oh, my." She drew her hand from his and held it up to the moonlight. "Holy mother and all the saints. Are you crazy, Ace? It's the size of a hen egg!"

He gave a low chuckle. "Do you like it?"

"Like it?" Caitlin dragged her gaze from the ring to his dark face. "I can't accept it. You must have spent a—"

"Small fortune," he finished for her. "And you're worth every cent." He caught her chin in his hand. His eyes glinted with determination as he bent his head. "I think it's time I got a kiss. Don't you?"

Caitlin could think of a dozen reasons why that might not be a champion idea, but he didn't allow her time to voice them. His silken mouth settled over hers, his breath warm and steamy and sweet with the taste of coffee. His large hands came to rest at her waist, drawing her close against the hard length of his body.

She felt as if he waged an attack on all her senses at once. His chest brushed lightly over the tips of her breasts, sending ribbons of electricity trailing down her spine to pool like fire in the pit of her stomach. With the tip of his tongue, he tickled the sensitive inner edges of her pursed lips, trying to coax them apart.

Remembering Bess's description of her first kiss—of how the young man had thrust his tongue in her mouth and nearly made her vomit—Caitlin braced herself, making tight fists on the front of her husband's shirt. Unless he forced the issue, she was determined not to open her mouth. Exchanging slobber with someone didn't strike her as a highly appealing activity.

After a moment, Ace drew back slightly, his gaze twinkling in the moonlight. Behind him, aspens that grew along the creek swayed like spangled dancers in the wind. Caitlin gazed up at him, her heart going *kerwhump—kerwhump—kerwhump*. She could tell by his expression that he wasn't wholly satisfied with her response.

"Caitlin, have you been kissed very many times?"

Except for their wedding kiss, she'd suffered through the experience only once, but that one time had been so awful, she figured it counted for a thousand. "Mmm," she murmured noncommittally.

"I see," he said, his tone implying that he didn't

believe her for a second. "How would you feel about a little . . . friendly instruction to perfect your execution?"

Caitlin took a deep breath for courage. "I'm not going to let you poke your tongue in my mouth. The very idea is disgusting."

The dimple in his right cheek flashed as his lips lifted in a smile. "Put that way, I have to admit it does sound disgusting."

"I'm glad we agree."

He arched one dark eyebrow. Caitlin had known him long enough to realize that boded ill. "Kissing properly is a very important prelude to lovemaking," he said huskily. "If you don't learn how to do it properly, it's very unlikely you'll ever want to do more."

Caitlin thought that was indeed a possibility.

"I'll tell you what," he said. "Allow me to direct you, hm? If I do anything you find disgusting, tap me on the shoulder."

Caitlin clenched her teeth. His smile deepened. Grasping her by the chin, he pressed in at her jaw joints, gently but firmly, with his thumb and forefinger. To lesson the discomfort of his grip, she had no choice but to open her mouth slightly. He bent his dark head and settled his firm, silken lips over hers. Just as she had feared, the next instant his tongue came into play, tickling the inside of her lips, tracing the shape of her teeth. When he touched the tip of his tongue to hers, she moaned and thumped his shoulder with the heel of her hand.

No response. She thumped him harder. This time, he responded, but instead of lifting his head, he deepened the kiss by drawing sharply with his mouth. Her tongue, which she'd curled back against her tonsils, was sucked forward. She tasted coffee and the steamy essence of man. Then she forgot everything but the sensations.

Making fists in his shirt, she leaned against him, opening her mouth wider, accepting his thrusts. An odd, heavy, excited feeling rolled through her. Her heart started to pound even more wildly. She developed an ache low in her belly. And then her legs felt as if they turned to water. Water that defied the laws of gravity and surged uphill to the juncture of her thighs, making everything within her feel liquid and strangely hot.

Ace released her chin to encircle her with his strong arms. Caitlin was glad of that, for she was no longer certain she could stand without the support of his body. He bent slightly at the knees and drew her up along his torso, his hips pushing forward to grind against hers. Caitlin gasped and then moaned at the sensations that rocked her.

When he finally drew his mouth from hers, she was breathless and light-headed. Acutely aware of their hearts pounding, his a sturdy thrum, hers an erratic patter, she gazed stupidly at the aspens that swayed behind him.

"Oh, my," she whispered. "That was—astounding."

He laughed low in his chest, the jerk of his broad shoulders shaking her clear to her toes. She realized she had melted over him like a pat of butter on a flapjack. "You're right. It was astounding."

As he set her away from him, he kept a firm grip on her arms. "Are you all right?"

Caitlin gazed up at him, her senses slowly orienting themselves. Her eyes shifted to his mouth, which was tipped into what could only be termed a very satisfied grin. Ace Keegan was dangerous, she realized. More dangerous than she'd ever dreamed. "Yes, I'm fine," she lied.

The truth was, she feared she might never feel truly all right again.

After that, at least once every day, and sometimes far more frequently, Ace would catch her unawares someplace in the house, whereupon he anchored her to the spot and pressed a sensual assault. Kissing her neck. Nibbling lightly on her ear. Whispering sweet nothings. He'd told her once that he knew his way around a woman's body, and Caitlin realized he hadn't lied. He knew exactly how and where to kiss her, finding all the most sensitive places and teasing them with a tantalizing relentlessness. It took all her concentration to keep her head clear and to resist the melting sensations.

But resist them, she did. By remembering another man, and another assault. Those memories alone were enough to make her quake with dread. One of these times, when she least expected it, Ace's ardor would find her struggling beneath him in the locked master bedroom, her screams stifled by one of his large hands.

That never happened. Instead, just when she felt absolutely certain he was so aroused he wouldn't stop, he always moved away. Sometimes he did so with his jaw clenched in obvious frustration, but he moved away all the same, his brown eyes filled with twinkling amusement, whether at her or himself, she was never sure.

What truly began to alarm Caitlin about those sensual parries was that eventually she stopped feeling breathlessly frightened by them and started to enjoy the tingling feelings he elicited within her. It was nothing earthshaking, just little urges to let her head droop sideways so he might have better access to the curve of her neck, to lean against him so she might absorb the hard strength of his body, to draw his hands from their resting place at her waist and pull his arms around her.

She had to be going absolutely mad to feel such inclinations.

When those traitorous urges came upon her, she could usually chase them away by conjuring up her awful memories. No matter how gently Ace touched her, she couldn't bear the thought of having a man use her like that again.

Caitlin started to feel as if she were perched on an emotional seesaw. Up and down, her emotions went, keeping her off balance, sometimes making her feel as if her heart was soaring, other times as if her stomach had dropped to the floor and lay quivering at her feet.

She hated Ace for toying with her feelings so mercilessly. She absolutely despised him for it. She said those words to herself at least a dozen times each day. And then he would walk into the house and do something so unexpected, so incredibly, impossibly sweet, that her heart ached.

One memorable, sunny afternoon while she was busy in the kitchen, Ace returned from a trip to town. As always, she recognized the odd shuffle of his footsteps when he entered the house, and knew it was he without even turning from the stove. Giving the stew she was simmering a final stir with a long-handled wooden spoon, she set the utensil aside and stepped to the archway between the kitchen and living room to call a greeting. When she clapped eyes on her husband, the greeting died in her throat.

Was this Ace, or some stranger who had sneaked in uninvited? Gone were his jet-black shirt and trousers. He stood before her dressed from head to toe in what looked to be brand-new clothing, the blue jeans still sporting fold creases above the knee, the light blue chambray work shirt so stiff with starch, it fairly crackled when he moved. Cocked at the usual jaunty angle atop his dark head was a new, camel-brown Stetson.

"Ace?" she queried, unable to conceal her incredulity.

"It's me." He glanced down at himself with a rueful expression. After taking a swipe at one trouser leg, he looked back up at her, a question shining in his eyes. "Well, what do you think?"

Caitlin didn't know. He looked extremely handsome in the new clothes, of course. Ace Keegan was so attractive, he could have worn just about anything and still drawn a woman's eye.

It was just that the outfit was so totally unlike what he usually wore. Caitlin had always suspected he favored satanic black because it gave him an intimidating air. A man who had a reputation with a gun was always some upstart's target, and looking fearful had probably kept Ace from being shot at more than once.

"You look very nice," she said hesitantly. "But why the change?"

He met her gaze, his hard mouth curving slightly.

"You have to swear you won't tell the boys. As far as they're to know, I just got a hair up my ass and bought new clothes."

Caitlin inclined her head slightly. "I won't tell them anything."

He drew the Stetson off, gave it a turn in his large, brown hands, then plopped it back on his head. "I guess it's sort of stupid, really."

Caitlin had never known Ace to do anything stupid.

She shot a glance at the gun he wore strapped low and always ready on his thigh. Without the black clothing, she feared that some young man looking to make himself a name might challenge Ace to a gunfight. Didn't he realize that by changing his attire, he might be inviting trouble?

"It's just that—" He broke off and gave a low, self-derisive chuckle. "Lucky and I—we, um, had ourselves a long talk. During the course of our conversation, it became absolutely clear that he isn't able to change his color. Since he can't, and his shedding is obviously going to continue, I decided maybe I ought to change my color. Black clothing isn't very practical around a yellow cat."

Caitlin felt as if he had slugged her right in the solar plexus. An awful, suffocating sensation grabbed hold of her throat. Her eyeballs started to throb with breathlessness. She stared at him, unable to speak, unable to move.

He had done this because of Lucky? Most men would have tossed the shedding cat out of the house on its ear. Tears started to burn behind her eyelids. And then she started to shake. With a low cry, she darted past him and ran to the bedroom.

"Caitlin!"

She heard Ace following right on her heels. When she tried to slam the door closed, he shoved a boot past the doorjamb to stop her. Half blind with tears, she flung herself full length on the bed and buried her face in the pillow to stifle her sobs. She knew it was madness. But now that the tears had started coming, she couldn't for the life of her make them stop.

She felt the mattress sink under Ace's weight as he sat down beside her. A second later, one of his big, heavy hands settled at the center of her back.

Something within Caitlin, an awful, aching, cold something, seemed to break apart at his touch, the shards exploding outward to slice cruelly at her insides with razor-sharp points. His hands were so wonderful. So awfully, horribly wonderful. So warm and strong. So gentle, yet capable. Never once had he used them to bring her pain. Never once. And yet he was hurting her worse than anyone else ever had in her entire life.

By making her love him.

"WHAT THE HELL'S EATING YOU?"

Joseph's question earned him a furious glare from Ace, who had entered the tack room of the barn in a frustrated rage and started throwing things around with a startling violence. "What the hell do you care? Just leave me alone!"

Never one to err on the side of caution, Joseph sauntered on into the tack room to lean his hip against a saddle that had been left on a sawhorse for future stirrup replacement. Folding his arms, he settled a somber gaze on Ace, his full mouth drawn into a grim, unrelenting line.

"If you weren't taking your foul temper out on all of us, I wouldn't care. Unfortunately, that isn't the case, and somebody's got to find out what's wrong. I've been elected."

"I haven't been taking my temper out on anyone!" Ace kicked a half-empty gunnysack out of his path. Grain went flying. The sight of it made him even madder. He gave the bag another kick, just for good measure. "Just get away from me. I mean it, Joseph. Right now, I'd just as soon stomp the hell out of you as look at you."

"Exactly," Joseph remarked, as if that said it all.

Ace shot him a warning glance. "Get off my back. I mean it, little brother. If you've got a bone to pick with me, now isn't the time."

Joseph hauled in a deep breath and slowly exhaled. "Ace, you've been acting like an ass for days. Snapping at all of us. Snarling whenever we ask you a simple question. If there's something needling you, get it taken care of. It isn't fair to take it out on us."

Even as angry as he was, Ace knew Joseph was right. That didn't make it any easier for him to swallow. Afraid he might do something stupid that he would keenly regret later, he upended a bucket and sat down on it. Propping his arms on his knees, he knotted and relaxed his fists, aching to smash them into something. He just didn't want it to be his brother's face.

"It's Caitlin, isn't it?"

Ace ground his teeth so hard, he heard the enamel on one molar grate. Glaring at the hay-strewn floor, he ignored the question. Joseph settled himself more comfortably against the saddle and crossed his feet.

"You know, big brother, trying to be patient is all fine and dandy. But a man only has so much, and then something has to give. I think you've run plumb out."

"Thank you so much for that illuminating observation."

Joseph chuckled. "Any time. I'm always here to tell you what you already know. The trouble is in making you face it. You can't go on like this. And neither can Caitlin."

"Go on like what?"

"Playing this stupid game of cat and mouse." He laughed again. "And, no, I didn't mean that as a pun."

Recalling Lucky's attack on his manhood, Ace found himself smiling slightly in spite of himself. After a long moment, he finally met his brother's gaze. "I'm at the end of my rope. I've done everything I can think of, and nothing I do seems to reach her. She's in there sobbing her heart out right now. So hard she can't even talk. And the worst of it is, I don't have a clue what I did to make her cry. You'd think I broke her heart, for Christ's sake, and all I did was buy myself new clothes!"

Joseph gave him a slow perusal. "Real nice duds. Why did you buy them? That's the question."

"Because of the goddamned cat. I got tired of its shedding. Wearing black is a bitch when you're around Lucky all the time."

Joseph arched an eyebrow. "And did you tell Caitlin your reason?"

"Yes. Whereupon she immediately started bawling. Jesus." Ace jerked off his hat and raked a hand through his hair. "That girl is driving me crazy, you know it? Nothing I do suits her. All that yardage I bought her? She stuck it in the closet, right along with the new clothes, and she's never so much as looked at any of it since." He sighed and leaned his head back. "I don't understand her. In all this time, she's never once ventured off the ranch. Not even to see her brother, and I know she'd love to. She won't even go into town with me. Every time I invite her, she makes up some excuse. It's as if she's hiding out here. As for how things are between us? I don't know what to do with her, Joseph. I just plain don't. No matter how hard I try, I can't make her happy."

Joseph seemed to ponder that. "Maybe it's just the opposite, Ace. Maybe everything you do suits her a little too well. You ever think about that?"

"How does that make sense?"

Joseph smiled. "You remember when I was a little kid and you were trying to teach me how to swim? You'd get out in the water and hold up your arms to me. 'Jump, Joseph!,' you'd say. 'I'll catch you! Come on. Don't be afraid.' And I'd stand up on that rock, so scared my knees were knocking, wanting to take the leap, yet hating you for trying to make me."

"What has that got to do with Caitlin?"

"Because you're trying to make her jump." Joseph looked deeply into Ace's eyes. "She's scared, big brother. Scared spitless. And there you are, holding out your arms, telling her to go ahead and take the leap, that if she'll just trust you enough to do it, you'll be there to catch her. It's an awful feeling, thinking about trusting someone that much. You have to risk everything. The tension builds up until you can't hardly stand it. You almost make yourself push off. Then at the last second, you lose your courage and run like hell."

Ace sighed. "Yeah, well, you've got that much right. She's running like hell."

"Do you remember how you finally got me into the water?"

"I grabbed you by an ankle and pulled you in."

Joseph pushed away from the saddle. He said nothing more, just turned and left the tack room. Ace sat there, staring at the empty doorway, his thoughts on the girl inside the house.

After a long while, Ace finally pushed to his feet. Maybe Joseph was right. Maybe he was trying to handle Caitlin all wrong. He had inalienable rights as her husband. How long did he plan to wait until he insisted she be a real wife to him?

He gave the gunnysack another kick. Dust from the grain billowed upward and stung his eyes. Inalienable rights? Somehow, he didn't think exercising them was going to set very well with his wife.

SUPPER THAT EVENING WAS A TENSE AFFAIR. CAITLIN HAD burned the stew. She had also burned the biscuits. Ace was mildly surprised she hadn't decided to set fire to the table as well.

When she sat down with them to partake of the ruined meal, she was wearing a face beyond salvation. Her eyelids were so purple and swollen from crying, she seemed to be looking at everyone through the sweep of her auburn lashes. Her cheeks were stained with great, red splotches. And her mouth looked as though she'd sunk her teeth repeatedly into the inside of her bottom lip. To make matters worse, her expression was sullen, the set of her mouth grimly resentful.

Since it was obvious to everyone present that there was trouble afoot, no one felt at ease enough to engage in conversation. A heavy silence blanketed the table, broken only by the occasional slurping noise as someone sucked stew broth from a spoon. Until now, Ace had never realized that Joseph's jaw popped every time he chewed. He'd also never noticed Esa's infuriating habit of sniffing constantly and rubbing his nose.

By the meal's end, Ace knew he had to get out of the house before he exploded. After taking his bowl to the kitchen sink, he exited by way of the back door, taking the six-foot jump with a crazed disregard, not really caring if he broke a leg in the process. After landing without mishap, which was almost a disappointment, he struck off for the hanging tree. Listening to the rustle of the oak leaves and feeling close to his stepfather always soothed Ace, and tonight he sure as hell needed soothing.

Once at the tree, he found a perch on the huge boulder he usually sat on, swinging a leg over an outcropping. After settling himself comfortably, he leaned his head back and closed his eyes, concentrating on the sound of the rustling leaves and his own breathing. Caitlin. She hung in his thoughts, no matter what he did or where he went. He didn't know what to do about her. Yet he had to do something. Joseph was right about that. They couldn't go on as they were.

Calmed by the feel of the evening breeze washing over his hatless head, Ace gazed out across the Paradise, his thoughts as distant from where he sat as the horizon. What was going through Caitlin's mind right now?

Ace supposed, with a stretch of his imagination, he could believe she'd accidentally burned dinner. But even as he tried to make that stretch, a feeling in his gut told him she'd done it on purpose. Why? To get back at him? If so, for what? Buying new clothes for himself wasn't exactly a major offense, especially when he'd done it because of her goddamned cat. He'd been trying to be nice. If this was the result, she might level the whole house if he ever did something really rotten.

Did she hold a grudge against him because of Patrick? The bastard had never yet let his shadow darken Ace's doorstep. Maybe she didn't believe he'd left Patrick a note, welcoming him to the Paradise. Maybe she blamed him because she never got to see her brother. As far as Ace was concerned, it was a good miss. Could that be the problem? That she sensed the animosity he bore Patrick? After all, how could he expect her to develop feelings for him and learn to trust him when she believed he reviled the very blood that flowed in her veins?

Revenge. For so many years, it had been all that Ace

had lived for. Now, it seemed, his thirst for it had become the one thing that stood between him and his reason for living. Caitlin . . .

God, he loved her. It had come upon him like a flash flood in the beginning, its depths slowly increasing with each passing day, until he no longer felt he could keep his head above flood level. He was slowly drowning in hopelessness. Without her, he wasn't sure he could survive.

Stupid, that. He'd never really believed a man's feelings could run so deep. But falling in love with Caitlin had proved him dead wrong. What was the purpose in doing anything, in accomplishing anything, if he couldn't share it with her? Jesus. He wanted to give her his babies. Him, the fellow who'd never screwed a woman without wearing a sheep-gut condom. Even worse was that he knew damned well those babies he wanted so badly would be half O'Shannessy. Little redheads, possibly. Christ. He could end up with a son who was a dead ringer for Conor.

Ace had hated the man so blindly for so many years, he had never stopped to consider what it was doing to him. He'd sacrificed so much for hatred. Was he willing to sacrifice the rest of his life?

"You got any room up there for company?"

Joseph's voice made Ace jerk. He glanced around, sought out his brother in the darkness, and flashed a rueful grin. "I reckon. Just be forewarned, I'm not in the best of moods."

"I figured as much." Joseph swung up onto the rock, face toward the mountains, boot heels hooked over a protrusion of stone. After watching the tree sway for a while, he said, "I thought maybe you'd like to talk." He reached inside his shirt and drew out a flask. Popping the cork, he took a generous swig, then handed the flask to Ace. "Join me?"

Ace chuckled and accepted the container. "Why the hell not? Maybe getting my hat cocked will make me feel better."

"I doubt it. But maybe you'll better enjoy your frustration."

Ace wiped the mouth of the flask. "I'm frustrated, all right. You would be, too, if you were walking around with a stiff third leg bent double in the crotch of your jeans."

Joseph chuckled. "The way I hear tell, it's more the size of Caitlin's little finger."

Ace took a gulp of whiskey, which burned like fire from the back of his throat clear to his belly. After whistling air through his teeth, he said, "Doesn't she just wish?"

"Well, I guess one of you is doing some wishful thinking." Joseph took the flask back when Ace proffered it. "I'm just not sure it's Caitlin."

Ace narrowed an eye, watching as his brother took another belt of whiskey. "I've got a hundred bucks that says mine is bigger than yours, you cocky little bastard."

Joseph handed the whiskey back to Ace. "You've got the cocky part right. I may be little, big brother, but I'm hung like a goddamned horse. The way I figure it, God took pity when he was fashioning me. He said to Himself, 'I gotta give this boy some kind of edge.'"

"My ass."

Joseph laughed goodnaturedly. "Yeah, well, you'll never know for sure, will you?"

Ace swallowed more whiskey. It no longer seemed to have such a bite. "I didn't eat enough supper. This is hitting me like a sixty-grain slug."

"Enjoy."

Ace decided that was the best advice he'd heard all day and took another drink. Handing the container back to his brother, he said, "Don't make me feel lonesome."

"I don't intend to."

The calming effect of the alcohol was beginning to embrace Ace like a blanket. He hauled in a huge lungful of air. "You know what?"

"Nope, what?"

"I'm thinking about throwing it all over."

"Throwing what all over?"

"Everything. Revenge isn't sweet. I thought it would be. All these years, I truly thought it would be. But it isn't."

Joseph said nothing. Ace took his silence as an unvoiced objection.

"I know you boys may feel pretty disappointed in me if I give up on everything right when it's almost finished. I can't blame you for that. But I—"

"Hold it! Hold it just one goddamned minute." Joseph leaned forward slightly to peer at Ace through the gloom. "Did I hear you right? That we're the ones who'll be disappointed? Excuse me, Ace, but where the hell did you ever come up with that idea? This whole business was never our idea. It was yours. You were the one who saw Pa get hung. You were the one who watched Ma get raped. And you were the one who had to look at a messed-up face every morning in the mirror."

"What the hell are you saying?"

"That you were the one obsessed with coming back here. The one who lived to see the bastards who killed our pa grovel. We were so little when it happened, none of us ever really gave a shit if we ever clapped eyes on this place again."

"You've all been behind me a hundred percent."

"We sure as hell have. You're our brother. When we were too little to fend for ourselves, you damned near sold your soul to feed us. When we got older, you were the closest thing to a father any of us had, and you did a damned fine job of raising us. Do you think we can forget that? Hell, no. We're behind you, right or wrong. And I have to tell you, there's been a few times when I thought you were wrong."

"Wrong?"

"Absolutely." Joseph gazed out across the ranch. "Sometimes I feel like you're so focused on avenging Pa that you've forgotten everything he stood for. Everything the Paradise was supposed to stand for. Our pa wasn't a violent man. Fact is, he'd have walked a mile to avoid doing another man harm. When he came here to this place, he was leaving the hell of war behind, not looking for a new one. He wanted a fresh start. A clean start. This land was a defeated man's dream come true. A second chance to live his life the way he wanted, upholding the laws of God, not breaking all of them."

"Are you saying I have?"

"I'm saying that's why you came here, to give back as good as we got. To inflict hurt on the people who hurt us. If that's what you want, more power to you. We'll all stand behind you or die trying. But don't put it off as being our idea in the first place, because it sure as hell wasn't."

Ace couldn't quite believe what he was hearing. "You sat with me, night after night, planning and conniving, until we were so tired we could hardly see. And now you're telling me none of this ever mattered to you?"

"It mattered. Not because it was important to me, but because it was to you." Joseph shot him a glance. "You want to throw it all over? Fine. It's about time you came to your senses, if you ask me. Pa never would have wanted you to avenge him. He would've wanted you to get on with your life. A good life, dammit. With a wife you love, and a passel of kids. Church on Sunday, and a heartfelt blessing of the food at every meal. A clean life, Ace. Not one of gambling and womanizing and killing a man before he kills you. How can you possibly think otherwise?"

Ace ran a hand over his face. Twenty years. He'd breathed and eaten and slept revenge for twenty years. Now it all seemed stupid. Stupid and pointless and completely misguided. A silence settled between him and his brother. A loaded silence that seemed permeated with one question. Where did he go from here?

"You know," Ace said softly after a long while, "I'm going to have to tell Caitlin. About everything. From the very start, I've kept things from her. About our sister. *Her* sister, for Christ's sake. About my real reasons for coming here. I have everything in position to financially ruin half the people in this town. She's liable to hate me for that when she finds out."

"Not if you fix things before you tell her." Joseph took another swig of whiskey, then handed the flask to Ace. "The people here have invested in land along a railroad spur route that won't ever be built. All you have to do is actually build it."

"Build it?" Ace said incredulously. "Have you lost your mind? That'd cost me a goddamned fortune, with no real means of recouping my investment. It'd be financial lunacy."

"You have the money." Joseph took the flask after Ace was finished with it and shoved the cork back into its mouth. "Instead of being so bent on ruining lives, why not invest a big portion of that money into building one for yourself? You've got a nice spread here. In the future, you'll have a lot better chance to make it as a cattleman if you can ship your cows by rail to Denver instead of driving them overland. These poor bastards around here lose a number of head every time they make the drive. You will as well. If you build a spur, that won't be the case any more."

"It isn't a sound business move, Joseph. I'd be throwing away money."

"Would it break you?"

"Hell, no. But I worked my ass off to get that money. Not one damned cent of it came easy. I might as well walk out there and chuck a fortune in the creek. Just a second ago, you were throwing it in my teeth about the kind of life I've led. Well, I didn't do it on a lark. I sweated and scrimped and sold my soul."

"You haven't sold your soul yet. It's just a little tattered around the edges." Joseph fixed a silvery blue gaze on him. "Will I still be able to say that if you end up losing Caitlin?"

Ace shifted his gaze to the mountains. His brother had no idea what he was suggesting. It wasn't just the money that he'd be throwing away, but a big piece of himself.

"You love her, don't you?"

It took Ace a long time to answer that question. "Yes, goddammit."

"If she was standing on an auction block, what kind of price would you put on her? How high would you bid?"

"She's not a hunk of meat, Joseph. You don't buy a woman!"

"That isn't the point. The point is, what's she worth to you? A fourth of your money? Half? If it came to a choice between your goddamned money and a life with her, which would you take?" Joseph fell silent a moment. "I don't give you advice very often. It's usually the other way around. But I'm going to now, and I hope you listen. Get your head on straight. Figure out what it is in this life that really matters to you. If you decide it's your money, you're going to end up being one sorry son of a bitch."

Ace closed his eyes. "You have to know that I would never choose money over my wife. I'd rather lose everything than lose her."

"Really?"

Ace cracked open one eye. "I get the point. Don't drive it into the ground. What you're failing to see is that there's far more involved than me dumping a bunch of money into a railroad spur. If I go ahead and build, the sons of bitches who hung your pa are going to come out smelling like roses. I can turn loose of my plan to get revenge, but I'll be damned if I'll buy back land from those bastards so they can make a profit."

"Then don't. Only make offers equal to what they originally invested."

"They'd refuse to sell."

"If they do that, you can threaten to sit on it and foreclose when they can't make their mortgage payments. They'll sell. If they don't, they'll lose their asses. You've got the advantage of time on your side, Ace. You can hold out until they go under." He gave a low laugh. "Just think how it'd be for those dirt farmers who have managed to hold on to their spreads. If you actually build that spur and buy their land at decent prices, they'll think Christmas came in August."

Ace smiled slightly. "I reckon they would, at that."

"Think about that side of it, all the people you'd make a miracle for, including one for yourself. It's not often a man gets a chance to play Santa Claus on that grand a scale."

"With money I made with the sweat of my brow."

"You can love money, Ace, but it ain't gonna love you back. On a cold winter night, you can't cuddle up to it for warmth. It can buy you a lot of things, but as you pointed out, it can't buy you a woman, and it can't give you children."

Ace mulled that over. "On down the road, if I build that spur, those bastards will be able to ship their cows to Denver right along with mine. I'll be providing them with a means of economic growth."

"Every cattleman in these parts will ship his cows on that rail. You can't pick and choose. You've got to turn loose of it, Ace. Let bygones be bygones. Punishing those men isn't going to bring our pa back. All it'll do is mess up the rest of your life. Let God be their judge. He'll settle up with them when they try to get through the old pearly gates."

On the tail of a long, drawn-out sigh, Ace said, "I'll think about it, Joseph. That's all I can promise."

"Do me one favor?"

"What's that?"

"If you decide to build that spur, don't be an idiot and go telling Caitlin anything until you've rectified matters." Joseph swung down off the rock. "You're right. At first, she may hate you. The only way you'll be able to convince her not to is to have proof, in black and white, that you've had a change of heart."

With that, he struck off for the house.

Ace remained sitting on the fence in the semidarkness, his thoughts turned back in time, not to the night of his stepfather's death, but to all the gentler, happier times before that, times that Ace had allowed to be overshadowed by a single, awful memory. After a lot of soul searching, he concluded that Joseph was right; their pa never would have condoned this madness. He would have long since put the tragedy behind him and gone on to build a happy life on a foundation of love, not hatred.

Now Ace had a chance to do just that with Caitlin. How much was she worth to him? *You place a very high price on yourself, Miss O'Shannessy.* He wouldn't go bust if he built the railroad spur, but doing so would put a very large dent in his capital.

He remembered Joseph's burning gaze and the stern

expression on his face. No one knew Ace quite as well as his brother. *The point is, what's she worth to you? A fourth of your money? Half?* Joseph never had learned to pull any of his punches. This was one time Ace was glad he hadn't. He couldn't put a dollar amount on Caitlin's worth. If he had to throw away everything, right down to the last dime, he'd still feel like a lucky man if she was in his arms.

Ace decided then and there that a railroad spur would be built between No Name and Denver, after all. No foreclosures or financial ruin for anyone if he could avoid it. Just a gigantic investment in the future. His and Caitlin's.

Ace felt as if a thousand pounds had been lifted off his shoulders. Sliding down off the boulder, he struck off for the house to get Caitlin. As Joseph had so cleverly pointed out earlier that day, it was high time Ace grabbed her by an ankle. They might both end up going under. The girl had a load of problems, and Ace wasn't at all sure he was strong enough or smart enough to help her fix them. But, by God, he was going to try.

21

As ACE APPROACHED THE HOUSE HE SAW THAT ALL THE doors and windows had been flung open. Given the coolness of the evening, that struck him as strange. Then he smelled smoke. Thinking that Caitlin must have burned something else, he took the steps two at a time, strode quickly across the porch, and came reeling to a stop as he entered the living room.

Peering through the haze, he saw that the top of the table was covered with stew. It looked as if someone had upended the pot and smeared the contents everywhere.

Juice and clumps of scorched vegetables had dripped from the table onto the benches. Worse, his beautiful varnished floor was covered with water.

Joseph stood in the middle of the mess, a sopping wet towel clutched in one hand. The front of his chambray shirt bore smears of stew juice. The look on his face was nothing short of murderous. A number of towels and blankets, which he'd evidently thrown on the floor to soak up the water, lay around him. From the kitchen, Ace could hear David and Esa cursing a blue streak and pounding on something.

"What the hell happened?" Ace asked. He glanced worriedly around. "Where's Caitlin?"

His brother waved to a hand clear smoke from his face. "Caitlin happened."

"What?"

With a swing of his arm, Joseph indicated the mess. "Caitlin did all this."

"What the hell do you mean, Caitlin did all this?"

"I mean she purposely dumped the stew on the table, smeared it everywhere, and then said, 'Oops! What a terrible mess!' Then she wiped her hands off on me and said, 'Oh, dear, I seem to have gotten stuff all over your shirt!' *That's* what I mean."

Ace felt a cold sensation seeping through his boots. He glanced down to see that he was standing in at least an inch of water.

"The flood came after the stew and the stove," Joseph said as he bent to grab another towel. "Excuse me, but your precious varnished floors will be ruined if I don't get this water up, and I'm a one man wring-out brigade. David and Esa are trying to open the fucking flue damper. She built up the fire, closed the draft, then beat on the handle with the poker until she bent it so bad you can't work it." As he strode toward the kitchen, Joseph threw Ace a glance over his shoulder. "She said you have a penchant for clearing the air and calming the waters, or some damned thing like that."

Clearing the air and calming the waters? Ace gave his boot a shake. "Where the hell did all this water come from?"

"She overflowed the bathtub."

Ace followed Joseph to the kitchen. David and Esa, who were trying without success to open the stove damper, had so much soot on their faces they looked like raccoons. Smoke billowed from the oven door and up around the hole covers.

"Do you know where the pliers are?" David asked Ace. "We can't get a good enough hold on this lever with our bare hands to turn it."

So stunned he could scarcely grasp what he was seeing, Ace waded back through the house to the water closet, found the pliers where he'd left them earlier in the week, and returned to the kitchen. As he handed the tool to David, he said, "Do you guys seriously expect me to believe Caitlin did all this? What actually happened here?"

Joseph turned from the sink, his hands still wrapped around a towel. "When I got back to the house," he said acidly, "she was banging things around in the kitchen. At first I thought she was just cleaning up the pots and pans or something. But the banging kept getting louder, the way it does when someone's slamming stuff around to get attention. When I asked her what was wrong, she came out to the table, looking mad as blazes, and said nothing was wrong. That nothing ever went wrong around here, and she was sick to death of it. Sick to death of us. Sick to death of you. Sick to death of all the pretense."

"The pretense?" Ace echoed, glancing incredulously at the stove again, which was still puffing smoke. "What the hell did she mean by that?"

"She's *your* wife. How are we supposed to know what she meant!" Joseph turned back to the sink to wring out another towel. As he gathered the cloth in his hands and gave it a twist, his furious stance left Ace with little doubt he wished he had his hands around Caitlin's neck. "All I know is, she was mad, and she made a hell of a mess."

Raking a hand through his hair, Ace stepped to the archway and stared at the destroyed living room. As his gaze came to rest on the floor, he felt a rush of anger. Three coats of varnish, possibly ruined. Hours of work, down the privy hole. He swung back to his brothers.

"I realize it may sound like a really stupid question, but where were you while she was doing all this?"

"Which part?" Esa asked, rubbing soot from under one eye. "While she was throwing stew, beating on the stove, or flooding the house?"

Ace felt anger building within him—a hot, surging anger. Why would Caitlin have done this? It was the sort of destruction one might expect from a spoiled, intractable child, not a grown woman. It was madness. He shot glares at all three men. "Where were all of you?"

"Well, I was standing right about where you are while she beat on the stove. That came after the stew, so Joseph and David weren't in here."

"Where were they?"

"Out by the table. Just sort of—" Esa broke off. "Geez, Ace. We all just kind of stood around and didn't know what to do. Why are you mad at us? We didn't make the mess!"

The stove belched a cloud of smoke. Ace coughed, waved a hand before his face, and stepped over to jerk the pliers from David's hands. As he set to work trying to turn the stove damper, he said, "I cannot believe that three grown men just stood and watched while one small, timid woman wreaked havoc. Why didn't one of you stop her?"

"I asked her to stop!" Esa said defensively.

"And?" Ace demanded. He could feel his eyes bugging a little and knew he should calm down. If he didn't, he would be sorely tempted to warm Caitlin's little backside when he finally got his hands on her.

"She wouldn't," Esa replied with a shrug. "She just kept swinging the poker and saying, 'Sick, sick, sick to death!'"

"For Christ's sake!" In his anger, Ace wrenched on the damper handle with all his strength. The lever gave unexpectedly under the onslaught, throwing him completely off balance. As he regained his footing, he said,

"You outweigh the girl by eighty pounds, Esa!" He threw the pliers onto the stove top, metal clanking loudly against metal. "I can't believe you just politely asked her to stop and didn't do anything! Why didn't you take the poker away from her, for Christ's sake?"

"You're repeating yourself," Joseph observed drily from where he worked at the sink. "Why is it when you get pissed, all you can think of to say is 'for Christ's sake'? or 'Jesus Christ'?"

"Shut up, Joseph. Right now is not the time for your smart-ass comments." Ace returned his gaze to Esa. "I asked you a question. I'd like an answer. Why didn't you stop her?"

Esa coughed and wiped his mouth with a sleeve. "Well, Ace, the truth is, I was kind of afraid she might— well, you know—hit me."

"Afraid she might *hit* you?" Ace couldn't believe his ears. "That girl doesn't have a mean bone in her whole body." He raised an eyebrow at Joseph's back. "And while she was smearing stew all over God's creation, Joseph? What were you and David doing?"

Joseph glanced over his shoulder. "Esa has it pretty much right. We just stood and watched. What else could we do, short of physically trying to stop her? Thanks, but no thanks. I've tangled with Eden a few times when she was in a temper. I learned the hard way, it's better to stay out the way."

David snorted. "You got that right. A man doesn't stand a chance."

Ace ran a hand over his hair again and cast another disbelieving glance at the destruction. Caitlin—sweet, timid little Caitlin—had done all this? "How on earth did she manage to flood the house this bad? Couldn't you have at least turned off the water spigot?"

David shrugged. "We were so busy trying to fix the stove and get rid of the smoke, we didn't notice the water until she came back from the bedroom carrying Lucky. By then, the hallway already looked like a damned river at flood stage."

Esa grabbed a towel from the wall rack to wipe his

hands. "On the way out, she asked me if I still thought she was a keeper. Can you believe it?" He rubbed the rectangle of soot-streaked linen over his face. "If I didn't know better, I'd swear she did all this just to piss us off."

Ace felt as if a fist had closed around his throat. He planted his hands on his hips and closed his eyes. Then, in a strangled voice, he said, "Jesus Christ!" Only this time, he was no longer certain if he was cursing or praying.

A keeper. A person or thing that had value. Someone or something others wanted. Caitlin wasn't sure either definition applied to her.

ACE LOOKED FOR CAITLIN NEAR THE HOUSE FIRST. WHEN HIS initial search turned up no sign of her, he widened his circle, each sweep taking him farther and farther from the yard and outbuildings. He couldn't help but grow concerned. Colorado was harsh, wild country. There were all manner of beasts running at large, especially at night, some of them predatory.

Do you still think I'm a keeper? Her parting shot at Esa went through Ace's mind a dozen times as he combed the area for her. *Caitlin.* She was like an intricate puzzle, and every time he thought he finally had her figured out, he realized a couple of pieces were missing.

She'd told Joseph she was sick to death of them all. Ace suspected just the opposite was true, that she was coming to care for them very much and was terrified of being hurt. After all, who in Caitlin's life hadn't hurt her? In her mind, if she allowed herself to trust again, she would be making herself vulnerable. That had to be pretty damned frightening.

Ace finally found her sitting on a log next to the creek. He approached quietly from her right, affording himself an opportunity to study her upturned face. Clutching Lucky protectively to her chest, she gazed at the moon and star-studded sky as though she were searching for answers to a multitude of questions. She was clearly troubled, and he had a hunch her concerns were all about him.

Ace wondered how she was going to react when she saw him. He didn't want to frighten her any more than she probably already was. He decided that casual congeniality would be the best approach. "Hi, there."

She gave such a start she nearly fell off the log. "Ace!"

Leaping to her feet, she bent to release the cat, giving him a pat on his rump to shoo him away. God forbid that Lucky should be caught in the middle and get hurt. Such were her expectations, that Ace would fly at her in a rage, just as her father had always done. It was written all over her face. In her pallor. In her huge, frightened eyes, which looked like molten silver in the moonlight.

Ace yearned to scold her for having come out here alone, but under the circumstances, he didn't think that would be a very smart move. There would be time enough later to discuss his concerns for her safety.

"I was starting to get a little worried," he admitted. "Of course, it took me longer to find you than it probably should have. Up near the house, I kept retracing my steps, thinking maybe I'd missed you in all the smoke."

She hugged her waist, her body rigid. "So you *have* been to the house?"

Ace nearly chuckled at the look on her face. He was clearly not reacting in the anticipated manner. "Oh, yes. I've been there. You made one hell of a mess, you know."

She stared at him for an interminably long moment. Then, keeping only one arm around her waist, she began to toy nervously with the buttons on her bodice, her gaze watchful and wary. "Aren't you—" She moistened her tremulous lips. "Aren't you angry?"

Ace placed his hands on his hips, not missing the fact that she flinched when he moved. "A little. Like I said, you made a hell of a mess. If they don't get that water up fairly fast, the floors will have to be sanded and revarnished. That'll be a lot of unnecessary work."

"I'm sure your brothers are all furious," she said in a quavery little voice.

"They are that. Right about now, they'd probably like to send you back to Patrick by pony express."

She became unaccountably interested in a small rock, nudging it around with the toe of her shoe. "And you? Are you wanting to send me back to Patrick as well?"

Ace regarded the top of her bent head. "It's not going to be that simple, Caitlin."

That brought her head up. She fixed him with a wary gaze. "Pardon?"

"You heard me. That's why you did all this, isn't it? To make me so mad, I'd either send you packing or lose my temper. Since we've already been over the first possibility and I've made it clear I won't give you an annulment, I have a feeling you were counting on me to do the latter. After all, if I act like a total ass, you'll be able to hate me. Right?"

"I—I don't know what you mean."

He searched her gaze. "Oh, I think you do." He waited a beat to lend that emphasis. "Caring about people is dangerous business, isn't it?"

A muscle under her eye started to twitch. She returned his regard with a stony expression that revealed nothing, yet told him more than she could possibly know, namely that he'd hit the mark dead on.

Ace sighed and leaned his head back. The vastness of the star-studded sky above them was soothing. They truly were all actors on a stage, each of them playing a role, each with a special purpose. His was to make this girl happy, and God help him, he didn't know how.

He lowered his gaze back to her pale face. "The long and the short of it is, your rash behavior tonight has accomplished nothing. I'm not going to lose my temper so you can hate me, and I'm not going to send you home to Patrick. You're stuck with me."

She wrapped both arms around her waist again, looking so fragile and shaken that he wanted to gather her into his arms. "It won't work, you know," she said softly.

"What won't?"

"This elaborate scheme of yours. I won't love you. No matter what you do. No matter how convincing you are." She hugged herself more tightly. "Go a thousand nights without touching me! Let Lucky sit smack dab in the center of your supper table to eat. Buy me an ocean full of chocolate, new clothes to fill every closet in the house, and enough yardage to make wall-to-wall rugs! I don't care. It won't work! I'll never love you, not in a million years!"

Her lips were saying one thing, her eyes something else entirely. His heart broke for her. "Caitlin, what is it you're so afraid of? Do you even know? Have you ever sat down and taken your fears out in the light of day to examine them?" He hesitated a moment, searching her frightened gaze. "Do you know what I think? I think you're so confused, you don't know which way's up. How can I help you deal with any of this if you won't be honest with me?"

"I don't want to be dealt with," she retorted shakily. "I just want out."

"Out of the marriage, you mean?" He gave a low laugh. "Is that how you've dealt with problems, by running from them?"

"I'm not running. I've stayed and honored my commitments."

"Have you? Pardon me for mentioning it, but we've yet to make love, which is one of your duties as a wife. You're running, Caitlin. Maybe not in a physical sense, but emotionally, you've been making tracks ever since I put a ring on your finger. Do you call what we have a marriage? Think again."

"I'm not ready for intimacy. I may never be."

"Sooner or later, you're going to have to face whatever it is that's making you so afraid. Problems don't solve themselves. You can't just pretend they don't exist and hope they'll go away." He fell silent, struggling for calm. When he could modulate his voice again, he said, "I'd like to help you, if you'll let me." He held out a hand to her. "Come on. Let's sit down and talk. We'll take one issue at a time. Together, Caitlin. There's nothing we can't whip if we tackle it together."

She fastened tortured eyes on his. "Don't you understand?" she cried in a thin, tremulous voice. "*You* are my greatest fear. You! How can you possibly help me face that? It's all or nothing with you. You already have control over my life. Why can't that be enough? But, oh, no, you have to have my heart and soul as well!"

"Damn straight."

"You see?" She flashed him an accusing look. "You want parts of me I'm unable to give!"

"Unable, or unwilling?" He thrust his hand out to her again. "Come on, sweetheart. Let's sit down and discuss it. You'll be surprised how much it helps to talk things out."

Instead of taking his hand, she cupped a shaking palm over her eyes. "Do you think my mind is like Joseph's vegetable garden, with everything in neat little rows? How can I separate things when they're all jumbled together and—" Her voice broke and she hauled in a ragged breath. "You make it sound so simple, but it isn't! Why can't you just let me go, Ace? Please. Before it's too late!"

"It's already too late. I'm in love with you."

She dropped her hand and fixed imploring eyes on his. "How can you say that?"

"Because it's true. I love you, Caitlin. With all my heart. You want to torch the barn next? Maybe level the house? It'll all be for nothing, because when it's over, I'll still be standing here, saying the same thing. I love you, and nothing is going to change that."

"I'm Conor O'Shannessy's daughter. Have you forgotten that? On down the road, you'll rue the day you ever met me!"

"That's crazy."

"Is it?" she demanded shrilly. "Try bad blood on for size, Mr. Keegan! If you keep me in this marriage and have things your way, I'll give you children one day! And those children will be Conor O'Shannessy's grandchildren. Your sons may be redheads. They may look just like him. Even worse, they could *be* like him. Bad seed, Ace. How are you going to feel about me then? My father was an *evil,* vile man!"

"Evilness doesn't run in families. People choose to be evil. They aren't born that way."

"What do *you* know about evilness?"

Ace wasn't sure, but he thought she'd just paid him a high compliment. "I know that most behavior, good or bad, is learned."

She swung a hand in an all-encompassing gesture. "Look at Patrick. Sober, he's the nicest person I've ever known. After a few drinks, he's crazier than a loco horse. Just like my father was!"

"Exactly. Young men tend to pattern themselves after their fathers. Point in fact, when have you ever known Patrick to have only a few drinks? I'll wager the first time he touched a bottle, he drank the whole damned thing. That's all he knows, drinking until he's corned. His father drank that way, so he does. His father behaved badly when he drank, so he does. There's not a damned thing wrong with your brother that a good, swift kick in the ass wouldn't cure. Bad blood, Caitlin? If you believed that, you wouldn't love him like you do."

"I love him in *spite* of it. Faults and all. Not because I think he's perfect!"

Ace saw that opening and leaped at it. "I love you the same way," he said huskily. "Faults and all, Caitlin. Why can't you trust in that?"

"Because you don't know all there is to know about me."

"Then, for Christ's sake, enlighten me."

"Maybe I should!" She said that as if she were issuing a threat. "Would you treat me like something special then, I wonder?"

"Sweetheart, you *are* special. A sweet, beautiful—"

"Stop it! Just—stop it!"

"Caitlin . . ."

She held up a hand. "You told me once that eventually you wanted no more secrets between us. Do you remember that?"

"Yes."

"Well, I have one. An awful one. More awful than you can imagine! And if I ever tell you, you'll—" Her voice cracked again and she gulped. "You'll never look at me the same again. Never."

Ace raked a hand through his hair, shifted his feet, his gaze never leaving hers. "I'll tell you what. Let's strike a bargain, shall we? You tell me your awful secret, and if I feel any differently about you after I hear it, I'll not only give you your goddamned annulment, I'll help you pack and put you on the first stage to San Francisco. I'll even kick in enough money for you to live on for a good long while. Sound fair?"

"You'd do that?" she asked shakily.

"You've got my word on it." Feeling fairly sure there was nothing she could possibly tell him that would have the power to shock him that badly, he said, "So, out with it. What is this *awful* secret of yours?"

She was already so pale, he didn't think she could grow any paler, but she did. Her eyes looked like splashes of black against her white skin. He saw her throat work, saw her lips part. But the words evidently refused to come. She passed a shaking hand over her eyes.

In a barely audible voice, she said, "Do you remember asking me if the man who—who raped me paid for it? And my saying he paid dearly?"

"Yes."

"I deliberately misled you."

"You mean he waltzed off scot-free?"

"No, he paid. Just not in the way you thought I meant. He gave my father six cases of whiskey."

"What?"

"He gave my father six cases of whiskey," she repeated thinly. "That was how much he paid."

Ace felt as if a horse had kicked him in the guts. The ground vanished from under his feet. He stood there, staring at her, not quite able to assimilate what she'd said to him. Then, slowly, like lethally sharp razors, the words cut their way into his brain. "Oh, Jesus, no."

It was all he could say, and at the words, she flinched as if he'd struck her. She took a stumbling step backward, still hugging her waist, the muscles in her face drawn taut over bone, making her look almost skeletal.

"You see?" she whispered.

She whirled to run. Ace was still so stunned, it took him a moment to react. By then, she'd already put several feet between them.

"Caitlin! Come back here!"

She ran as if the devil were at her heels. Ace struck off after her. He knew damned well she couldn't see that well at night, and he feared she might trip over something if she didn't stick to the open areas.

No such luck. Like a terrified, injured animal, she sought the cover of the trees and undergrowth that grew along the creek. *Darkness.* Ace plunged in after her, swatting limbs from his face, cursing beneath his breath.

"Goddammit, Caitlin! Stop! Not into the trees! Caitlin!"

If anything, his warnings and the sound of his footsteps so close behind her spurred her to a greater speed. Ace lengthened his stride, bending forward at the waist, reaching for her as he closed the distance between them. He got so close, he could hear her labored breathing. But every time he grabbed for her, she managed to evade his hand.

Then he saw them. Rocks. Fifteen feet ahead of her, a bed of jagged rock in the bend of the stream. She was running right for them, blind to the danger, oblivious to his shouts.

With a speed he didn't know he had, Ace closed the last few feet between them. She gave a startled *umph* as he caught her around the waist in a flying leap. Twisting in midair so he would land beneath her and take the brunt of their fall, he hit the ground with her locked in his embrace.

"Let go of me!" she shrieked. "Let go of me!"

Elbows. Knees. Ace had never been jabbed into so many places at once. When he rolled to pin her beneath him, she went for his face with her fingernails. He caught her wrists just before she found her mark, pinning her arms above her head. "Goddammit, Caitlin, stop it!"

She threw her head from side to side, straining every muscle in her body to break his hold. He took her wrists in the grip of one hand so he could grasp her by the chin. Moonlight slanting into the clearing illuminated her face. "Stop it, I said!"

Left with no other way to avoid his gaze, she closed her eyes, her expression one of utter despair. "Let go of me," she cried again, this time piteously. "I mean it! Let me go!"

She fought him with surprising strength. Unfortunately for her, she was no match for him physically. He held her down easily, scarcely exerting himself while she pushed herself closer and closer to exhaustion. When she finally had no more energy left with which to fight, she shuddered and went limp, her face mirroring her defeat.

Ace gazed down at her tortured expression. Dear God in heaven. He couldn't conceive of anyone doing something so heartless to her as selling her body for whiskey.

"Ah, Caitlin . . . sweetheart." Holding her chin firmly clasped so she couldn't look away, he locked his gaze on hers. "I want you to listen to me." He bent his head to kiss her forehead, then looked deeply into her eyes again. "It doesn't matter. It tears me apart that such a thing happened to you, but it doesn't change how I feel about you. Not one whit. Do you understand? If your father had traded you for whiskey a hundred different times, to a hundred different men, it still wouldn't matter. I'll always love you. Always. The most awful secret in the world won't ever change that."

With a suddenness that startled him, she burst into tears. Not delicate, ladylike crying, but wrenching sobs that cut clear through him.

Rolling onto his back, Ace drew her into his arms, cupping the back of her head with one hand, pressing her shuddering body full-length against him with his other arm. In their struggle, her hair had come loose from its pins. With a texture like the underside of silk, the freed strands fell across his wrist and down his forearm.

"It's all right, Caitlin. Shh, sweetheart, it's all right."

Only, of course, it wasn't. Caitlin, the intricate puzzle that had always seemed to have pieces missing. Now, suddenly, all those missing pieces had fallen together. Her sense of inadequacy. Her low opinion of herself. Her refusal to trust. Little wonder she'd been unable to separate and conquer her fears of him. *Sold for six cases of whiskey.* She'd been nothing more than a possession to Conor O'Shannessy, a marketable commodity. How could Ace expect her to believe he cherished her when her own father had sold her to another man?

I pray I can forget.

Turning his face against her hair, Ace closed his eyes, hard. He couldn't remember the last time he'd cried. Not since boyhood, he guessed. A man didn't easily give way to his emotions. Only he was crying now. With her. For her. He tightened his hold on her, aware in the back of his mind that he should be careful not to hurt her, yet feeling compelled to hold her tight and never let her go.

To his surprise, she hooked an arm around his neck and clung to him. He wasn't sure how long he held her like that, only that time passed and eventually her sobs ebbed away to occasional hiccoughs. The way she hugged his neck no longer felt quite so desperate. She surrendered to the caresses of his hands on her back and arms, making no protest when his palms brushed close to the sides of her breasts.

"It happened in the study," she whispered.

Ace pressed his lips against her hair. "Tell me," he whispered softly.

He didn't really want to hear the details. He knew it was going to be an ugly story, one that would probably haunt him until the day he died. The coward in him recoiled. But he also sensed that Caitlin might never be able to put it behind her until she talked about it.

She feathered her fingertips over the hair that grew along the back of his neck, her touch tentative and exploring. Then suddenly her nails dug in slightly, pricking his skin. "Pa was sitting at his desk with his whiskey," she said thinly. "That was all he cared about, whiskey."

Ace closed his eyes again, fighting back rage. Later. Later he could get angry. Shove his fist through a wall. Yell until he was hoarse. But not now. She needed him. She might never again need him quite so desperately.

"He t-told me to stop squalling," she said. "That was all! To stop squalling."

Ace swallowed back a curse, then stared sightlessly at the sky. The words spewed from her now, a purging of heart and soul that was six years late in coming. She spoke of the pain, then of the shame she'd felt. Ace tried to picture it and was a little more successful in that endeavor than he wanted to be. A young girl, brutally raped while her father slouched at his desk, swilling from his whiskey jug. It was inconceivable. Yet he knew it had happened. The hatred and bitterness in her voice were evidence of that, so thick in the air he could almost taste the emotions every time he drew breath.

March 12, 1879. There'd been no one to hold her then, no one to comfort her. To get Patrick out of the way, Conor had sent the boy on a cattle drive. Cruise Dublin had shown up that first night, shortly after dark, with the six cases of whiskey in the back of his wagon.

Ace clenched his teeth when he heard the name. Dublin had been one of Conor O'Shannessy's sidekicks, one of the four men involved in swindling Joseph. A bastard. Most likely a cruel bastard. Any man who could stand by and watch while a boy was bludgeoned with a rifle butt and a helpless woman was sexually violated had to be cruel. Not to mention that Dublin had participated in the hanging of an innocent man.

Ace could almost picture him. A short, stocky fellow with blunt features and a ruddy face. He tried to imagine him putting his hands on Caitlin and couldn't. What kind of man did such a thing? Ace considered himself to be as hot-blooded as the next fellow, but he drew the line at rape. There was no excuse, none whatsoever, for a man to take by force what could be purchased at nearly any saloon with a five-dollar gold piece.

Not that he considered Caitlin to be on the same plane with sporting women. She was sweet and precious and beautiful—the kind of woman a lot of men could only dream of touching. Cruise Dublin had done more than dream.

"How old were you, Caitlin?" Even as he asked that

question, Ace remembered the date in her diary and knew she couldn't have been very old. "Fifteen, sixteen? How old?"

"Sixteen," she said shakily. "Old enough to be married, Pa said."

As if that excused what Conor had done. Sixteen . . . In Ace's books, that was barely past childhood, a time in most girls' lives when they'd just put away their dolls and started to wear their hair up. An innocent time. A curious time. A time when wounds ran deep. So deep they sometimes never healed.

She went on to describe the attack itself, the futility she'd felt, the brutality Dublin had resorted to when she nearly succeeded in escaping him. "He hit me. And when that didn't make me stop fighting, he hit me again. After that, I just lay there in a daze. It was like a nightmare, only I was awake."

Ace angled one arm under her fanny and lifted her more firmly against him, trying in the only way he knew to comfort her. With his closeness. With his strength. She had so little of her own. He wanted to kill Cruise Dublin. So help him, maybe someday he would. The man didn't deserve to live.

She went on to tell him how she'd felt afterward. About the nightmares that haunted her sleep, and the irrational fears that made her leap at shadows during the day. "By the time Patrick got home from the cattle drive a week later, I was feeling better," she whispered. "The bruises were nearly gone. I was all right by then. As all right as I'd ever be, anyway. So I never told him."

Ace wondered if she'd been afraid Patrick would feel differently about her if he learned what had happened. "Why, Caitlin? Were you ashamed to tell him?"

"No," she said softly. "Never that. Not with Patrick. I know he hasn't shown it, but he loves me. More than most brothers, I think. When we were children, all we had was each other."

"Then why?" he pressed. "Why didn't you tell him?"

She hauled in a deep, tremulous breath. "I didn't want him to be hurt."

"Hurt?"

"Yes, hurt. It wasn't easy on Patrick, being the only son and looking so much like our father. People were constantly saying, 'That boy's a regular chip off the old block.' And every single time, Patrick looked as if they'd slugged him. Sometimes I'd catch him staring at himself in the mirror, looking into the reflection of his eyes, as if he were searching for something. I think he was terrified of what he might see."

"That he might see something of his father in himself, you mean?"

"Yes," she whispered. "And that's why I never told him about what happened to me. He had convinced himself Pa wasn't really a bad man, that it was just the whiskey that made him so mean and crazy. I didn't want to take that away from him. Sometimes, believing in a lie is all that keeps us sane."

Ace tried to imagine what it must have been like for Patrick, being raised by such a man. Until his stepfather's death, Ace had always had a man in his life to admire and try to pattern himself after. "I'm sorry, Caitlin. I never meant to hurt your brother by coming back here. I just wanted to clear my stepfather's name."

"I know that."

Ace placed a hand on her shoulder. "I admire you for trying to spare your brother by keeping the truth from him. But I have to say, it wasn't very wise. What if your father had tried to do the same thing again?"

"If Pa had tried to send Patrick away on another cattle drive, I would have had no choice but to tell him. Luckily, it never came to that. The ranch began to prosper a little, and money was never quite so scarce again. As long as our father had plenty of whiskey, he was content to drink himself stupid and knock us around occasionally."

"More than occasionally, from the sound of it."

"Yes," she admitted, and then went on to share bits and pieces of her memories.

By the time she wound down, Ace had an entirely different picture of Patrick O'Shannessy. "Your brother sounds like quite the fellow. No wonder you love him so."

"He'd give up his life for me," she whispered. "He took more beatings to protect me than I can count on all my fingers and toes."

"Would your father have done the same? Would he have taken a beating to spare someone he loved, Caitlin?"

She gave a bitter laugh. "My father? He never loved anyone but himself, so it's a moot question."

"Then Patrick is nothing like him, is he? Not in all the ways that really count. He can't handle his liquor, and he acts like an ass when he's drunk, but essentially he's nothing like your father."

She dug her elbows into his chest to push up and look him directly in the eye. "What are you saying?"

Ace traced the contours of her sweet, tear-streaked countenance with a fingertip, loving her in a way he wouldn't have believed possible two months ago. He felt his manhood harden at the pressure of her hips against him and willed the erection away. *Not now.* It felt so good, having her lie on top of him. Not seeing any fear in her eyes. He didn't want to spoil it.

"Bad seed, remember? There's no such thing, Caitlin. Patrick is no more tainted by the O'Shannessy blood in his veins than you are." He rubbed his thumb across her slightly swollen mouth. "Another thing, Mrs. Keegan. I think your red hair is beautiful. If you give me a half-dozen redheaded babies, I'll count myself one hell of a lucky man."

She shifted her hips slightly, her eyes going wide with startlement. "I think I'd better get up."

Realizing that she'd felt his sudden hardness, Ace looped an arm around her waist to anchor her. "Don't even think about it."

"But I—"

"I'm not going to hurt you, Caitlin. It feels nice having you against me, that's all. My body, unlike my brain, doesn't realize this is an inappropriate moment to react."

She nibbled her bottom lip. "Are you certain?"

"Trust me," he said silkily. "I get this way practi-

cally every time I get close to you. I smell your hair
or feel your softness, and the next thing I know, I want
you."

"Oh, dear." She pushed harder with her elbows,
levering her torso upward and swinging a knee to the
ground. "I really think I'd better—"

"Caitlin, stay put," he said firmly. "Wanting you and
doing something about it are two different things. Sooner or later, you have to learn to trust me. There's no time
like the present."

"Tomorrow might be better."

He laughed in spite of himself. As his mirth ebbed, he
grew solemn and searched her worried gaze. "What is it
you're so afraid may happen, Caitlin? Can you tell me
that? What was the first thought that came into your
mind a second ago when you felt my hardness?"

"That you might hurt me."

"So your greatest fear of making love is that I'll cause
you pain. Is that right?"

She averted her gaze. "Mostly, yes."

He caught a tendril at her temple and let it curl around
his finger. "Caitlin, how much do you love me?"

The question itself was a gamble. A short time ago,
she'd vehemently denied even feeling the emotion and
might very well do so again. To admit to loving was to
open one's self up to hurt, to make one's self vulnerable.
He wasn't sure she was capable of doing that.

"A lot," she said in a hollow little voice.

It wasn't exactly the most poetic avowal of love he'd
ever heard, but to Ace, knowing how dearly the admission cost her, it was beautiful. *A lot.* As high as the
mountains? No. As deep as the sea? No. Just a lot. But
for him, it was enough.

"Do you love me enough to trust me?" he asked her
softly.

She stirred slightly. A dimwitted young woman, she
wasn't. Not even in her present state, which was probably half numb. She knew a danger signal when she felt
one. "I'm trusting you right now."

He bit back a smile. The wariness in her gaze was

unmistakable, and he knew she'd like nothing better than to put a safe distance between them. "I guess you are, at that. I'm just hoping you'll trust me a bit further."

"How do you mean?"

He tightened his hand on her shoulder. Through the worn cloth of her dress, he could feel the strap of her chemise, the ball of her shoulder beneath his thumb, the network of feminine muscle that shielded the bone of her upper arm. A bone that he could undoubtedly snap with the crush of his grip. He took a deep breath.

"I'm just thinking about striking another little bargain with you," he said softly, slowly, so the words could sink into her mind and begin to make sense before he went on. "How would you feel if I were to swear that I'll never touch you in any way that you don't wish for me to?"

A measure of tension left her body. "Never?" she asked, the hopeful note in her voice unmistakable.

Ace smiled again, ruefully. "Never," he assured her.

"I guess that would be—" She broke off, her eyes shimmering and filled with questions. "You would do that?"

"Absolutely."

"You swear it?"

"In return for a promise from you, yes, I'll swear it."

A sudden flicker of distrust darkened her eyes to a gunmetal blue. She had a right to feel wary, Ace knew, but he mourned the fact, even so. "What kind of promise?"

"An all-inclusive one, I'm afraid. It won't be an easy promise for you to make, and it will probably be even harder for you to keep."

"What?"

Ace swallowed. Here went nothing. "I want you to promise me you'll never object or ask me not to touch you in a particular way unless it brings you pain. If it does, I'll stop. No questions, no arguments. I'll just stop and never touch you like that again."

Her heartbeat escalated. He could feel the rapid thrum of her pulse beneath his fingertips, against her ribs, across his hips. "I-I don't know. I don't really—"

"Don't answer off the top of your head," he warned. "It's more than most husbands offer, for one. For another, it's a damned good deal, if you'll just think about it. A guarantee from me that I'll never, under any circumstances, hurt you. You just said that's what frightens you most, the thought of being hurt."

"It is. The main thing, anyway."

"Well, then?"

She pushed up a bit more, supporting more of her weight on her elbows. "If—I promise that, you'll swear never to hurt me? Not even a teeny bit? Not even for a second?"

Ace felt almost guilty. He knew damned well that her memory of Dublin's attack served her well. Probably acutely so. The thing that undoubtedly loomed most frighteningly in her mind was the pain the bastard had inflicted. A man couldn't rape a struggling woman without his every touch being brutal. She clearly believed she would suffer the same abuse again if she allowed her husband liberties with her body. Little did she know that nothing, not even Ace's invasive possession of her, was likely to cause her any discomfort.

In short, he was tricking her, and later, when it was too late, she would undoubtedly realize it. Hopefully, by that time, he would also have had a chance to prove to her that she had nothing to fear from being in his arms.

"Caitlin, I'm willing to swear on my very life—hell, I'll even swear it on the Bible—that I will do nothing, absolutely nothing, that will cause you so much as a twinge of discomfort. Never. And if, by some accident, I start to, all you'll have to do is tell me and I'll stop instantly."

The incredulity in her eyes made his throat tighten. What in God's name had the poor girl been imagining he might do to her?

She took a deep, shaky breath. "I think I'd like it better if you'd simply agree not to touch me at all. At least for a while."

Ace gulped back a chuckle. Simply? She had no idea. "That isn't an option, honey. That's basically what we've been doing this last month, and just look at you. You're a bundle of nerves. And I've been snapping my brothers' heads off every time they look crosswise at me. We can't go on like this. And if you'll think about it, I'm sure you wouldn't want to. As long as I never hurt you, what have you got to lose, hm?"

She fell silent for a while, clearly weighing her options, which were few. "All right," she finally said. "We have a deal."

Ace nearly whooped for joy. Not a wise idea. Instead he kept his expression suitably solemn and said, "You'll never regret it. I swear that as well."

GOLDEN LANTERN LIGHT ILLUMINATED THE WINDOWS OF THE house, beckoning to Ace like beacons in a safe harbor as he carried Caitlin across the yard. Exhaustion had finally taken its toll on her about halfway home, and he'd been left with little choice but to carry her. Luckily, she didn't weigh much.

At some point along the way, she'd fallen asleep. Her head lolled on his shoulder. One of her arms dangled limply at his side. He figured it was just as well. This way, she wouldn't have to face his brothers and could wait until morning to apologize for the mess she'd made of the house.

His brothers. Sanity awaited him inside. For the first time in his life, the darkness seemed evil to Ace—a cold, cloying dimness filled with shifting, mocking shadows.

When Ace kicked open the front door, he could smell only the faintest traces of smoke. With a quick glance at the room, he saw that the water and spilled stew had been mopped up. His brothers, who were sitting at the table, froze in various positions, their startled, questioning gazes locked on the woman in his arms. Joseph was the first to finally move.

"What the hell happened?" He jumped up from the bench and strode toward Ace. "Did she fall? What?"

Ace shook his head slightly, trying to say with his eyes what he couldn't with words. Joseph's steps faltered, and he shot another look at Caitlin, his expression growing more concerned. Ace moved past him toward the hallway. There would be time later to answer their questions.

🐉 22

FOR A SECOND, CAITLIN WASN'T SURE WHERE SHE WAS. Softness beneath her. Ace's strong hands gripping her by the shoulders. With a dim awareness, she concluded that he'd put her on the bed, that he was holding her upright. She opened her eyes and concentrated on his face, etched by moonlight and defined with shadow. His expression was so grim. Her heart caught at the way he avoided looking into her eyes.

She had told him . . .

Something inside her tightened like a fist. Her darkest secret—the one thing she'd never told anyone. What on earth had possessed her? Every time he looked at her now, he would think of it. He'd never feel the same about her. Never. A shiver ran through her body. She wanted to hug herself to ward off the sudden chill, but her arms felt like strips of wet rug hanging from her shoulders.

Coolness brushed over her shoulders, then across her breasts. She blinked and glanced down, surprised to see that Ace was tugging her arms from her dress sleeves. Numb. No hands. No legs. No feet. There was only that awful fist of pain inside her stomach. Suddenly the world seemed to turn topsy-turvy. A pillow embraced her cheek. Lying down. She was lying down.

Tap, shuffle. Tap, shuffle. She peered through the gloom, watching as Ace stepped into the dressing room. He returned a moment later with something white trailing from his hands. As he bent back over her, he said, "I'm going to pull your nightgown on over your head before I completely undress you, honey. No need to feel embarrassed. Okay? I'll keep you covered."

No need to feel embarrassed? All Caitlin felt was the hurting. A huge, awful kind of hurting that radiated upward from her middle into her chest. Her head fell back as Ace lifted her to a sitting position again. She struggled to put some starch in her neck, to help hold herself upright with her hands. No part of her body seemed willing to cooperate.

Up went one of her arms. She felt her hand double over as he tried to stuff it down a sleeve. Her wrist panged.

"Christ. I'm not very good at this. I'm sorry."

Caitlin watched as he tried to push his own hand up the sleeve from the opposite direction so he might grasp her fingers and fish her arm through. But, of course, his hand wouldn't fit. The cuff formed far too small an opening for that large fist of his. He struggled to unfasten the three pearl buttons.

Suddenly it all struck Caitlin as being funny. The fearful Ace Keegan, trying to undress a woman without baring any part of her body? She remembered all the times she'd trembled in fear of him, and a shrill laugh burst from her. He glanced up, his eyes filled with questions.

"What?"

Caitlin slumped forward, bumping her brow against his. "You . . ."

His mouth twisted in a smile. "Yeah, I'm pretty amusing, all right. A damned bungler, that's me." He finally managed to draw her arm down the sleeve. Then, keeping a firm grasp on that shoulder, he turned his attention to her other cuff. After fumbling for a moment, he popped the buttons free. Within seconds, he got her other arm into the gown, and the next thing she knew, her upper body was swathed in white cotton.

Jerking the quilt and sheet aside, he flipped her over onto her back and proceeded to divest her lower body of clothing, tugging off the dress first, then her petticoats, and lastly her bloomers and stockings. The cotton drawers, ribbed hose, and garters ended up in fat rolls at her ankles, which he jerked off over her feet, taking her unlaced shoes along with them. That done, he drew the covers over her and tucked them in around her shoulders.

Caitlin stared up at him, longing to ask him not to leave, but unable to articulate the thought. Planting a hand on either side of her, he leaned down over her, his dark eyes glinting.

"I'll be right back. Okay?"

She tried to reach for him, but his weight on the quilt held her arms anchored to the mattress at her sides. The next thing she knew, he had gone. She turned her gaze to the open door, where the faint glow of lantern light coming from the front room cut an amber swath across the floor. She could hear voices, but her mind wouldn't focus sharply enough to make sense of the words.

WHEN ACE RETURNED TO THE BEDROOM, CAITLIN WASN'T IN the bed. When he'd left her, he would have sworn she was too emotionally spent to move. He spun in a half-circle, his gaze searching the shadows. He spotted her standing at the window, barely visible against the backdrop of white curtain.

"Caitlin?"

Setting a bottle of liquor and tumbler on the bedside table, he stepped over to grasp her shoulders. She was trembling. "Sweetheart, what are you doing out of bed?"

"Just thinking," she said hollowly.

From somewhere at the front of the house, Ace heard a door slam closed. He'd asked his brothers to retire early, and he guessed they'd just left. "Come on," he whispered. "Let's get you back under the quilt before you catch your death."

As usual, the chill Colorado night wind had dropped the temperature in the room. At the bed, he released her wrist to fumble with the bedcovers. After giving the sheet and quilt a sharp snap, he drew both back out of the way. Moonlight from the window fell over her as she submitted to his guiding hands and lowered herself into a huddled ball on the mattress. He drew the covers over her and tucked them snugly around her.

He stepped quickly to the bedside table and lit the lamp. When the light flared, he went back to sit beside her, then reached for the whiskey jug. After sloshing out a measure into the glass, he slipped a hand beneath her neck and lifted her head. "Drink."

She wrinkled her nose at the smell. "Whiskey!"

"Drink," he said firmly. "I mean it, Caitlin. Drink or I'll pour it down you. Your choice."

She took a large gulp of the liquor, then wheezed for breath. Ace pressed the rim of the tumbler back to her lips. "All of it."

She shot him a look, her eyes quickening with tears. "It burns."

"Keegan's remedy for whatever ails you," he said softly. "Drink."

She took two more swallows, nearly draining the glass. Ace figured he'd gotten one or two shots down her. It wasn't much by his standards, but he guessed it would be enough to relax her and help her get a good night's sleep. She shuddered as the whiskey settled on her stomach. Then she sank back against the pillow and closed her eyes.

He set the tumbler and jug back on the table. Then he touched a fingertip to the column of her throat. "A penny for them," he whispered.

She lifted an arm and angled it over her eyes. Ace studied her for a moment, then hauled in a deep breath. "Caitlin, won't you look at me?"

The corners of her mouth tightened. "I shouldn't have told you," she said.

"I'm damned glad you did. I can understand you a little better now, at least."

She kept her arm over her eyes. "Every time—" She broke off and swallowed, the muscles along her throat convulsing. "Every time you look at me now, you're going to think of it."

Ace pushed up off the bed and stepped around to

douse the lamp, unbuttoning his shirt en route. When darkness cloaked the room, he divested himself of his clothing, leaving on only his drawers. He felt her gaze on him as he walked back to the bed. He knew by the sudden tensing of her body exactly when she lowered her gaze to the region of his hips.

"Ace?"

"There's nothing to be afraid of," he told her huskily.

He drew back the covers and lowered himself onto the mattress beside her. She tried to scoot away as the quilt settled over them, but Ace was determined to have none of that. He clamped a hand over her side. The touch of her cool skin through the worn nightgown burned his palm.

"You're freezing, sweetheart." He drew her toward him, moving halfway to meet her. "Let me get you warm."

She gasped and tried to rear back when the chilled tips of her breasts touched his hot chest. "Don't!"

He angled an arm beneath her head and pulled her even closer. "Don't what?"

"I'm naked under my nightgown."

He smiled slightly, recalling all the times she'd come to bed wearing nearly enough clothing to attend church. His wife, the temptress. "I think that's the way you're supposed to be, Caitlin."

"But it makes me—nervous not having anything else on."

He had noticed that, yes. "Caitlin, am I hurting you?"

She ceased her wiggling and fastened accusing eyes on his face. Realization had struck. Ace refused to feel like a skunk.

"Well, am I?"

"No," she admitted faintly.

"Then stop squirming."

"I'd really like my pantalets, please."

"And I'd really, really like to feel my wife for a change, instead of layers of cotton." He pushed up on his elbow and bent his head to kiss her. She planted the heels of her hands on his shoulders to hold him off. "Caitlin, you promised. No objections unless I hurt you."

"Not tonight," she pleaded in a pitiful little voice. "Please, not tonight."

"Why?" he countered. "So you can imagine I'm looking at you and thinking you're anything less that perfect? Or so you can slip out of bed after I'm asleep and chill yourself to the bone, gazing out the window and thinking things that have no basis in fact? I don't think so."

He touched his lips to her fair brows, then to her eyelids, smiling at the way her lashes fluttered. "You're beautiful, Caitlin. Sweet and absolutely precious to me." Nuzzling his way downward, he found the curve of her neck and traced it with the tip of his tongue. "You can't run away from the memories, honey. But I can love them away, if you'll only let me."

Love them away? Caitlin felt as if her heart might slam straight up her throat, yet for the life of her, she didn't have the strength or will to move. Her head had fallen back over his arm, giving him free access to her neck. He nibbled at the tender spot with firm, satiny lips that set her skin afire.

"Ace?"

She gazed at his dark head, at the blur of his chiseled features. Broad, muscular shoulders, gilded with moonlight, flexed and rippled every time he moved. His body made her think of carved walnut, rubbed with oil to a burnished sheen. She ran a hand from his chest, which felt so hard it really might have been carved from wood, to test the bulges along his upper arm. The strength she felt there was frightening. How could anyone have so much muscle and still move as fast as he did?

Somehow, the buttons of her nightgown had come unfastened. With expert fingertips, he parted the plackets. She felt cold air puckering her nipple. The next thing she knew, his mouth trailed to the beginning swell of her breast. Caitlin held her breath to keep from begging him to stop. Instead, she waited for the pain, certain it would come, absolutely convinced it would. Memories flashed. Of cruel hands, of biting fingers, of teeth torturing her flesh. As he trailed light kisses in a slowly diminishing circle around her nipple, her flesh shriveled in self-defense and she braced herself for an assault. Instead, Ace kissed only the orb of her breast, continuing to avoid its throbbing, expectant crest.

The agony of waiting soon had her arching toward him, her body responding even though her mind recoiled. He ran his hand from her side down over her hip. Then his fingertips blazed a swath the length of her thigh. Afraid he might thrust his hand between her legs, she forgot all about the gentle assault he waged on her upper torso and concentrated on clamping her knees together.

It was then that she felt the silken, wet heat of his mouth close over her nipple. She gasped. He drew on her sharply, teasing the tip of her breast into an aching, throbbing erection, which he then seized lightly between his teeth and flicked with his tongue. Caitlin felt as if every nerve in her body was being stroked. She jerked and quivered, unable to even think clearly, let alone anticipate what he might do next.

It was heaven. It was hell. She had been pinned to the mattress by a thick wall of warm muscle. Somehow, he'd insinuated a knee between both of hers, forcing her thighs apart. She reached down to grab his hand, only to forget her aim when he suddenly switched his attention to her other breast. He had a dozen hands, she thought dizzily. And all of them were eliciting responses from her body she'd never dreamed possible.

Fire pooled low in her belly. She heard herself moan. The next thing she knew, she had made fists in his hair, not to shove his head away, but to draw his wonderful mouth more firmly to her breast. Every time he flicked her with his tongue, she nearly cried out. Nothing had ever felt so good. Nothing. And yet it also made her ache. A frustrating, confusing ache for things she couldn't name.

She lifted her hips, wanting more of the grinding pressure of his hand on her pelvis. It was madness, this wanting, and yet she couldn't resist. Heat. Shooting little shards of sensation that took her breath. She arched higher, seeking more, needing to feel the hardness pressing against her.

Ace lifted his head to gaze down at Caitlin's face. Her lashes had drifted low. Her lips were softly parted, inviting his kiss. He bent his head to taste her mouth, then returned to suckle her breasts, enjoying the mewling noises she made when he drew on her and teased her with his teeth. God, she was sweet. He wanted to touch every inch of her, taste every inch of her.

He hadn't intended to actually finish the act when he'd first started to make love to her. But then, he'd never expected this kind of response. Shoving the hem of her nightgown higher, he ran his hand over the soft thatch of curls between her thighs, gently parting her folds with a fingertip. Moist heat. He closed his eyes against a rush of longing. God, he wanted her. He'd never wanted any woman this urgently.

She cried out when he delved deeply into her with his touch. Not a cry of fear, but one of surprise. He abandoned her breasts to rain light kisses over her face, whispering reassurances to her.

"It's all right, Caitlin. Shhh. Relax, sweetheart."

She tightened her thighs around his hand to inhibit its thrust. Sensing that he needed to spend more time arousing her, he withdrew and touched his fingertips to the already swollen flange of flesh just above her channel. At the contact, she dragged in a breath and wriggled her hips, trying to escape. Ace followed with his hand, pressed his thumb against her, and began a slow, light rotation.

Under his teasing ministrations, her sensitive flesh slowly hardened and thrust upward, begging for firmer handling. Ace increased the pressure and escalated the pace. In a gesture as old as womankind, she lifted her hips, seeking the pleasure his hand could give her. Ace didn't withhold it from her.

She ignited like sun-dried pitch touched by a match flame. As the first shock of sensation rolled over her, she grabbed hold of his shoulders and arched her back, her breath coming in increasingly quick little pants.

"Ace?"

"Shhh, sweetheart, it's all right."

He smiled slightly, watching the expressions that flitted across her face, her initial startlement, a flash of fear, and then oblivion as passion caught her in its grasp. Along with her climax came shudders that ran the length of her slender body.

Ace drew her close afterward, stroking her hair, whispering gently to her. She pressed her parted lips against his neck, shivering and breathing unevenly. He waited until the residual shudders finally stopped. Then, and only then, did he pull away from her.

Pulling off his drawers, he positioned himself over her. At the first nudge of his manhood against her, she blinked and focused. He didn't give her time to become frightened. With one smooth thrust, he buried himself inside her. In all his memory, nothing had ever felt quite so good. She shrieked and dug her fingernails into his skin.

"Noooo!"

Ace felt her body convulse and spasm around him. Every muscle in his own knotted with his effort not to move. "Caitlin? Sweetheart, did I hurt you?"

She stared up at him, her face aglow with passion, her eyes dark splashes against moon-silvered skin. "Ace?"

Who the hell did she think? He clenched his teeth, acutely aware that the reflexive clasping of her tight little passage was about to send him over the edge. Then, explosively and with a force that snapped his whole body taut, he erupted.

"Christ!"

Ace tried to stop it. He would have had more luck trying to make water flow uphill. Like an untried lad, he spent himself inside her without even taking a stroke. Muscles quivering, heart pounding like a bunch of Cheyenne war drums, he lowered himself onto her, trying without much success to bear most of his weight on his arms.

God, what a great lover he was. Next thing he knew, he'd start hopping like a damned rabbit.

"I'm sorry, Caitlin. God, sweetheart, I'm so sorry."

She angled her head to hook her chin over his shoulder, probably to keep from suffocating. Ace knew he was probably squashing her and tried to lift himself away. His arms had turned into wet noodles.

"Why are you sorry?" she asked in a shaky voice.

Ace groaned, finally managed to roll off of her, and planted his face in the pillow. She obviously didn't know what she had missed. Egotist that he was, he wasn't about to enlighten her. Later, he promised himself. When he got some strength back. From the way he felt, that would only be a day or so. A week, tops.

Jesus. Never in all his life had he made such a poor showing and felt so drained afterward. In the past, with other women, he had been able to keep up his rhythm for prolonged periods of time, and he had always gotten it off at least twice. Why, with the one female who mattered, had he been such a Nancy-boy? He felt as drained as a sink with no stopper.

"It's nothing," he mumbled into the ticking. "I just— it's nothing, sweetheart."

Seconds passed. He felt her roll onto her side. Another long silence. "Oh, Ace," she whispered. "I feel so silly."

She felt silly?

"After all my worrying," she said, "and there was hardly anything to it!"

🙰 23

THE FOLLOWING MORNING, ACE WAS ALREADY UP AND dressed by the time Caitlin came sailing from the bedroom. Because he'd asked his brothers to hit the sack early last night, they had already guessed that Caitlin's and his evening together had been momentous. Her entrance into the front room confirmed their suspicions.

"Good morning, everyone!" she fairly chortled as she

moved toward the table. Coming to a stop near Ace's elbow, she let her smile dim slightly. She glanced at each of his brothers. "I, um, guess I owe you all an apology. You're probably still pretty mad at me, huh?"

Joseph narrowed one eye at her. "Do I look mad?"

"No," she said cautiously.

"Well, then, I guess I'm not." The corners of his mouth quirked. "Looking back on it, I wouldn't have missed it, actually. I've never seen anyone attack a stove pipe with a poker before."

"Does that mean I'm forgiven?"

Ace's brothers smiled. "Only if you promise not to burn supper again," Esa compromised.

"Never on purpose again, anyway," Caitlin vowed, then continued toward the kitchen. "Isn't it an absolutely glorious day?"

Joseph yawned, scratched his head, and cast a glance out the front window at the overcast sky. "Oh, yeah . . ." When Caitlin disappeared into the kitchen, he batted his eyelashes and grinned at Ace. "You give a little swimming instruction last night, big brother?"

"Shut up."

Esa stopped chomping on the toast he'd just stuffed into his mouth. Around the half-chewed chunks, he said, "Where'd you go swimmin'? In the creek?"

Joseph chuckled and scratched beside his nose. Caitlin reentered the room just then, a steaming mug of coffee cradled between her palms. She sat at the table near Ace's elbow, flashed him a shy smile, and proceeded to turn an alarming shade of crimson.

Why she was blushing, Ace didn't know. Hardly anything had happened, after all.

He lifted his mug, took a giant swig of coffee, and burned the hair off of his tongue clear back to his tonsils. Tears rushed to his eyes, and he coughed. Everyone at the table, expect Joseph, turned a curious gaze on him.

Ace motioned with the mug. "Now that's hot coffee."

Caitlin gingerly took a sip. "Mmm." The blush on her face began to recede. She glanced around at each of his brothers. "What're everyone's plans for the day?"

Ace intended to make proper love to his wife the first chance he got, but he had business to tend to first. "I have to spend the morning in town."

"Esa and I have a stretch of fence to mend," David put in.

Joseph shrugged. "I thought I'd fix the wagon wheel and do some weeding in the garden. After that, wherever my nose leads me, I guess."

Caitlin flashed another smile. "I thought I'd make cinnamon rolls. Does that sound good?"

It didn't sound as good as getting her off alone in the bedroom and tossing up her skirts, Ace thought wryly. With any luck, he'd pour it to her so hard and fast, he'd make her yeast bread fall.

Hardly anything to it? Jesus H. Christ.

WHEN HE GOT TO TOWN LATER THAT MORNING, ACE TETH-ered his horse out behind the livery stable, his hope being that he could slip down the street to the office of Barbary Coast Mortgage without anyone noticing. The fewer people who saw him entering the building, the better. Until he got things straightened out here in No Name, he couldn't afford for anyone to connect him with the company that had financed the purchase of so many parcels of land along the proposed railroad spur route.

Although his and Caitlin's relationship had taken a definite turn for the better last night, it was still fragile. A girl who'd been betrayed so cruelly by her own father wasn't likely to take any man on faith. He couldn't risk her accidentally learning of his many deceptions until he had rectified matters. Then, and only then, would he tell her the truth about everything—when he had proof in black and white that he'd had a change of heart.

Despite his tension about being seen, Ace was amused to catch John Parrish, the supposed proprietor of Barba-ry Coast Mortgage, in the middle of writing a letter to his fiance, Eden. A love letter, if the flush that crept up John's neck when he saw Ace was any indication. After stuffing the stationery in a drawer, he shot up from his desk as if the chair were piping hot.

"Ace!" He glanced worriedly at the windows. "What're you doing here?"

Except for one other time, Ace had never paid John a visit at the office. In the past, any time he had needed to speak to the younger man, he'd shoved a note through the mail drop in his hotel room door to arrange a meeting elsewhere.

"There's been a slight change in plans," Ace told him lightly. Turning the straight-backed chair in front of John's desk, Ace straddled the seat and folded his arms over the back. "You got a few minutes?"

Neat and businesslike in his tailored tweed suit, John stepped over to the lock the door and draw the shades. Watching him, Ace concluded it wasn't any wonder the people in No Name had so easily accepted John in his role of lien holder; he'd been born to play the part.

"You're taking an awful chance coming here," he said. "What if someone saw you and guesses what we're up to?"

"I tied my horse in back of the livery, and I was careful. Unless someone just happened to be staring out a window, chances are I wasn't seen." Ace trailed his gaze over the desk. "Where'd your portrait of Eden hare off to?"

John's mouth tightened as he resumed his seat across from Ace. "After Joseph sent me a note telling me of her uncanny resemblance to Caitlin O'Shannessy and your certainty that Eden is O'Shannessy's daughter, I was afraid to keep her picture sitting out. People do come in here to see me about loans, you know. I was afraid someone might notice Eden's picture and start putting two and two together."

"Good thinking," Ace observed. Meeting his future brother-in-law's gaze, he added, "Caitlin's last name is no longer O'Shannessy, you know."

John smoothed a hand over his dark hair and pushed his spectacles higher on his nose. "Yes, I know. Joseph got word to me of your marriage. Not that I wouldn't have heard. For weeks, it was all anyone talked about around here." He met Ace's gaze. "I heard you gave her a toss in the hay and had to marry her. Can you believe the lies people tell when gossip starts running thick? And about a man like you. It fairly boggles the mind."

Ace bit back a sheepish smile. "Yeah, well, there's just no figuring folks sometimes. Caitlin isn't the kind of young woman to take a roll in the hay with a stranger. I can't imagine anyone who knows her very well saying such a thing."

John nodded, then frowned slightly. "I have to admit, I was surprised to hear you'd married her. As much as you hate the O'Shannessys, well . . ." He lifted his hands. "You could've knocked me over with a feather."

"A man doesn't choose who he falls in love with. It just happens. She's a wonderful girl."

Ace rubbed the stubble along his jaw. Before going home to Caitlin, he'd need a shave. In his mind's eye, he pictured the hayloft in the barn, filled to the brim with fresh hay. His thoughts went from there to images of Caitlin as she'd looked last night, her slender body arched up against him in ecstasy. A roll in the hay, hm? The idea had its merits.

With a start, he realized John had been talking. He jerked himself back to the present. "Say what?"

"I just asked what the change in plans might be," John repeated. "Are you wanting me to start the foreclosures ahead of schedule?"

"No. In fact, I've decided there aren't going to be any foreclosures. I've changed my mind, John. Now that I'm married to Caitlin, I feel a little differently about things. Revenge is a shaky foundation to build a marriage on. I've decided to give it up. In short, we're actually going to build that railroad spur."

John's blue eyes widened. "You're kidding." When he saw that Ace was serious, he whistled. "Holy Jehosha-phats! That'll cost you a bloody fortune."

"Please spare me the lectures. I already know it isn't a sound business move. I'm willing to suffer the losses."

John studied him for a long moment. "We're talking some fairly heavy losses, Ace. Are you sure you've thought this through carefully?"

"I'm sure. I'm thinking of it as an investment in my future. Being able to ship my cattle to Denver by rail will decrease the number of cattle I'll lose. But that's not my only reason. It's mainly personal. I've decided there are more important things in life than money. I can't expect Caitlin to be happy with a man who sets out to financially destroy all the people she knows, including her brother. Now can I?"

"Instead of destroying them, you'll be making them heaps of money, and they're all crooks," John observed. "Patrick O'Shannessy included. All the men who invested in land along that spur route did so at the expense of small-time dirt farmers. Before, I could look at that and figure the farmers had gotten money for their land they wouldn't have been offered otherwise, that they were better off because of this hoax than they ever could have hoped to be. But now?"

"I've already considered that. I'm going to offer those particular investors exactly what they paid for the land, not a penny more. If they refuse to sell, I'll threaten to sit on things until they're unable to make their mortgage payments, then foreclose. They'll knuckle under, and they won't make a dime on the venture."

"Ace, money doesn't grow on trees. You can't start throwing it away. True, you're a wealthy man, but as rich as Croesus, you're not."

"You're a financier to the marrow of your bones, John. That's why I originally hired you into the corporation. But there are times when wise financial ventures and a man's personal feelings don't mix. This is one of them. I have to do this. I need you to help me."

John puffed air into his cheeks. "All right, Ace. Far be it from me to tell you how to spend your money."

For the next two hours, the two men discussed what they'd have to do before construction of the railroad spur could get underway. At the conclusion of their meeting, John said, "I'll start sending out inquiries immediately. It takes a lot more to build a spur than just money, you know."

"I appreciate the fact that it won't be easy." Ace

pushed up from the chair. "Just remember that speed is of the essence. For the sake of my marriage, I want this process off and running as quickly as you can manage it."

As Ace left the mortgage company, he spotted Patrick O'Shannessy exiting the feed store across the street. Their gazes locked. Ace couldn't quite bring himself to smile, but he did tip his hat to his brother-in-law before he turned and headed down the street toward the saloon.

With every step Ace took, he could feel Patrick's gaze boring into his back. How long had his brother-in-law been in town? he wondered. Had Patrick seen him enter Barbary Coast Mortgage? Shit. Of all the people to have seen him, why did it have to be Patrick?

When he reached the bat-wing doors of the saloon, Ace shot a surreptitious glance back down the street. Just as he'd suspected, Patrick was still standing on the boardwalk watching him, his face creased in a thoughtful frown. Ace swore under his breath and pushed the saloon doors open.

The interior of the drinking establishment smelled just like a hundred others Ace had frequented. Stale smoke, even staler whiskey, and the stench of unwashed bodies. Little wonder he found the smell of barnyard manure preferable.

The instant the doors swung shut behind him, a blonde in a red sequin gown appeared, seemingly from out of nowhere, to clasp his arm.

"Hello there, goodlookin'. What'd'ya say to buyin' l'il ol' me a drink?"

Ace smiled down at her. "Sorry, honey. I have other fish to fry at the moment." Casting a glance at the men bellied up to the bar, Ace shook free of the woman's grasp. Just as he'd hoped, the individual he was seeking was standing there, nursing a glass of whiskey. Ace strode over to the counter and elbowed his way in beside the stout, ruddy-faced man with blunt features and grizzled brown hair. "Bartender, I'll take a whiskey, please."

The barkeep slapped a shot glass onto the counter and

slid it over the well-varnished oak surface toward Ace. The fact that the glass spun to a stop directly in front of him gave testimony to the fact that its sender had been serving whiskey for a good long while. Grabbing a half-filled bottle off the shelf behind him, the man stepped over to slosh out a fairly precise measure of liquor. "That'll be two bits."

Ace reached into his trouser pocket and fished out change. He laid the requested amount of coin on the bar, picked up the tumbler, and downed the whiskey in one gulp. As he set the glass back down, he turned to gaze at the portly man beside him.

"Seems the clientele in here hasn't much improved since my last visit," he said softly. "Do you come in just to pass the time of day, Dublin? Or could it be you have to drink to live with your conscience?"

Cruise Dublin looked up, his bloodshot blue eyes filled with equal parts surprise and wariness. "Are you addressing me, Keegan?"

"Sure as hell am." Ace ran his gaze down to the man's paunch, which was so considerable it stressed the buttons of his shirt. "You're a piece of shit. I don't know about everyone else in here, but I don't much like rubbing elbows with a turd."

Dublin's face went angry red. "If you're trying to pick a fight with me, I'm not that stupid or that drunk. I've heard about your skill with a gun."

Ace smiled. "Have you, now?" He reached to unfasten his gun belt. After putting the weapon on the bar, he said, "What's your excuse now, Dublin? Cowardice?"

"I have no quarrel with you."

"That's where you're wrong." In a voice pitched so low no one else could hear, Ace added, "There's the little matter of a sixteen-year-old girl you raped, mister. You made her life hell for six long years. It's one of those things I just can't let go. You understand?"

"She's lying!" Dublin said with a hiss.

"I wouldn't call my wife a liar if I were you. That's liable to make me real mad."

"She's mistaken, then."

"I don't think so. A woman doesn't tend to forget the man who raped her. It's one of those things that tends to linger in her mind."

Dublin squared off with the bar again and picked up his jigger of whiskey with a trembling hand. "What do you want from me? An apology? Fine. You have it. Now leave me alone."

Ace curled his hand over his holster. "I'm giving you a choice, you miserable little sack of shit. You can fight me like a man, or I'll put my gun back on and blow you straight to hell. Take your pick. I'll even let you have the first punch. How's that for a deal you can't pass up?"

Giving no advance warning, Dublin snorted and tossed the whiskey in Ace's face. The liquor got into Ace's eyes, temporarily blinding him. Swinging away from the bar, he gave his head a shake and blinked. In the blur, he saw Dublin grabbing up a chair. The next thing he knew, his head exploded with pain. He went down like a felled oak, landing flat on his back. Dublin buried a boot in his ribs, then kicked him again. And again. The breath whooshed from Ace's lungs. He rolled to his knees, tried to gain his feet. Dublin sent him down face first again with another swing of the chair.

"Fight! Fight!" someone yelled. Ace heard running footsteps. Then a voice called, "Get the marshal! Quick!"

As the sting of the whiskey in his eyes dissipated, Ace regained some of his sight. Enough to see Dublin's boot coming at him again, anyway. Before the well-placed kick could reach its target, Ace snaked out a hand and grabbed the bastard by the ankle. With a forceful twist, he brought the other man down. Dublin landed hard on his back. He was so fat, he looked like a turtle lying there, belly upthrust, his short limbs thrashing uselessly.

Ace sprang up and grabbed Dublin by the lapels of his jacket. Jerking the man to his feet, he planted a fist square in his mouth. The sound of his knuckles connecting with teeth made a very satisfying sound. For Caitlin, Ace thought. For all the tears she'd shed. For all the heartache she'd suffered. For all the times she'd been afraid because of what this son of a bitch had done to her.

At any other time, Ace would have held himself in check. There was no denying he had a physical advantage over the older man, that it wasn't really a fair match. Dublin was short, fat, and twenty years Ace's senior. No contest. Ace usually picked opponents who could give back as good as they got.

Not this time. He thought of Caitlin, of her fragile build and bony elbows. He envisioned her big blue eyes, always so filled with shadows and dark with fear. This bastard had raped her, not caring that she had no strength with which to fight back. Not caring if he humiliated her, or terrified her, or caused her pain. Not a fair match. Now Dublin was going to find out how it felt.

Ace looked into Dublin's frightened eyes, drew back his fist, and hit him again. And then again. After that, he stopped counting.

At some point, one of the other men who had been standing at the bar grabbed Ace by the arm. "Whoa, partner. Unless you mean to kill him, I think he's had enough."

Ace let go of Dublin's jacket and watched the man crumple. He landed with a thud, one side of his face against the floor. Blood streamed from his nose and mouth. Breathing as hard as if he'd been running, Ace stood there, feet spread, hands knotted, gaze fixed on the unconscious man. It wasn't finished. It would never be finished. He'd meant to make the little bastard crawl. To see him grovel, the way he'd undoubtedly made Caitlin grovel. To hear him beg. Instead, he'd beaten him into a senseless stupor.

Ace doubted that Caitlin had been so lucky. There'd been no escape into unconsciousness for her. No way to block out the pain. That was one of the most terrible things about rape; it didn't initially kill a woman. That came later, when she had to live with the memory of what had happened and the feeling she'd never be able to rid herself of the taintedness.

"Never enough," Ace muttered under his breath. With that, he buried the toe of his boot in Dublin's side. Viciously. With all his strength. It was another first. Ace never took shots at an unconscious man. When the fight was over, it was over. "Rot in hell, you miserable piece of garbage."

Staggering back to the bar to get his gun, Ace wiped his face with his shirt sleeve. He had just buckled his gun belt and was tying down the holster when No Name's estimable marshal came crashing through the doors. Estyn Beiler. Like his cohort, Dublin, he was a stout man who had gone soft around the middle. Ace fixed a hate-filled glare on him. Though he'd met the man countless times on the street since his return to No Name, Ace still felt a nearly overpowering revulsion when he saw him. He would never forget the night of his stepfather's death, or the faces of the men who'd been responsible.

Glancing down at Dublin's unconscious form, Beiler yelled, "You're under arrest, Keegan."

"What's the charge?"

"Assault."

Ace glanced around the saloon, looking several of the men near him directly in the eye. "You all saw it. Dublin attacked me first."

"That's right," one of the men confirmed. "Cruise took the first swing. Went crazy. Picked up a chair and worked Keegan over good."

Beiler's face went angry red. "Cruise isn't that big a fool. You're twice his size and half his age."

Ace sneered. "I realize he generally picks on people who can't fight back. I guess this time he decided to make an exception."

Ace glanced around for his hat, which had gone flying when Dublin had beaned him. He spotted it lying under a table and stepped over to collect it. After straightening the crown, he set the Stetson at an angle on his head, then politely tipped the brim. "Gentlemen."

With that, he made his exit. Despite the fact that his head hurt like the blazes, Ace was smiling when he stepped out onto the boardwalk. He stood there for a moment, not caring a whit that the sky was still overcast. Caitlin had nailed it right on the head this morning; it was an absolutely glorious day.

24

"OH, MY GOD! WHAT HAPPENED?"

Ace hadn't realized he looked that bad. Caitlin's startled greeting told him otherwise. Stepping into the house, he pushed the door closed behind him and sailed his hat toward the table. "Nothing much."

"But you have blood all over your upper lip!"

Tossing a towel down on the bench, she came running over to him, her eyes wide as she regarded his face. Ace gave his nose a wiggle, recalling how he'd done a face plant on the barroom floor. "I do? Hmm."

She clasped her hands at her waist and went as white as chalk. "Patrick," she said softly. "You got into it with Patrick."

All the way home, Ace had debated whether or not to tell Caitlin about his set-to with Dublin. On the one hand, he didn't want to sound like a puffed-up braggart. The man had gotten what was coming to him. That was the end of it. On the other hand, Ace had wondered if she wouldn't want to know. Though he'd had a personal change of heart just recently, he still maintained that revenge could sometimes be awfully sweet, and if anyone on earth had call to want a taste of it, Caitlin did.

"Not Patrick," Ace assured her.

Some of the color returned to her cheeks. "You promise?"

Ace grinned. "Have I ever lied to you?"

"I haven't caught you yet, anyway."

"Such faith." Ace stepped past her and headed for the

kitchen where he dampened a towel to wash his face. He gazed down at the surprising amount of blood that came away on the linen. No wonder so many people in town had stopped to stare at him as he sauntered along the boardwalk. As he laid the towel aside, he said, "You got anything to eat? I'm starving."

"Just that? You're starving? You've been in a fight. I want to know with whom."

Ace sighed. "I'm not sure I should tell you. It'll either make you glad or mad. I'm not sure which. I'd kind of like to stay on your good side."

She narrowed an eye. "It *was* Patrick. You promised me, Ace. You promised."

He caught her by the chin and looked deeply into her eyes. "And I don't make a habit of breaking my promises. The fight wasn't with your brother. I had a bone to pick with a certain individual. I picked it. It's finished. Let's leave it at that, all right? I'm sorry I walked in with blood on my face and got you all upset. I'm not hurt. So let's get on with our day and not worry about it."

"Who?" she persisted.

Ace chuckled. "Curiosity killed the cat, you know. Where is he, by the way?"

"He's in the study window sill having a nap."

Reaching around her, Ace snatched a square of cornbread out of a pan sitting on the range's warming shelf. He shoved the morsel into his mouth. "Mmm." Glancing toward the yeast dough she'd set out to rise on the counter, he swallowed and asked, "How long before the rolls are done?"

"About an hour after you tell me who you got in a fight with."

Ace wiped his mouth with the back of his hand. "Cruise Dublin," he mumbled.

Her eyes went dark. "Cruise Dublin?"

"That's right." Ace felt heat inching up his neck. He'd always hated it when he heard men brag about their prowess in a fist fight. It was disgusting. A real man didn't fight and tell. He just took care of business and kept his mouth shut. "I stomped the fire out of him."

"You did?"

Ace squared his shoulders. "It wasn't all that big a thing."

Her expression said it was. A very big thing. Tears filled her eyes. "Tell me."

"Tell you what?"

"The details."

Ace saw that she had her hands clenched into fists at her sides. "I shoved a couple of his teeth down his throat." No brag, that. Just fact.

She squeezed her eyes closed. Tears trailed down her pale cheeks. Then her mouth lifted in a tremulous smile. When she looked at him again, Ace felt a few inches taller than he had a second before. "Did you break his nose?"

"Probably." Ace smiled, too. What the hell. A man was allowed to brag just once in his life. "When I got finished with him, he looked kind of like a dead pig on a platter. Minus the apple, of course. I didn't have one handy."

Her smile faltered. "Was it—I mean—well . . . ?"

"What?"

"When you beat him up, did you do it because of what he did to your stepfather? Or because—"

"I did it for you," Ace interrupted. "And I made damned sure he knew it before I started. If I'd wanted to kick the shit out of him because of what he did to my stepfather, I'd have done it months ago."

She closed her eyes again. "For me," she whispered. "And you told him before you hit him?"

Ace grinned. "You want me to go back and kick the shit out of him again?"

Her eyes popped open. "Would you?"

"If you twist my arm."

"Can I watch?"

Ace threw back his head and laughed. "That can be arranged."

"What I'd really like—" She broke off and touched her tongue to the corners of her mouth. "What I'd really, really like is for you to hold him while _I_ hit him."

Ace shook his head and drew her into his arms. "I'm sorry. I should have taken you with me. It never occurred to me that you'd want to be there."

"I've dreamed of beating him up a hundred times."

"Let's go," he said in all sincerity. "But only if you use a stick. I don't want those pretty little hands of yours messed up."

She reached behind her to grasp his wrist. Drawing his hand up, she stared at his broken knuckles. "Oh, Ace . . ." Tears filled her eyes again. She swallowed convulsively. "I know it's awful of me. Really awful. But I'm so glad you did it!"

"He had that coming, and worse. If there were any justice in this old world, he'd have hanged for it."

She pressed tremulous lips to his barked knuckles. "No one has ever fought for me before," she whispered. "Not ever."

"You're my wife now. If anyone ever hurts you again, it'll be over my dead body. And even then, if I go down, you'll still have the Paxton boys to kick ass for you. Joseph is one ornery little son of a gun when it comes to defending one of his own. You'll never have to feel afraid again, sweetheart. Or fight a battle without plenty of reinforcement to back you up. That's a promise."

She stepped onto the toes of his boots and looped her arms around his neck. "That makes me feel very safe. I haven't felt safe in a long time. It's a very good feeling."

It didn't escape Ace's notice that she finally felt safe in his arms. He guessed they both had reason to feel good. Mighty good.

"Tell me all the details," she whispered. "What did you say to Cruise right before you hit him?"

He chuckled. Sometimes, there was just no help for it. A man had to brag his ass off. He spent the next five minutes holding his wife in his arms while he related the entire incident to her, from beginning to end. The only thing he neglected to share was that he'd almost gotten his butt kicked. A man hesitated to tell that kind of thing to his lady, especially when he had every intention of making love to her as soon as he could possibly manage it.

AFTER ACE HAD SHAVED AND WASHED UP, HE HOLLERED FOR Caitlin to join him in the bedroom. When she entered, he was waiting for her just inside the door, which he promptly closed and locked. She turned a startled gaze on him.

"Why'd you do that?" Her attention shifted to his bare shoulders. "What happened to your shirt?"

Ace rubbed his chest. "I took it off."

He moved slowly toward her, smiling slightly as she took a step back in retreat. "What?" she whispered.

"You know damned well what," he said huskily. Running an arm around her slender waist, he pulled her firmly against him. "You aren't scared, are you?"

She leaned her head back. "Surely you don't mean to—well, you know." She shot a worried look at the drawn curtains at the window. "It's the middle of the day! We can't do that in broad daylight."

"Why not? There's hardly anything to it."

With his free hand, Ace set himself to the task of unfastening the buttons of her dress. When his knuckles grazed the silken swells of her breasts, his shaft sprang taut. This time, he vowed, he wouldn't embarrass himself. No way. He was going to make love to the girl until she lay limp with exhaustion. She wouldn't leave this bedroom again, thinking there was "hardly anything to it." That was for damned sure.

"You didn't answer my question," he whispered against her hair. "Are you scared?"

"Not at all."

She did sound a little breathless.

"You sure?"

She shivered as he peeled the gown away from her shoulders. Creamy skin. Ace bent to nibble along the edge of the chemise strap at her shoulder, then down around the scooped neckline. The undergarment was cut low. With his teeth, he caught the ribbon that gathered it closed. Cloth began to puddle on the floor at her feet.

Dress. Petticoats. Bloomers. Ace's heart started to slam. He moved her around to stand against the wall. Dragged the chemise off over her head and gave it a toss. Oh, yes.

"Ace? It's not dark in here."

He'd noticed that. He bent on one knee to unfasten her shoes. Her silken thighs were inches from his nose. Flesh plumped up at the tops of her garters. White, sensitive-looking flesh that begged to be kissed. As he tugged her ribbed hose down her slender calves, he sat back on his heel to look at her.

Her face pink with embarrassment, she cupped a palm over the thatch of red curls at the apex of her thighs and angled an arm over her chest, her hand splayed to hide one breast. Ace slid his gaze slowly over her, allowing it to linger at certain points along the way. One nipple peeked out at him from under her elbow. It was as rosy as a strawberry. Strawberries had always been his favorite fruit.

He left her feet trapped in the tangle of hosiery and cloth. The better to catch her, just in case she decided to run. Pushing erect, he planted a hand against the wall on either side of her. He bent his head, touched his nose to hers. "Wanna make some baby snots with me?"

She giggled. "You're awful!"

She hadn't seen anything yet. Ace touched the tip of his tongue to her pouted lips, ticking her sensitive flesh. "May I kiss you, Mrs. Keegan?"

"I don't think I want to—well, you know—in the middle of the day. I'd rather wait until dark so we can turn the lights out."

"Why? Are you hiding something from me?"

Her face turned a shade pinker. "I'm trying."

Ace pushed back, glanced down. His throat felt oddly tight. God, she was pretty. He could have spent an hour just looking. With one hand, he grasped her wrist and pried her fingers away from her breast. Her nipple hardened instantly at the touch of cool air. He tweaked it gently and smiled at the way she sucked in her belly and held her breath. Between his fingers, that hardened nubbin of flesh throbbed with her every heartbeat.

Ace settled his mouth over hers, drove his tongue deep, tasting, savoring, establishing a rhythm of thrust and withdrawal. Meanwhile, he toyed with her nipple, his body quickening when she moaned and opened her mouth wider to him. He kissed her until she hung between his chest and the wall, nearly too limp to stand. And then he moved downward, kissing her throat, her breasts. She gasped when he nipped each nipple with his teeth. Made fists in his hair. Clung to him.

"Oh . . . yes," she cried. "Oh, Ace, yes."

It was all the invitation he needed. Capturing the peaks of her breasts between his fingers, he rolled them, watching the expressions that flitted across her small face until he saw complete oblivion. Then he resumed his earlier position at her feet. She had both hands in his hair, which left the glistening thatch of red curls between her thighs unguarded. Vulnerable.

He pressed close, found the sensitive place he sought with the tip of his tongue. She shrieked and nearly jerked his hair out by the roots.

"Wha—? Oh, my God! Nooo!" Even as she protested, she arched her back to press her shoulders against the wall and angle her hips forward, surrendering herself to him. "Stop! Don't! You mustn't. Nooo!"

Tightening her fists, she drew him closer, nearly suffocating him with her sweetness. It was a hell of a way to go. He caught her between his teeth, increasing the pressure as he dragged his tongue over that throbbing protrusion of flesh.

"No! Oh, God!" With a low cry, she began to undulate her hips. As her body began to spasm, she said, "Yes. Oh, yes!"

The next instant, her knees buckled, and she started to slide down the wall to join her clothes in a puddle on the floor. He grasped her beneath the arms. Slid her back up to a standing position. Held her there with his chest while he unfastened his trousers and jerked her slender feet free of the tangle around her ankles.

She shrieked again when he brought her legs up around his hips and thrust the full length of his shaft up inside her. This time, Ace knew better than to stop and ask if he'd hurt her. No way. He withdrew slightly and buried himself to the hilt again.

"Oh, dear God!" She dug in hard at his shoulders with her fingernails. "This is—you can't—oh, my God!"

Pressing her fanny against the wall, Ace established a driving rhythm, jarring her until her cries became soft grunts. She arched at the waist, tossed back her head. He laved her breasts with his tongue as he pushed with his hips, taking her and himself closer and closer, higher and higher. When her body convulsed, he couldn't hold back any longer.

His release was so explosive it left him weak. He slid down the wall with her, landing hard on his knees. She hugged his neck, her head lolling on his shoulder.

"Christ!"

The girl was going to kill him, no two ways about it. He'd never experienced sex like this. Always before, he'd been able to engage in foreplay, give and take satisfaction (always twice, sometimes more), and then leave directly after. With Caitlin, sex was like being run over by a freight train.

She sighed. A sweet, drawn out sigh of sheer bliss. Ace glanced over the top of her curly head, searching for a spot to collapse. Rolling onto his back to take the brunt of their weight, he went down, still holding her clasped to his chest. She gave a final shudder and stretched out over him like a blanket that was too short to cover his feet. He smiled and ran his hand down the curve of her spine. He had only one clear thought before exhaustion claimed him. He kind of liked being run over by trains.

AN HOUR OR SO LATER, ACE WOKE UP. CAITLIN SLEPT ON, her limp body plastered against his, her cheek burrowed against his chest. It took some doing, but Ace managed to stand up with his slumbering wife cradled in his arms. Big problem. He'd never gotten around to shucking his pants. He hobbled over to the bed, feeling like an idiot. There was nothing more undignified than trying to walk, bare-ass naked, with your britches around your ankles. She was definitely a new experience at every turn. Ace Keegan, the debonair gambler, taking baby steps.

As he stripped back the covers and deposited her gently on the bed, her lashes fluttered. Then she opened her eyes, her expression like that of a cat who'd just lapped its fill of cream. Ace grinned. He couldn't help himself. For a girl who'd so studiously avoided the intimate side of marriage, she was sure as hell taking to sex like a duck to water.

"Hi," she said drowsily.

Ace bent to kiss the end of her nose. While his head was lowered, she hooked an arm around his neck. He didn't resist the inviting tug. Lowering himself over her, he tasted the kiss she offered, then suckled the nipple she pressed upward. She made tight fists in his hair again, as if she feared he might try to get away. At this rate, he would probably go bald before he was forty. Not that he gave a shit.

He made love to her again with his boots still on. At some point between foreplay and climax, he drew another astute conclusion. His sweet little wife was a shrieker. He could only hope Joseph was still outside tending the garden. Otherwise, he would hear Caitlin's shrill cries of pleasure and know damned well what was going on behind the locked bedroom door.

Not that he gave a shit.

JOSEPH WAS NOT TENDING THE GARDEN WHEN ACE FINALLY exited the bedroom. Nor had he been tending to his own business, judging by the grin he wore when Ace entered the living room. He was sitting at the table, smoking a cigarette and having a cup of coffee, his blue eyes twinkling.

"Howdy."

Ace narrowed an eye. "You could have stepped out-side."

"You want me to pitch a tent out there, or what?" He shrugged a muscular shoulder. "Hell, I went out and stayed out for nearly an hour. When I came back,

everything was quiet. Then all hell broke loose again."
At Ace's growl, he chuckled. "It's raining out there, big
brother. I didn't want to catch my death."

"I can only wish. Is the barn leaking or something?"

"No. But it is colder out there than a witch's tit. This
is Colorado, remember? At the end of June and the first
part of July, Mother Nature still hasn't gotten a firm grip
on the idea that it's summer."

Ace took a seat across from him. "One word to Caitlin
and you're a dead man."

Joseph chuckled again. "My mama didn't raise me in
no barn. I do have some couth." He gestured with his
mug. "Want some coffee?"

Ace rubbed a hand over his face and propped an
elbow on the table. "We got any blood fortifier around
here anywhere?"

⁊ 25

HEAVEN . . . WHEN CAITLIN OPENED HER EYES THE FOL-
lowing morning, that was her first thought, that she had
found her own private corner of heaven. Ace lay beside
her, his dark face inches from her own on the pillow.
Glistening black hair fell in lazy waves over his high
forehead to touch his sharply arched brows. Thick,
ebony lashes lay in a feathery sweep on his cheeks. In the
wash of morning sunlight that played over his face, she
could see the tiny lines that etched his lips, the creases at
the corners of his eyes, the faint knot along the bridge of
his nose. He was, she decided, as close to being beautiful
as a man could get.

Moving her gaze lower, she took stock of his shoulders, which bulged with muscle even in his sleep.
Bronzed and with a natural sheen to his skin, he looked

as hard and smooth as polished teak. She liked the fact that he wasn't covered from head to toe with lots of body hair. There was a light furring of black across his well-padded chest that tapered to a V at his waist, and his thick forearms were covered with silky hair as well. But otherwise his skin was bare.

And kissable . . .

She pushed up on an elbow, wondering what magic this man had worked within her. Two days ago, she wouldn't have been caught dead naked in bed with him. Now she wanted to draw his hands to her body, wanted to feel his silken lips running over her skin, needed to feel the hard length of him pressed against her and into her. She felt like a greedy child who had just gotten her first taste of candy. She wanted more. And more. If he made love to her a million times, it would never be enough.

She rubbed the tip of her nose against his and smiled when he went, "Mmm," in his sleep. The tips of her breasts skimmed his chest. His dark brows drew together in a slight frown. Grinning, she ran her palm down his flat, ridged abdomen to the coarse hair at the apex of his thighs. Her fingertips encountered a rigid, impressively large shaft that sprang upward, eager for her touch.

His lashes lifted. Sleepy brown eyes focused blearily on her face. Then he smiled slightly. "Better watch out, Mrs. Keegan. That might get you."

"Promise?"

He chuckled. "For a girl who didn't want any part of this, you sure have developed a liking."

"It was the same way with liver. When I first tried it, I hated it. Then I tasted it again years later and couldn't get enough."

"Are you comparing me with liver?"

"It's my favorite."

He rolled up onto an elbow, flipping her onto her back as he moved. "I'll forgive you, then." Coppery shoulders eclipsed the sunlight streaming through the window as he bent his head to kiss her. "My favorite is strawberries."

"I'll grow you some next year," she promised.

"You already have," he said as he dipped downward to taste the crest of one breast. "With these to taste every morning, I'll be a happy man."

Caitlin felt heat building within her and arched up to press her body against his. "Make love to me, Ace."

"I am."

"No, I mean now."

"Don't rush me." He switched his attention to her other breast. "My God, I can't believe how sweet you are."

Caitlin closed her eyes on a rush of yearning.

"Keegan!"

The shout from outdoors brought Caitlin's eyes open and Ace's head up. They stared at each other for a moment. Then, together, they said, "Patrick!" She groaned. He cursed. They both flew from the bed, grabbing for their clothes.

"Is it my imagination, or does this seem to be becoming a habit?" he asked as he thrust a leg into his trousers.

"A bad habit," she agreed, dragging on her bloomers. "He has rotten timing, my brother."

Ace finished dressing before she did. Patrick was still yelling. He sounded drunk.

"Wait!" she cried when Ace started to leave the room.

He turned from the door and retraced his steps to the bed, bending to help fasten one of her shoes. "I can handle him, you know."

She nodded. "I'd just prefer to be out there. Do you mind?"

He pushed at her tousled hair and smiled. "Sweetheart, I like having you with me, no matter what."

As she stood up, he checked to make sure she'd fastened all her buttons. She glanced worriedly at the gun resting at his hip. He caught her chin on the edge of his hand.

"One of these days, you're going to start believing me when I tell you something. Trust me, Caitlin. Please?"

Their gazes locked. For a long moment, they simply stood there, ignoring Patrick's shouts, completely lost in each other. Then she smiled. "I do trust you. More than I've ever trusted anyone."

They left the bedroom together, Ace leading the way. At the front door, he paused to wait for her. They stepped out onto the porch side by side, presenting a united front for the first time.

Patrick, typically, was standing in the yard, his long legs spread, his red hair tousled, his eyes wild. He'd been drinking heavily. Caitlin didn't need to smell his breath to know that.

It broke her heart to see him like this. Again. She doubted she would ever be able to accept it. This was the brother she'd once rocked to sleep. The brother whose diapers she'd changed when she was barely out of diapers herself. She'd practically raised him. She definitely loved him. But, more than that, she pitied him. The whiskey worked on him like poison. When he drank, he wasn't Patrick any more, but a madman she didn't know and didn't wish to know.

Maybe it was a weakness in his blood. Or perhaps it was learned behavior, and the alcohol simply provided him with an excuse. She preferred to believe the first. The Patrick she loved was sweet and gentle and fair. The man he became when he drank was a monster.

"What do you want, Patrick?" she asked.

As he strode in a drunken path toward the porch, he jerked open his shirt and drew out what looked like a bunch of papers. With a violent sweep of his arm, he threw them in the dirt at the bottom of the steps. "I came to show you what a fool he's made out of you! Look at them, Caitlin!" He jerked his glittering gaze to Ace. "I broke into Barbary Coast Mortgage last night! I found out some very interesting things, namely that your husband came back here to destroy all the men he thinks killed his stepfather, not to mention their families, you and me included."

Caitlin moved slowly down the steps, her gaze fixed on the drifting sheets of paper and the ornately framed portrait of a young woman that had landed face up on the dirt. For a moment, Caitlin thought it was a likeness of herself, so great was the resemblance. But as she drew closer, she realized the girl was a stranger.

"Oh, yes, that's another thing!" Patrick said with a

raucous laugh. "Meet your half-sister, Eden Paxton. Our father's by-blow, sired the night he raped Ace Keegan's mother." He drew several sheets of folded stationery from his shirt pocket and stepped forward to shove them into Caitlin's hands. "Read that letter. It'll pretty much explain everything. It's from John Parrish, the guy at Barbary Coast Mortgage. Come to find out, he's betrothed to Eden Paxton. Quite a coincidence, right? In it, he breaks the terrible news to her about her parentage. God forbid that she should have come here not knowing she had O'Shannessy blood running through her veins."

Caitlin glanced down at the letter Patrick had handed her. It was dated the day before, and when she flipped to the last page, she saw that it had never been finished.

"Don't read that, Caitlin." Ace came down the steps behind her. "Unless I'm mistaken, John was writing that letter at the office yesterday morning when I stopped in to see him. If I hadn't interrupted him, I'm sure he would have posted it. Instead, he stuffed it in his desk drawer. It was never meant to fall into Patrick's hands. John and Eden are engaged to be married, and I'm sure John's letters to her are of a private and romantic nature. Not the sort of thing intended for anyone else's eyes."

Patrick gave a loud snort. "And we should care about John Parrish's privacy? Think again, Keegan. You just don't want Caitlin seeing what it says, because it'll damn you in her eyes."

"Please, Caitlin, don't read it," Ace said again. "Patrick's right. It probably will damn me. If you're going to learn the truth, then I want you to hear it from me."

The fact that he was admitting there was a truth he hadn't yet told her was a slap in the face. She glanced back down at the upturned portrait of Eden Paxton, undeniable evidence that Ace had been lying to her, if only by omission. A half-sister? Her father had raped his mother? She felt sick. So sick, it was all she could do to stay standing.

"He's used you!" Patrick cried. "Used you. Made a fool of you! Why didn't you listen to me? Instead, you stayed here with him, let him make a whore of you."

Ace touched Caitlin's arm, but she jerked away. She

felt so horribly sick. Heaven? Hysterically, she found herself wondering if he hadn't given her a hell on earth instead.

A sense of unreality gripped her as she lowered her gaze back to the letter. She flicked a glance over the masculine script. *Why Ace or your mother hasn't told you the truth, I'll never understand. You have a right to know who your real father was, after all.* She skipped a few lines. *I don't want to live here in No Name after all of this business is finished. How can I help ruin people's lives and then hope to live amongst them? I think we'll be happier in San Francisco. Don't you? Especially now that we know about your relationship to the O'Shannessys. Here, you would be bound to run into Caitlin frequently. The resemblance would be an awful reminder every time you saw her.*

"I can explain everything, Caitlin," she heard Ace say. She ignored him. "I swear to God, I can explain everything."

Farther down the page, she read, *I don't know what possessed Ace to marry the girl. I'm afraid for him, honey. It isn't enough to make them all think there will be a railroad spur built so he can swindle them out of their money. He's so consumed with hatred, he will stop at nothing to get even. I heard he raped the poor girl. I know it doesn't sound like him. But, then, does any of this? Maybe he actually did it. Maybe, in some twisted way, he sees her as the personification of Conor O'Shannessy. By hurting her, he feels as if he's getting at Conor. Reaching beyond the grave, so to speak.*

Caitlin refolded the stationery and made a fist over it. She didn't need to read more. Woodenly, she turned to look at Ace, who stood on the step above her. His dark face. The lopsided curve of his mouth. His lying lips. In the beginning, before he'd convinced her to place her faith in him, she wouldn't have been surprised by such a betrayal. Now it hurt more than she could say.

"I'll pack my things, Patrick," she said hollowly. "Please don't leave without me."

As she started up the steps, Ace caught hold of her arm. She kept her gaze averted. It hurt too badly to look at him. Once, a man had raped her with brutal force. She'd believed then that nothing could shame her more. Now she knew differently. Ace Keegan had raped her with gentle, treacherous lies. Had he been silently laughing when she arched her body up against his mouth? Had he found it satisfying when she cried out in the throes of ecstasy?

Conor O'Shannessy's daughter, playing the whore for him. To her eternal mortification, Patrick had been right from the very beginning.

"Caitlin, you owe me at least five minutes to tell you my side," Ace said gently. "Please. Give me at least that much."

The plea in his voice brought her gaze up to his. She felt as if a giant fist had slammed into her stomach. "I think I've given you quite enough of my time, Ace. I hope you're satisfied, that your taste for revenge has been appeased."

"Caitlin . . ." His hand tightened slightly to keep her from moving on up the steps. "You're my wife. Doesn't that mean anything? Five minutes, please."

She stood there for a moment, gazing up at the face she'd come to love so very much—the face of her betrayer. Why was it that the two men she'd loved the most had broken her faith so utterly? "Your wife?" she whispered. "I think people will call me something quite different. Keegan's whore, possibly?"

She jerked her arm from his grasp and continued up the steps. As she reached to draw open the front door, his voice stopped her dead. "Keegan's lady," he corrected. "I'll kill any man who says differently. No matter what you're thinking right now, no matter what you believe I'm guilty of, you're a lady. You always have been, and you always will be."

Caitlin could scarcely see for the tears as she let herself back inside the house.

FIVE MINUTES LATER, SHE HAD NEARLY FINISHED GATHERING her things. There were clean underclothes in a basket in the kitchen that she'd carried in from the line yesterday and never gotten around to folding. She still had to collect those. And then, of course, she had to find Lucky, who was evidently asleep somewhere.

Caitlin glanced around the room to be sure she hadn't forgotten anything. Memories. So many memories. She clamped a hand over her mouth and swallowed back a sob. Only a few short minutes ago, she'd been so happy. So incredibly happy.

The door crashed open. Caitlin whirled, half expecting to see Ace. Instead Joseph strode into the room, his bullet-straight blond hair lifting from his shoulders with each step. His eyes were fiery with anger, his usually tanned face a pasty white. He came to a stop in front of her.

"My brother is out there taking the beating of his life for you!" he said, grabbing a stack of clothing from her hands and throwing it on the floor. "Get out there, goddammit. Put a stop to it! If you don't, Patrick is going to kill him."

Caitlin backed up a step. She'd never seen Joseph angry, and she couldn't help but feel intimidated. Before she could retreat any further, he seized her by the arm and propelled her toward the door. There was no sense in trying to resist him. He was far too strong, for one thing, and too angry for another.

As she raced through the house, trying to keep up with his long strides, Caitlin went back over what he'd said. Patrick was going to kill Ace? It made no sense. None at all. If she had concerns for anyone, they would be for her brother. Ace was larger and stronger than Patrick, not to mention that he was stone-cold sober. In a physical confrontation, there would be no contest between the two men, and it was a foregone conclusion that Patrick would lose.

As Joseph dragged her out onto the front porch, Caitlin stared at her brother and husband, who faced each other in the yard. Joseph hadn't lied; Ace was taking a beating. Patrick was throwing punches that were knocking Ace nearly off his feet. As soon as Ace regained his balance, Patrick would hit him again.

Though she was seeing it with her own eyes, Caitlin

couldn't quite believe it. There was so much blood streaming from Ace's nose and mouth, he was almost unrecognizable. Yet as far as she could tell, he was making no attempt to defend himself. She turned a horrified gaze on Joseph.

"Do something! Make Patrick stop, Joseph. You have to do something."

"You still don't understand, do you? I can't do anything. He forbade any of us to interfere." His lips drew back in a disgusted sneer. "He promised you, remember? That he'd never lift a hand to your brother. He broke that promise once. He's determined not to again. He'd rather let Patrick kill him!"

Caitlin whirled back around. Ace had fallen to his knees. She watched in frozen disbelief as Patrick drew back a boot and kicked her husband in the stomach. "Stop it! Patrick, for God's sake, stop it!"

Taking the steps in a flying leap, Caitlin raced out into the yard and threw herself at her brother. "Stop it, I said! Stop it!"

Patrick shoved her aside and started toward Ace again. Caitlin staggered to get her balance. Now that she was standing at a closer proximity, she could see that Ace's face wasn't merely bleeding, but badly battered. There was a cut above his eyebrow. His lips were already swelling and streaming blood, as was the scar along his cheek. Dear God, it even looked to her as if his nose had been broken. Yet Patrick seemed bent on inflicting more damage.

She couldn't believe Ace was putting himself through this. Couldn't believe anyone would go to such lengths or endure so much, merely to keep a promise.

A few minutes ago, she'd been absolutely convinced of Ace's treachery. She'd seen the evidence of it with her own eyes. John Parrish's letter. The likeness of Eden Paxton. Patrick's accusations had to be true. What other explanation was there? And yet . . . there was her husband, on his knees in the dirt, taking the beating of his life, all because he refused to break his word to her.

She threw a frantic glance at Ace's brothers, all three

of whom stood at a distance, their grim expressions stony with anger. Maybe they had been forbidden to interfere, but no such strictures had been placed upon her.

She whirled and ran toward the garden where a pile of scrap lumber lay. She grabbed up one of the shorter lengths of board, pivoted, and raced back to the center of the yard. Just as she got there, Patrick drew back to kick Ace again. It was a kick that never found its target. Caitlin swung the board with all her might, hitting her brother flatly across the chest. The impact of the blow sent him reeling. He landed on his back in the dirt, shaking his head, looking surprised.

"Caitlin?"

He rolled and came up on his knees. Caitlin drew back and clobbered him again, this time on the arm. "How dare you, Patrick? How dare you! I'm ashamed to even claim you as my kin!"

Patrick grabbed his arm, his expression one of stunned incredulity. "You'd take his side against me?"

"Without batting an eye," she retorted. Drawing the board back in a threatening manner, she said, "Get out of here! Do you hear me? Now, before I decide to knock some sense into that head of yours."

"Caitlin . . ." Patrick gained his feet, then staggered sideways to catch his balance. He was so drunk, he seemed unable even to focus properly on her.

Revulsion filled her. And disgust. This was her brother, her own flesh and blood. He had to have realized Ace wasn't fighting back. He couldn't possibly be so drunk he hadn't been able to determine at least that much. Yet instead of turning and walking away, he'd pressed his advantage, pummeling an opponent who offered no resistance. What kind of man did such a thing? A month ago, she might not have known the answer to that question. She did now. Her brother was no kind of man at all. Not when whiskey did his thinking for him.

"Go, Patrick. Go, and don't come back. You're no longer welcome here."

Patrick shot a look at the board she held. Caitlin

tightened her grip. He seemed to realize, even in his state of drunkenness, that she meant business, for he turned and staggered toward his horse.

This time, Caitlin didn't gaze after him in tearful despair. The tears that sprang to her eyes were all for Ace. He knelt in the dirt, one arm hugging his middle, his dark head hanging. Patrick had beaten him almost senseless. If he was aware of anything that was happening around him, he gave no sign of it.

With a low sob, Caitlin tossed down the board and ran to her husband. As she sank to her knees beside him, she felt as if her heart might break. When Patrick had tossed those papers and Eden's portrait at her feet, she'd turned her back on him, refusing him even so much as a chance to explain.

In her mind, he'd been guilty. Now she was no longer certain. And even if he was, what did it matter? What he'd done in the past wasn't important. What counted was right now, this minute, and how he intended to go on from here. By keeping his word to her, at so great a cost to himself, he'd told her all she needed to know. She could count on him, no matter what.

And he loved her better than he loved himself . . .

"Ace? Oh, Ace, I'm so sorry. So awfully sorry." She caught his battered face between her hands. "Please forgive me. I'm so sorry."

"Cai'lin?" He mumbled her name through swollen, bleeding lips. One of his eyes was a mere slit. "I di'n't lif' a hand."

"No. I know you didn't." Tears welled in Caitlin's eyes. In that moment, she realized just how much she had come to love him. So much she felt as though she might die from it. "Oh, Ace, can you ever forgive me?"

His response was to pitch forward. Caitlin caught him, but only just barely, and she wasn't any too sure how long she could support his weight. "Help me!" She threw Joseph a pleading glance. Her brother-in-law still stood on the porch, his expression unreadable. He was clearly beside himself, as angry with Ace as he was with her. "Hurry, for God's sake. He's unconscious."

As Joseph came down the steps and started across the yard, there was no mistaking the fact that he was still in a temper. With every other step, he sent dirt flying. "He's a damned fool, that's what. Taking a beating like that. He's crazy!" He shot Caitlin a scathing look. "All I can say is, I hope you're worth it. If any woman did me like you just did him, I'd help her pack and say good riddance!"

Caitlin moved back as Ace's brothers lifted him to carry him inside the house. Was she worth it? Right now, she doubted it. But from this moment on, she would try to be.

All her life, she'd yearned to be loved by someone. Not just when it was convenient, but in the difficult times as well. She'd wished . . . Oh, God. She pressed the back of her hand over her mouth. She'd wished on stars for half her life, always yearning for the same thing—one person who would love her so much, so completely, that she could trust him with her life. Someone who would fight for her. Someone who would never lie to her. Someone who would put her happiness before his own.

A hero . . . That had been her wish. Someone who'd sweep her up and carry her away from the trap her life had been. Someone who would make her bad memories fade and give her new, magical ones. Someone who would make her feel like a princess.

Long ago, she'd grown to accept that it was a stupid, little girl's wish. An impossible wish. Heroes existed only in fairy tales. Magic was a child's fantasy. There were no princesses in real life.

And then Ace Keegan had stormed into her world. He'd given her all her wishes. Made all her dreams come true. Taught her to believe in magic again. He hadn't done it with flourish. He'd waved no sparkling wand. Just day in, and day out, doing little things, performing little bits of magic that didn't really seem like magic when they happened.

Ace Keegan, her hero . . . She'd almost turned her back on him. Almost rejected every sweet thing he'd so selflessly offered her. Love. A family. Promises to last a lifetime. Gentleness. Unfailing kindness. A sense of safety and security that was absolutely priceless. In short, a life filled with magic.

I wish I may, I wish I might, have this wish . . .

Caitlin closed her eyes. She felt all the old bitterness break apart inside of her. It had been a very long while since she'd given thanks to God for anything. She thanked Him now. Not for who she was, but for who He'd given her the chance to become.

Ace Keegan's lady.

26

BY LATE AFTERNOON, ACE WAS SITTING UP IN BED. JOSEPH had bandaged his ribs, suspecting that one might have sustained a hairline fracture. Caitlin had cleaned the cuts on her husband's face and applied poultices to his bruises. The rest would be left to Mother Nature and the healing process of time.

Holding a spoonful of broth to Ace's split lips, Caitlin found herself staring at his face, still appalled at the amount of damage Patrick had inflicted. It made her feel sick when she thought about it. She could only wonder how many times Patrick must have struck Ace, how many times Ace must have staggered from the blows, only to regain his balance and allow Patrick to hit him again.

"It was a very stupid thing you did, letting him beat you like that," she said shakily. "I realize you made me a promise, but if you'll recall, you did qualify it by stipulating you'd defend yourself if Patrick threatened your life. If he had continued hitting and kicking you like that, he might have killed you."

"He didn't. That's all that matters. My sweet little wife ran him off with a two-by-four." Placing a palm over his midriff, he carefully shifted his shoulders against the pillows. "Knowing you took up for me like that makes it all worth it. I'm proud of you, Caitlin."

"Proud of me?" That he could say such a thing after the way she'd behaved made her want to hide her face in shame. "How can you possibly feel proud of me after the way I treated you?"

"I just am, that's all. I've never gotten to see you when your dander's up. It's a shame I had to miss it."

One twinkling brown eye settled on hers. The other eyelid was an alarming shade of purple and nearly swollen shut. And his nose—his beautiful nose. Joseph had tried to straighten it, but it looked to Caitlin as if it were listing to one side. She could only pray that was due to the swelling.

"I'll never forgive myself if your nose mends crookedly."

"I'll just have to remember not to follow it."

"I don't know why you're joking. It isn't funny."

"You're still here, aren't you?" He leaned his head forward for more broth, trying, without much success, to tighten his sore lips over the spoon. As he swallowed, he swiped at the trickle that ran down his chin. "Patrick won the fight, but I got the girl. Who's complaining?"

"Lucky you."

He tried to smile, then winced. "That's me. One lucky fellow."

Caitlin couldn't hold the tears at bay any longer. She blinked, trying to dry her lashes. "Joseph said if he'd been you, he would've helped me pack and said good riddance. I can't say I blame him."

"Caitlin, would you stop?" He took the cup of broth from her hands and set it on the bedside table. Then he wrested away the spoon, the end of which he used to lightly thump her on the forehead. "I happen to love you. And not to discount Joseph's sage opinion, mind you, but I think I know you a little better than he does.

"After what your father did to you, is it any wonder your faith in me got a little shaken? You're still here, sweetheart. That's what I'm concentrating on. That you stood up to Patrick to defend me, and that you're still here now, taking care of me. So far, you haven't even demanded an explanation. Do you think that's lost on me? That I don't know how hard it is for you to take me on faith?"

"On faith? I wouldn't even listen to your side of the story. I was just going to leave!"

"That's my fault, not yours. I should have had the guts to tell you the truth before you heard it from someone else."

"Are you saying everything Patrick told me—everything in that letter—that it's all true?"

He regarded her for a long, tension-laden moment. "If I say yes, am I going to lose you? I think I could become a very accomplished liar, if that's the case, because the plain truth is, I don't know if I can—" He broke off and sighed. "I guess it's silly to say I won't be able to live through it if you leave me. But that's how I feel. My life won't be worth a damn without you."

That was all Caitlin really needed to hear. The sudden knot of fear that had formed inside of her loosened, melted. She managed a tremulous smile. "If you truly love me, Ace, none of the rest really matters. What hurt me the most was thinking you'd been toying with me. That nothing between us had meant anything to you. That maybe you'd been"—her throat went tight—"amusing yourself with me."

His one good eye narrowed. "Caitlin O'Shannessy Keegan, you are the sweetest, most wonderful thing that's ever happened to me, and don't you ever forget it. Amusing myself? Jesus H. Christ."

"Well . . . ? That's how it sounded in John Parrish's letter. He told Eden he thought—well, that he was afraid you might be using me to get revenge against my father."

"Revenge against your father? After sleeping in the same bed with you for a month and never being able to so much as touch you?" He chuckled and grabbed for his ribs. "Oh . . . God! Don't make me laugh."

Caitlin waited until his mirth subsided. "Would you mind sharing the joke?"

Still holding one arm clamped over his midriff, he said, "It's nothing, sweetheart. Just a man thing. I'm not laughing at you. Honestly. It's just—well, if anyone got revenge, it was probably your father."

Realization started to dawn, and Caitlin felt heat rising up her neck. "I see."

"I doubt it," he said with another low laugh. "Just trust me when I say you were worth waiting for." He took a deep but careful breath. "Definitely worth waiting for."

His swollen mouth tipped into a crooked smile. "Come here," he said in a low, husky voice. "You're looking a little bruised around the edges. I didn't mean to hurt your feelings." He set the spoon aside and reached to grab her hand. "Come on. Over here."

"But what about your ribs?"

"To hell with my ribs." He gave a hard jerk, pulling her toward him. "I need to feel you close to me."

Caitlin allowed herself to be drawn onto her knees, whereupon she twisted at the waist to sit beside him with her back to the pillows. He curled an arm around her shoulders.

"There. That's better." He glanced down at her. "Now I have a good hold on you, just in case you decide to take off."

"I'm not going anywhere."

"You're liable to be tempted after I've told you everything."

Caitlin swallowed. "Then don't tell me. There's nothing I need to hear, except that you love me. I know you have your reasons for wanting revenge against the men who killed your stepfather. I won't let that come between us. No matter what you choose to do, I won't let it ruin things for us."

His arm tightened around her. "Thank you for that. It means more to me than I can say."

She leaned her head against his shoulder so she could see his face. "I know how it feels to hate someone because he's hurt you. To feel almost sick with the need to get back at him. When you sought out Cruise Dublin and beat him up, you did it for me—because you understood I'd never be able to feel it was completely finished until he had paid for what he did. If you want your own revenge, I won't try to stand in your way. Those men killed your stepfather, and the way I see it, they have whatever they get coming to them."

He ran his hand lightly up and down her arm, his touch making her feel warm and wonderfully safe. "I'm glad you feel that way. Maybe it'll make it easier for you to understand everything I've done."

Caitlin could tell by the tightness in his voice that he truly was still afraid he might lose her. "I already understand." When she didn't feel any of the tension ease from his body, she quickly added, "I'll even go a step farther than that and help you get even."

He cast her a startled look. "You'll what?"

"I said I'll help you. Just tell me what I can do. I can't beat anyone up for you, but I can do other things. If you're bent on going through with this, then I'll stand behind you every inch of the way."

After a long moment, he relaxed against the pillows, head back, eyes closed. "Caitlin O'Shannessy Keegan, you are a treasure. I don't deserve you. You know it?"

"I think it's the other way around."

Another long silence fell. At last he said, "I have so much to tell you, and I'm not sure where to start."

"At the beginning," she said softly.

He dragged in a shaky breath. "The very beginning was clear back in St. Louis, when Pa ran into two men who had some prime range land to sell for a thousand dollars. It was a steep price, but the land sounded like a paradise, and he was willing to pay it. The next thing we all knew, we were heading west."

And so the story began. In the minutes that followed, Ace told her everything. About the night Joseph Paxton Sr. was hung. About how his mother had bargained for her husband's life with her body, only to watch him be murdered anyway. About how Conor O'Shannessy had struck Ace with the butt of Joseph's rifle and then kicked him while he lay half-conscious in the dirt.

"So that's why you shuffle one foot when you walk," Caitlin whispered. "Because your hip was injured?"

As if he sensed the remorse she felt, he said, "It really doesn't bother me all that much, Caitlin. And even if it did, it wasn't your doing."

"But it was *my* father who did that to you! How do you think that makes me feel?"

He ran his hand up to her shoulder and drew her more snugly against him, resting his chin against her hair. "If you're going to blame yourself, I'm not telling you the rest."

"The rest?" Caitlin felt sick. Sick to her bones. "About Eden, you mean?"

"Yes, about Eden."

He went on to tell her about his mother's giving birth to a baby girl shortly after they settled in California, how she'd lied to her children all these years, claiming that Eden's red hair and fair complexion were inherited from a deceased aunt on her side of the family.

"I never realized the truth—that she was Conor's child—until the night I first saw you," he said. "I guess maybe I suspected once or twice, but I shoved the thoughts from my mind. I didn't want to believe it. I loved my little half-sister, and just the thought that—" He broke off and sighed. "When I saw you, I couldn't deny the truth any longer."

"Oh, God, how angry you must have felt. No wonder you were so hateful. You must have despised me!"

"Yeah. For at least five minutes." He craned his neck to see her face, his expression tender and slightly a-mused. "After that, it was a losing battle. I think I started falling in love with you that very night. I was just too damned dumb to know it."

"In love with me? Oh, Ace . . . After what my father had done?"

"It was the third button that got me, I think." His swollen mouth lifted awkwardly at one corner. "When I realized you really meant to take off that nightgown. I kept thinking you'd run, that you'd throw Patrick to the wolves and save your own hide. You were Conor

O'Shannessy's daughter, after all. I figured you'd renege. But in the end, I was the one who hightailed it. I came back here feeling like the lowest kind of skunk, and I couldn't rest until I apologized to you."

"So you sought me out at the social?"

"And then couldn't work up my nerve to say I was sorry. There you were, ostracized by everyone in town, and I knew it was all my fault. An apology just didn't seem like enough."

She turned her head to rub her cheek against his chest. "So you decided to follow me home and offer to marry me."

"Hell, no. Me, marry an O'Shannessy? All during the wagon ride out to your place, I was trying to think of some way I could make amends."

She stirred and glanced up. "Amends?"

He looked a little sheepish. "I was thinking that maybe some money might put us square."

"Money?"

"Now, Caitlin. Don't get mad. It was just a thought that went through my mind." He cast her a glance and quickly added, "A very fleeting thought. I never offered you any, did I?"

"No, but—money? For ruining my reputation? No wonder you felt like a skunk."

He chuckled. "I knew you probably wouldn't take it. I just toyed with the notion for a few minutes."

"Probably wouldn't take it? I would have shoved it down your throat."

"Right. You were so scared, you were jumping at your own shadow. It was when I realized *why* you were so scared that I decided to marry you."

"Because I was afraid of making love?" She arched her eyebrows. "What are you, sadistic or something?"

He barked with laughter, then grabbed for his ribs. "Oh, ouch! Caitlin, I told you, don't make me laugh."

"Well?" she said at the tail end of a giggle. "What else am I to assume, but that you decided to torture me for a month?"

"I tortured *you*?" He shook his head. "That isn't

exactly the way I remember it. And as for your question, I didn't marry you because you were afraid to make love, but because you intended to go through with it that night. In spite of how you felt, to keep the bargain we'd made."

"*That's* why you married me?"

"Absolutely." His expression turned suddenly serious, the glow in his eye tender. "You were being so brave." His mouth quirked at one corner. "Ready to sacrifice yourself to honor our bargain. From that second on, I was hooked. All you had to do was start reeling me in."

"Oh, my. You poor man. Talk about getting hood-winked. I wasn't going to make love with you just because I felt obligated to keep our bargain. I was afraid if I didn't, you'd find Patrick off somewhere alone and shoot him to get back at me."

He looked surprised. "Are you serious? That was why, because you were worried I'd hurt Patrick?"

"Of course, that was why. It was an unholy bargain you'd struck with me. I didn't feel honor bound to keep it. The only thing you had hanging over my head was my brother."

He clicked his tongue. "And all this time, I thought—" He shook his head. "Well, hell, I may as well throw you back then. I got gypped."

She tweaked his chest hair. "You certainly did, you poor man."

He caught her hand, enclosing her fingers in his. The teasing twinkle in his eye had become cloudy with emotion. Caitlin's smile faded, for she sensed that this time, his mood truly had turned serious. She lifted her gaze to his, and what she saw there made her heart catch. *Love.* He didn't need to say the words. His expression said it all.

"All teasing aside, Caitlin, you truly are one of the most loyal people I've ever met. And you do have a deep sense of honor. If it hadn't been for that, you would have gotten an annulment and we wouldn't be here, having this conversation right now. You'd be back at your place, working the ranch and scraping to make ends meet. And

I'd be sitting here, counting my money and laughing my ass off at all the fools I was about to foreclose on, your brother included."

Caitlin searched his gaze. "You've changed your mind, haven't you? About the foreclosures."

"I've decided to actually build the railroad spur. I own Trans-con Railway, you know."

She couldn't believe she'd heard him right. "But, Ace, why? What about your stepfather? What about——"

He tightened his hand on hers. "It's over, Caitlin. Done and finished. This last month, I've come to realize there's more to life than getting even. A lot more. I want to build a future. With you. Not spend all my time and thoughts and energy on the past. It's time to put what happened behind me. I should have a long time ago."

She could see he truly meant that. "Oh, Ace, are you sure? No one can blame you for hating the people who hurt you and your family so badly."

"We can't build a life on hatred. Believe me, I know. It's all I've had for nearly twenty years, and it's a mighty empty existence. I want more than that. A lot more. Until I met you, I didn't realize all I had been missing."

Tears rushed to Caitlin's eyes. Tears of happiness.

"Patrick mortgaged his ranch, you know," Ace added. "To invest in land along the spur route. If I ruin the others, he'll go down with them."

She swallowed and averted her gaze. "Yes, well . . . Patrick has done a lot of things I don't approve of. I can't protect him forever. Sooner or later, he has to start paying the price."

"But not at my hands. He's your brother. Someday he'll be the uncle of my children. I know you're very angry with him right now, but under all of that, your feelings for him run deep. As your husband, I have to respect that."

"I told him today not to ever come back here."

"Never is a mighty long time. Tempers will cool. Your feelings will change. I don't want to burn any bridges. In fact, as soon as I can get up out of this bed, I want to go over and see him. It's time he and I bury the hatchet." He smiled slightly. "If for no other reason, I want to

shake his hand for all the times he took a beating to keep
you from getting one. I admire him for that, Caitlin, and
no matter what he's done since, I can't easily discount
it."

"After what he did to you today, you can say that?"

He grew thoughtful for a moment. "Truthfully? It's
going to be really hard for me to be nice to the man. But
there's another part of me that wants to get to know him
a whole lot better before I pass judgment." He sighed
and passed a moment of silence toying with her fingertips. "I've always maintained that a man's being drunk is
no excuse for bad behavior. But you seem to believe
otherwise, that Patrick truly goes crazy when he drinks
and that he isn't entirely responsible for what he does."
He looked over at her. "I've just been doing a lot of
thinking about it. After all Patrick has done for you, I
think he deserves the benefit of the doubt."

"Patrick hasn't quit drinking."

"No. But he might. I know you've talked to him, and
it hasn't seemed to do much good, but that doesn't mean
the words have fallen on deaf ears." Ace pushed a tendril
of hair back from her cheek. "Tomorrow when he wakes
up, he's probably going to remember his sister lighting
into him with a two-by-four. If he loves you half as much
as you love him, that's bound to eat at him. Who knows?
Maybe that was exactly what he needed all along. He
may not swear off whiskey tomorrow, but he may later. If
you stick to your guns, at some point he's going to realize
what the drink is costing him."

"Oh, Ace, do you really think so?"

"Yes, I do." He flashed another awkward grin. "And
when that day comes, I don't want him to have any more
reason to hate my guts than he already does." He
shrugged a shoulder. "Besides, I'm in the cattle business
now. I'll make a lot more money if I can ship my beef by
rail to Denver. Not much point in cutting off my nose to
spite my face. It'll be better all the way around if I go
ahead and build the spur. Don't you think?"

Caitlin nestled her head in the hollow of his shoulder.
"What I think, Mr. Keegan, is that you're the most
wonderful man I've ever met."

"How wonderful?"

She slanted him a questioning glance. "Wonderful, wonderful."

"Wonderful enough that you'd go lock that door and come back to me wearing nothing but that glorious smile of yours?"

"What about your ribs?"

"To hell with my ribs."

❧ 27

ON THE THIRD DAY OF HIS CONVALESCENCE, ACE INSISTED on getting out of bed. Directly after Caitlin had fed him and his brothers breakfast, he took his rifle from the rack above the mantel and informed her he meant to ride fence line with David and Esa the remainder of the morning.

"I'll get so sore I can't wiggle if I don't force myself to move around."

"But your ribs! What if you take a tumble from the horse or something? You could end up puncturing a lung."

Ace took her by the shoulders. "Sweetheart, I haven't taken a tumble off Shakespeare since I broke him to ride. As for my ribs, I think they're just bruised."

Looking up at his dark face, which had become so incredibly dear to her, Caitlin couldn't quite rid herself of the feeling that something awful might happen if he left the house. She tried to tell herself it was only because she loved him so much. After all, what would she do if she lost him? How would she go on living if he rode off someday and never came back? She couldn't go back to her prior existence. Not now. Not when she knew firsthand how incredibly wonderful life could be.

Foolishness. Ace was a tall, strapping man—well muscled, healthy, skilled with weapons, intelligent. He wasn't likely to suffer some fatal accident while out riding fence line. And yet . . . Gazing up at his handsome face, still so bruised from the beating he'd taken from Patrick, she couldn't ignore the fact that he wasn't invincible. He could be injured just like any other man and leave her a widow.

A widow. The word struck terror into Caitlin. Now that she'd discovered love, she was desperately afraid of losing it. It felt so good to fall asleep at night in his strong arms. To feel cherished and safe. To know that tomorrow would be another wonderful day, filled with laughter and closeness and sharing. The feeling of family Ace had given her was something she'd never had, a sweet and beautiful gift. Now that she'd had a taste of it, she couldn't help but fear fate might snatch it away from her.

Fate. Caitlin's hadn't been particularly kind thus far. Perhaps, she reasoned in an attempt to make herself feel better, it was her turn to be happy. Maybe in the giant scheme of things, people had to suffer a certain measure of heartache before they found true happiness. If so, then she'd already had her share of sorrow. Perhaps now only good things were going to come her way. It was time she stopped letting her past tarnish her present and her future, time that she concentrated instead on being the kind of wife Ace deserved. This was her home now, not someplace she was merely visiting. It was up to her to see that everything ran smoothly.

On that positive thought, she chased the sense of impending doom from her mind and concentrated instead on straightening the house and preparing lunch, a huge pot of chili beans. Shortly before noon, she put a pan of cornbread into the oven to bake.

By the time Ace and his brothers came in from doing their morning chores, the house was filled with the delicious smells of piping hot food, ready to be served.

"Wow, Caitlin, this does taste good!" Esa mumbled around a mouthful of cornbread.

"Thank you very much, Esa. I'm glad you like it. But,

please, don't talk with your mouth full," Caitlin admonished. To David, she said, "And get your elbows off the table, David. It isn't seemly."

Every man at the table, including Ace, stopped chewing to stare at her. Their expressions ranged from surprised to disgruntled.

"Well . . . ?" Caitlin flashed them all a smile. "When your mother joins us here, do you want her to think I've no understanding of etiquette and proper table manners?"

"We'll mind our manners when Ma gets here," Esa said. "Until then, why can't we just be ourselves?"

"Because I have requested otherwise." She met the gaze of each man. "When you sit down at my table, you will all be gentlemen, or you won't eat. New cook, new rules."

Ace's mouth quirked. He bent his head to shovel in another mouthful of beans. Caitlin arched an eyebrow. "The ceiling should never see your nape, Mr. Keegan. With concentration and a certain amount of coordination, it is possible to carry a spoonful of food to the mouth without putting one's face nearly in the bowl."

Broad shoulders straightened. Brown eyes met hers. After a long, tension-packed moment, he said, "Yes, ma'am."

For the remainder of the meal, everyone's manners were exemplary. After they finished eating, the men helped Caitlin clean up the kitchen. When the last dish was dried and stowed away in the cupboard, Ace said, "How about a walk along the creek?"

Caitlin removed her apron and hung it on a hook Joseph had screwed into the wall near the back door. The cheerful sunlight that lanced through the window over the sink beckoned temptingly. Going for a walk with her husband sounded heavenly. "You promised you'd rest this afternoon," she reminded him.

Though most of the swelling had left, Ace still sported a beauty of a black eye. He gave her a teasing wink. "What's the matter? Am I too ugly to go walking with, or what?"

Ugly? With his dark skin, the bruises on his face were

noticeable, but not glaringly so. His was the kind of face that could sport bruises and still manage to look attractive. Caitlin thought the extra color gave him a rugged appeal, especially around his mouth. The nearly healed splits made his firm lips look vulnerable and kissable.

"I think I could be convinced to take a walk with you," she told him lightly, "but only if you promise you'll lie down for at least two hours when we get back."

He glanced from the kitchen toward the table, where his brothers had gathered to partake of some after-dinner coffee. Looking back at her, he whispered, "Only two hours? I was really hoping for three. You will lie down with me, won't you?"

Caitlin felt herself blush. "You, sir, are impossible."

"Yeah, well, I can't get enough of you. If that makes me impossible, I guess I am. I'll happily lie down when we get back, Mrs. Keegan, but only if you agree to lie with me." He wiggled his eyebrows, clearly trying to look lecherous. "And I do mean that in the biblical sense."

As it turned out, they didn't wait to make love in the privacy of their bedroom. Ace found a grassy spot along the creek that was sheltered from view by a thick copse and promptly began unfastening Caitlin's buttons.

"What are you doing?" she asked in a voice gone high-pitched with nervousness. "We can't do anything out here. It's broad daylight! What if one of your hired hands happens along? Or one of your brothers? Are you out of your mind?"

"I'm crazy as a loco horse. But is that going to stop me? Hell, no." He opened her chemise, baring her breasts to the sunlight. "My God, you are beautiful."

Caitlin shivered at the rasp of his thumbs over her puckered nipples.

"Cold, sweetheart?"

"No, it's just—" Her lashes drifted slowly downward. When he touched her like this, she forgot everything but the sensations he elicited. "It's indecent, doing things like this, right out here in front of God and everybody."

"God, maybe. There's no one else around. As for indecent?" Still toying with her breasts, he claimed her mouth in a long, slow kiss that sent ribbons of excitement clear to her toes. "Making love is a sacred rite between a man and wife. There's nothing indecent about my touching you, sweetheart. When our flesh joins, it's a holy thing. A precious gift from God that He'd want us to enjoy. Don't you feel it?"

Caitlin felt it, all right. An incredible sweetness. She arched her back over his arm to accommodate his lips as they trailed down her throat to her breasts. With one flick of his tongue over her nipple, he drove any lingering concerns about propriety from her mind. Within seconds, she was moaning. Minutes later, he'd divested her of all her clothing. There on the grass, with the sunlight warming their skin, they made passionate love, followed later by a more languorous joining.

"It is holy," she whispered to him as they put their clothing back on. "Nothing that feels so wonderfully right could possibly be wrong."

As they strolled arm in arm back to the house, her thoughts turned to the future. She looked out across the endless stretches of ranch land, imagining her children romping in the sunshine, their voices ringing with laughter.

"Oh, Ace, I want babies," she said with a sigh.

He tugged his arm free from hers to encircle her waist and draw her close in a hug. "I'm working on it. I've always heard practice makes perfect. What do you think?"

She gave him a saucy grin. "I think I'll beat you back to the house. You did promise you'd lie down for two hours this afternoon."

"Only if you'll join me."

She slipped from his grasp and lifted her skirts to skip ahead of him. "Why do you think I'm so anxious to get there?"

CAITLIN AND ACE WERE DISTURBED FROM THEIR "NAP" by a sharp rap on the door. Caitlin dived under the covers. Her husband jerked the sheet up over her bare shoulders and flopped onto his back beside her, pretending to yawn loudly.

"Yo?" he called. "What do you want?"

Stifling a giggle, she snuggled up to her pillow. A second later, Joseph poked his head into the bedroom. His gaze shot from Caitlin to Ace, his expression knowing.

"Sorry to disturb you, big brother, but you have to oust out. We've got company coming, and it looks to me like trouble's riding double behind them."

"Who?" Ace asked, still feigning sleepiness.

"Marshal Beiler. He's got about twenty men with him, all of them packing rifles."

All pretense vanished. Ace sat bolt upright. "Shit."

The instant Joseph shut the door, Ace leaped from the bed, Caitlin close on his heels. As they threw on their clothes, she said, "What do you think he wants?"

He flashed her a disgruntled look. "God only knows."

Caitlin shoved on her shoes, forgoing stockings for the first time in her recollection. Recalling her fears of the morning, her throat went tight. "You don't think Dublin pressed charges against you for assault, do you? It'd be just like him."

Ace shook his head. "He took the first swing, and there were witnesses to the fact. Even if he did press charges, he couldn't make them stick."

By the time they finished dressing and left the bedroom, Joseph was already out on the porch speaking to Beiler, who'd dismounted and stood at the bottom of the steps, a rifle cradled at the ready in his arms. David and Esa, who'd evidently been doing something out in the barn, stood off to one side at the right end of the porch.

Glancing out through the window at Beiler and his cohorts, Caitlin shoved nervously at her tousled hair. Long strands had escaped her bun to trail along her neck. "Oh, Ace," she said worriedly. "What on earth do you think he wants?"

"Don't worry about your hair," he told her as he bent to tie down his gun holster. "You're staying in here. I don't like the looks of all those rifles."

Caitlin glanced back out the window. She had to

admit, she didn't like the looks of them, either. At a quick count, Beiler was accompanied by about fifteen armed men.

Caitlin had known most of those men all her life. Some attended the community church. All were ranchers and family men. But this afternoon, their faces seemed oddly unfamiliar—hard and resolute, their glittering gazes rife with anger and resentment. Something had them all riled up. She could only wonder what.

"Oh, Ace, I'm scared. Why would they come here with rifles? Something's wrong."

He bent to quickly kiss her forehead. "You stay in here, all right? Whatever it is they're wanting, I'm sure it has nothing to do with you."

Caitlin clutched his shirt to keep him from turning away. "Nothing to do with me? Anything that involves you is my concern as well."

"Then be concerned. Just do your worrying from in here."

"They've come for you! I just know it! Something to do with Dublin, probably, and they're going to take you away! You have to get out of here. The back door. Go out the back door."

He grasped her firmly by the wrists. Caitlin knew he meant to pry her hands from his shirt, so she held on more stubbornly. "Caitlin, don't be silly. I haven't done anything."

"Neither did Joseph Paxton!"

The words hung between them, a silent testimony to the fact that Caitlin had turned her back on everything she had once believed, namely that Paxton might have murdered Camlin Beckett, just as he'd been accused of doing, and that he'd deserved to be hung that fateful night so very long ago. She knew better now. After knowing and loving Ace Keegan, how could she not?

"Sweetheart, a man can't run every time trouble comes calling." Gently, Ace worked her hands free from his shirt, his gaze holding hers. "We just have to trust in God, hm? I haven't done anything wrong."

"Estyn Beiler was there that night, Ace." Caitlin heard the hysteria in her voice, but for the life of her, she couldn't control it. "He stood by while my father bludgeoned and kicked a little boy! What kind of man could do that? He means you harm. I just know it. I can see it on his face. He hates you for telling the truth, for revealing the part he played in it. Don't you understand? You've put a mark on his record. Made him look bad. The only way he can completely regain his standing in the community is to discredit you."

He stepped away from her. "Be that as it may, I can't run. It isn't in me, Caitlin. You have to understand that."

What she understood was that those men out there had come here to do him ill. She didn't have to step out there and hear what they had to say to know that. "Foolish pride won't protect you. Not from a man like Beiler."

"Call it foolish if you want, but without his pride, what does a man have?"

He cracked the door. To Caitlin, the creak of the hinges was an ominous sound, a prelude to disaster. She was shaking. Shaking horribly. Not with fear for herself, but fear for him. He threw her one last glance before opening the door all the way. "If anything does happen," he said softly, "you stay with Joseph. Do you understand me, Caitlin? He'll take care of you."

Her gaze clung to his. He knew. She could see it in his eyes. He sensed it as well—that something awful was about to happen, that those men out there had come to take him away. "Ace . . . I love you."

He smiled slightly. That wonderful, crooked smile. "I know you do. Promise me? That you'll stay with Joseph. I know he'll take good care of you."

This was insane. Caitlin wanted to grab him by the arm and jerk him back inside. She wanted to bolt the door. Make him listen to her. Convince him to run. But if he did that, he wouldn't be the man she loved. There was none of the coward in him. He could no more hightail it than he could stop breathing.

"I promise," she whispered.

He gave a slight nod. "My brothers . . . they're your family now. Don't forget that."

"I won't."

He turned then. Straightened his shoulders. Took a deep breath. Caitlin realized in that moment that he was as scared as she was. As he drew the door open and stepped out onto the porch, her mind filled with silent cries of protest she couldn't voice, wouldn't voice, because being his woman demanded that she be as strong as he was.

As the door swung shut, she went to stand at the window so she might watch and listen to what Beiler had to say. Ace moved to stand beside Joseph. There was nothing in his stance to indicate he was the least bit shaken by this unexpected visit or that he felt threatened by the presence of so many armed men.

"Marshal," he said, his voice pitched low, his tone questioning. "What brings you clear out this way?"

Beiler's face twisted into a sneer. "What brings me out this way? As if you don't know." He studied Ace's face for a moment. "Patrick O'Shannessy was in town yesterday morning. Told anyone who wanted to listen that you and him had a hell of a set-to the morning before and that he beat the daylights out of you. Judging by those bruises, I'd say he was telling the truth."

Ace inclined his dark head. "That's right. We had a confrontation of sorts."

"And you got the worst end of it."

Again Ace nodded. Caitlin felt so proud of him. Most men would have rushed on to explain *why* they'd gotten the worst end of it. Ace just let it ride. He knew the truth; evidently that was enough for him.

"Where were you this morning?" Beiler asked.

Ace rubbed his slightly swollen his nose. "I went out to ride fence line with my brothers."

"Were you with them the entire time?"

Ace hesitated before replying, "No, not the entire time. Why do you ask?"

Caitlin's heart began to pound.

"The time when you weren't with your brothers . . ." Beiler shifted his rifle in his arms. "How long, would you say, were you apart from them?"

"An hour, maybe two. I didn't keep track."

Beiler's eyes began to glitter. "So you would have had time to ride over to the O'Shannessy place this morning?"

"I would have had time, yes."

The marshal smiled. "I'd venture a guess you not only had time to do so, but that you did."

Ace started to speak, but Beiler cut him short.

"There's no sense lying about it. Cruise Dublin saw you riding away from the O'Shannessy place. You were there."

"I have no intention of lying. I went over to see Patrick this morning. What of it? For my wife's sake, I hoped that he and I could settle our differences. As it happened, he wasn't around, so I left."

"It's a little hard to talk to a man when he's been shot in the back, ain't it?"

Caitlin felt as if her legs had turned to water. Patrick. She dug her nails into the window sill. Oh, dear God . . .

"Shot in the back?" Ace repeated slowly. "Patrick O'Shannessy?"

"Don't bother to play innocent with me," Beiler said with a snort. "There's bad blood between you and O'Shannessy. Has been since you first came back here. Everyone knows it."

Ace gave a low, incredulous laugh. "Are you accusing me of shooting my brother-in-law in the back?"

Caitlin gave a low, agonized cry. She couldn't help it. Her brother. Her baby brother. For all that he'd done, she still loved him. Oh, God, was he dead? Was that what Beiler was saying? That her brother had been murdered?

Ace heard her cry and turned back toward the house. Beiler yelled, stopping him dead. "Oh, no, you don't. You stay right where you are, you back-shooting son of a bitch."

"My wife is in there. She needs me right now. Patrick is her brother, in case you've forgotten. That was a hell of a way to deliver such terrible news!"

There was no mistaking the cold fury in Ace's voice or the venom in Beiler's expression.

"She turned her back on her brother when she became your wife," the marshal said. "I doubt she's all that shaken up."

Ace stood on the porch, clearly afraid to make a move, yet longing to come inside to be with her. Caitlin stared at him through the glass, holding her breath to keep from sobbing, afraid that if she made so much as another sound, he would risk getting shot to come to her.

"I wanna see your rifle," Beiler said. "Where is it?"

Ace jabbed a thumb over his shoulder at the house. "Over the fireplace."

Beiler glanced at Joseph. "Go get it, mister. And no funny business. My deputies here have been instructed to shoot first and ask questions later."

Joseph curled a lip as he turned toward the door. "Marshals like you always shoot first and ask questions later, Beiler. It keeps your jails from getting crowded."

As he stepped inside, Joseph paused to look deeply into Caitlin's eyes. "I'm sorry about your brother, sis."

Sis? The word seemed to have slipped from him without thought. She could also tell by the ache in his eyes that he truly did feel awful about what had happened to Patrick. That he would spare a thought for that, or for her feelings, when his own brother was being accused of the foul deed told Caitlin more than a hundred pretty speeches could have. She couldn't speak for the tears that were dammed up in her throat, so she merely nodded.

Joseph stepped over to the fireplace to retrieve Ace's Henry from the rifle rack. As he turned back toward her, he once again met her gaze. "Ace is no angel. I won't claim he is. But one thing he'd never do is shoot a man when his back was turned. No matter what Beiler has to say, I hope you'll remember that."

Again, Caitlin could only nod. She knew Joseph was warning her. If she let her faith in Ace be shaken a second time, if she turned her back on him again, it might do irreparable damage to their marriage.

Hefting the rifle in his hands, Joseph strode back to the door, the heels of his dusty boots tapping out a brisk tattoo on the varnished floor. At the door, he paused for a second, glanced her way, and winked. Caitlin knew he was trying to tell her not to be afraid, that one way or another, they would get through this.

Beiler moved up onto the steps to take the rifle when Joseph exited the house. Holding the Henry in one hand, the marshal took a long, slow sniff of the weapon's barrel, his gaze fixed on Ace. "This gun has been fired recently."

Caitlin saw Ace's back stiffen. "That's right. When I was out riding fences this morning, I saw a coyote after one of my calves. I shot it. There's no law against that, is there?"

Beiler's smirk spoke volumes as he returned the Henry to Joseph. "You're under arrest, Keegan. For the murder of Patrick O'Shannessy."

One of Beiler's riders straightened in the saddle. "He ain't dead yet, Marshal. The charge is only attempted murder until he dies, ain't it?"

At that news, Ace took a step toward Beiler, his stance threatening. "You heartless bastard! He isn't dead? How dare you let on he was. Have you no concern at all for my wife's feelings?"

Beiler flashed a cold smile. "You mad because you think maybe I upset her without cause? Or because Patrick isn't dead yet and might be able to identify his murderer before he dies?"

Ace's hands knotted into fists. Caitlin knew that if it hadn't been for all the rifles trained on him, he would have shoved the question back down Beiler's throat. "I wish to God he could identify the shooter, because it sure as hell wasn't me."

"We'll let you sing that song to a judge." Beiler jerked a pair of handcuffs off his belt. "You're going to jail, Mr. Keegan."

"Oh, no, he isn't," Joseph said softly, his hand hovering over his gun.

At the end of the porch, David and Esa assumed shooting stances as well. Joseph inclined his head at Beiler. "The last time you got your hands on one of ours, you hung him without a fair hearing. I'm not letting you take my brother anywhere."

"Joseph," Ace said softly, "stay out of this."

"No, goddammit! I won't stand by and let history repeat itself. You're a worm, Beiler! The lowest kind of worm."

Fifteen rifle barrels swung toward Joseph. He spread his feet, his gun hand still hovering over his holster. "Go ahead, you bastard. Give them the signal to shoot. I'll go down, sure as shit, but I'll take your miserable ass with me. They can't kill me fast enough to stop me from getting off at least two shots. I'll put them both right between your beady little eyes."

Beiler's cowardice started to show. His face drained of color, and his eyes began to dart from side to side, as if he were looking for an escape route. There was none. After a moment, he said, "If he goes for his gun, gentlemen, shoot the girl."

All the rifles shifted aim. Caitlin found herself staring out the glass at fifteen barrels.

"You miserable son of a bitch," Ace said acidly.

Beiler held up the cuffs. Ace stood there for a second, then moved down the steps, his wrists thrust forward. Beiler cuffed him, then jerked him roughly out into the yard. "Hamilton, Petrie, Hobbs! Cuff the brothers. We're hauling them all in!"

"On what charge?" Joseph cried.

"Interfering with a law officer! Ain't no way I'm gonna have any trouble out of you boys over this. With your butts cooling in the hoosegow, I won't have to worry none, now will I?"

Caitlin couldn't believe her ears. Beiler meant to arrest them all? Forgetting her promise to Ace, she ran outside onto the porch. "No! Marshal Beiler, please! They didn't do anything!"

Three of Beiler's men dismounted and moved toward Ace's brothers. As Hamilton came up onto the porch, Joseph glanced at all the rifles, then at Caitlin. In the end, he held out his hands, allowing himself to be cuffed. David and Esa followed suit. The minute all three Paxtons had their hands safely bound, Beiler motioned for them to be disarmed. The rotund marshal removed Ace's gun from its holster himself.

"You boys don't look quite so fearsome without your side arms, now do you?"

"You can't do this!" Caitlin cried. "You can't just arrest people when they've done nothing wrong! I'm a witness. They did nothing. Absolutely nothing!"

Ace spoke up. "At least leave one of the boys here, Beiler. No woman should be left alone on a ranch this far from town. Her brother's just been shot, for Christ's sake. She needs someone to stay with her!"

"She made her bed." Beiler gave Ace a vicious shove, nearly knocking him off his feet. "Mount up behind Morgan. And shut your trap. When I want to hear more out of you, I'll let you know."

Morgan moved his horse forward and leaned sideways in the saddle to grasp the short length of chain between Ace's wrists. Removing his foot from the stirrup, the rancher gave his prisoner only time enough to get a foothold before he jerked him upward. Ace winced at the rough treatment, but managed to swing up a leg and settle himself on the horse behind the shorter man. His dark gaze sought Caitlin's.

"I know this looks bad, but I didn't shoot him," he called. "I swear it, Caitlin. You have to believe that. I went over there this morning to try to talk to Patrick. That's all. When I didn't find him around, I rode back. End of story."

Trust. In the past, it had been a commodity in short supply in Caitlin's heart. But now? She looked deeply into Ace's eyes. There were no shadows there. No furtiveness. Only a heartfelt plea that she try to believe in him.

Through blinding tears, Caitlin managed to give him a shaky smile. "They won't get away with this, Ace. I don't know who shot Patrick, but if it's the last thing I do, I'll find out."

Beiler shot her a hate-filled look as he mounted his bay gelding. Joseph, David, and Esa were hauled up onto horses behind three other men. "First, you'd best get into town to see that brother of yours. He's mortally wounded. Unless I miss my guess, he won't live to see another sunrise. He's at the doc's."

The marshal signaled to his men to ride out. Caitlin stood on the porch, tears streaming down her cheeks. Doom. Somehow, she'd sensed its coming. Now it had arrived. Dust billowed around the horses and riders as they became small specks on the grassland that stretched endlessly beyond the yard. She'd never felt quite so alone. Her husband gone, his brothers gone. Patrick near death. Fear lanced through her. An awful, bone-chilling fear.

Oh, God . . . She cast an imploring glance at the sky. She didn't know what to do. Her brother shot in the back? Who would do such a thing? And why? The questions circled dizzily in her mind. She had no answers. And without them, she would lose her husband. Beiler would hang Ace without so much as blinking an eye. Caitlin knew that. Just as he'd taken part in hanging Joseph Paxton twenty years ago. She had to do something. Only what?

Caitlin straightened her shoulders. One thing was for sure. She would accomplish nothing here. Her brother lay close to death in town. She needed to go see him. While she was there, she would take stock of the situation. Possibly think of some way to help her husband.

She couldn't let him die at the end of a rope.

It had taken twenty-two years, but God had finally sent her a hero. She wasn't about to lose him. Not if she could help it.

ℬ 28

By THE TIME CAITLIN REACHED TOWN, A MOB OF ABOUT twenty men had already gathered in front of the jail. As she made her way down the street toward the doctor's office, she could hear them yelling, "Let's hang the bastard! Justice, Beiler! We want justice!"

She paused on the boardwalk outside the doctor's office, her gaze fixed on the small, barred windows of the marshal's domain, just across the way. Ace and his brothers were in there somewhere. She imagined them sitting in cheerless cells, their gazes fixed on the bars that held them prisoner. They had to be frightened. She knew she was. Those men wanted blood, and from the sound of it, they wouldn't be satisfied until they got it.

For a crazy instant, Caitlin entertained the notion of breaking her husband and his brothers out of jail. She was a good shot with a rifle. It wasn't beyond the realm of possibility that she could—

Foolishness. Utter foolishness. She could no more take on twenty armed men than a pig could fly. It was stupid to even consider it, and Ace would be the first to tell her so.

A sense of helplessness flooded over her. She felt cold inside. Her husband—her whole life—was over there in that jail, and there was nothing she could do to help him.

It took all Caitlin's strength of will to turn her back on the jail and enter the doctor's office. Patrick lay wounded. He might very well die. She needed to be with him right now. And deep down, she knew it was what Ace would want her to do. If he knew she'd even entertained the notion of a jail break, he'd be horrified. Are you out of your mind? he'd ask. And the sad truth was, he'd be right. Whether she liked it or not, she had little choice but to do what women had been doing since the beginning of time—wait and pray.

Doc Halloway's office was just as Caitlin remembered it. A clutter of medical books lined the walls of the waiting room, holding court over utilitarian chairs with metal legs and worn leather seats. Next to the scarred oak door that led into the examining rooms and surgery there hung a picture of a small girl with red jam smeared over her face and the front of her white pinafore. Over the years, Caitlin had stared at that picture for countless hours while she waited for Doc to finish with his other patients so he might treat her injuries.

Once, she'd come to him with a broken wrist. Another time, lacerations on her back and legs from her father's belt buckle had driven her to seek Doc's help. She'd even come to him once with loosened front teeth, which he'd saved by rigging her up a wire retainer to hold her teeth fast until they healed.

Doc. He'd always patched her up and never asked questions. He had even forgone his usual fees most of the time, understanding that she'd come to see him on the sly and that her father would raise Cain if he found out. Conor O'Shannessy had been strange that way. After his drunken rages, he'd wanted to pretend they never happened, and he had wanted her to do so as well. Sometimes, due to her injuries, that simply hadn't been possible.

Stepping to the door that led to the interior medical rooms, Caitlin hauled in a deep, bracing breath before she knocked. Almost immediately, she heard another door open and shut somewhere, followed by the familiar shuffle of Doc's footsteps. A second later, the oak panel creaked open, and Doc was standing there, just as he had a dozen times over the years, his kindly expression filled with silent understanding. Only this time, Caitlin doubted he was going to be able to fix what ailed her.

"Caitlin! Come in, lass. Come in."

Stooped with age and overweight from restricted physical activity, the old man scratched his grizzled head and pushed his spectacles farther up on his bulbous nose as he moved back to allow her entry. His blue eyes were cloudy with sadness behind the thick lenses of his glasses. That had always been one of the nicest things about Doc; he truly empathized with people. Caitlin gave him a quick peck on the cheek.

"Hi, Doc. It's been a while."

"And aren't we glad of that?"

Caitlin couldn't help but smile. Shakily, to be sure, but a smile just the same. She truly did love this old man. Because of his profession, he was the one person in town who knew just how bad things had been for her sometimes. Except for Cruise Dublin's attack, of course. Even though she'd bled badly for days afterward, she'd been too ashamed to seek treatment that time. Until Ace, she'd never told a single soul about that night.

Ace. Caitlin realized she'd been blocking out the belt buckle had driven her to seek Doc's help. She'd even sounds of the men's voices across the street. Refusing to accept what their angry shouts portended. She guessed women had been doing that since the beginning of time as well—fooling themselves, pretending things weren't as bad as they actually were in an attempt to stay sane.

"How is Patrick?" she asked, suddenly feeling as though she were looking out at the world through a thin layer of cotton.

Doc shook his head. "Not good. He's got a high fever, honey. I've done all I can. Cleaned the wound. Stitched him up, inside and out. Now it's up to God."

"I'd like to sit with him a while. Will that be all right?"

"Sure, it will."

Doc shuffled along in front of her, the cuffs of his gray trousers dragging the floor. He wore suspenders, but, typical of Doc, he'd pushed the bright red straps off his shoulders, letting them hang uselessly at his waist. He'd never been one to be overly concerned with appearance. He had greater concerns, namely his patients.

"This way, lass. I have him on a cot in here in my surgery."

The smell of disinfectant and ether assailed Caitlin's nostrils as she stepped into the dimly lit room. At its center stood an operating table, over which three unlit lanterns were suspended. Many had been the time she'd lain on that table, blinded by the lights overhead, while Doc chased away her pain.

"I doused the lights," Doc explained. "Thought he might rest better that way." He stepped over to the cot, then turned to fix her with a thoughtful look. "He hadn't been drinking when they brought him in." He shrugged. "I just thought you might like to know that. He's been hitting the jug pretty heavily the last few months. You can't have been too happy about that, not after the way liquor did your father. Never met a nicer man than Conor O'Shannessy sober. Crazier than a loco horse when he got drunk, though. Patrick's the same way, I'm afraid."

Caitlin pressed a hand to her waist, glad for anything

to distract her from the lifeless form on that cot across the room. It was almost more than she could face. Her stomach turned, felt burning hot. "He, um . . . didn't smell of whiskey when they brought him in? Are you sure?"

"I can smell the stuff a mile off. It's my guess he hadn't touched a drop for a couple of days. It lingers on a man who imbibes heavily. A doctor develops a nose for it after a while."

Her next words came hard. "He—was drunk—crazy drunk—when I saw him three days ago. We had words. I told him I never wanted to see him again."

"Ah . . ." Doc glanced down at his patient. "That probably explains it, then. I can't say a lot for the boy, his behavior being like it has the last few months, but no one can doubt that he loves his sister. Must have shaken him up pretty bad, you telling him something like that."

"Yes. Well, I don't really know. I guess, maybe."

Doc winked at her. "I'd say he tried to quit drinking. That's nice for you to know, hm? No matter how this turns out?"

Nice? Caitlin wanted to sink to her knees and sob. To think that her brother had spent the last three days thinking of her, that he'd tried, once again, to stay away from the whiskey . . . and this time, without her help. Oh, God. Now he lay dying, and she couldn't even be sure he would hear her if she told him how much she loved him.

Death was so final. It gave no second chances. Caitlin braced herself as she moved across the room to look down on her brother. In the gloom, his skin was so pale it reminded her of the underbelly of a fish. His tousled hair looked glaringly red against the starched white pillowcase. "Oh, Paddy," she whispered shakily. "Oh, God."

Doc rested a hand on her shoulder. "Now, now, Caitlin, lass. He might just surprise us and pull through, you know. Let's not be giving up hope. He's young and strong."

Caitlin sank onto the straight-backed chair Doc had

pulled up beside the cot, the seat of which still felt warm. She realized the doctor had been keeping a vigil beside her brother's bed. She should have known. Doc always went the extra mile. On a small table, close at hand, sat a basin of water. With shaking hands, she wrung out the rag and bathed her brother's feverish face.

"Caitlin!" Patrick cried out suddenly. "Have to tell . . . Have to."

"He's been talking out kind of crazy," Doc warned her. "Saying your name a lot and all kinds of strange things. With such a high fever, that's to be expected."

Caitlin drew back the crisp sheet to stare at the bandage that swathed her brother's torso. She was horrified to see that blood had seeped through the strips of cloth. No stranger to bullet wounds, she knew the damage that could occur when lead entered at one side of the body and exited out the other. Patrick had been shot in the back.

"Oh, dear God. The bullet went clear through?"

"Now, now. It's not as bad as it looks. Better this way, actually. The bullet made a clean pass and did most of its damage on the way out instead of inside him somewhere. He's not spitting up any blood, which means it didn't get a lung. If you'll look more closely, you'll see that the lead glanced off to one side. Probably because of the angle from which it was fired. If there's any such thing as a good bullet wound, this one is it."

Caitlin focused on the bloodstain and saw that the darkest part of the seepage was indeed off to the right. "Do you think it hit anything vital?"

"I pray not. Only time will tell. Just be thankful the lead passed all the way through. I didn't have to do any excavating. That's a plus. And you have to remember, a bullet does the most damage where it lodges inside a man or as it makes its exit. In this case, I think it made a clean pass. Truly, I do. Even a vital organ can heal, you know. I've seen it in my day. Then again, I've seen flesh wounds kill a man. Like I said, it's up to God at this point, honey."

Up to God . . . Caitlin closed her eyes on that. When

she looked back at the old physician, she asked, "Do you know how it happened, Doc? Where Patrick was when he got shot?"

"They said he was out by the pigpen. Probably slopping the sows, would be my guess. The sniper was up on the hill behind your house, according to the good marshal's calculations. Shooting a high-powered rifle, that's at fairly close range."

The doctor said "good marshal" with unmistakable sarcasm. Though Estyn Beiler had managed to be re-elected year after year, there were a lot of people in No Name who didn't think highly of him. Not many men had the temperament to be in law enforcement. As in most small towns, the risks were high, the wages low. At election time, Beiler's was usually the only name on the ballot. The man had a penchant for drinking and playing poker that wasn't strictly admirable in an elected official, but people tended to overlook that. Someone had to wear a badge and uphold the law.

Caitlin felt a rush of anger. "I hate that man. If he has his way, my husband's going to hang for this. And, I'm telling you, Ace didn't do it. I'm not pretending he doesn't have it in him to shoot someone. We all know that's not true. But he wouldn't hide on a hillside and sight in on a man whose back was turned. Only a coward would do such a thing, and my husband is no coward."

"I agree."

Caitlin glanced up, unable to conceal her surprise. "You do?"

Doc smiled. "That's another thing I've become a fair hand at over the years, judging people. I've watched Ace Keegan since he came to town, taken his measure pretty carefully. I'd say he's a hard man, but a good one."

"Oh, Doc! I should have known I'd have a friend in you. Will you help him? Please? Go out there and talk some sense into those men! Make them stop this craziness."

"Ah, honey. A friend, I definitely am. But not a very influential one, I'm afraid. To people here, I'm just the eccentric old doctor who has trouble keeping his trousers up. They come to me for their ingrown toenails and for the occasional serious illness. Otherwise, they think I'm battier than a belfry."

Caitlin knew he spoke the truth. People liked Doc, but most of them were of the opinion that he was a little strange. Maybe he was. In Caitlin's books, it was a very good kind of strange.

She thumbed the diamond ring her husband had placed on her finger, aching with concern for him. "I love Ace Keegan with all my heart."

"I can see that you do." Doc rubbed his chin. "And I'd help him if I could. Honestly, I would."

"I know." Caitlin meant that. When had she ever come to Doc that he hadn't tried to set her world aright? Once he'd even offered her a home with him. She'd refused, of course, afraid her father might fly into a rage and take it out on Doc if she tried to leave home. But she'd never forgotten. This old man would have fought the devil himself for her, even if he had known beforehand that he'd probably lose. "I know you would, Doc. Thank you for that."

"Yes, well . . ." He smiled wryly. "I guess I developed a special fondness for you over the years. I have to admit, I was a mite worried when I first heard Keegan had married you. Then, after thinking it over, I decided maybe it was the best thing that could have happened to you. I'm glad to see I was right. It's about time you had a man treat you decent."

"He treats me a whole lot better than just decent." Caitlin focused on the sounds coming from across the street. Angry shouts, calls for justice. "Oh, Doc, if only Patrick could tell us who shot him. They're going to storm that jail. I just know it. And Beiler probably won't do a blooming thing to stop them."

"No, probably not," Doc agreed, looking concerned. "Knowing him, probably not."

Doc drew up another chair and sat beside her, his gaze fixed worriedly on Patrick. After a long while, he said, "Even if Patrick could talk, he might not know who shot him. Like you say, the man who did it was a coward. He probably hid in the brush where Patrick couldn't see him."

"And they"—Caitlin gestured toward the jail—"think Ace Keegan did it? Just listen to them. Where are their heads at?"

"Most of those fellows out there are good men, Caitlin. They're angry right now and not thinking straight, that's all."

"I wish I could feel so charitable."

Doc sighed. "I'm not defending them. Don't take me wrong. It's just bad business, this. Most of them are older men. Men who knew and liked Camlin Beckett. They were outraged over his murder."

"That happened nearly twenty years ago! That doesn't excuse their behavior now!"

"Doesn't it?" Doc arched an eyebrow at her, his spectacles catching light from the small surgery window positioned high on the wall. "In their minds, history has repeated itself. The Paxton bunch came back to No Name, and the first thing they know, one of their own has been shot in the back again. Naturally, they're angry, and in the heat of their anger, they want justice."

Caitlin hadn't looked at it in quite that way. She tried to do so now. "All I know is, they'd like to lynch my husband, and he's innocent. Anyone should be able to see that."

Doc rested a hand on her knee. "And you're angry with them for being so blind. I don't blame you for that. At the same time, even though they're wrong to want to take the law into their own hands, I can't really blame them, either. Back shooting, like I said, is nasty business. It's too bad that—" He broke off and shook his head. "Ah, nothing."

"What?" Caitlin pressed.

"Oh, I was just thinking out loud, that's all. Wishing there were some way to prove . . . ." His voice trailed off and he shrugged. "There isn't, though. Twenty years is a long time."

Patrick tossed his head upon the pillow and began

muttering under his breath. Something about Beiler and his losses at the poker tables. Caitlin wished she could pull him from his nightmares.

When Patrick finally quieted, she shifted her focus back to the physician. "You said something about proving something, Doc? Proving what?"

"I was just thinking how great it'd be if you could prove that Joseph Paxton might have been innocent. That is what Keegan claims, right?"

"Yes."

"Well?" Doc met her gaze. "It's a shame you can't prove it. Or, at least, put some doubt in their minds. That'd take the wind out of those fellows' sails. Make them step back and do some serious thinking. It's a terrible thing, hanging an innocent man. None of them would want to do that. If they'd calm down for a few minutes, they'd all have second thoughts."

Caitlin had dared to let herself hope. Now she felt crestfallen. "That's only wishful thinking, Doc. How could I possibly prove Joseph Paxton was innocent? He and Beckett have been dead and buried for so long."

From the front waiting room came the sound of a door opening, quickly followed by footsteps. Doc pushed up from his chair. "Summer cold season. Sounds like I've got another patient." He shuffled toward the door. "If you need me, honey, I'll be a skip and a jump away. Don't hesitate to holler. Unless an emergency comes in, there'll be nothing all that urgent going on out here."

Caitlin gazed after him until he disappeared, the door closing softly behind him. Then she devoted herself to Patrick, smoothing his hair, trickling cold water over his feverish skin. At least for her brother, she could do something useful.

She was surprised when she heard the door open again. Glancing up, she saw her friend Bess slipping into the room. Their gazes locked. Bess's eyes were swimming with tears. "Surely, you knew I would come," she said softly.

Caitlin nodded. Bess was that kind of friend. Always had been. She patted the chair beside her. Bess sat down, her moist gaze fixed on Patrick.

"Oh, Caitie. I'm so sorry. So very, very sorry."

Caitlin wrung out the rag again, striving to maintain control. "He may not make it, Bess."

"I know. I heard about Ace, too. Are you, um . . . upset about that?"

"Oh, Bess. I love him so much. I'm afraid those men out there are going to hang him, and there's nothing I can do to help him."

Bess laid a hand on her shoulder. She said nothing. There was nothing to say.

Silence fell. Bess's presence was a comfort to Caitlin as she bathed Patrick's feverish skin, wondering with every breath she took if he would live or die.

As she worked, Caitlin's mind kept circling back to what Doc had said. Proof. Now that the thought had been planted in her mind, it refused to be dislodged. It would be so wonderful if she could actually help Ace. She owed him so much. To stand helplessly by while he faced this trouble nearly broke her heart.

Doc was absolutely right about one thing. If she could put a trace of doubt into those men's minds—just enough to make them question Paxton's guilt—they might not be quite so eager to hang Ace. Right now, they were thinking of him as a chip off the old block, the stepson of a back shooter who'd grown into a man with the same cowardly tendencies. If she could make them wonder, even for an instant, if Paxton had actually shot Beckett, then they might reconsider. No one wanted to be responsible for hanging an innocent man.

Ceaselessly running the cloth over Patrick's brow and face, Caitlin shared with Bess what Doc had said. "I wish I could prove Paxton's innocence," she whispered in conclusion. "Oh, God, if only I could."

"I don't see how. It all happened so long ago."

Bess was right, Caitlin knew. Still, she couldn't help but wish.

As she bathed her brother's arms, Caitlin went back over everything Ace had told her about the past. About Joseph Paxton paying a thousand dollars for the Circle Star in St. Louis. About their trip westward and its tragic conclusion when they finally arrived here. If only there were some way for her to cast some doubt. Some way to make those men out there ask themselves some difficult questions. What if Paxton had been innocent? What if her father and his friends had hung a guiltless man? What if Paxton actually had paid a thousand dollars for the Circle Star? What if he really had been swindled?

At the coldness of the cloth, Patrick flung his head back and forth on the pillow, rambling senselessly, just as Doc had warned her he might. "Damned cat," he muttered, making Caitlin smile. She knew her brother must be dreaming about Lucky. "Gonna rain. Gotta get the grass hay cut." He licked his parched lips, then frowned. His expression turned suddenly tormented. He knotted his hands into fists and jerked his arm from her grasp. "Caitlin. Have to tell . . . her. Journals. In the journals. Go . . . Beiler. Tell Caitlin."

"Patrick," Caitlin murmured soothingly. "Just dreams, Paddy boy. I'm here. The hay's all cut now. The monthly ledgers can wait. It's all right. Don't worry. Shhh."

At the sound of her voice, Patrick thrashed more violently and opened his eyes, which seemed to hold no recognition. "Have to listen," he said in a raspy voice. "Read—ledger, Caitlin. And the journal. Don't—not Beiler. Promise me?"

"I promise, Paddy. I promise." Caitlin pressed a hand to her brother's hot forehead, believing his words to be the result of delirium. "I love you, Patrick. I didn't mean what I said the other morning. I love you so. Do you hear me? I love you, Patrick. No matter what, I'll always love you."

His eyes seemed to grow clear for a second. He stared up at her face, his expression beseeching. "Forgive—me. Forgive me, Caitlin. Sorry. So sorry. No more— whiskey. I swear it. No more."

"I know. I know," she whispered. "You'll never drink again. Not ever. I know. Now, hush, Paddy boy. Sleep. You have to get well."

It was all Caitlin could do to keep the tears from her

eyes. It hurt so badly, seeing him like this, knowing he probably wouldn't live. He was so young. And, just as she'd told him, she loved him and always would, no matter what.

"Go to sleep now," she urged. "I'll stay right here, Patrick. Right here. Go to sleep."

He caught her hand and gripped it with surprising strength. "No. You have to—go home. Read—journal. Promise?"

Caitlin felt a chill run up her spine. Delirium? Or was her brother trying desperately to tell her something? "What journal, Patrick? What are you talking about?"

Bess sat forward on her chair, her eyes gleaming with excitement. "Caitlin, he's trying to tell you something!"

The muscles along Patrick's throat grew distended. He gulped for air. "Pa's journal. Like Doc said. Proof—in—there. Home. Go home. Promise."

"All right. I promise." Caitlin gave his hand a squeeze and glanced questioningly at Bess. "I promise, Patrick. It'll be all right now. Go to sleep. Rest."

His lashes fluttered closed. His hand relaxed over hers, then went limp. For a long moment, Caitlin and Bess simply sat there, staring down at him.

"Doc warned me crazy talk was to be expected with such a high fever," she whispered to her friend.

Bess's green eyes looked huge in her pale face. "Is it crazy talk? That's the question. Uncle Bart may have been listening with only half an ear. As a doctor, he often has his mind on treating his patient and scarcely hears what they say to him. Oh, Caitlin, maybe you should go out to the ranch. Go through those ledgers and journals."

Caitlin was almost afraid to place any importance on the mutterings of a delirious man. "Oh, Bess, do you think so?"

Bess snatched the wet rag from her hand. "I'll sit here with Patrick. Go, for heaven's sake. What have you got to lose?"

Nothing, Caitlin realized. Absolutely nothing.

She pushed slowly to her feet, her heart racing. It was

a long shot. Probably a total waste of time. But what was she accomplishing here? Their father had kept daily journals and monthly ledgers. They were on shelves in his study, gathering dust. Had Patrick found something in them? Something that might have gotten him shot in the back for his trouble?

History repeating itself, Doc had said. Dear God, how could she have been so stupid? Someone had murdered Camlin Beckett twenty years ago. If not Joseph Paxton, then who? Bullets weren't fired by phantoms. Someone had shot Beckett in the back. Someone who might still be alive. Someone who probably wouldn't hesitate to kill again if he felt threatened with discovery.

Caitlin hurried from the surgery room. "Doc? Doc! I need to speak with you."

"Just a second!" he called. He spoke in a lower voice to someone else, then stepped out into the short hallway where Caitlin waited for him. "What is it, lass? You look as if you've seen a ghost."

Caitlin grasped both his hands, so excited she had to swallow before she could manage to speak. "Doc," she whispered urgently, "don't think we're crazy, but Bess and I think maybe Patrick found something at home in our father's journals, something to prove that Joseph Paxton didn't shoot Beckett!"

The elderly physician tightened his hold on her hands. "I know he's been rambling about some kind of journal, honey, but you can't put any stock in that. He's out of his head."

"Is he? Or has he been trying to tell us something?" She closed her eyes for a moment, striving to calm down. "Oh, Doc, I have to try. I'm going home to see what I can find. You mustn't tell anyone what I'm doing. Promise me? If Bess and I are right, that may be why Patrick was shot."

"Good Lord." The doctor's eyes grew dark with concern. "I never thought of that. Ledgers and journals. That's all he's talked about ever since they brought him in."

Hope welled within Caitlin. An almost violent hope.

"Doc, it could take me hours. Meanwhile, those men out there—they could go off half-cocked and hang Ace before I can get back. You have to go over there and talk to them. Try to calm them down. Keep them from doing anything stupid. Will you do that for me? Please?"

Doc drew his hands from hers and grasped her shoulders. "I'll try, honey. For you, I'll try."

Caitlin threw her arms around his neck and gave him a fierce hug. "Thank you! I'll never forget this. Never!"

She spun and ran from the building.

29

IT WAS AFTER DARK BY THE TIME CAITLIN FINISHED THE search of her father's study and returned to town. She headed straight for the jail in hopes of catching Marshal Beiler before he left for the night.

She was at first puzzled, then alarmed, when she saw the crowd that had gathered under a large oak at the end of Main Street. In the bobbing torchlight, she could see a man astride a horse under one of the tree limbs. Even in the dusky light, the set of his shoulders and the way he held his head struck a chord within her. Ace. She would have recognized him anywhere.

Caitlin broke into a run. History was indeed about to repeat itself. Like Joseph Paxton twenty years earlier, Ace was about to be lynched by an angry mob.

A painful stitch lanced Caitlin's side by the time she reached the edges of the milling crowd. In her peripheral vision, she saw Doc standing off to her left. He had obviously failed in his attempt to calm these people down, for his expression was a mixture of apology and grim resignation. Men were yelling. Women were huddled together in groups talking. All of them seemed eager for the show to begin. The thought sickened

Caitlin, and she wanted to scream at them, revile them. A man's life was on the line. Didn't they comprehend that? This wasn't some kind of circus show, staged for their entertainment.

Caitlin knew she'd never be able to make herself heard above the rumble of the crowd unless she did something to get everyone's attention. Digging into ribs with her elbows and shoving at broad backs, she pressed toward the shifting ring of torchlight, waving the papers she'd ripped from her father's ledgers and journals above her head.

"Stop it! Stop this madness! You have to listen to me. All of you! You have to listen to me!"

"It's the O'Shannessy girl," she heard someone shout. Another man yelled, "Let her through. She should get to watch the bastard swing. It's her brother who's about to die, after all."

The throng of bodies suddenly parted, making a path for her. Caitlin stumbled forward into the circle of illumination. Her gaze swung immediately to Ace. His dark eyes held hers for a long moment, the bruises on his face barely visible in the shadows cast by the torchlight.

When he spoke, his Adam's apple made the knot in the noose around his throat bob up and down. "Go home, Caitlin. Please, sweetheart. I don't want you to see this."

He could have said anything else, and maybe it wouldn't have brought tears to her eyes. But to know he was concerned about her at a time like this, that was her undoing. His life was about to be forfeited. Didn't he comprehend that? These men hadn't notched the rope as he had done the night he nearly hanged Patrick. When the horse he was sitting on lunged forward, he would either get his neck broken or choke to death, neither of which was a pleasant way to die. He should have been quivering in terror. Pleading for his life. Maybe even furious. Instead, he was focused on getting her out of there. If Caitlin had ever needed proof of his love for her, she had it now. It made the thought of losing him all that much harder to bear.

Clutching the papers more tightly, she gulped for

breath and grabbed for control. Now was no time for histrionics. No time to lose her perspective. Turning from her husband, she faced the crowd. "Where is Marshal Beiler?" she cried, shaking the papers in the faces of the men who stood closest to her. "Get him out here right now. This man didn't shoot my brother! And I can prove it! If you hang him, you'll carry the guilt of it to your graves. Do you understand me?"

"How can you prove it?"

The speaker was Charley Banks, a big, brawny man whose eyes glowed with righteous anger. By his commanding stance, Caitlin guessed he'd been selected as the mob's ringleader and, as such, he was undoubtedly the most dangerous man present. On his say-so alone, the people in this crowd would either release Ace or go crazy with primal blood lust.

Reminding herself of what Doc had said—that all of these men were basically good people—Caitlin straightened her shoulders, gathered her courage, and strode directly to Banks. Thrusting the papers under his nose, she said, "The main reason you think my husband shot my brother is because you're convinced his stepfather shot Camlin Beckett. Isn't that right? The son of a back shooter following in his stepfather's footsteps?"

Banks darted a glance at the papers. "Might be. Might not. What have you got there, girl?"

Caitlin jutted her chin at him. "Proof in my father's own handwriting that Joseph Paxton didn't kill Camlin Beckett! And you'd better thank God I found it in time. You idiots have nearly hung an innocent man!"

"Caitlin, for God's sake, watch your tongue," Ace said from behind her. "These men are angry right now. Don't test their tempers."

Caitlin knew Ace was afraid Charley Banks would take offense and retaliate by striking her. At any other time, she might have quaked in her shoes. Right now she didn't care. She'd taken the punishment of a man's fists before.

She shook the papers under Banks's nose again. "If it tests their tempers to be confronted with the truth, then that's their problem, not mine. You're about to do something incredibly stupid, Mr. Banks. Something you'll regret until your dying day! Mark my words, I will press charges against you if you lynch my husband. And with evidence like this"—she shook the papers again—"there isn't a court in the land that won't convict you of murder! A hanging offense, Mr. Banks! And so help me God, I'll help build the gallows myself to see you executed!"

"Caitlin!" Ace exclaimed, his voice taut with warning.

Banks growled and snatched the papers from her hand. "What kind of evidence?" he asked sarcastically. "Something you hatched up to save his hide? It's a sad day, I'll tell you, when a woman tries to save the man who shot her own brother in the back!"

"That's right!" someone yelled. "Let's get on with it. He's guilty. We all know it."

"He's no more guilty than you or I!" Caitlin cried.

Banks was holding the ledger and journal pages up to the torchlight that flickered behind him. A strange expression crossed his face. "Hold on just a minute, boys. This is Conor's handwriting. I seen it often enough to know." His gaze sliced back to Caitlin. "What have you got here, girl? What is it you think you've found that's so important?"

A sudden hush fell. Caitlin knew it would take Banks as many hours as it had her to find the discrepancies in her father's ledgers, that he might have difficulty figuring it all out even if she pinpointed the entries for him.

A bluff. That was what was called for. The most important bluff of her life. And if she didn't carry it off, her husband would die.

"Those are pages from my father's journals and ledgers, as you can see. His entries substantiate the fact that Joseph Paxton, my husband's stepfather, paid good money twenty years ago to purchase the deed to the Circle Star Ranch. Yet when Paxton arrived here, he was ordered off the land. A swindle, plain and simple. And Paxton wasn't their only victim! My father worked in cahoots with four other men, Beckett, Dublin, Connel and Beiler. All of them were in on it, not once but several times, swindling innocent people out of their hard-earned money. Read for yourself!"

Banks gave a ledger page a quick once-over, his brows drawing together in a frown. "Show me."

"It's all there," Caitlin cried. "In black and white. Joseph Paxton came here to possess land he'd purchased in good faith from Camlin Beckett back in St. Louis. Almost immediately after he got here, my father and his friends, all armed to the teeth, paid him a visit and told him to leave. Paxton was a peaceful, God-fearing man, and he feared for his family's safety, so he agreed to go. But before he could, Beckett was shot in the back, and Paxton was accused of the murder.

"Stop and think!" she implored the crowd. "In my father's own hand, the admission is made. He and his four friends swindled people to make extra money. You all know how hard it is to make ends meet here, farming and raising cattle. Most of you originally came here hoping to find gold. Many of you were poor Irish immigrants like my parents, driven from your homeland by famine. You came here chasing a dream. Quick fortunes in gold! The very name of our town is testimony to that, a mining community gone bust so soon it never even got a proper name. My father and his friends discovered a way to earn money on the side, by swindling innocent people! That's how they always seemed to turn a better profit than the rest of you, by the sweat of someone else's brow."

"My God," a man in the crowd yelled, "I wondered how Conor always managed to get his hands on money. Drinking and gambling like he did must have cost a small fortune."

The man's outburst was the first sign that any of these people were even listening to her. Caitlin nearly went limp with relief. Then someone cried, "So that's why Paxton shot Beckett! He'd been swindled!"

"That's right. You've just proven Paxton's guilt, girl, not the other way around. He shot Beckett to get revenge! Just like Keegan did your brother."

"No!" Caitlin cried. "How can you people be so

blind? Ace Keegan doesn't need to shoot anyone in the back. Why bother? There isn't a man amongst you, including my brother Patrick, that he couldn't gun down in a fair fight. Use your heads! Think! You know what I'm saying is absolutely true."

Before anyone could interrupt her, Caitlin rushed on to ask, "How many of you believe there can be any honor among thieves? There is none, I can assure you! If men will steal together, they will steal from one another without blinking an eye." She waited for that to sink in. "And that's exactly what happened. When Camlin Beckett sold the Circle Star to Joseph Paxton in St. Louis, Paxton paid him a thousand dollars. Yet when Beckett returned to No Name from St. Louis, he reported a sale of only five hundred. A swindler swindling the swindlers! It's right there, in black and white. Undeniable proof."

"How do you know how much Paxton actually paid?"

Someone else yelled, "Yeah, are we supposed to take Keegan's word for it?"

Caitlin gulped, praying no one would call her on her next claim. "I've seen Paxton's bill of sale with my own eyes! Ace Keegan kept the paperwork all these years. I didn't have time to go out to his ranch and fetch it, but the deed and bill of sale are there. I've seen them, I'm telling you. Paxton paid a thousand dollars! Not five hundred. And Camlin Beckett attested to that himself with his signature. Yet according to my father's journal entries, which Mr. Banks holds in his hands right now, Camlin Beckett returned to No Name with only half that amount."

"Beckett cheated the others out of five hundred dollars?" another man in the crowd asked.

"Yes, and he was dancing with the devil, believe me. My father was no one to cross, as all of you well know."

"You sayin' Conor killed Beckett?" someone asked.

"I'm saying one of them did," Caitlin admitted. "One of them discovered that Beckett had cheated them. I maintain it was that man who shot him in the back. Not Joseph Paxton. My father and his friends hanged an innocent man!"

Caitlin began to search the crowd for the faces of the

men responsible for Paxton's death. So far, they'd held their peace, probably because they were hoping the situation might still swing in their favor. Caitlin hadn't managed to completely convince this crowd of her claims as yet. As long as her story was being met with opposition, Paxton's killers undoubtedly felt safe.

She spotted Dublin first. His face was one from her nightmares, round and florid, his beady little eyes like those of a snake's. She expected him to be glaring at her, enraged because she would dare to sully his good name. Her rapist. Dear God, how she hated him. Even in the torchlight, the injuries Ace had inflicted on his face were apparent—puffy discoloration along his cheekbones and around his eyes, a swollen blue welt at the bridge of his nose. Caitlin doubled her hands into fists, wishing it had been she who'd pummeled him.

To her surprise, Dublin wasn't even looking at her. Instead, his gaze seemed to be fixed on a point at the edge of the crowd. Someone stood in the shadows of the buildings. A faceless someone who was watching the goings-on, but not taking part.

Caitlin squinted, trying to make out the man's face. The brightness of the torchlight frustrated her. Before she could move to see better, Aiden Connel's voice rose from somewhere in the crowd.

"How do you explain the difference in money?" he demanded of the shadowy figure. "You went to St. Louis with Camlin. How was it you didn't realize he'd filched some of the proceeds?"

"Because her whole story's bullshit! That's how!" the man retorted, stepping into the light as he spoke. Caitlin recognized that voice even before she could see the man's features. Estyn Beiler, the marshal. "The girl's grasping at straws, trying to save her husband's miserable neck! A discrepancy in her father's ledgers? Ha! Have you found it yet, Banks? Hell, no. She's fabricated the entire story, trying to make us doubt the rightness of what we're about to do, which is to hang a cowardly back shooter!"

"I fabricated nothing!" Caitlin cried.

"The truth is," Beiler retorted, "Joseph Paxton was as guilty as sin. He shot Beckett in the back, just like Ace Keegan shot your brother. Like father, like son. As for the members of our little association being swindlers? How dare you tarnish your father's good name, and him in the grave, unable to defend himself. Have you no loyalty at all? Though why it surprises me, I wouldn't know. Your brother is dying, and here you are, defending his killer! You're no kind of daughter. Or sister, for that matter. You've sold out, heart and soul, to that back-shooting bastard. You're the worst kind of whore, turning your back on your own family."

Scenes from over the years flashed through Caitlin's mind, making her shake with impotent fury. "That's right! I've sold out, heart and soul. I'd rather be Ace Keegan's wife than my father's daughter, any day. Conor O'Shannessy was a black-hearted, cruel bastard, and all of you know it."

Gasps of shock rose from the crowd. Caitlin turned on the masses. "You know it's true. All of you saw the bruises on me, time after time. You knew what happened when he staggered home, reeling drunk. But did any of you lift a finger to help me? Never. You were all afraid of him, just like I was." Caitlin met the gazes of the men who stood closest to her. "Well, I'm not afraid anymore. He's dead and buried, his only legacy to this town a host of atrocities none of you want to admit even happened! Call me Ace Keegan's whore, if you like. I'll bear the title with pride. My father wasn't fit to lick my husband's boots."

Beiler bellowed with laughter. "Do we have to stand here and listen to this tripe? Sing Ace Keegan's praises if you want, but not where we have to hear them. As for the way your father abused you?" He pressed a hand over his heart. "We weep rivers of tears. You seem to be in fine form now. If he had been as black-hearted as you claim, you'd have the lasting injuries to prove it.

"As for this entertaining story you've hatched up, I will remind you that I was there, young lady. I have my faults, but no one in his right mind would ever accuse me of being a thief. I jail the thieves around here, in case you've forgotten. I've been putting my life on the line for the people in this town for years, upholding the law. True, we sold Paxton some scrub land. When he got here, he didn't like the parcel we'd selected and tried to squat on the Circle Star, which was a piece of Conor's prime ranch land. We ordered him off. He got mad, came gunning for us, and shot Camlin in the back when he caught him off alone. That's the real story. I was there. I ought to know."

Looking into Beiler's eyes, Caitlin saw a burning hatred. Fear mushroomed inside her. There was no mistaking that look. Beiler wasn't simply standing aside, letting the mob have their way because he could do nothing to stop them. He wanted Ace to be hung.

Why? She no sooner asked herself that question than she knew the answer. She'd guessed wrong. Oh, God, she'd guessed wrong. It hadn't been Camlin Beckett who'd purloined half the swindling proceeds twenty years ago. It had been Beiler. Camlin Beckett must have accompanied Beiler to St. Louis and somehow discovered his treachery. To keep him quiet, Beiler had shot him in the back and blamed the murder on Paxton.

Terrified that the men around her would believe Beiler and not her, Caitlin cried, "I have proof, Mr. Beiler. My father's ledgers. Look at them, Mr. Banks. It's all there. Our wonderful marshal is lying through his teeth."

Beiler laughed again. "Right. And how can we know Paxton paid a thousand dollars for the land? She claims there's a deed and bill of sale back at Keegan's place, but you don't see it, do you? Are you going to take Keegan's word for it? Or hers? One look at her face, and anybody can see she's crazy in love with the bastard. Hell, she's even admitted as much. Keegan's whore, and proud of it!"

A man at the back of the crowd yelled, "I say let's go ahead and hang him. She has no real proof. Just a bunch of supposition! Keegan shot Patrick O'Shannessy. Who else would have done it?"

"That's right!" someone else yelled.

"Make him pay," a woman cried.

Caitlin's gaze swung back to Ace. He looked deeply into her eyes. "Go home, Caitlin," he called huskily. "Please. Do this one last thing for me. Go home."

A man who'd been leaning against the oak tree stepped over to Ace's horse. With unnecessary roughness, he checked to be sure his prisoner's hands were still securely tied behind his back. It hit Caitlin then. She'd given it her best, and she'd failed. They were actually going to hang her husband, and there was nothing she could do to stop them.

After checking Ace's bound wrists, the man stepped up into one of the stirrups to check the noose around Ace's neck. Ace jerked his head to one side, his expression frustrated, his eyes never releasing hers. "Please, honey. I don't want you seeing this. Go home and wait for Joseph."

"I can't," Caitlin cried raggedly. "Don't ask me to. You don't abandon the people you love! And I love you, Ace. With all my heart!"

Ace jerked his gaze from hers to look out over the crowd. Caitlin was so terrified it took her a moment to register that a tense silence had blanketed everything. She turned to follow her husband's gaze.

"You may love him, sis, but I sure as hell don't," a weak voice called out. "Fact is, I hate the man's guts, and everyone here knows it. That's why what I've got to say is so important. Folks know I won't defend him without good reason."

Caitlin's heart nearly stopped. Patrick. She went up on tiptoe, trying to see through the crowd. She glimpsed her brother's shock of red hair, Doc's grizzled gray head bobbing beside him. "Patrick! Dear God, what are you doing here?"

Much like the sea for Moses, the crowd suddenly parted between her and her brother. Faintly illuminated by flickering torchlight, Patrick stood there, wearing faded denim trousers and the bandage that swathed his chest. He was clearly too weak to stay on his feet without the doctor's support. His face was deathly white, his eyes a smoldering blue.

"Bess told me what was happening out here. I just

came to set the record straight, that's—all." His knees buckled. Doc grabbed to keep a hold on him, making Patrick wince. "You folks—" He broke off, his quavering voice trailing away into silence. He let his head loll, then with obvious difficulty, forced it back up. "You're about to—hang the wrong man."

Caitlin took a step forward. Her brother was clearly in no shape to get up out of bed. The fact that he had done so was all the proof she needed that he was sorry for everything he'd said and done. So sorry that he was willing to risk his life to rectify matters.

"Oh, Patrick." Caitlin could barely see for the tears. "I can't believe you're doing this."

"Wait just a damned minute!" Beiler shouted. "Patrick's out of his head with fever. Anyone can see that! Nothing he says right now can be taken as fact."

Doc held up his hand, silencing Beiler and anyone else who might have tried to interrupt. "He's not out of his head. The fever's broken. The way I see it, if the young man wants to talk, the least you folks can do is listen. Where's the harm in that?"

The crowd went quiet again. Patrick worked his mouth, swallowed, took a careful, tremulous breath. Finally, in a raspy voice, he said, "The other day, I came into town, bragging"—he broke off to take another breath, obviously so weak that every word cost him dearly—"that I had kicked Ace Keegan's ass. The truth is, it was real easy to kick 'cause the man wouldn't fight back. He just stood there and let me—hit him. Back when he first married my sister, he promised her he'd never lift a hand against me. I heard him say it. The other morning, he kept that promise and just stood there while I beat him half stupid. I was so drunk I didn't care. Just took advantage of the situation."

Conversation began to buzz at this revelation. Caitlin closed her eyes to blink away the tears. Patrick. No coward, her brother. And she felt sure no sister had ever been more proud. It wasn't just that he'd dragged himself up from bed to come out here. It was that he was willing to humiliate himself to set his wrongs aright.

When she opened her eyes again, Patrick was looking

directly at her. "That and the fact that my sister disowned me got me to thinking. Ace Keegan couldn't be as bad a man as I thought, not if she'd grown to love him that much, not if he'd go that far to keep a promise to her. After I sobered up, I started going through my father's records, found the discrepancies Caitlin has been trying to tell you about. If Paxton paid a thousand for the Circle Star, like Keegan claims, what happened to the other five hundred?"

Patrick let that question hang there for a moment while he caught his breath. During the lull, Doc shifted his hold so he might bear more of Patrick's weight.

"Like my sister," Patrick finally continued, "I figured Beckett had filched the other half of the money. That one of his friends, maybe even my own father, had caught him red-handed and shot him. Last night, I came into town to confront Marshal Beiler with what I'd learned, to demand that he find out who really killed Beckett and clear Paxton's name. He said he'd think about it, that he'd try to figure out which of his friends had done it, Connel or Dublin."

"Me?" Dublin roared from amongst the crowd. "I never shot Camlin. He was my best friend."

"This is absurd!" Beiler cried. "The man's out of his head, I tell you. He never talked to me about anything! Who're you going to believe, me or someone crazy with fever?"

Patrick riveted his gaze on Beiler, who stood on the boardwalk illuminated by torchlight. "This morning, bright and early, I went out to feed my hogs. As I bent over the trough, I saw a man up on the hill. I thought he'd come to talk to me. Only he shot me, instead." Patrick bared his clenched teeth as he struggled to raise his arm and point. "That man was Estyn Beiler!"

Everyone started to talk at once. Beiler shook his fist. "He's lying! That's a bare-faced lie, I tell you!"

"Not a lie. I saw you, Beiler." To the crowd, Patrick said, "Caitlin and I both guessed wrong. It wasn't Beckett who filched the five hundred dollars. It was Beiler. You all know he likes to drink and gamble, and that he usually loses. How could he afford those gambling losses in the early years before he had investments to bring in extra income? He got paid a pittance as our marshal, and we all know it." Patrick hauled in another breath. "I'll tell you how he afforded it! By cheating his friends. Camlin must have discovered the truth, and Beiler shot him to shut him up. Just like he shot me."

"You little bastard," Beiler shrieked with rage. "I should've made the first bullet count!"

Then, before anyone could anticipate what he meant to do, Beiler drew his revolver and took a wild shot. Patrick went down like a felled tree, Doc Halloway crumpling on top of him. Women in the crowd screamed. Men cursed. In retaliation, one of the men in the crowd drew his gun and fired back at Beiler. "You murderous son of a bitch! We elected you marshal. We trusted you!"

An incredulous expression passed over Beiler's round face. The next second, Beiler clutched his stomach and crashed to his knees.

Horrified by all that was happening, Caitlin was only dimly aware of a horse whinnying. Then the sound finally registered. She whirled toward Ace. The two men who'd been standing near the tree were trying to control the gelding, but the gunfire had spooked it. As one of the men leaped up to grab for the bridle, the horse flung its head, evading the man's grasp. And then before anyone could stop it, the animal bolted straight into the crowd, trampling everyone who got in its way.

Screams. People running. In the confusion, no one seemed aware of the man who dangled at the end of a lynching rope.

Caitlin had eyes only for him. Ace, swinging in the torchlight, his long, powerfully muscled legs jerking in a macabre dance of death. "No!" she screamed. "Oh, my God, no!"

In a nightmare of slowness, she dodged the horse and shoved people aside, desperate to reach her husband, knowing with every breath, every heartbeat, every step she took that she would be too late. He was strangling. Strangling before her very eyes.

It seemed to her time had stopped, that she ran toward him through a great void of nothingness with only the labored whine of her own breathing to break the awful silence. In those seconds, scenes from the last month flashed before her eyes. Ace, smiling down at her. Ace, walking into the house, dressed in all new clothing, just so her cat's hair would no longer show on him. Ace, throwing back his dark head to bark with laughter. Ace, making gentle love to her. He'd given her so much. And now his life was being snuffed out.

It was like looking at him through plate glass. Ace on the other side, beyond her reach. Needing her help. She would never reach him in time.

"No!"

Caitlin finally reached the tree. In a frantic attempt to save her husband, she hugged his legs and pushed upward, trying in the only way she knew to take the tension off the rope. Too late. Too late. His body already felt limp.

"Help me. Dear God, help me!"

Her screams finally drew attention away from the marauding horse back to her husband. Men rushed forward. Stronger arms than hers grabbed Ace's heavy body. Someone leaped up to cut the rope. Caitlin fell back, sobbing wildly, as her husband was gently lowered to the ground.

"Jesus H. Christ!" Banks cried. "Petrie, why didn't you have a better hold on the goddamned horse! We hung him. We hung the poor fellow."

Wailing with grief, Caitlin sank to her knees and gathered her husband into her arms. He couldn't die. He couldn't leave her. Not after making her love him as he had. He couldn't. He just couldn't.

Cradling his dark head on her lap, she caught his face between her hands. Her tears spilled onto his burnished skin, glistening like diamonds in the torchlight. "Ace! Oh, please, God. Take me. Not him! Please, not him!"

In a desperate attempt to bring him back, Caitlin pressed her mouth over his lax lips and heaved with all her might, trying to force breath into lungs that no

longer had life. He'd made her a gift of his love. And
now it was being torn away. She couldn't bear it.
Couldn't live without him. If he was going to leave her,
she wanted to go with him. It was as simple and as
horrible as that.

"Caitlin. Miss Caitlin?" Gentle hands grasped her by
the shoulders, trying to pull her away from her husband.
"It's too late, honey. You have to let him go."

She wrenched away, fierce in her need, determined not
to give up. Resetting her lips over Ace's, she forced her
breath into him again. And again. Until her head spun.
Until she felt weak. And still, he just lay there, completely lifeless.

Gone. The word slipped into her mind, cutting at her
brain like an ice shard. He was gone, and death gave no
second chances. Let him go, someone had said. Only she
couldn't.

Finally giving up, Caitlin threw back her head and
screamed. Screamed until it felt as if the sound were
ripping her throat out. "Ace! Ace! Don't leave me!
Please, God. Plea—ease, don't ta—ake him. Please!"

Someone grabbed her forcefully by the shoulders.
Caitlin felt Ace's body being dragged from her arms. He
was gone. Just like that. Gone.

Ace felt as if he were drowning in darkness. Far away
from him, he saw a needle point of light. He wanted to
move toward it. But he was tired, so awfully tired. A part
of him wanted to surrender to the blackness. To rest and
be at peace.

Only something tugged him back. He wasn't sure
what. Then he heard it. Caitlin's voice. She sounded
miles away. Her cries echoed and bounced off the
darkness. "Ace! Ace! Don't leave me. Please, please!
Don't leave me!"

Ace didn't want to leave her, but sometimes a man
had no choice, and the darkness seemed to be pulling
him deeper, its hold on him growing stronger. And yet
he couldn't disregard Caitlin's voice.

He focused on the pinpoint of light, and in that tiny

halo of gold, he saw Caitlin. She was weeping. Struggling to escape the arms of some man. Ace tried to move toward her. He'd sworn never to allow anyone to hurt her again. And now some man had his filthy hands on her.

Before Ace realized what he was doing, he was trying to reach her. Fighting against the drowning sensation, trying to pull himself through it toward her. Caitlin. God, how he loved her. There was nothing that had a stronger pull on him than that. Nothing.

"Don't leave me!" he heard her screaming. He tried to tell her he wasn't. That he was coming. Only the blackness seemed to have no end. No matter how he tried, he couldn't escape it. He went down into it. Down, down. And then, nothing . . . just an airless blackness that wouldn't turn loose of him.

"Holy shit, he's coming around!"

"The hell he is!"

"I saw him move, goddammit!"

The voices exploded inside Ace's brain. Simultaneously, an awful pain swelled in his chest. He gagged. Grabbed frantically for breath. Something was choking him. He wrapped both hands around his larynx and rolled onto his side, coughing, wheezing, trying desperately to get oxygen.

"Ace! Oh, Ace!"

Just as he dragged breath into his lungs, Ace felt Caitlin's arms come around him, felt her tears on his face. Air . . . and Caitlin. He couldn't live without either. It seemed right, somehow, to take that first breath and feel her body press so sweetly around him at the same time.

Ace blinked, tried to see her face. As she swam into focus, he managed to lift an arm, put it around her shaking shoulders. Caitlin. She was weeping. He wanted to comfort her, but right then, the need to breathe was far more consuming.

Slowly, inch by inch, reality came back to him. The faces of the mob. The rope that swung from the tree limb above him. Caitlin, crying as if her heart might break.

Ace blinked again, then tightened his arm around her shoulders, remembering the man who had so roughly held her. She was his. His. No other man was going to touch her. Not as long as he had anything to say about it.

"I'm all right," he managed to rasp. "All right, sweetheart. Don't cry. Please, don't cry."

Kisses . . . Sweet kisses, all over his face. The taste of her, like sun-warmed honey, seemed to linger at the back of his tongue. He smiled and drew her closer. "It's all right, Caitlin. Shhh. Don't."

She hugged him fiercely and continued to weep. Staring up at the empty noose that swung above them, Ace realized he'd been hanged. He remembered the horse bolting, then the awful pain. No wonder his throat hurt like hell. Jesus. He'd almost died. Would have died. Only Caitlin had called him back.

Gunshots. Someone had fired a gun, and the horse had spooked.

Patrick.

Ace stiffened, tried to sit up. Beiler had shot at Patrick. He'd fallen. Oh, God. Caitlin had suffered enough grief in her short life without losing her brother.

Commandeering all his strength, Ace pushed her away and managed to sit up. The world became a swimming blur of faces and bobbing torchlight. He blinked, swung onto his knees, hauled in a deep breath. Patrick. As everything came back into focus, Ace mustered all his willpower to stand. Staggering sideways, he swung his head, searching for his brother-in-law in the swarm of people. Caitlin jumped up to grab his waist.

"Ace, don't. You should lie still."

"Patrick," he told her hoarsely.

He felt her body snap taut and knew she'd forgotten all about her brother until he'd said his name. "Oh, dear God. Paddy!"

Ace half expected her to bolt into the crowd to find her brother. He would have understood if she had. Instead, she quickened her pace, tightening her hold at his waist and helping him to walk with her. The group of people that had gathered around Patrick and the doctor parted at their approach. Realizing that Caitlin meant to keep an arm around him, Ace pried her loose and gave her a little shove.

"Go on," he said softly.

It was all the encouragement she needed. With a low cry, she sank to her knees beside her brother. Patrick lay in Doc Halloway's arms, his expression like that of a cat who'd just swallowed a canary. Despite his chalky pallor, he met Ace's gaze and winked. "I'm okay, Caitlin," Patrick said shakily. "After the way I've acted, dying would be too easy on me. Beiler missed."

"Missed?" she repeated shrilly, then gave an hysterical laugh. "He missed? Oh, thank God!"

She ran her hands lightly over her brother's shoulders, then touched his bloodstained bandage. "You're bleeding, Paddy. Badly."

He flashed a weak smile. "I'll make it, Caitlin. Ask Doc. He'll tell you."

Caitlin glanced up at the elderly physician. "The blood, Doc. We have to get him back to the surgery."

Doc glanced around at the men who stood nearby. "I'll need help carrying him."

Ace yearned to step forward, but he barely had the strength to stand himself. Four other men volunteered. Caitlin fell back to get out of their way. When she stood, Ace slipped an arm around her waist. He could feel her trembling, and he knew how frightened she was.

As the men jostled for position to lift Patrick between them, the younger man searched out Ace's gaze again. "I don't suppose saying I'm sorry will count for much after what I did, but consider it said, Keegan."

Ace couldn't help but grin. There was still a trace of underlying animosity in Patrick's voice. "No apologies necessary," Ace replied in a voice so hoarse from the hanging noose it was little more than a gruff whisper. "Let's just consider it a disagreement between brothers and forget about it."

As the men carried Patrick away, Ace heard his brother-in-law muttering something under his breath about his not being related to any damned Keegan. He shook his head and glanced down at his wife.

"He's going to be all right, sweetheart."

She turned huge, luminous eyes on him. That look was all Ace needed to restore his strength. She needed him. More now, possibly, than she ever had.

"Trust me," he whispered. "He's going to make it."

With a stifled sob, she wrapped both arms around him and buried her face against his chest. Ace drew her close. He held her for a very long while, trying to regather his own strength while he bolstered hers. When she finally stopped crying, he whispered, "Come on. Let's wait inside the doctor's office. As soon as Doc's finished patching your brother back up, I'm sure he'll want to let us know how he's doing."

"What about *this* brother?"

Ace turned to see Joseph standing there, his leather riding hat drawn low over his head, blond hair drifting in the night breeze around his shoulders.

"Hey, Joseph. How'd you get out?"

"Some kind soul happened to remember we were locked up and fished the key out of Beiler's pocket." Joseph flashed a look at Caitlin, who still clung to Ace, her face hidden against his shirt. "He's dead, you know."

"I figured," Ace said hoarsely.

Joseph stepped closer and put a hand on Caitlin's shoulder. "Hey, there, girl. What're you crying now for? The worst part's over."

To Ace's surprise, Caitlin turned and threw her arms around Joseph's neck. "Oh, Joseph! They hanged Ace. I thought he was dead!"

Evidently, Joseph was as taken aback as Ace was, for he just stood there for a moment looking dumbfounded, his hands hovering over Caitlin's shuddering back. He was obviously leery about touching her. He shot another glance at Ace. Then he closed his arms around his sister-in-law. "He isn't dead, though," he said softly.

"I don't know what I would've done!" she wailed.

Joseph smiled and gave her a pat. "I guess I would've had to marry you. Couldn't let a catch like you get away. I like your cooking too much."

Caitlin laughed, the sound wet and choked. "You're impossible. Your brother almost died, and you're cracking jokes."

"I'm not joking. He just beat me to the draw and proposed to you first."

Ace cocked an eyebrow. "Any time you get tired of hugging my wife, Joseph, I'll be happy to take over."

Joseph chuckled. "Go find a post to lean on. I'll be a while."

David and Esa walked up just then. "How's Patrick?"

"I was just suggesting we might go see," Ace said.

Caitlin drew away from Joseph, wiped her cheeks, and then fell into David's arms to cry some more. Esa's shirt got a good soaking next. By the time Ace got his wife back, he was beginning to feel a little green around the edges. Determined not to relinquish her to one of his brothers again, he cinched an arm tightly around her waist as the five of them walked to the doctor's office.

The prognosis from Doc was good. "Patrick didn't break the wound open," he assured them. "Not all that much blood loss from moving around, which is a miracle. What with his fever breaking the way it did, I'd say he's on the road to recovery."

"Can we see him?" Caitlin asked.

"Sure, you can. He's still awake. Just don't stay long. I don't want him overtaxed. He's had a rough night as it is."

Ace moved to follow his wife to the surgery, not realizing until they reached the door that his brothers had all tagged along. "What is this, a convoy? Who invited you yahoos?"

"Nobody," Joseph replied. "We don't need an invite. He's part of the family."

The grateful look in Caitlin's eyes forestalled Ace from saying more. When the five of them entered the room en masse, however, Patrick evidently felt no such compunction. "Holy mother, the whole damn bunch of you? I'm supposed to be resting. With you fellows in here, I'll be afraid to shut my eyes."

"Be nice, Patrick." Caitlin went to sit on the edge of

his cot. After gazing at her brother a moment, she flashed Ace a radiant smile that was just a little damp around the edges. "He looks better. Don't you think?"

"Absolutely."

Joseph shuffled the sole of his boot on the floor, then planted his hands on his hips. "Well, O'Shannessy, I hate to have to say it, but what you did out there tonight earned you my respect."

"Who says I want it?"

"Patrick!" Caitlin scolded. "I said be nice. Joseph is part of my family now, just like you. Someday soon, when I start having babies, you'll all be uncles together."

Patrick met Ace's gaze over the top of his sister's russet head. "You go havin' kids, and they'll all be half O'Shannessy. Redheads, probably. And ornerier than the day is long. You'd better think twice."

Ace laughed in spite of himself. "O'Shannessys are kind of like warts. They grow on you." At Caitlin's reproachful look, he added quickly, "I'm only joking, Caitlin. A good measure of O'Shannessy blood stirred in with the Keegan will be a great mix. Like I told you once before, if you give me a half-dozen redheaded babies, I'll be one happy man."

Patrick smiled slightly and took his sister's hand. "Well, I guess if you're gonna go throwing babies into the bargain, I'll have to bury the hatchet."

"Deep," Caitlin stressed. "No more fighting."

"No more fighting," Patrick agreed. His smile broadened. "I busted up all the whiskey jugs. Swore off. I mean it this time."

Caitlin leaned over to give him a hug. "Oh, Patrick, I hope you make it."

"I will."

Joseph stepped over to the bed and extended his hand. "I don't want to tire you, Patrick, so I'll be going. First, though, I'd like to say thank you for what you did out there tonight. You saved my brother's life. I won't forget it."

Patrick stared at Joseph's outstretched palm for a long moment. Then he finally extended his own. The two men clasped hands and looked dead into each other's eyes. When Joseph moved away, David and Esa stepped forward to follow suit. Patrick was beginning to look pale by the time all the handshaking was over.

"Out of here," Ace told his brothers. "Go on, all of you. We'll be right out."

When his brothers had exited the room, Ace went to stand beside his wife, one hand resting lightly on her shoulder. He gazed down at Patrick for several seconds in solemn reflection.

Patrick lifted an eyebrow. "I look a lot like my father, don't I? You gonna hold it against me?"

Ace gave the question careful consideration. When at last he replied, he answered from the heart. "No, Patrick, I don't believe I will."

A few minutes later, when Ace and Caitlin stepped outside the doctor's office into the chill night air, she cast him a questioning glance. "You meant it, didn't you? Somewhere along the way, you've made your peace with my father and everything he did."

Ace drew her into the circle of his arms and gazed at the craggy peaks of the Rockies, illuminated by moonlight in the distance. For so long, he'd been consumed with hatred and anger. Now all of it was gone. It felt damned good.

He bent to press a kiss to Caitlin's forehead, then looked deeply into her eyes. "Your father gave you life," he said huskily. "And you are, without question, the sweetest thing that's ever happened to me. How can I not make my peace with him?"

Tears filled her eyes. Then she went up on her toes to hug his neck. "I used to wonder if I'd ever feel free of him, if I'd ever stop jumping with a start, thinking he was standing right behind me." Her arms tightened in a fierce hold. "A cloud of fear hanging over me, that was how I thought of him." She fell silent for a moment. "And now, guess what? The sun has finally come out and the cloud is gone. I can't remember the last time I forgot he was dead for a second and felt terrified. I think it's because, since marrying you, I feel truly safe for the first time in my whole life."

"Ah, Caitlin . . ."

"It's true," she whispered. "I don't feel afraid any more. I don't think I ever will again. He no longer has a hold on me."

She wasn't the only one who felt as though he'd been set free.

As Ace closed his arms around her again, a sense of rightness filled him. Conor O'Shannessy's daughter . . . the most precious gift he'd ever received. He buried his face against her hair and inhaled its sweet scent, remembering how he'd come here, itching to get revenge.

Holding this girl in his arms definitely settled the score.